"I'm surprised you want
mumble as I turn back to the

"Why wouldn't I?" he questions.

"I haven't exactly been nice to you. I don't know if I'd be as patient as you've been." I turn to him, curiously. "Why did you stick around, keep trying to be my friend? Especially when you had every other girl in town hot to be the center of your attention."

A peculiar look crosses his face, and he glances away from me. After a moment, he looks back and grins. "I'm a sucker for punishment?" he offers.

"I don't think so," I laugh.

"I've been angling for another pie?" He ducks as I lob an apple at him, swiped from the basket on the counter, neatly catching it above his head.

"Try again," I say.

He shrugs, and looks at me more seriously. "I thought you were cute. Which—" he holds up a finger to silence me when I open my mouth to protest, "—would not have kept me coming back, just so you know. I'm not that shallow. But I saw how much your friends cared for you, the way they listen to you, and I decided there was more to you than you were letting on."

"Oh," is my brilliant response.

He steps closer to me, and I instinctively step backward, my progress stopped by the sharp hardness of the counter. I reach back, resting my hands against the edge. He places both hands on the counter, trapping me between them. My heart immediately starts to race.

"Have you ever been kissed?" he asks quietly.

Immortal Mine

Cindy C Bennett

Books by Cindy C Bennett

Geek Girl (Sweetwater Books)

Heart on a Chain

©2011 Cindy C Bennett USA

Cover design by Cindy C Bennett

To my husband, my own high school sweetheart, who has given me the kind of life I could only have imagined, and who has made it possible for me to reach for my dreams. It's a great thing to not only love the one you've bound yourself to, but to actually like them as well. And, honey, I like you a lot!

Prologue

Sam

We pull up to the building, the one my uncle and I scouted out and purchased before making the move to this town. It sits ten miles outside of town, an old, abandoned motel. No one knows of the purchase—we've kept it looking exactly the same. Same broken windows, same graffiti covered walls, same faded "for sale" sign out front, all of it covered in a layer of disuse.

She looks at me oddly, but doesn't question as she climbs out of the truck. I follow her, taking her hand and leading her to the only room that has been altered. The alterations are invisible from the outside.

"So, is this the latest venture in the Coleman dynasty?" she teases. I'd hoped that was the conclusion she would come to. I knew that if I tried to tell her the truth, she would run as fast as she could, away from me. The truth isn't something I can tell her . . . it's something I have to *show* her.

"I want to show you something," I say, tugging her gently toward room three, pulling the key from my pocket.

"Okay," she agrees happily, and I feel a tinge of guilt for the deception.

We stop outside the door. I twist the key in the lock, but turn to her before I push the door open.

"Before we go in, I want to tell you something," I say. "I want you to remember that I love you, and that no matter what happens, everything is going to be okay."

For the first time, a small amount of wariness creeps into her expression.

"Okaaay," she answers, hesitant, skeptical. "Is everything okay, Sam?"

I smile at her, and push the door open. She steps in ahead of me, and I close the door behind us, the lock automatically clicking into place. She is staring at the bed, which suddenly seems overwhelmingly large in the room, and I can see what she might think of my bringing her here. She turns toward me, and the worry on her face confirms my suspicion.

"No, it's not . . ." I begin.

"You know how I feel . . ." she says at the same time, laughing nervously as our words overlap.

I walk up to her, place my hands on her shoulders.

"I do know how you feel, and I would never do anything that would cause you to compromise your values for me. I didn't really think about how this would appear."

Relief floods her eyes, and she smiles as she leans into me, wrapping her arms trustingly around my waist.

"I know that, Sam. I shouldn't have doubted you."

I swallow over the lump in my throat at her words. What I'm about to do is much worse . . . She leans back and looks up at me, trust and love shining in her unusual eyes. Those eyes are the reason we are even here. They are what made me first believe that she could be like me . . . that she could be the one I've been waiting centuries for, the hope amplified when I met her grandmother and knew what *she* is. Those are the eyes that I had fallen in love with so quickly.

And, pig that I am, I take advantage of that love and lean down to kiss her.

I pull one of the two chairs that sit next to the table out, pushing her down gently to sit in it. I back away until I'm standing near the bed, across the room from her.

"I want you to trust me," I implore. "Just stay there, just . . . wait. And remember what I said before: everything is going to be okay."

The smile on her face falters as I pull the gun from my pocket.

"Sam, what—" I can hear the fear sliding up her words.

"I'm not going to hurt you, I promise." I flip the cylinder of the revolver open and show it to her. "Only one bullet."

She begins to rise out of her chair.

"I think you should stay sitting," I tell her, trying not to sound threatening. She hesitates, but when I don't turn the gun her way, she continues to a standing position, slowly moving toward the door, hands raised toward me, as if she's the victim of a hold-up. My heart breaks at the fear that shrouds her entire body.

"Sam, I don't know what you're planning, but I think this has gone far enough." Her words are soothing, but firm. I feel a moment's fierce pride at her courage.

I slide the cylinder back into place and she reaches for the door knob. It turns, but the door doesn't open.

"Sam," she says, her voice exerting authority, even over the tremor of fright. "Unlock the door. I want to leave now."

I almost give in, but can't now. She has to know, has to *see*.

"Just trust me—" I see the change in her face at my words, and quickly revise. "Just *give* me ten more minutes. Then I'll let you out, and we'll go home."

"I don't like this. I want to go now." The pleading that has crept into her voice nearly undoes me, but I have to follow through. Her eyes haven't left the gun since I closed the cylinder. I take a breath and turn the gun toward my chest.

"No!" Her response is immediate, and she takes a step toward me, hand reaching as if to stop me. I can't let her get any closer, in case something goes wrong. It's not her time yet.

"Everything will be okay," I reiterate, and pull the trigger.

Chapter 1

Niahm

Six Months Earlier

Some people might call my little town of Goshen a dying town. The population steadily decreases—along with the size of the ranches and farms—as people move away, looking for a better living elsewhere. I know it will always have a population of at least one—me.

My family made a living originally as sheep farmers. My grandfather wasn't a very good businessman, though, and sold large parcels off to pay his debts even before my father became the owner. My father didn't have much of an interest in farming the creatures, and sold off most of the rest, including the sheep. We went from over a thousand acres passed to my grandfather, to the fifty acres that will be left to me. I plan to spend the rest of my life on my fifty acres.

"You're crazy for wanting to stay, Niamh Parker," my

friends have all told me, at one time or another.

Yes, that's me—that's truly my name. Not pronounced nee-uhm like you'd think. It's an old Irish name pronounced neeve—which totally makes sense if you throw out everything you've ever known or been taught about phonetics. If you don't think that's caused me any amount of grief over the years! My name, though, is one of the reasons I love living in a small town so much—no one new to try to explain my name to.

I don't even have Irish ancestry. Solidly English, with smatterings of German, Scottish, Dutch and Norwegian sprinkled in here and there. My name is reflective of my mother's romantic nature. She claims she named me Niamh because it means radiant. I think she read it in a romance novel. She's fond of those.

I looked it up on the internet once—not easy, as it kept telling me I had typed it in wrong—and read that it means snow, which I guess *is* radiant in the right light. So that's me, the radiant snow girl. Guess with my peculiar name, strange was written in the stars.

Currently, there are exactly 376 residents of Goshen. Once in a while that number might increase because of a birth, but more likely it drops as people leave. You might be able to understand, then, why such a big deal is made when Shane Coleman and his nephew, Sam, move into the old Stanton place.

There's a flurry of activity upon their unexpected arrival. They bought the place from Barbara Glissmeyer, the only realtor in town—she also works in four other nearby towns, which probably each do more business in one week than we do in Goshen in a year—and swore her to secrecy on the sale. That in itself is cause for rampant speculation and burning the phone lines up with gossip when it's discovered.

But then there is Shane and Sam themselves. Mrs. Bradley was the first on their doorstep with casserole in hand, arriving almost simultaneously with the moving truck and the

Coleman's themselves—pretty amazing considering her lack of knowledge concerning their arrival, but she lives nearest, half a block down and across the street from the old ranch. It's completely understandable that she'd have a casserole ready to go—we all have something food wise we can deliver at a moment's notice. After rolling out the welcome carpet in her exuberant and overbearing manner, she hurried home to call Mrs. Yonkers. Within thirty minutes, everyone in town had received a phone call from someone or other.

I receive my call from my best friend Stacy.

"Did you hear yet?"

"Hear what?" I ask breathlessly, having just run in from feeding my chickens. I glance at the tile floor, grimacing at the mud tracks sprinkled with chicken feed—and chicken poop—that I tracked in. I grimace at the mess. I should have taken the extra seconds to peel my boots off, but patience is not one of my virtues, you'll find. The situation is made worse when Bob, my big, black retriever, runs in through the door that I left hanging open in my hurry, tracking in the same mess, because he'd been with me in the coop. He sneezes and a few chicken feathers float into the air, making me smile. He does love to chase them around, tormenting them for his own amusement.

"About the new guy," Stacy prompts.

I search my memory, not able to think of anyone who might be considered new. Unless she's speaking of the Fredricks's new baby? Was it a boy?

"Um . . ." I respond, and she huffs irritably.

"I swear, Vee, you live in your own, happy little world, unaware of what goes on around you." She calls me Vee for the simple reason, she says, that she can spell it without having to call me for verification. Of course, that was in the first grade. She can spell it by now—I think. But Vee is just old habit.

I can't really argue with her summation of my inattention to the world around me.

"Some new people just moved into the old Stanton place."

"Really?" she's piqued my interest now. No matter how

loyal I am to the greatness of my little town, I'm well aware that folks tend to move *out*, not in. "Who?"

"It's a guy named Shane Coleman, and his nephew, Sam."

"That's weird," I say, leaning against the counter, crossing my feet and settling in for the details as I pick up an apple (from my own apple tree) and bite into it. "Where's the rest of the family?"

"No one knows," Stacy says, her words shocking me into a straight posture.

"What? Hasn't Busybody Bradley been there yet?"

"She has." Stacy's tone is rife with intrigue.

"Okay, Stace, spit it out. I need details."

"That's the weird thing, Vee. There aren't any details. They bought the place some time ago, but Glisten"—our nickname for Ms. Glissmeyer, partly because of her name and partly because she covers herself with glitter powder—"is being all tight lipped. She says she's sworn to silence. All she would 'fess up is that they bought the place, paid some cleaning company to come in and get it ready. She claims she wasn't even sure of the exact move-in date."

"No!" This is the best gossip we've had since Melissa Stratton gave birth to a purportedly two-month premature baby—that weighed nine pounds, two ounces.

"Yes, but that isn't all. Busybody Bradley claims that the uncle is beyond gorgeous, which has been verified by nearly every other woman who's seen him. They say he's nice enough, but doesn't seem interested in turning in his single status any time soon."

"Oh, yeah?" I place my forgotten apple absent-mindedly on the counter, where it's immediately snatched up by Bob. I vaguely notice the mess he's making on the floor as he chomps noisily on it. Oh well, what's a little more mess? "Bet that ticks off all the single oldies."

"I get the idea he's not that old. And it's being said that his gorgeousness is surpassed only by that of his nephew," Stacy pauses dramatically. "His *seventeen-year-old* nephew!"

"No way!" I exclaim. "Who told you that?"

"Ashley heard it from Heather *and* Hilary."

"Wow," I breathe. If the double-H—the two most popular girls in the school, and thereby the foremost experts on what can be considered gorgeous—claim it, well, that's something of weight.

"How soon can you go?" I don't need to ask what she means. A lifetime of friendship has created enough of a short-hand between us that she doesn't need to expound. I still have chores to do, animals to feed, stalls to muck, and no one to help me.

That all can wait, I decide in an instant.

"I'm going to need thirty," I say, knowing that I'll have to rush. I have to get the farm smell off me, put on some make-up and try to do something with my hair. All this in order to be presented to someone the double-H has given a stamp of approval to in thirty short minutes, someone our own age—a *boy* our own age.

"*Thirty?*" Stacy moans. "No way. I can't wait that long. I'll give you fifteen."

"Fifteen! I can't—"

"I'll pick you up. Bye." Stacy cuts me off, and I know that means I really only have, like, ten minutes. I look at the mess on the floor—that really shouldn't wait. My parents won't be home from their latest work excursion to Egypt until Friday, three days from now. That gives me time—I always have time before they'll be home again, it seems. It too can wait, I decide.

"Outside, Bob," I command. He gives me a forlorn look, so I grab another apple and toss it out the door. He happily bounds after it, tail wagging and tongue lolling. I shut the door behind him—no need to lock up. I don't think anyone in Goshen could actually tell you where the key to their house is. Locks are pretty much archaic around here.

I hop around, quickly shedding my boots. Running up the stairs, I pull off clothes as I go, leaving a trail behind me. I don't have time for a full-on make-up job, so I pull the mascara wand across my pale blonde but thankfully thick lashes. A couple of swipes with the blush-brush, gloss slid across my lips and I have to call it good.

What to do about the stench? I can't go over smelling like old MacDonald. Looking around, I have sudden inspiration. I grab a can of Febreeze, spray a curtain of it in front of me and step into it. The chemicals can't be especially good for me, but it proclaims the ability to rid odors. Then, afraid that might not be quite enough, I douse myself in perfume. I gag and cough a little at the smell. A glance at my watch confirms I don't have time to wash it off. Oh well, I'll just have to hope for the best.

I pull on some jeans—what else does anyone around here wear, except a skirt to church—and waste three precious minutes pulling top after top from my closet in indecision. I finally settle on a dark blue peasant blouse that makes my gold eyes look more blue than their unusual color, pulling it over my head.

A brush pulled through the tangles of my long, dark blonde hair make it clear that it's beyond hope. I hurriedly twist a couple of thin braids into the front, then twist the whole, heavy disordered length up into hair band, leaving pieces dangling. A dark blue silk flower pinned into place completes the masterpiece—okay, so it's more like a masterpiece created by Picasso than by . . . well, almost anyone else. I'm going to try to pull it off as one of those hairdo's that are artfully disarrayed that really take hours to do, rather than one which is just plain disarray.

I leap back down the stairs—a game from when I was a child that I only do if I'm alone, which is often—and pull one of my famous apple pies from the fridge. I made it with my own home-grown apples. Frantic honking from the direction of the front of the house confirms my suspicions about the ten minutes.

Stacy is waiting for me in her old Mustang—which bespeaks of the urgency for speed that we're taking a car rather than our ATV's—applying gloss to her own lips as I climb into her car.

"What took ya, pokey?" she asks, as if it hasn't been, like, three seconds since she honked.

"Just try not to kill us with speeding, okay?"

She rolls her eyes at me as she jams it into reverse. Bob comes running around the house, probably thinking he's coming with. When he sees that it's Stacy behind the wheel, he turns tail and heads the other way.

Smart dog. He learns lessons the first time.

We can avoid Main Street between my place and the Stanton place. It's pretty much all dirt, though, and Stacy leaves a cloud behind as she pushes the old beast to its limit on the bumpy road.

"If you cause damage to the pie, you're not my friend anymore," I threaten. I might think she didn't hear me from her deafening silence, if it weren't for the fact that she immediately swerves to hit a particularly bad rut. I hold the pie aloft, letting it bounce with the motion. Stacy's revenge can be vicious.

When we pull out onto the paved street, Stacy slows down. Officer Hill told her that if he has to write her one more speeding ticket, she's going to lose her license. Officer Hill is a fair man, and honest. So that means if he catches you breaking the law, you're going to be fined or ticketed. Stacy knows he means business. Therefore, after running only *one* stop sign and a left turn that I think we made on the two outside tires, we arrive at the Stanton place.

Chapter 2

Niahm

We pass most of the Stanton's acreage, grass beginning to brown from the early chill of September nights, before actually coming to the house. One of the reasons the Stanton place hasn't sold is because it has two-thousand acres, and the Stanton heirs all live in New York City. They priced the land as if it were in a thriving region—like, the Hamptons, or something—rather than here, in no man's land. The land is overgrown. It wouldn't be good for farming without a couple years of good, hard work. Then it would take another twenty or thirty years to recoup the money for the purchase and cleanup before it would turn a profit. No one ever thought it would sell. The new people—Coleman's, I think Stacy called them—must have negotiated a better deal.

We reach the main house—a traditional farm house, large and roomy with dormers and a large wrap-around porch. It even has a three-car garage; the only one in Goshen, I believe. A falling-down barn and two rusty silos are visible not far behind the house. I notice with chagrin that there are several cars, pick-up trucks and ATV's already there. I hoped, foolishly, that most of the crowd would have died down by now.

My pie is miraculously unscathed as we climb out of the car. Stacy's mother already brought their offering, leaving her empty handed. Crowds of people mill about in the front porch. I wonder if the house is just too full to admit anymore, but gather rapidly from the murmurs that no one has been invited in.

I realize there is a cluster of people on the far end of the porch, and I get my first glimpse of the infamous Shane Coleman. Busybody was right—he's movie-star good-looking. Of course he's an old guy . . . well, not so old. He looks about thirty or so, but definitely old for my seventeen-year-old self.

"He's dreamy," Stacy sighs. I glance at her and see that she, too, has spotted Shane Coleman.

"Dreamy?" I scoff. "What, have we been transported back to the fifties?"

She scowls at me, bringing us firmly back into the present.

"What would you call him?" she demands.

"He's pretty cute," I admit. At her snarl, I laugh. "He's *extremely* cute," I amend. "But, seriously, Stace, the guy's like, old enough to be our dad."

"No, he's not," she refutes, punching me in the shoulder.

"Ow," I complain, rubbing the spot, even though it was little more than a tap.

"Wuss," she utters, her response rote. "He is *gourgeois*."

"That's not a word, and you're not French. Besides, it'd be illegal if he looked at you as anything other than a kid."

"Only for the next three months, my young friend. Then I'm a legal-eagle."

"You're sick," I tell her—or rather, I tell the back of her head since she's walking away, pushing through the crowd toward her dream man.

A table under a large window seems to be the collecting place for the array of food items being pressed upon the Coleman's. With a smirk, I add my pie to the pile that couldn't be eaten by a family of twelve in a month's time, let alone by this little family of two. Poor Coleman's. I don't even know where they'll put everything, unless they brought five refrigerators and freezers with them. There are no charities in town where they can share their wealth of victuals, either.

"You're adding to the pile, when you should be taking away," a voice from my right informs me.

I turn and catch my breath. This has to be the nephew. He's someone I've never seen before. Actually, I've never seen anyone *like* him before. He stands easily six feet tall. His skin is clear and smooth. This might seem a strange observation, unless you take into account his red hair. It's an amazing shade of red, not bright, not dark, more of a copper. Straight, shagged, sweeping just above his clear green eyes, curling just slightly over his ears and collar. Despite the red hair, there are no freckles to be found. Just a strong jaw with great cheek bones, beautifully shaped eyes fringed with dark red lashes, full lips that are smiling at me.

He doesn't seem real in his beauty.

"I'm just kidding," he offers, leaning slightly toward me when I remain silent, staring.

I start, "Oh, sorry. You . . . you took me by surprise," I say, inanely. I sweep my hand toward the table. "I hope you're hungry. Actually, I hope you're ravenous."

He laughs and my belly does a little flip-flop. Even his laugh is beautiful. I mentally shake myself; I don't intend to become one of the simpering, giggling females who will surely be fawning over him in no time.

"What's that smell?" he asks, wrinkling his nose.

I take a little step backward, hoping he won't realize it's my chicken feed/Febreeze/perfume concoction.

"So, which one is yours?" he questions, moving closer. I have to look up at him, and revise my opinion of his height. He must be six-three, at least.

"The, um . . . the pie," I stutter.

"This one?" he points to another pie, one that looks like it's cherry or blueberry by the dark jelly oozing out of the top. It's sloppily put together, without an embellishment to be seen.

"Of course not," my indignation is clear in my voice. I know it's not fair; he can't know how much pride I take in my pies. "This one," I say, pointing to my beautiful pie (if I do say so myself).

"Wow," he says, leaning closer to get a look at it. He traces one of the leaf shapes I hand cut and baked on top of the shell. "Where did you get it?"

I bristle at his words.

"Out of my oven," I tell him, annoyed by his assumption that I could not have made such a thing myself.

His eyebrows shoot up, lost behind the copper hair, and I have an overwhelming urge to brush the hair back. Then I remember that he's offending my pie, and the urge vanishes.

"Really? You made this?"

"Don't sound so incredulous. I'm not a complete imbecile."

My tone finally registers with him, and he glances at me sideways, frozen in the act of reaching for the pie in question.

"I'm sorry," he sounds perplexed. "Did I offend you?"

"Of course not. Who would be offended over a pie?" My voice is dripping with affront.

"I just meant it looks too beautiful to eat."

"So don't eat it," I say, crossly.

His grin disarms me. "Oh, but now I must try it," he purrs. I almost fall for his charm, until he dips two fingers into the pie, pulling a large bite up to his mouth. My mouth drops open in shock.

He closes his eyes in ecstasy. "Delicious," he mumbles around the large bite of pie shoved in his mouth, looking at me with hooded eyes.

I stamp my foot—yes, I mean that literally. Immediately I glean the childishness of the act, but can't take it back. I can't even pretend he didn't notice, since his eyes widen and he freezes in the motion of licking his fingers. I'm embarrassed, but jut my chin up, daring him to say anything.

"You must be Samuel." A feminine hand extends past me. I turn to see Stacy next to me, trying to signal that I should introduce her.

"Uh, yeah, I am. Just Sam, though." He wipes his fingers clean on his jeans, reaching for her hand and enclosing it in his.

"Oh . . . Sam, then. I thought it was Sam, but your uncle was calling you Samuel, so I thought maybe you preferred that. Or maybe, that we had just heard wrong." Stacy is babbling, trying to fill the obviously awkward silence.

"Yeah, well, he's a little formal. I prefer Sam."

"Hm." Stacy glances at me again, but my mouth is clamped. I can feel my temper just below the surface, experience has taught me that the best way to control it is to pretend my mouth is made of stone and can't be opened.

"You are . . . ?" he asks, withdrawing his hand from hers. She seems to realize she'd been holding on for longer than was necessary, and she smiles.

"Oh, um, yeah, my name is Stacy. Stacy Bowen." She glances at me again in concern. "Vee, are you okay?"

"I'm afraid she and I may have gotten off on the wrong foot," Sam informs her, pointing to the destroyed pie. I feel my ire rise to flaming heights at his words. *The wrong foot?* I want to scream.

Stacy looks at the pie, at my face that I can feel heating up—which I'm all too aware is visible—and then at Sam. Understanding dawns, and she links her arm firmly through mine, and drags me away from a stunned Sam.

"Okay, well, it was nice to meet you Sam. We have to be going now. Welcome, and I guess we'll see you at school."

Her words shock me out of my self-imposed stupor.

"*School?*" I screech, and Stacy tugs me even harder, until we're actually running for her car. "I have to go to *school* with that arrogant, insensitive, unfeeling . . . " I'm searching for the proper adjective as she shoves me in and slams the door.

"... Jerk!" I explode as she climbs in her side.

Stacy drives silently, letting me vent, not even attempting to stop me.

"The nerve! Seriously, who does he think he is? He thinks he can offend me; insinuate that my pie is *store bought*," I spit the offensive words. "Thinks he can just sidle up to me, ooze charm and I'll just let him drive his fingers into it, as if it's of no consequence, as if I can just churn them out in minutes—"

"You kind of can," Stacy interjects quietly.

"*He* doesn't know that! Does he think he can do anything he wants just because he's . . ." I trail off, a thousand adjectives running through my head.

"Cute? Gorgeous? Stunning? Good-looking? Beautiful?"

My head snaps toward Stacy when she uses the very word I had been thinking of him earlier.

"No excuse!" I fume.

After a few minutes of silence, Stacy looks my way.

"Done, now?"

I fold my arms petulantly.

"Yes," I grumble.

"The Coleman's are new, Vee. He doesn't know you or your pies, right?"

"So?" I grouse.

"*So*, give him a break. Seriously, girl, you need to relax a little. It's just—"

She cuts herself off, and I shoot her a sharp glance.

"Don't you dare say it, Stace. Don't you dare say it's *just* a pie."

"Okay, I won't." Silence. Then, "But it is, Vee."

I blow out a heavy breath.

"Yeah, I know." I look at her and smile, embarrassment lighting my cheeks. "I really lost it, didn't I?"

Stacy shrugs. "Could have been worse." We burst out laughing.

"I'm such an idiot," I moan.

"I'm almost afraid to ask; what did you say to him? Was it bad?"

I don't answer for a few long minutes, while Stacy fiddles with the radio—kind of pointless since we are only able to receive about five different stations with any kind of clarity.

"Nothing he didn't deserve," I finally say. Stacy, true friend that she is, groans, punches me, then bursts out laughing again.

Chapter 3

Niahm

Someone should do something about the lukewarm, stale water that spouts from the water fountains in the school, I muse, as I fill my mouth with the less-than-appealing liquid.

"Niahm?" I hear my name from nearby, the tone questioning and almost . . . disbelieving.

"That's my name, don't wear it—" I turn, snapping my mouth closed as I see a coppery head turning my way, from where he'd been reading the names of the school officers off the information board, astonishment in every line of his face.

"*You?* You're Niahm?" he questions, incredulity coloring his words.

"I suppose a girl who can't bake pies can't have a name either?" I turn and walk away, rolling my eyes at my inane response. I'm usually better at returning insults than that.

"Wait," Sam calls, jogging to catch up with me. "I just . . . I thought your name was Evie. That's what Stacy called you yesterday."

I stop and his momentum carries him past me. He swings back, moving to stand in front of me, forcing me to look up. I decide he must be more like six-two. I glance away, not liking this weird . . . *pull* . . . I feel when I look at him.

"Not Evie; she called me Vee. It's her nickname for me, short for Niahm. Want to insult that also?"

He opens and closes his mouth twice, then blows out a breath.

"I didn't mean to insult you again. I was just surprised, that's all. It's an unusual name. I'll bet there's not another person in America who has that name—spelled that way, anyway. At least, I've never heard it."

"And I suppose you're some big world traveler?"

"I get around," he says, an odd look on his face. "I'm just saying, it's very unique."

"And someone as *common* as me is hardly worthy of such a *unique* name, right?"

"I'm . . . no . . . that's not—" he stammers.

"Wait a minute—how did you know how to pronounce it?" I interrupt, swinging my eyes back up to his face. I'm awed and a little suspicious. No one ever knows how to say it when they see it.

"Um, I . . . ," he trails off, looking distinctly nervous, suddenly interested is something over my shoulder.

"Sam! There you are," the double-H come around the corner, immediately honing in on Sam. "You know Niamh?" Hilary asks.

"I . . . we—"

"No," I interrupt, "he doesn't know anything about me."

I stalk away, feeling as if he's staring after me—though that's probably my egotistical imagination. Or rather, I try to stalk away. I'm trying to maintain my angry walk, but it's difficult. I curse Stacy for convincing me to wear her high-heeled red shoes just because they match my red shirt perfectly. I'm not really a high-heels kind of girl under the best of circumstances. After a slight stumble, I glance back and see Sam watching me. With a grimace in his direction, I kick the shoes off, scooping them up in my hand. Now I can stalk.

"I better get to class," I hear Sam tell them.

"We'll walk with you," Heather tells him.

"Small school; most of us share most of our classes," Hilary confirms.

I groan as I realize the truth of their words. There are a total of ninety-three kids in our school—and that's grades K-12. In our senior class we have eight.

Nine, now.

We share classes with kids of a variety of ages and abilities. Our teachers have to be extremely flexible in their teaching methods. Sam, Hilary and Heather follow me into the English classroom.

"Sit here, by us," Heather tells Sam, scooting an empty desk a little closer to her own.

"Thanks," he says, sliding in and sliding a smile over her at the same time.

I roll my eyes in disgust and turn back toward Stacy, who's idly doodling in her notebook.

"What a jerk," I mutter. No response. I lean toward her, reaching out to tap her arm, get her attention so she can listen to me complain. But my hand never quite reaches its destination; my close proximity brings her doodling into view.

"Are you crazy?" I murmur fiercely under my breath, snatching her notebook from under her pen, slamming it closed.

"What?" She's all innocence.

"You cannot write Shane Coleman's name, all decorated with hearts!"

"Why not? He's so—"

"Stace! Stop." She grins at me, unrepentant. I sigh, giving up. I throw a glance over my shoulder at the nephew of Stacy's obsession, and see him completely engaged in conversation with the double-H, as well as a couple of the juniors.

Show off.

✳ ✳ ✳ ✳ ✳

"Guys, we really need to decide what play we want to do," I interrupt . . . well, pretty much everyone at the table. We're sitting at lunch, at our definitely more crowded than usual table. Kids here tend to sit with their age group. Usually we have eight at our table. Today we have fifteen.

The reason isn't hard to divine. In fact, that particular reason is leaning his coppery head toward two giggling juniors, who are interlopers at our table. I sigh in disgust, earning me a warning look from Stacy.

"What?" I demand. "If we don't get going on it, we won't be prepared."

"You're right," Hilary pipes up. "That means anyone who's not a senior needs to leave the table." Not only is Hilary probably the most pumped up about the production, she doesn't look too happy about the attention the other girls are getting from Sam.

The two juniors throw her a regretful look, but that's another great thing about my great little town; no need to explain the importance of our discussion, or why they need to make themselves scarce. The only one who looks confused is a certain beautiful jerk—and he's staring right at me, like the whole thing is my fault.

"It's tradition," I fairly growl towards him, refusing to meet his gaze. "Which you would know about if you were from here."

Stunned silence greets my words, and I'm horrified at my tone. Seriously, I'm *never* like this—or at least, not much. I also can't back down with him looking at me like that.

"What she means," Stacy tells him, looking at me like I've grown an extra head, before turning her attention to Sam, "is that this is a big deal for us. Every year we put on a big production. As seniors, we get to decide what show to do, and we run the whole thing. It's a pretty big deal; if we can't out-do last year's show, well, we might get flogged or something, I guess."

I shoot her a baleful look.

"Huh," Sam sounds astonished; apparently I'm the only one who takes offense to it. "So, what kind of show are you talking?"

"I think we should do *Cats*," Heather pronounces enthusiastically. A chorus of groans just as enthusiastic greets her.

"Ugh! Boring!" This is Stacy, which is somewhat ironic since she will choose to have as small a part of the production as possible. For someone so dramatic, she really isn't into theater.

"Seriously," Hilary says, "who wants to watch a bunch of cats prance around the stage? I think we should do *Oklahoma*."

"Too old fashioned," Jon, who will probably play the part of the male lead, looks pained at her suggestion.

"*Mama Mia*."

"Absolutely no Abba," Kevin strongly interjects.

"*Lion King*."

"Too expensive."

This volley goes back and forth with suggestions and rejections from everyone—well, nearly everyone. Sam silently watches, and I keep my mouth clamped, afraid I'll be mean again. I'm watching Sam unobtrusively, noticing that he's eating a home lunch. I guess with all that food foisted on him and his uncle, he'll be eating meals from home for some time.

"What about *Les Miserable*?" At this suggestion, everyone falls silent—but only because of who suggested it, in perfectly accented French, I might add. *Pretentious jerk.* All eyes turn to Sam, and I can feel it; they're considering it. Really, am I the only one left with a brain in my head?

"Three years ago." That's all I have to say to bring them to their senses. Three years ago when we were lowly freshmen, the seniors—a rather large class at eighteen students—put on a production of *Les Mis* without allowing any of the younger students to be part of it. That was cause for contention enough, but when it turned out so spectacularly, the bar was raised to almost impossible heights.

Groans and moans round the table.

"Am I missing something?" Sam asks.

"Long story," Stacy tells him. "Besides, who could sing the part of Jean Valjean?"

"Well, not to brag, but I could," he tells her, smiling in a way that's both charming and modest. I nearly gag, but the other girls at the table all melt and make googly eyes at him. I can tell they are considering it again.

"Let's do *Grease*," I tell them, rolling my eyes.

"Yes, *Grease*. You can play the part of Sandy, Niahm." Hilary leans forward excitedly.

"I don't—"

"You have to," Stacy informs me. "You're the only one with a strong enough voice. And you're blonde. And *sweet*." I glance toward Sam to see what he thinks of that assessment, but to his credit, he doesn't roll his eyes, though his jaw tightens a little. He doesn't even glance at me.

"Jon, you'll be Danny."

"No way," he argues. "I wanna be Kenickie. He's the cool one. That's where I'm at," he laughs, bumping fists with Kevin.

"Well, that leaves you, then, Sam." I sit up straight in my chair at this pronouncement by Heather. "If you can sing Jean Valjean"—she pronounces it in a very Americanized way rather than with the French inflection—"then you can surely do Danny Zuko."

"Wait, no, I don't think that's a good idea—" my protest is lost in the flurry of voices as they start choosing parts. I'm about to speak up louder when Sam does something very odd.

He opens a small Tupperware container—then immediately slams it shut with a quick look my way, his cheeks flushed. What in the world—then it becomes clear. I know exactly what is in that container. He grabs it with the clear intention of putting it back in his bag.

Before I'm completely aware of my intention, my hand shoots out, grabbing his wrist, roughly stopping him. I push the container back to the table with a thump.

"Don't stop eating now," I snarl. All conversation stops, eight pairs of eyes coming to rest on me. Sure, *now* they hear me.

In the silence, their eyes dart back and forth between my irate face, and his chagrined one.

"I'm . . . uh, actually, I'm full," he stammers, still avoiding eye contact.

"What's in the container?" I question, snarky.

"I . . . um, oh, it's . . . .nothing," he finishes lamely.

"Pie?" I purr.

"Just . . . it's . . . um, yeah."

"*My* pie?" I clarify. His cheeks are flushed, and I can't tell if he's embarrassed . . . or angry. Both, maybe.

"Oh, Sam, if it's Niamh's pie, you definitely don't want to pass on it. She makes the best pies around. Probably the best pie you could get *anywhere*," Hilary pronounces, clearly still trying to be the center of his attention.

"I . . . I don't have a fork," he says unconvincingly, pulling his hand and the container from beneath my own, which was still in place, I realize belatedly.

"You don't really need one, do you?" I ask mockingly. "Just use your fingers."

This is met with a moment's stunned silence at my rudeness. Not saying anything, he puts the container back in his bag. Before he can close the bag, Heather is shoving a fork at him.

"Here, you can use mine. It's clean. Hill isn't kidding when she says you don't want to miss out on it, if it's one Niahm made."

Sam doesn't have much choice now but to open the container and eat the piece of apple pie residing within. Normal conversation resumes for the most part. Sam eats the

Cindy C Bennett

pie slowly, glaring my way momentarily then turning a charming smile on Heather. He manages to convey utter pleasure at the taste, while maintaining a distantly angry look. It becomes difficult to watch him, but I refuse to look away, even if he won't return my look—even if I am ashamed at my stupid temper tantrum. No one seems to notice this little drama occurring in their midst—except for Stacy, who is kicking me under the table.

Yeah, that's gonna leave a mark.

Chapter 4

Sam

I lower myself into one of the kitchen chairs, throwing the remainder of the apple pie on the table in front of me. I pick up the fork and dig in like a starving man.

"How was school?" Shane smirks, and I throw him a dirty look. He laughs. "That bad, huh?"

He takes a seat across from me, jerking his chin toward the pie.

"Gonna share?"

I growl at him, and he laughs again.

"Guess not. Want to talk about it?"

"No," I mutter, shoving another bite in my mouth. How can someone so wicked make something so heavenly? "I mean, I really don't know what I did to her."

Shane's eyebrows shoot up, but he remains otherwise calm. "Her?"

"Niahm . . ." I break off, realizing I have no idea what her last name is.

"Eve?" Shane repeats.

"No, Niahm. N-I-A-H-M. Niahm."

Shane sits up a little straighter at the spelled name.

"Samuel . . ." his voice is a warning.

"No, I know. I know it's not her. *Trust* me I know how much it isn't her."

"Meaning?"

"Meaning the Niahm I knew was sweet, kind, loving. This one is . . . *not*."

"Well, that clears it up," Shane's teasing tells me he's off guard once again, as he relaxes back against his chair back.

"She just . . . no matter what I say, she takes offense."

"And you care because . . .?"

I'm silent as I continue devouring the pie, and Shane gives the table a little rattle.

"I don't, okay?" I growl at him.

"Look, Samuel, I know you're used to girls just throwing themselves at your feet—" his sentence ends in a grunt as I push the table with severe force into his ribcage. He lifts his hands in surrender as he tries to catch his breath. To be fair, I may have cracked a rib with the force of it, and though I know it will be healed within minutes, I feel bad about the pain that I know came with it. I gulp down the last bite and shove away from the table, tossing the empty pie pan and fork into the sink.

"Wash those," he says, his voice nearly back to normal.

"You're not my father," I say, but pull out the sponge and begin washing them anyway. Shane and I have lived together, moved around together for most of our lives. There are times when we grind on one another's nerves enough that we have to be apart for a time. Shane really *is* my uncle—my *great* uncle.

It's more convenient to live with him in the paternal role and myself in the teen role, to keep our story more feasible.

But with two men, who've lived as long as we have, there are bound to be some conflicts. So we might take a few decades apart, but somehow always find our way back together. Just one family member, no matter how authoritative, is better than the crushing loneliness.

"Cheer up, Samuel. Your babies are coming today."

I turn at his announcement, feeling lit up inside.

"Today?"

"Yup," he confirms. "I got the name of a local stable where we can board the horses until we get our own stable refurbished."

Shane knows me well enough to know how much this announcement can change my attitude. It's been a while since I've been able to have my own horse, Autumn Star, with me, as we've been living in large cities. Moving to a small town was my request. Shane didn't have to come, he could have chosen to go his own way, but loneliness doesn't just affect me.

"You said *horses*. The Irish is coming as well?" I clarify as I dry the plate and place it back in the cabinet. I haven't seen the new stallion yet. I look forward to the distraction of breaking him.

"Yes, he is. They weren't supposed to be here for another week, but if we don't take possession today, we lose the Irish."

"You say there's somewhere here in town to keep them?" I ask, placing the newly cleaned glass into its place.

"I asked around and was told the only place in town that stables for rent is the Parker farm."

"Shane?"

"Mm-hm?"

"Sorry about the ribs."

Chapter 5

Niahm

What was *with* you today?"

I plop into the recliner, tucking the phone between my cheek and shoulder, absently rubbing Bob's head resting on my knee.

"What do you mean?" I ask, knowing Stacy will never buy my feigned innocence for one minute.

"C'mon, Vee. You were like a triple W"—by which I know she means the Wicked Witch of the West—"with Sam today. What did he do to you to make you hate him so much?"

I sigh, without a good answer for her.

"Nothing, Stace. I really don't know why I—hold on, I've got a call on the other line." I push the call-waiting button on the phone, grateful for the reprieve. "Hello?"

"Oh," a surprised voice answers, rich and deep. "I'm not sure I have the right—I'm looking for the Parker Stables?"

"You've got them," I answer.

"Oh, great. I'm new in town—"

"Let me guess—Mr. Coleman?"

"Shane," he corrects, and I can hear the smile in his voice. "It's not really hard to guess who I am when I tell you I'm new in town."

"Let me put it this way, Mr. Col—Shane, I'm seventeen and there hasn't been anyone move into town for my whole lifetime."

"Well, that's quite some time, isn't it?" His voice rings with irony. Strange. "Is your father in? I'd like to speak to him about stabling my horses."

"No, sorry. He's out of town. I can help you, though. How many horses?"

"Uh . . . two." He seems hesitant to deal with me.

"That's fine. I have four empty stalls right now. One-fifty a month for both. That includes usage of the wash bay and the arena either for exercising them yourselves, or for letting them loose in. I'll feed and water them daily, but you'll have to muck the stall yourself." I use my best business woman voice. It works. When he answers, his tone turns businesslike, the hesitation gone from his voice.

"That will be fine. My nephew and I will make sure one or the other is there daily."

My stomach drops. Shoot! I forgot just whose uncle I was speaking to. I should have kept my wits about me and told him the stable was full.

"How soon will you be bringing them by?" I force myself to ask, hoping he doesn't notice my sudden hesitancy.

"Actually, they arrived unexpectedly today, a week early. Can I bring them now?"

Relived by his use of the word "I," I relax. At least I won't have to deal with the arrogant Sam today.

"Sure. I'll give you directions."

When I'm finished, the phone buzzes, reminding me that Stacy is waiting.

"You'll never believe what—" I cut myself off. If I tell her Shane Coleman is coming to my house, she'll rush over, making a fool of herself over him. I don't want to contribute to her going down that particular path.

"What?" she demands impatiently when I'm silent.

"You'll . . . you'll never believe . . . what Bob did," I spout with sudden inspiration. "He got into—"

"No, please!" Stacy wails into the phone. "Not another Bob story. I swear you love that mutt more than you love anyone else."

I laugh at her completely predictable response. "Not more than you, lovey."

"Yeah, yeah, whatever," she grumbles, somewhat appeased.

"Gotta go, Stace. The chickens don't feed themselves."

"Stupid chickens, you should train them better."

"Ha, ha," I mock, hanging up.

❋❋❋❋❋

I am in the middle of the chicken coop, spreading feed when I hear the truck turn up the drive. I'm wearing one of my father's large beat-up flannel shirts to protect my clothes, and my knee-high rubber boots, hair twisted up into a messy bun, protected by an old John Deere cap. I briefly consider running in and shedding all the "farm-girl" accessories, then realize that's what Stacy would do for the exalted Shane Coleman.

"C'mon, Bob," I say, backing out of the coop. Bob is momentarily dejected at having to leave one of his favorite pastimes—torturing the chickens—but always willing to go forth with the hope that an even greater adventure awaits him.

I hang the feed bucket on its nail, wiping my hands on my jeans. I walk around the front of the stable, where the signs direct folks to the stables—not that most people need them. I arrive to see a massive black pick-up, pulling a matching black horse trailer, clearly expensive. For the first time, I wonder what Mr. Coleman—Shane—does for a living.

The driver's door is open, and he's nowhere to be seen, so I head to the rear of the trailer. Its door hanging open gives away his location. A chestnut Thoroughbred with white half-stockings of nearly the same length and a white star between his eyes is led from his other side. He's one of the most stunning horses I've ever seen—feisty, if his black mane tossing is any indication. His legs lift in a spirited prance. It doesn't take a practiced eye to see the value of this stallion.

Shane turns the horse toward me, and stops. Because I'm staring at the horse, I don't pay particular attention to Shane.

"Wow, he's a beauty." I finally pull my gaze from the horse so that Shane can see the sincerity on my smiling face, considering removing my sunglasses so he will see the same emotion in my eyes. The smile drops, along with my shoulders, to be replaced by a grimace.

It's not Shane.

Chapter 6

Sam

et me guess," I say, ironically. "Niamh *Parker*?" I realize I never asked her last name.

"What are you doing here?" she demands.

I raise my brows at her, and jerk my head toward the horse. She rolls her eyes.

"I thought your uncle was coming."

"He had some business to take care of so he sent me," I mutter, wondering if he somehow *knew* whose stable he was sending me to.

"Great." I can hear the sarcasm in her voice. Almost reluctantly, she says, "Follow me, I'll show you where to put him."

She stalks off, not waiting to see if I follow. She leads into the stable, opening one of the stall doors. No words, just a sweep of her hand to show me the way as she holds the door open. I narrow my eyes at her, wondering if she'll trip me or slam the door on me, finally leading the stallion in. I turn the horse, clucking and making soothing noises to the horse that's a little nervous in this place with strange smells. I take the halter off the horse and step out as she closes the door behind me.

"Name?" she asks.

"Sam Coleman, as you well know," I respond irritably.

"Not yours, id—" she stops herself from calling me the name, her cheeks flooding with a charming shade of pink. I'm well aware of the name she'd been about to call me. "The horse's name?"

"Autumn Star," I reply, nearly smacking my forehead in consternation. Of course she meant the horse's name. Guess I am kind of an idiot. She lifts her chin, stubbornly refusing to acknowledge her words.

"You have another? Not name, horse I mean," she clarifies.

I grit my teeth at her tone, as if she were talking to an imbecile. "I knew what you meant. Where's he going to go?"

She points to the stall on the opposite side. I walk over and peer into the stall.

"That should do," I mutter, more to myself than to her.

"I be so surry, *Mr.* Coleman, if our stables aren't to yer likin'," she says, trying to sound like a backwoods country bumpkin—and doing a poor job of it, I might add. I've lived among people in the most backwoods of places, and she isn't even close in her impression. I throw a look her way, trying to let her know how poor her impression is, and turn toward the open stable door.

"That's not what I meant," I say as I walk away. It seems that whatever I say to Miss Parker, she takes offense.

She follows me out as I disappear into the trailer. I grab the Irish by the lead rope and he immediately rears back. The first stallion is my own; this one is new. Today is the first day I've set eyes on him. He's large, shiny black without an ounce of any other color on him—with the exception of pure white coronets near each hoof. He is magnificent.

I lead him out of the trailer with as much gentle persuasion as possible, to find Niahm peering around the corner, interest lighting her face. It's a look I haven't seen on her face before, and it completely transforms her. The horse rears up, front legs pawing the air in fright. My attention diverted, I give the Irish a little lead, but not too much. Niahm takes a quick step back.

She hurries into the barn, standing behind the stall door, ready to close it as soon as I get the beast inside. Smart girl. With a little work, and a lot of coaxing, I finally lead the stallion in. The horse's eyes are rolling, but I'm able to sooth him just enough.

Once the stallion is in the stall, Niahm pushes the door closed, trapping me within—exactly what she should do. I unclip the lead, backing toward the stall door, not looking, trusting her to open it. Once I'm out of the stall, I smile triumphantly in Niahm's direction—and to my surprise, she smiles back, sharing in my victory. Suddenly, the faux intimacy of the moment strikes us both, and she turns away.

"What kind of horse is that? I don't recognize it," she asks.

"He's an Irish Draught. Striking, isn't he?"

"He's absolutely gorgeous. I've never seen anything like him."

"I'm glad you like *him*," I say. She doesn't comment on *that* statement.

"What's his name?" she asks.

"He doesn't actually have one yet. He's new, not even green broke yet."

"That would explain the tantrum. You have someone coming to break him?"

"Yeah, me."

"You?" Surprise laces her tone.

"What, you don't think I can break a horse?" I throw her words back at her, though in a less harsh tone than she used on me.

She looks thoughtful, as if the question bears scrutiny.

"Actually, I believe you can."

I freeze in the act of hanging the lead, turning her way.

"What? Was that an actual *compliment* from the inimitable Niahm Parker?"

I can see her narrowing her eyes at me even through the sunglasses as she turns away, refusing to answer. I follow her from the stable.

"My uncle said to let you know that we'll only be keeping them here until we can get the barn rebuilt on our own property."

"Oh." Her response is almost—wistful. "Well, while they're

here, you can come over anytime. The stable is never locked."
She points to her left. "There's a paddock over there that you
are welcome to use. If you let them through the gate just over
there," she points again, "they can graze in there. The tack
room is right there," she thumbs over her shoulder.

"Sounds good," I say, watching her closely. I'm impressed
by her professionalism.

"I'll feed and water them, but I won't muck your stalls."

I laugh at her overly fervent tone.

"Gotcha."

Her shoulders drop, as if relenting. "That's not necessarily
the complete truth. If you're going to be out of town, or just
can't get over for some reason, just call. One of us will do it."

"One of us?"

"Me or, if they're around, one of my parents."

"Oh. Are they here? I'd like to meet them," I respond,
wondering about the type of people who could produce a
being such as Niahm Parker.

"No, they're in Egypt. They'll be home Friday."

"Egypt? What are they doing there?" That was hardly the
response I expected from the daughter of two small town
farmers.

"Work," she says. "My dad's a photographer, and my
mom's a writer. They write beautiful, interesting travel books."

"Why didn't you go with them?" I wonder aloud.

"Been there, done that. They dragged me all over the
world till I finally dug my feet in and refused to go anymore."

"I can imagine that," I mumble, well acquainted with said
stubbornness.

"I haven't been more than fifty miles from Goshen since I
was thirteen."

I stop, stunned. "They left you home? Alone?"

"I can take care of myself," she bristles. "Besides," her
voice pitches upward, mischievously, "I have a protector." She
whistles, and a black lab comes bounding in, tail wagging. I
laugh.

"*That's* your protection?"

"Get 'em, Bob," she says calmly. The dog immediately crouches forward, snarling, teeth bared aggressively. I take a step back—he can't really hurt me . . . at least, not too much. But I don't want witnesses to that fact. The dog, Bob, continues to move toward me, growling from deep within his chest, punctuated by threatening barks.

"Call him off," I warn calmly, continuing to back slowly away, my voice as calm and soothing as I used with the Irish.

Niahm cocks her head, looking for all the world as if she is rather enjoying this. "I don't think I will," she says with a smile. I take my eyes from Bob just long enough to give her a look, letting her know how crazy I believe her to be.

"Good dog," I soothe, clucking, turning my attention back to the snarling fury in front of me. The dog begins to back down, giving in to my cajoling, growls becoming whimpers.

"Get 'em," Niahm repeats. Bob steps up his assault stance. Just as he gets near me, and I'm wondering how I'm going to explain the healed bites tomorrow, he lunges—past me, continuing his growling threat to the tree behind me. I turn toward Niahm, perplexed. What just happened?

"Back, Bob," she says, and he comes bounding back, tongue lolling, waiting to be praised for his performance.

I look at her in stunned disbelief. And she's *grinning*.

"It's been a long time since I've been able to pull that trick on anyone since most folks around here know it by now," she grins. Anger floods my entire being.

"Are you *kidding* me? Is that supposed to be funny?"

"It was to me," she laughs.

"You're protection is some . . . some *party trick*?" I think of all the things that can happen to a young, beautiful, teenage girl left alone . . . apparently with the knowledge of the whole town that not only is she alone, but also that she is protected by an overgrown puppy.

She shrugs, and my anger surges dangerously close to fury.

"You didn't know he wouldn't hurt you. Most people

would've turned tail and run. You're either really brave or really stupid. Which is it, Sam?"

"I believe you're completely insane," I half-yell. When she doesn't respond, my frustration boils over. "I think you're Sybil reincarnated."

"Who?" she asks, reaching up to tuck a stray hair behind her ear.

"You know, Sybil . . . multiple personalities . . . it was a movie . . . based on a true story . . . Sally Fields?" I'm holding my hands out toward her in supplication and, realizing the silliness of the gesture, I pull them back and tuck them into my rear pockets.

She shakes her head, "Sorry, never heard of it."

Her words stop me. Frustration has made me careless. What seventeen-year-old kid would know about an old movie? I rock back on my heels, cursing my stupidity.

"I guess it was an old movie, from the seventies, I think."

"You're into old stuff?"

I look at her, trying to push the anger back into a manageable place.

"Maybe I am."

"Okay, *grandpa*," she jokes, and I feel the anger boiling up again—mainly because she has no idea how close to the truth she is.

"You are either like her, with about twelve different personalities," I spit, "or you're just plain schizophrenic. Either way, certifiably insane."

With that, I stride to my truck, annoyance radiating from me in waves. I glance back while driving away, and if I didn't know better, I would almost swear Niahm looks as if she feels the smallest bit of regret for baiting me.

She has no idea how close she came to forbidden territory.

Chapter 7

Niahm

"Y"ou are my sunshine . . . " The booming, off-key song comes from the front porch. I light up at the sound, pushing away the slight irritation at their lateness. They were supposed to be here early this morning. It's now nearly noon.

"My only sunshine," I holler back, jumping up from the gray-carpeted floor where I'd been lying, watching TV.

"You make me happy," the male voice cracks on the high note.

"When skies are gray." I pull the front door open.

"You'll never know, dear—" he sings, extremely off-key, with a wide grin.

"—how much I love you," I join in with him, "Please don't take my sunshine away."

I launch myself into my father's arms, which close around

me in a bear hug.

"You two are beyond ridiculous," my mother says, grinning at us both. I release him and throw my arms around her. She's right, and I would never in a million years admit to my friends this strange little coming-home ritual we have. I would miss it if we were to stop—almost as much as I miss them when they're gone.

"I'm so glad you're home," I say with absolute sincerity.

"You know, honey, I'll sing with you anytime you want. It doesn't just have to be on our homecoming."

"And have them run us out of town?" I tease. My father is well known for his completely off-key, tone-deaf voice, which he happily shares at the drop of a hat. "How was the sphinx?"

"Beautiful, as always," they intone together.

"You guys spend way too much time together," I grimace, watching as my father drops to vigorously rub the sides of Bob's neck, letting Bob lick his face unheeded. "And that's really gross, dad. I wish you wouldn't let him do that. Then he thinks he can do it to anyone."

"How did everything go while we were gone?" Mom asks, giving my father's shoulder a little push to move him into the house, as he completely ignores me, not pushing Bob away.

"Great. No problems. Got two new horses in the stable."

"Oh yeah? Who bought new horses?" Dad asks.

"The people who just moved into the Stanton place."

That stops them both in their tracks. I have their complete attention now; my father even pushes Bob down off him, Mom stops trying to get him to move. Bob gives a snort of disgust then tromps happily off, probably to chase butterflies.

"Someone bought that old, rundown place?" my mother asks at the same moment my father says, "Someone moved into town?"

"Yes and yes."

"Okay, spill," Mom exhorts, practically pushing me back into the house, followed closely by my father.

"Guy named Shane Coleman, and his nephew Sam."

"Uh-oh," my father says. "What have they done to offend you already?"

I hate that my father can read me so well.

"Nothing. Shane is really nice, from what little dealing I've had with him."

"The nephew, then," my mother says to him.

"Do I need to pull out the shotgun?" my dad asks. I laugh aloud at the thought of my father with a gun in his hands. I myself can shoot a pop can dead-center from a hundred yards, but he would not even know how to load the bullets.

"No, he's not *that* bad."

"Let me guess," my mother says, opening the fridge to pull out a bottle of water. "He's your age, or close to it, good-looking, and all the girls are falling all over him."

I grimace, then admit, "All but the *good-looking* part."

"Must be gorgeous," my father mutters to her.

"Dazzling," my mother confirms with a wink.

"I'm in the room," I complain. "I can hear you."

"What did he do, darling?" Mom says. I think about telling them about the pie, but realize how ridiculous it will sound. And knowing they will laugh at me. And that they will have every right to—it was a stupid reaction to such a trivial thing. I'm still unsure of why I react the way I do to Sam Coleman.

"Nothing. He's just really annoying."

"Hum," they both murmur meaningfully at the same time. I choose to ignore them.

"You should come out and see the horses. They're amazing."

I knew that would distract them.

✳ ✳ ✳ ✳ ✳

Church in Goshen is as much about worshiping as it is about socializing. I'm not sure exactly when it started—long before I existed, anyway—but church always ends at noon, to be followed by a picnic, when the weather holds, or by a potluck in the gym if the weather is bad. No matter your degree of belief, everyone shows up at least for the food. Unless you're new in town and don't understand the rules, that it.

I guess Mrs. Bradley forgot to inform the Coleman's about this particular ritual as they aren't at church, or the picnic following. In a town like Goshen, this isn't just worthy of being noted, it's cause for gossip and speculation. Of course, because they aren't here to hear, the gossip runs rampant.

"Did anyone tell them what time services begin?" Mrs. Wittmer whispers—loudly enough to be not really a whisper.

"I'm sure they were informed, I believe I told them myself . . ."

"Do you think they are *anti*-social?"

"Maybe they're hiding something . . . what do you think it could be?"

Stacy and I wander around, listening to the ridiculous gossip, mimicking some of the more meaningless chatter. I have to admit, Stacy is good at imitating voices, almost to perfection, definitely to my amusement.

After the picnic, I meet up with Stacy and the double-H on my ATV—and them on theirs—to go for a ride. It's one of the beauties of having my parent's home—a little freedom. It's Stacy's turn to lead the way, and we dig in. When Stacy leads, you can count on a fast, wild ride. We're speeding down dirt roads, me eating the dust of the other three, when suddenly she stops. As the person in the rear, this requires me to do a little panicked turn off to the side to avoid a collision, into the soft dirt which gives me a final spray from forehead to chest to knees.

I pull my sunglasses off, which are now almost impossible to see through, wiping them on the underneath of my t-shirt before replacing them, glad for the reprieve as I backhand the dirt off my mouth and loudly cough up what feels like dirt clods.

"Well, hey there, Coleman's, fancy meeting you here," Stacy's voice, full of saccharine, oozes.

I look up in horror, stopped short by Stacy's words in the

act of about to let loose the stream of muddy spit that I've worked into my mouth, my horrified eyes snapping up to see Sam and his uncle working on a fence—their own fence—right in front of her.

Shane chuckles. "Not exactly a surprise to find us on our own property, though, is it?"

Stacy looks around in mock surprise. "Gee, I didn't realize we'd come so far."

I roll my eyes. Stacy doesn't ever end up anywhere that she didn't explicitly intend to. I risk a glance at Sam, to see him watching me, a slightly amused look on his face. I get the distinct feeling that he is more than cognizant of the sludge currently residing behind my teeth. I straighten a little, throwing him a look intended to make him feel inferior. It only makes his grin a little wider. I slowly slide my sunglasses back on, turning Sam into a slightly smudged version of himself.

"Well," Shane sweeps us all with a glance, "Samuel and I were just about done." The look Sam shoots him negates his uncle's statement, but he doesn't say anything. "Would you girls like to come up to the house for some lemonade?"

I begin to roll my eyes at the silliness of the request as well as at Stacy and the double-H's over-enthusiastic response, until I notice Sam doing the same thing. I try to stop mid-roll, refusing to agree with him on anything. I don't know if you've ever tried to stop an eye-roll smack in the middle. It's quite painful. My eyes immediately begin to water. I reach up to wipe the pain-tears away, only after dragging my fingers through the grit remembering about the dirt on my face.

Great, now I have mud streaks down my face. I look at Stacy, whose face is virtually clean and at the double-H, also clean. I guess my refusal to wear a bandana over my face beneath my glasses is my payment for my current predicament.

"We'd love to," Stacy gushes, echoed by Hilary and Heather. I risk another glance at Sam, who is grinning openly at me now. I'm sure it has something to do with the wet, muddy track now leading from the corner of my mouth. He cocks an eyebrow at me, as if daring me. Stacy and the double-H swing gracefully off their bikes, and follow Shane toward the ranch. Sam stays behind to mock me.

"Coming, Niamh?" he asks, laughter in his voice.

I nod, glaring.

"I'm sorry, what? I couldn't hear you," he laughs. "Got something in your mouth?"

I stand up slowly, straddling my bike. Not taking my eyes from his, I slowly swing my leg over. Climbing down, I walk toward him. His eyes widen slightly, but the grin never leaves his face. As soon as I am right in front of him—standing this close I decide he must really be at least six-five—I pucker, and breathe in through my nose. Then I spit the whole, disgusting muddy mess—right next to him. I admit it; I seriously considered spitting it on him, or at least on his shoes. I chickened out.

Whether Sam knew my original intention or not, he bursts out laughing. "All right," he yells, punching the air with his fist. I wipe my mouth with my sleeve, and intensify my glare as I push past him. Only a guy would think spit is something to cheer, rather than a disgusting act.

I manage to ignore Sam's cheerful whistling as he casually strolls behind my aggressive stroll. Very noble of me to refrain from shoving him, I'd say. When I arrive on the doorstep, however, I'm checked in my anger. Shane and the others have already entered, the screen door having swung closed behind them. Whatever else I am, I can't ignore my polite upbringing, which requires me to knock before entering the house of someone I'm not that familiar with. I debate the silliness of knocking, when Sam is quickly coming up behind me, and can open the door to his home himself, versus knocking rather than waiting for him to do so.

His arrival takes the decision out of my hands. He reaches past me to grasp the door handle. I am uncomfortably aware of his nearness, and the faux intimacy of the gesture. When he hesitates, I glance up at him irritably—to see him looking at me, brows raised, infuriating grin still in place. His face is far too close to mine for ease.

"What?" I demand, when he continues to look at me.

"I *could* pull the door open," he says, winking at me. *Winking* at me! My face flushes. "But it would likely smack into you, and that would be rather rude, don't you think?"

My brows furrow in confusion. *What?* Finally, my brain does its job and processes, but only after I glance back at the screen door and realize I'm standing directly in front of it—and it swings toward me. Embarrassed, I step sideways, out of the half-circle formed by his arm. He chuckles, and pulls the door open, waving me to enter ahead of him with his free hand. I give him my best haughty look and sweep into the house, following the sounds of laughter into the kitchen.

They glance up at my entrance, except for Shane who is squeezing lemons into a pitcher. The remaining three sets of faces change from smiles to looks of horror as they spy me. Assuming they think it's rude to wear my sunglasses in the house, I push them up on top of my head. Their eyes go wider.

"Uh, Vee, the restroom is just around that corner," Stacy informs me.

I shake my head at her. "Thanks, Stace, but I don't need. . ." I trail off as she begins making circular motions and pointing at her face. My dirty face is suddenly brought to my recollection and I grimace. "Right, gotcha. I'll be back." I refuse to glance Sam's way as I follow her pointing finger.

I walk into a bare bathroom. By bare, I mean there is nothing within besides the toilet, sink, and a towel hanging from the rack. Not a single picture, rug, or anything personal to break up the monotony. I step in front of the mirror, and gasp when I see myself.

My hair is tangled and knotted, hanging all askew. But that's nothing compared to my face. Muddy streaks cover the entire surface—even my forehead. I look like I've been rolling in it, and eating it, my lips and corners of my mouth caked with it. I think of Sam, teasing me, of my haughty defiance, and humiliation floods me. I'm sure he must be having a great laugh at my ill-placed pride.

I turn on the water and lean down, scrubbing my face with my hands. Mud swirls down the drain. When it's finally clean—albeit a little red from my scrubbing—I dab it dry with the towel. I pull my hair tie out and try to finger comb my hair. It doesn't help. I wrap it back up and exit the bathroom.

"There you are," Shane says, affably. He hands me a glass, and indicates I should sit at the table with the others. Sam is seated between Heather and Hillary, whether by his choice or theirs I don't know. I suspect it was theirs, but he doesn't exactly look sorry to be there. Shane returns to lean against the edge of the counter, feet crossed, one arm propped behind him, the other holding his own glass. In his pose, he appears much younger than he must be, and I can see why Stacy thinks he's hot—even if it is still, like, eww.

I plop down next to Heather, with mumbled thanks.

"You've gotta try these, Vee," Stacy says, pushing a plate of cookies across the table to me. I glance at the large, fat cookies stuffed with oatmeal and raisins.

"Joan Ames?" I ask, picking one up and taking a bite.

"Mmm-hmm," Stacy answers around her own mouthful of cookie.

"How did you know?" Sam asks, wonder in his voice.

"If there's one thing Niamh knows, it's baked goods," offers Hilary, leaning closer to Sam.

"And horses," Stacy puts in sardonically.

"She can tell you who made just about any kind of cookie, cake or pie, because she's better than most. Everyone else tries to bake as well as she does," Hilary ignores Stacy's comment, not willing to forgo the absolute attention being bestowed on her by Sam, even if the attention is caused by extolling my cooking virtues.

"Chickens, too," Stacy says, smirking.

"But she still can't beat Joan's cookies," Hilary finishes, as if

Stacy hadn't spoken, nudging Sam's arm, as if sharing some great secret.

"Sheep, not so much," Stacy adds, cynically.

"Too bad you don't have some of Niamh's pie here," Heather pipes up, wanting to draw Sam's attention to herself. I freeze at her words. "Her apple pie is the best in the state, five years running."

"Is that right?" Shane asks, turning toward Heather.

"Grows the apples herself," Hilary says, not willing to relinquish the spotlight, blushing as Sam turns her way once again.

"She knows apples," Stacy's inane comment is given with humor lacing her voice.

"We had an apple pie brought the day we moved in," Shane says. "But I didn't get any of it. Samuel ate the whole thing himself, within two days I believe."

I risk a glance at Sam, only to see that he's suddenly, intensely interested in tracing the pattern on the tablecloth with one long finger. I throw him a glare, anyway. His cheeks redden over his clenched jaw, as if he can feel the weight of my look.

"Was that one yours, Niamh?" Shane asks. Stacy shoots me a warning look. I narrow my eyes at her, then turn to Shane, the sun glaring in the window directly into my eyes tempting me to replace my sunglasses, rude or not.

"Probably not," I say. Sam finally looks up at me, unable to ignore the super-sweet tone of my voice. "It was probably store bought."

Stacy chokes on her lemonade; Sam narrows his eyes at me.

"If so, I'd like to know where it came from," Sam says. "It was the best pie I've ever had."

Chapter 8

Niahm

Chucking a single cookie at Sam wasn't too harsh a reaction, I didn't think. Maybe grabbing five more of them and following suit while he dodged and deflected with both hands was a *little* overboard. Heather and Hilary were horrified by my actions. Stacy looked horrified, and Shane laughed so hard he was bent in half.

Sam was stunned into silence. At least, that was the last expression I saw before turning and fleeing from their house. I ran to my ATV, jumped on and gunned it toward home.

"What is it with you and Sam, Vee?" Stacy asks me later, when she calls on the phone.

I give an exasperated huff of breath.

"I don't really know, Stace. Every time I'm around the guy, it's like my brains just fall out of my head. But, seriously, what he said today—"

"Would have made you laugh if anyone else had said it," she interrupts.

I sink down to the floor, and Bob immediately has his muzzle in my face, tempted to lick me but knowing better. He settles for nuzzling me with his wet nose.

"Maybe I'm just having some kind of raging, hormonal reaction to red hair," I groan.

"I believe it's hormonal, but it's not just red hair causing it," Stacy answers.

"What do you mean?" I am immediately defensive.

"I *mean*," she explains slowly, as if I'm an imbecile, "that you are attracted to him, and you hate it."

"I am *so* not attracted to him," I argue, even while visions of his amazing eyes and great smile dance in front of me. I smack the palm of my hand against my forehead, trying to erase said vision. "Why would you even think that? I can hardly stand to be near the guy."

"Classic story," she says, "pretending to hate one another, when really you're madly in love."

"Give me a break," I say, pushing Bob off me and standing. "This isn't some cheesy, dime-store, romance novel. This is my *life*. If I liked him even a little, don't you think I would—"

"No, I don't," she interrupts yet again, as I wander to my window, looking down, ironically, on my mini apple orchard—which I need to pick. That brings to mind my pie, his comment, the cookies . . . I swing away from the window, pulling the string to drop the blinds. "I know you better than anyone, Vee," she continues, "probably better than yourself."

"And?" I ask, wishing I could take the word back as soon as it leaves my mouth.

"And I think you've got the hots for this guy."

I roll my eyes, wishing she could see the gesture. "Okay, first of all, Stace, I'm not you and he's not his uncle. Second, if I had the hots for him, I'd be *nice* to him, not . . ." I hesitate at calling myself mean, "well, you know, angry at him all the time.

Your theory makes zero sense."

"Hear me out, my little chicky. Exhibit A: you have never had a serious boyfriend before."

"What does that have to do with—"

"You've never *had* a serious boyfriend because you are extremely independent. You've practically raised yourself, and so you don't think you need anyone. Not only does that keep you from hooking up, it intimidates the boys we know."

"Okay, *mom*," I begin, sarcastically. "Thanks for the—"

"Exhibit B: So far, all the boys you've known are planning to leave Goshen, a thought you can't stomach, so you're waiting to see who comes back, or who's willing to stay."

"That's not—"

"Finally, exhibit C: Sam and Shane are clearly not small town types, which means they probably won't stick around for long, and while that's a total turn on to me, you find it . . . *undesirable*. You don't want to fall for someone who doesn't share your dream of growing old and dying here—along with the town, I might add."

I'm silent as I desperately try to find my side of the argument. Finally, I settle on, "*Exhibit* C? What are you, a lawyer now?"

"Look, Vee, I'm just saying that being nice to the guy, hanging out with him and having a little fun isn't going to hurt you. *He* isn't going to hurt you. Just because you admit you like the guy doesn't mean you're going to marry him."

I take a deep breath, suddenly drained by the conversation.

"I've gotta go do my chores, Stace. I'll talk to you at school tomorrow." I hang up without waiting for her response.

"Come on, Bob," I say opening the door. "Let's go feed the chickens." At the word *chicken* he immediately perks up, tail wagging, nose pressed to the door in anticipation of being set free to pursue his favorite hobby, impatient while I pull my boots on. When I open the door, he beelines for the chicken coop, but at the last second, detours to the right, taking off at a dead run.

"Bob, come back!" I call, which he completely ignores. I grunt and follow his path, deciding I better discover just what caught his attention so fully. I come around the backside of the stable and stop in my tracks.

Sam is in the center of the enclosure, leading the Irish in wide circles. The stallion is agitated, leaping and bucking, pulling against the lead, glorious in his fury. I spot Bob, sitting outside the gate, watching the scene, as if he, too, is transfixed by the sight. I slowly walk toward him, not wanting to disturb their work.

As I draw near, I can hear Sam, clucking and talking in a low voice, soothing and hypnotic. For long minutes, the horse ignores him, refusing to give in to his call. I don't know how long he's been at it, but they are both covered in sweat and dust, his t-shirt clinging to his straining muscles. Sam is patient, slowly circling, giving the horse just enough freedom to keep his rage at bay, but holding on tight enough to make sure the Irish knows just who is in charge. I find myself holding my breath, trying to force my own will on the horse, compel him to trust in the hand that holds him.

The stallion begins to tire, and slows his pace. His breath heaves his sides loudly in the hot air, his eyes rolling still, but giving in to the persistence of his lead. Finally, he slows to a complete stop. He tosses his majestic head twice then drops his nose slightly; with a final huff, he gives himself over—for now.

I glance up at Sam, and his eyes meet mine across the distance. In his victory, he appears more like seven-feet-tall than his true . . . six-whatever. Suddenly, his face breaks out in a wide smile, victorious, complete joy radiating from his eyes. I can't help it; I smile back, my face reflecting his elation. He lifts his hand in a low wave, and I mirror the gesture. Suddenly I'm embarrassed at being caught watching him, and I quickly shove both hands in my back pockets. The intimacy of the moment strikes me, and abruptly I turn away, smacking my thigh twice to bring Bob to heel as I head for the chickens.

I think about Stacy's words, and realize how very wrong she is. I think, if I gave myself over to Sam as the stallion did, it would give him the power to hurt me . . . to hurt me very much.

I let myself into the noisy, squawking hens and try to ignore my pounding pulse, my thoughts that want to succumb to a certain hypnotic voice, my heart that squeezes painfully.

Chapter 9

Sam

I watch as Niahm hurries away from the paddock. For just a minute, as she shared in my victory, I saw something in her, something that she seems to try to keep hidden. I think about her parents leaving her home while they travel the world. It didn't take much asking to find out that they're gone more than they're home. Anger rises in my chest again, and I quickly push it back as the horse catches the scent of it and throws his head.

I would like to hold Niahm's hands, find out what is really going on in that head of hers—but I can see well enough how welcome that gesture would be. I can easily recognize the bond that is being formed between us. I think she feels it also, but she's fighting it with all her might.

It's not the first time I've felt a bond with a mortal . . . but it's definitely the strongest and fastest forming I've experienced. I should have run as soon as I first recognized it, the first day I saw her. After experiencing the wrenching loss that comes with bonding, I've learned to avoid it as much as possible. It's been decades. Maybe that's why this bond has felt so different.

As soon as I return home, I question Shane about it.

"Do you think you're feeling a genuine bond with this girl, or do you think you're feeling a bond to her *name*?" is Shane's first question after I explain my dilemma.

I give his question serious consideration. It's a valid question. Finally, I shake my head.

"No, it's her. I felt it before I even knew her name."

"Hum," Shane responds. "I don't know of anyone else who's had such a hard time getting a mortal to bond with them in return."

"Lucky me," I mutter, sarcastically.

"Can you leave?" Shane questions.

I huff out a frustrated breath. I know what he's asking—one word and he would either drop everything and leave with me, if I asked it of him, or stay and let me go, covering for my disappearance.

"No," I finally answer, misery in the word. "Not unless she asks it of me."

"Well, then," Shane responds, standing up. "I guess you better get to work charming that girl," he chuckles. But even though he's trying to lighten the mood, make me feel better, he pats my shoulder sympathetically, and in the weight of his hand I divine the burden of the task.

Chapter 10

Niahm

It's not an entire shock to me when it's decided that we will stay after school each day to begin planning our production of *Grease*—that's been happening since time immemorial around here. What does shock me is my own reluctance to be involved in the planning. The Senior Class production is almost hallowed, and I've looked forward to it since I saw my first production at age three. I try to think of excuses to get me out of the meetings, but can't come up with anything that would sound true. Everyone knows everything about me, and they all know that not only are my parents back in town—relieving me of some of my chores—but that I have time to donate to the cause. So instead I just refuse to participate in the planning, doodling in my notebook as the others plan.

Now, I sit across from Sam, placed near one another as we

are the two leads. For the first time in my life that I can recall, I wish I attended a large high school, where one would have to try out for a part, rather than having it *assumed* upon them.

My feelings regarding my forced-upon-me costar are a muddled mess. I'll admit, between Stacy's words and what I witnessed in the paddock yesterday, I'm having a hard time retaining my anger. I'm having a hard time really remembering why I was that mad to begin with. But, in my typical stubbornness, I refuse to admit to her—or myself—that she might have been just a little bit right.

I steadfastly refuse to look at Sam, except when he's not looking, of course. Then I can't help but look, as I try to puzzle out my confusion. There's definitely something different about Sam from any other boy I've ever known. Not just that he's, you know, totally gorgeous. Not that his amazing shade-of-red hair sweeps across his brow and curls lightly over his ears and collar. Not his lips, full and wide. I think I actually sigh looking at them. Not his perfectly masculine jaw or his eyes that have . . . *crap!* . . . just lifted to look at me, auburn brows drawn down in confusion at my intense perusal . . . and probably at his hearing my sigh.

I can feel the flames fan my cheeks as I quickly look away, trying to pay attention to the discussion. Honestly, though, I have zero creativity concerning writing a script or planning the stage props. I'm very creative in the kitchen, but this kind of creativity is better left to those whose input will actually be helpful. Put me on the stage and tell me what to sing or say, and I can hold my own pretty well, but that's the end of my talent in that area. I begin to sigh again, then realizing how it may sound to Sam, I try to suck it back in.

This, of course, causes me to choke. I begin coughing violently, attracting the attention of every set of eyes at the table. Yup . . . his, too. I stand and try to excuse myself around gasping for air. No one really pays attention when they see I'm not in mortal danger, so I make a quick exit.

In the hallway, I lean over, coughing and holding my

stomach. Just when I almost have it under control, I hear, "You should get a drink of water."

It's not the words, but the source of the words that causes me to gasp, and I begin choking anew. A set of hands reach out and guide me to the drinking fountain. I lean over and take a mouthful, swallowing it against my breath. I cough a few more times, between a few more swallows of water, and soon I'm able to control it.

"Thanks," I croak, avoiding looking up at Sam's towering height. I swear he must be, like, six-six as my eyes are right at chest level.

"No problem. Are you okay, now?"

Nervously, I realize his hand is still lingering on my shoulder.

"How tall *are* you?" I blurt out. He blinks in surprise, and it occurs to me that my tone sounds a little accusatory, as if he's been keeping it secret. I drop my voice to a murmur, "Not that I, you know, wonder about it very much, or anything."

"I'm six-three," he says. "How tall are you?" I glance up at him, and quickly away, but not before I see the grin and teasing glint in his eyes.

"About a foot shorter," I say.

"*About* a foot?"

"Fine, *exactly* a foot, okay?" I know I sound sullen, but I still haven't decided whether I should be nice to him or not—especially when I'm this confused about him. I've never been confused about a boy before. It's kind of embarrassing to admit, but I've never even kissed a boy before.

"Should I call you shorty, or shrimp?" he laughs.

I glare at his chest. "Should I call you lanky or Lurch?" I shoot back. Yeah, I know. Lame. But he only laughs more. Then he slips his hand from my shoulder and holds it toward me.

"You can call me anything you want if you'll agree to a truce."

I glance at his hand, at him, then back to his hand, suspiciously. "A truce?"

He shrugs. "We got off on a really bad foot, and I'm sorry about that. I'm sorry for offending you. But we have to figure out a way to co-exist peacefully, and I'd really like to be your friend."

I scrunch my eyebrows. "You sound like my dad," I grumble. Then I relent and place my hand in his, tired of being angry all the time. His long fingers close over mine, strong and warm. Then he's shaking my hand, as if we'd just met. I glance up into his smiling face, my gaze immediately sliding away, embarrassed.

"Hi, my name is Sam. It's nice to meet you."

I can't help but smile back at the silly charade.

"Niahm," I say.

"Hmm . . . Niahm. That's an unusual name."

I shrug. "I have unusual parents."

He gives my hand a squeeze and releases it.

"Should we go back in and help with the planning?" he asks.

I look toward the door. I can hear voices from within. Somehow, I doubt they'll miss me.

"No, I think I'm going to cut out for today. I should go home, anyway, and—"

"Feed the chickens?" he interrupts.

"Something like that," I smile.

"Mind if I go with you?"

"You want to feed my chickens?" I ask, perplexed.

He grins. "No, I want to work the horses." Oh, *duh*. "And I'd like to meet your unusual parents."

I shrug. "Okay, just remember you asked for it."

We leave without telling anyone that we're going. I'm not sure of Sam's reasons for this, but mine are clear. I don't want Stacy giving me that told-you-so look because this *isn't* what she thinks. This is just deciding to be nice to Sam, nothing more.

"So, what transportation did you use to get to school? Livestock or thumb throttle?"

"Ha, ha," I mock. "Except when it's snowing, my only transport is my feet."

"I live a little further, so I drove. Want to ride with me back to your place?"

"Uh . . . " His question stumps me. It shouldn't. I've caught rides with any number of people in town, and never thought twice about it. But this whole being nice to Sam thing is new, and instinct makes me want to say no. Thinking it feels a little too friendly also makes me want to say no. Being in a confined space so close to Sam makes me want to say no. Not wanting to explain any of that to him makes me finally mumble, "Okay."

He looks at me oddly. "I'm a pretty good driver. I promise to get you there in one piece."

"Oh, yeah, no . . . I know that. I mean, I *don't* know that, but . . . "

"But?"

But I'm feeling flustered by you right now. Why is that?

"No but, just . . . okay."

He narrows his eyes in confusion, but doesn't press the issue. He leads me to his truck—the same one he brought the horses to the stable in—and opens my door. Like that doesn't make me even more uncomfortable, as if we were on a date or something. What can I do, though, but climb in and let him close the door behind me.

❋ ❋ ❋ ❋ ❋

"I'm *not* rushing through my chores so that I can get out to the pasture to watch Sam with the Irish. I'm hurrying because . . . okay, maybe that's the reason a little bit. It has *nothing* to do with Sam. I just want to watch the horse. He's so beautiful. All six-foot-three, red-headed—" I gasp and break off, glaring at Bob as if he caused me to say that. He's trying to be a good friend, sitting at my feet, glancing at me as much as he possibly can while I ramble—not an easy task with the chickens in front of him, egging him on just by existing.

"I *so* did not mean that," his head, which had been inching back in the direction of the source of his divided attention, jerks toward me at my harsh tone. I smack my forehead with the palm of my hand—and grimace as I feel the grind of the chicken feed, which is now rolling down my face. I angrily brush the feed from my hand using the front of my jeans, then brush it from my face, as Bob tries to catch the miniscule falling pieces, pretty much just snapping air between his jaws—which makes me laugh.

I back out of the pen, calling Bob with me. His head hangs dejectedly as a result of my cutting into his chicken chasing time with my conversation, but once the gate closes behind us, he perks up and bounds off. I walk into the horse barn, peeking in on Sheila, my mare. She stands happily in her clean stall, eating fresh hay next to her full water trough. I know I should be happy my parents are back and that they've done some of my more time consuming chores, like cleaning Sheila's stall and feeding and watering all the horses.

I grunt and turn toward the sounds I can hear coming from outside in the paddock. I give in to the urge and follow the sounds out.

Sam is working the Irish in the same manner as the previous time. This time, I climb up on the top rung of the fence and watch more closely. Bob jumps up on his hind legs, paws at me once and whines, as if upset that I didn't bring him up to sit with me. I push a palm toward him and he backs down, settling for sticking his nose through the bottom rung.

The Irish continues his wild defiance, though not quite so harshly as previously. Sam just keeps on clucking and soothing, and while they are both covered in sweat once again, neither is breathing quite as hard once the stallion gives in. Sam grins at me, walks closer to the horse, shortening the line as he goes, continuing to talk in monosyllables as he nears. The Irish tosses his head and snorts, but allows the nearness. Sam urges the horse forward, walking next to him.

"What do you think, Niahm? Thinks he's ready for the saddle?"

It takes me a few seconds to grasp the question, since he delivers it in the same soothing voice, just slightly louder than his other words.

"I think that would be cruel," I say. "Look at the poor beast, he's sweating and exhausted."

"Best time to try it," he says.

"I think you'd do better to give him a name."

He grins at me again, and I look away, Stacy's words ringing in my mind again.

"Got any ideas?" His words pull my attention back to him.

I lean forward, hooking my feet behind the next log down, leaning my weight on my arms as I consider the stallion, now walking almost docilely next to Sam.

"I don't know. He's an unusual horse; he should have an unusual name."

"Yeah, that's why I haven't named him yet. Nothing's come to me that seems right."

"Doesn't your uncle have any say in it?"

Sam shrugs. "The horses are more of my thing than his. He likes to ride, occasionally, but he's not as crazy as I am about them."

"Oh yeah? Why are you so crazy about them?"

"I've been riding horses for so many years, that I guess it makes me feel like I'm home."

"So, where is that? Home, I mean."

Sam glances at me, wariness stealing into his face. I get the distinct feeling that he doesn't want to answer me.

"Is it a secret or—" I ask, when the silence lengthens.

Just then, the Irish gives a kicking buck, throwing his head.

"Whoa, there," Sam's attention is drawn back to the horse. "I think he's had enough for one day," he calls to me, struggling with the lead. "Can you get the gate for me, Niamh?"

I jump down and swing the gate open, stepping behind it as he leads the Irish through. I follow him into the stable and pull the gate open for his stall. Sam removes the lead, and gives the nervous horse a quick rubdown, before rewarding him with an apple from the bucket of apples I keep in the barn for just such things.

He hangs up the lead on the nail tacked outside the stall, then follows me back outside. Bob comes bounding over, bypassing me and waggling his tail enthusiastically for Sam. I lift my eyebrows at him. He grins, not so innocently.

"I just used a little bribery on Bob the couple of times I've been here. Wanted to make sure he wouldn't be attacking me again."

"Bob, you traitor!" I accuse. He glances up at me, his ears flattening in chagrin for all of about one-tenth of a millisecond. Sam and I laugh and I glance up at him. Suddenly the smile drops from Sam's face and he steps closer to me, alarm on his face.

"What?" I ask, my hands immediately going up to my cheeks, wondering what's wrong.

"Your eyes!" he declares, and I relax. I'm used to the strange reaction when someone really looks at my eyes for the first time, and realizes that they are clear, only ringed with gold which gives them the appearance of actually having color.

"Yeah," I smile, "I know my eyes are different, they're—"

"Colorless," he finishes, still sounding alarmed. I bristle a little at his summation. I've had them called unique, unusual, exceptional . . . any number if descriptive verbs, but never "colorless."

"They're not exactly colorless, they just—"

"There you are, kiddo." My father's words boom across the yard, and I realize how close Sam and I are standing as he stares into my eyes, and I take a step backward, a little freaked by Sam's intensely worried demeanor.

"Hey, dad," I say back, turning to see him and my mother striding across the yard toward us. I roll my eyes. Remember me saying how everyone in town wears jeans except on Sunday's? I should have qualified that with: except my parents. They always dress in one of two ways: as if they are on a safari, or they were headed to 4 o'clock tea with the Queen. Today, they are in Safari mode—my dad even has the hat, and the shorts with knee-socks.

As they near, smiling expectantly toward Sam, I turn back.

"Sam, these are my parents, Jonas and Beth Parker. Mom and dad, this is Sam Coleman."

Sam still looks stunned, and slightly nauseated. Somehow I doubt my eyes can be the cause of such a reaction, so there must be something else going on.

"How are you, Sam? Welcome to town," my father says, pumping his hand.

"Oh . . . yes, thanks," Sam's response is rote, distracted.

"Sam, would you like to stay for dinner?" This from my mother, who I love, but I groan at her invitation. Since I usually cook, it's extra work for me, not her.

"What?" That pulls Sam out of his reverie, though the furrow in his forehead doesn't ease. "Dinner? Uh, no . . . no, thanks. I . . . I have to go. I have to be . . ." He glances at me again, in an expression close to horror and I find myself caught up by it. Now he has me worried. Something is definitely wrong.

He turns away, striding toward his truck without a backward glance. He slams the door behind him and guns it down the driveway.

"Okay," I murmur, "that was odd."

"Well, isn't he a tall drink of water," my father teases, and I groan.

"Please, dad, that's creepy."

"Oh, but darling, your father's right. No wonder you've been in such a bind about him."

"Mom!" I head toward the house, but they follow, tormenting me.

"Did you see them when we came out? Gazing into one anoth—"

I slam the door behind me, shutting out the rest of my father's words, but not the sound of their laughter.

Sometimes, loneliness is the better option.

Chapter 11

Sam

I slam the door open, and Shane's reaction is immediate. He stands and steps toward the closet where we keep the weapons, his eyes never leaving me. Then, whatever he sees, he relaxes.

"Her eyes!" I explode.

His alarm turns to amusement as he looks at me.

"Do you have them in your hand?" he asks lightly.

"What?" His question throws me, until I follow his gaze down to my clenched fists. I relax them and blow out a breath.

"You wanna sit?" he asks, indicating the table.

"Yes," I huff, then proceed to pace beside the table, while Shane slides back into the chair he had vacated, where he was working on one of his blasted Sudoku puzzles. I can't stand the things myself.

"You want to tell me about it, or just wear a hole in the

floor?" Shane continues writing numbers, not lifting his eyes.

I grunt, not sure how to tell him. Finally, I just blurt it out. "They're colorless."

That stops Shane short, and he looks at me in some alarm.

"I thought they were unusual . . . gold. They appeared gold the few times I glimpsed them. Her rim is still large enough to give the impression . . . ." I stop pacing and drop into the chair across from him. I think back to all the times I'd seen her. She was either wearing those infernal sunglasses, or far away, or not looking at me . . .

"How did I miss it?" Misery laces my voice as I drop my head into my hands.

"That's no' hard to fathom. You weren't lookin', now, were ya?" I can gauge the strength of Shane's upset by the fact that he's allowed the slightest burr to creep back into his voice. "How long ha' it been since we've seen one?"

"Too long," I answer. "But why does it have to be her?"

We sit in silence for long minutes, both considering. When Shane speaks again, he's back under control, all traces of his true heritage lost in his American accent.

"Okay, well, it is what it is," he reasons. "It's not completely unheard of for an immortal to bond with another immortal."

"But we don't know for certain that she *is*. We only suspect. And there's only one way to find out for sure."

Shane nods. He understands instinctively what I'm talking about. It's bad enough to bond with a mortal, and have to watch them die. The only way to take that nightmare to a new level is to add in the possibility that she *might* be immortal, but not know unless she dies—and comes back—before her fifty-third birthday. To watch her pass that benchmark and not "die" beforehand means an eternity of living with *if*. To lose her before that and have her not be immortal is unthinkable.

Leave it to me to bond with a temperamental, stubborn, pig-headed, *possible* immortal.

Chapter 12

Niahm

Gotta love Saturdays. I can sleep in 'til six. I don't have to get ready for school, before I get up and start my chores. I don't even bother with makeup or doing my hair. I can get to that later.

"Hey, mom," I say as I walk into the kitchen. She's already up, making me breakfast.

"Morning, baby," she says, walking over to kiss me on the head as I drop into a chair. I don't get to be babied too often, so I take advantage when I can.

"Where's dad?"

"Oh, he's out in the stable, admiring those Coleman horses." She puts a plate of food in front of me—the kinds of food I never eat when I'm home alone, like bacon, eggs, and toast—and sits down across from me.

We talk about her and my dad's newest book, which the publisher is pushing for a completion date on, and I update her on the nothing new that's been going on around the farm and in town.

"Why don't you invite the Coleman's out to dinner, Niahm?" Mom asks, taking a bite of her dry toast. Ugh. I can't eat toast unless it's slathered with butter and jam.

I roll my eyes. "I'm sure they're inundated with invites, mom. I'll bet they haven't eaten at home once."

"Well, now, if everyone assumed that, they wouldn't be getting a single invitation, would they?" I huff out a sarcastic sigh at her words. "Just ask them, okay?"

She knows I won't deny her. It's so rare they're home, that when they are, there isn't much I won't do for them.

I stand up and kiss her on the head, as she had done to me. "Sure, mom, I'll ask. Just for you."

"You're a good girl, Niahm," she says as I walk out the door.

As I near the stable, I can hear my father talking. Not so unusual, for him to talk to himself, or Bob. I hear a familiar voice respond and pick up my pace. As I round the corner, my fears are realized as I see my father standing in conversation with Sam.

I'm surprised to see Sam here so early, especially after his strange behavior the day before. He seems happy this morning, his anxiety gone. He glances up at me and smiles, his smile open, but behind it just a tinge of the wariness resides.

"Hey, Sam, Dad, what're you two up to?" I ask, rubbing Bob who bounds over, excited, as if he hadn't just left my room thirty minutes ago.

"Well, there's my princess," my dad says, pulling me into a one-armed hug as he ruffles my hair. I groan—it's bad enough that he calls me that in front of Sam, but his ruffling of my hair recalls to my mind that I haven't even brushed it, let alone put a spot of make-up on. I guess I should at least be grateful that I brushed my teeth.

"Your dad was just telling me about his experiences, photographing other countries," Sam says, trying to hold back a grin at my obvious discomfort.

"Dad," I whine mockingly, "if you keep boring my friends with your stories, they are going to quit coming around. I've *told* you this."

He laughs at me, knowing I'm only teasing, dropping a kiss on top of my head.

"All right, I've got some photographs to develop. You kids have fun." I roll my eyes affectionately as he walks away. My dad is a complete dork. Who else would still use film rather than digital? He claims the photos lose something when pixilated.

"Nice guy," Sam says as my father leaves the stable.

"Yeah, he is," I agree. "I hope he wasn't boring you, though."

"No, his stories are actually quite fascinating."

"Uhm," I grunt noncommittally. My father's stories stopped being fascinating to me long ago, but I guess they would be new to Sam.

"So, is that what I am, now?" he asks, looking at me slantwise, "Your friend?"

I glance away, thinking of my thoughtlessly spoken words. I shrug, and decide to change the subject.

"You seem better this morning. You were a little freaked out yesterday."

"Oh, yeah, that." He looks uncomfortable. "That was . . . " He trails off then looks at me. "I can't really explain that."

He waits for my response, but I don't know what to say. It was definitely weird, but I guess everyone is entitled to their strange quirks. Instead of answering, I walk over to Sheila's stall. She comes to greet me, knowing I'll have an apple for her.

"Let's go for a ride," Sam says behind me, "on the horses."

I look at Sheila longingly for a moment, before turning back to Sam.

"I wish I could, but there's work to be done. If I don't do it, who will?"

He glances toward the open door that my father just exited from, but doesn't say anything. Good thing; I don't deal well with criticism of my parents.

"You can't take a break for a couple hours, have some fun?" he asks, instead.

"It's not like I *never* have fun," I defend. "It's just that there're things that need to be done."

"I'll help you, as soon as we get back."

"You don't understand, Sam. After I clean Sheila's stall—"

"Done," he interrupts.

"What?"

"That's what your dad was doing when I got here."

I glance toward Sheila's stall, surprised I missed that when I looked in before.

"Huh," I say. Brilliant, right? "Well, I've gotta milk Bessie and—"

"Wait, your cows name is *Bessie*?" Sam scoffs.

I narrow my eyes at him. "So?"

He bites back a laugh, "So nothing."

I shoot him my best dirty look, and continue. "I've gotta clean out the chicken coop, change the litter boxes, check my ducks and make sure they're doing okay, tend the garden, and start the apple picking—"

"Is that a normal Saturday for you?" Sam's stunned.

I shrug. "A little hard work never hurt anyone."

"Niahm, you're *seventeen*. A child. You should hardly be expected to run an entire *ranch* by yourself."

Of course, my anger rises.

"I'm not a child!" I explode, sounding very much like a petulant child, completing the illusion with my hands on hips. "And I've been running my *farm* since I was thirteen years old."

"Why don't you hire some help?" Sam questions, remaining calm in the face of my temper. I refuse to admit that my parents have tried to hire help multiple times, but it's become a matter of pride to run the place myself. I keep my lips clamped, not wanting to admit my stubbornness.

"Look, just come for an hour. We can run the fence lines, check them over." I'm about to argue; we don't really have any animals to be kept penned in, but then he makes an offer. "When we get back, I'll help you with whatever you need."

I glance at him. "*Any*thing?"

"Anything," he confirms, "for the rest of the day."

I narrow my eyes at him, "Why would you do that?"

"Because I'd really like to go for a ride, and I don't want to go alone." When I continue to look at him suspiciously, he grins. "And I have nothing better to do all day. What do you do for fun around here?" His city-slicker-ness is definitely showing. People who haven't been raised in small towns don't understand small towns.

"You can go to the movie," I say.

"It's been out on DVD for, like, six months," he counters.

"Bowling," I offer.

"There're only four lanes, and they have their league play today."

I'm impressed by his knowledge of that so quickly.

"Ma & Pa's Diner," I offer, starting to smile at him.

"All day in a diner?"

"You could hang out with old man Jones in front of the store." He grimaces at the suggestion, and I relent with a laugh. "Or you could go for a horseback ride."

"Ah-ha!" He grins. "That sounds like a fantastic idea. Now, if I only had someone to come along . . . "

I shake my head at him. "Fine, I'll come, but you're going to be sorry when you see how much work I manage to put you to."

He rocks forward onto the balls of his feet. "Do your worst," he teases.

Chapter 13

Sam

Niahm leads Sheila from a trot into a canter, taking the gait in her hips as any experienced rider would. Her upper body remains still, elegant in the saddle. With a gentle nudge of her calves, she urges Sheila into a run. Leaning slightly forward, she relaxes, a small smile playing across her mouth as we gallop across the fields, the cool air flooding her cheeks and nose with a charming shade of pink. I can't take my eyes off the grace with which she rides. She seems to understand instinctively when Sheila begins to tire, and brings her back down to a canter. She pulls up and stops after twenty minutes, near a stand of trees and the creek which runs across their property. We swing down off our horses and lead them to the cool, clear water.

"Having fun?" I ask.

She grins at me as she loops Sheila's reins over a low tree

branch.

"A little," she says, walking back to the stream where she drops to the green, grassy ground with a sigh of pleasure. I hurriedly tie Autumn Star off as well and join her. "There isn't anything quite like it, is there?" she asks. "It's so peaceful, almost quiet with the power of a horse beneath you. For a few minutes, anyway, you can forget about the world." The contented expression on her face speaks volumes, and not for the first time I wonder why a girl of seventeen needs an activity to take away worldly cares.

"How often do you take the time to do something just for you?" I expect her to bristle at the question as she does anytime someone questions her vision of her perfect life.

"Probably not often enough," she surprises me by admitting. "But I can't really complain, can I?"

"Why not?" I ask, genuinely curious why she would think that.

"Because I chose this life. I chose to stay home rather than globetrot with my parents. I chose to run things alone." She pauses. "I chose to not ask my parents to stay home with me."

I can hear the pain that laces her voice at the last admission. "Would they?" She glances at me. "I mean, if you asked, would they stay?"

She's silent for long moments, staring at the water that meanders by. "Of course they would," she mumbles. The doubt is clear in her tone.

"You do have *some* fun," I offer, changing the subject. She glances up at me, and I'm struck once again by her eyes. "You have been known to take a ride on your ATV and eat a mouthful of dirt."

She narrows her eyes at me, then bursts out laughing. "I can't believe you still speak to me after I nearly spit on you."

"Well, it wasn't so much the spit as the cookie grenades that were the low point of that day."

She looked chagrinned. "I'm sorry about that. It was a bit of an overreaction."

"And a waste of some really good cookies," I add.

"I'll make it up to you," she offers. "I'll bake you some cookies. They won't be as good, but . . ."

"How about a pie?" I venture, looking at her slantwise.

She narrows her eyes at me again, and her mouth tightens slightly.

"Kidding," I laugh, holding my hands up in surrender.

"Not funny," she mutters.

"No? Not even a little?" I bump her shoulder with mine; see the corner of her mouth lift. She pushes my shoulder with her hand, and I tumble away, as if she'd really pushed hard.

She laughs one quick laugh, then smothers it with her hand, though her shining eyes give her humor away. "You're *so* not cute," she laughs behind her hand.

I sigh dramatically. "I know. It's this dang red hair, everyone hates it—"

"Who?" she demands, almost angrily. "Has someone said something? They're wrong, Sam. Your hair is beautifu—" she stops abruptly, turning back toward the stream.

I crawl back over next to her. "I knew you thought I was cute," I tease and she smiles, cheeks pink. "I'll make a deal with you," I say, and she turns to me with curiosity, her embarrassment forgotten. "If I work really hard with you today, and don't make you angry once, you come with me next weekend, to dinner and a movie."

One corner of her mouth lifts wryly. "You mean the movie that's been on DVD for six months and the diner?"

"Nope," I say, pulling a blade of grass near my feet, splitting it with my thumbnail. "A *real* movie, and dinner at a *real* restaurant, in the city."

I look up to see her staring at me, stunned. "You mean, like, a *date*?"

I huff out a laugh. "You make it sound like I'm offering a disease."

"No, it's not . . . it's just . . . uh . . ."

"The correct answer," I tease, picking up her hand, ignoring the spark of energy that arcs toward me, placing the flimsy bracelet I've weaved from the blades of grass around her wrist, "is, 'Yes, Sam, I would love to go with you to the city to see a movie that no one else has seen, and to eat a dinner cooked by someone besides myself. Thanks for asking.'"

She looks down at the bracelet, pulling her hand away from mine before I can get a read on anything more than a jumble of confusion, fingering it lightly. "*This* is your idea of a bribe?" she asks, then looks up and I see the teasing glint in her eyes.

"There's more where that came from," I say, sweeping my hands around, indicating the field peppered with grass and weeds. "And the color looks great on you."

"Flattery will get you nowhere," she says, a small smile playing across her lips.

"Will it get me a date for next weekend, at least?"

"No," she says firmly, hopping up onto her feet. "But it will get you a *friend* to go with you—dutch."

I grin as I stand and follow her back to the horses.

Chapter 14

Niahm

*O*f course, I regretted telling Sam I'd go with him as soon as we arrived back at the house. No matter how much crappy work I gave him, no matter how hard I pushed him, he worked without complaining, without doing anything I could get mad at him for, making it that much harder to come up with an excuse to get out of it. He even talked to my parents, making sure it was okay if he took me, since it's an hour ride each way.

This is how I find myself sitting next to Sam in his truck, one week later, as we make the hour long drive. I guess there are worse things than a night in the city, seeing a real movie, sitting next to a tall, red-headed Adonis.

We stop at an Italian restaurant, which is not the nicest restaurant I've ever eaten at—that would be when we were the guests of a Sheik in Saudi Arabia when I was about ten or so—but it is leaps and bounds above Goshen's diner. The cloth napkins and Italian décor—complete with Italian opera playing—give the place a nice ambiance, a feel of luxury. They seat us smack in the middle of the room, as if on display. I look around at the other tables, mostly occupied by couples but with a few groups or families here and there.

"See that couple over there?" I ask him, pointing. The couple looks to be in their mid-forties, overweight and frazzled, and not speaking, let alone looking at one another. "They have eight kids, and this is their first night out without them. They're so exhausted they can't even muster the energy for a conversation."

It's a game I used to play with my parents when we traveled, making up stories about the people we saw. It doesn't really work in Goshen as I know pretty much everything about everyone.

Sam chuckles and says, "Not just exhausted, but it's been so long since they've spoken adult talk, they no longer know how." I laugh, glad that he caught on so quickly. "And there," he continues, pointing to a young couple, she texting madly on her phone while he appears utterly bored. "First date, she won't get off her phone, he's ticked that he has to pay for her dinner."

"Hi there, I'm Sauna, can I get you guys something to drink?" our server interrupts our laughter. Sam raises his brows at me as she gives her name, and I have to bite my lip. We order our drinks, and as she walks away, Sam say, "Did she really say her name is *Sauna*?" He gives me a huge, over-dramatic wink. "That's *hot*."

I groan, "Bad joke, Sam Coleman. Besides, I am the *last* person in the world to mock someone's name."

After she returns with our drinks and takes our order, Sam says, "Okay, what do you make of that?"

I follow where he's pointing to see a teenage couple sitting in a cove. Nothing unusual in that—if you discount that she's completely Goth and he's a complete nerd.

"Hmmm," I try to imagine what would pull such a couple together. "Someone dared him to ask her out, and she's too nice to say no?"

Sam grimaces at me. "Doubtful as far as her, I'd say, though I can buy someone daring him to ask her out. She's out with him because someone either bribed her, or made a bet with her that she wouldn't do it."

I watch as the couple leans toward one another, almost subconsciously.

"She likes him," Sam states, also watching them. "See how she leans toward him? She likes him, and she hates that."

I can't argue with that logic, since their body language seems to support his theory. I turn to another table. "See that group over there? They are on a double date, but the girl on the left side of the table really likes the guy on the right side, not the date she's with."

Sam's attention is drawn back to the game, away from the odd couple, and after we've made up stories about everyone in the vicinity, and when our food has been served, I ask Sam about himself.

"So, what's your story, Sam? Where did you and your uncle live before now?"

It may be my imagination, but Sam suddenly looks uncomfortable.

"New York," is his short, hesitant answer.

"Why in the world would you move from New York to *Goshen*? That seems like a *colossal* change."

Sam clears his throat, suddenly interested in the dew collecting on the side of his glass. "Shane was . . . *tired* . . . of the city, I guess. Wanted to move somewhere small."

"Well, he certainly accomplished that," I laugh, wondering at his strange behavior. "How do you feel about that? I mean, you must have friends in New York. Wasn't it hard to leave them?"

He glances up at me under his brow, and gives me a one-sided, wry smile. "It's different there. There are a lot of people,

Niahm. I wasn't particularly close to anyone who I didn't want to leave."

"That's kind of sad," I say. "What was your school like there?"

The waitress walks up to the table with our bill. Sam's attention is diverted while he pays her, completely ignoring my efforts to pay for my own meal.

"We should get going so we're not late for the movie," he says, standing and moving to pull my chair out. When I don't stand, he raises one of his glorious auburn brows at me in question.

"Sam, this isn't a date, remember? If you pay for me, and pull my chair out, then it becomes a date."

He leans down, his face near mine, and I'm struck again by his dark green eyes. For the first time, I wonder if he wears colored contacts. "Would that be so bad, Niahm?" he questions, and I forget to breathe for long seconds. He leans back a little, and the spell is broken.

"I'm paying for the movie," I inform him as I stand. He chuckles and shakes his head.

"Of course you are," he mutters. I choose to ignore the sarcasm as we leave the restaurant.

Chapter 15

Sam

Niahm insists on paying for our movie tickets, as I knew she would. I make sure I'm prepared when we get our popcorn and sodas so that she doesn't have a chance to pay. She glares at me for a second, but I smile as charmingly as possible. I really need her to be somewhat pliable tonight.

From the first moment I met Niahm Parker, I've been trying to figure out a way to get her hand into mine, palm to palm. It's unfair, I know, and I usually try really hard to avoid reading someone I plan to know for any length of time. It's a matter of privacy. But with Niahm, I have a vested interest, a need to *know*.

We make our way into the theater—reserved seating: brilliant!—and find our seats. We talk while waiting for the movie to start, Niahm entertaining me with their visit to the Arab Sheik when she was ten, from her point of view, of course. I can't help but laugh at her story—somehow I doubt the guy pulled the sheet directly off his bed to wear on his head, and the elephants and monkeys dining with them in his home are surely a stretch.

When the lights go down, I give her thirty minutes into the movie to finish the popcorn and relax as she gets involved in the flickering story on the screen. Then I make my move, casually taking her hand into mine, not looking at her, acting like it isn't a big deal. From my peripheral vision I see her glance at me, but she doesn't pull away. Once her attention is back on the screen, I close my eyes and let the arcing electricity flow into me, as my mind fills with images.

Every moment of Niahm's life flashes through my mind, even moments she has no conscious recollection of—those memories are dimmer, less clear. Light and laughter fill her childhood, deep love for her parents. I'd like to take the time to watch it all, but there is something specific I am looking for, so I bypass anything that doesn't pertain. I see her traveling with her parents, feel her frustration at always having to go when she really just wants to be home with her animals. I can feel the deep devotion she has to the creatures, her intense guilt over leaving them alone. When the pain comes, I'm completely unprepared. It isn't that I thought Niahm has lived such a carefree, charming life that she wouldn't have suffered pain, but this pain is the deep, cutting pain of betrayal by the two people she loves most—her mother and father.

Niahm may say that she doesn't mind her parents going on their working trips, but she's lying. She feels deep pain at their decision to continue to go, to leave her behind. I can feel her insecurity: that they don't love her enough to stay home with her, that she isn't good enough for them, that she isn't as appealing as the travelling. I feel her anger at a stolen childhood, first by being taken all over the world, then by being left to play the role of an adult at home, her jealousy over watching her friend be afforded that which she wanted most. Her stubborn pride in refusing to admit that she needs them extends to her refusing to accept help of any kind. To admit she needs help would be to admit she needs them home. Her fear stems from taking them away from what they love, even more from the fear that they might not choose her.

I look at her then, and as she feels the weight of my look, and glances at me, I see the astonishment on her face at whatever she sees on mine. I try to school my face into a smile, though it's probably more like a grimace. I turn back toward the screen, and after a few seconds, she follows suit.

I close my eyes again, still searching. I can't help but notice that the only person she feels a deep connection to besides her parents is her friend, Stacy. She feels a deep and abiding loyalty toward her. No boys. I wasn't looking for that *specifically*, but the fact that I find that makes gives me an unfair sense of relief.

I get a glimpse of her confused feelings about me, but quickly shy away from that.

I pull myself out of the images completely, knowing that Niahm can't feel the intense heat between our palms, as if they were on fire. Only I can feel it. I continue to hold her hand until the end of the movie, letting go when I have to as we stand and put our jackets on. As we're walking out of the theater, I take her hand again, just to see if she'll allow it. She does. What I really want to do is take her in my arms, shelter her from her pain, anger and disappointment. I can just imagine the outcome of *that* move.

As I open the door to the truck, closing it behind her then walking around to the opposite side, all I can think is, *she doesn't know*. She has no idea, not even in the deepest recesses of her imagination, of what she just might be.

Chapter 16

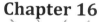

Niahm

"Sooo?" Stacy drags the word out, heavy with emphasis. We're in my kitchen, and I'm preparing the meal for later tonight for my parents, Shane and Sam, and, you guessed it, Stacy. She immediately invited herself as soon as I told her that at the end of mine and Sam's . . . well, I guess I have to call it date considering the hand holding and all, that I'd extended the invitation requested over a week ago by my mom.

I still can't believe I did invite them. I can't believe I let him hold my hand. Even worse that I'd enjoyed it! And mostly, I can't believe that I am anticipating tonight—maybe as much as Stacy.

"So . . . what?" I ask, cleaning the chicken over the sink. No, not one of *my* chickens. I'm not a sadist. It's not that I think the chicken purchased at the store was produced at the store and didn't come from an actual chicken; it's that I didn't love this chicken. I know it doesn't make sense, but I refuse to eat any of my own chickens.

She pelts the back of my head with a small wad of the roll dough that she is supposed to be kneading.

"Dude!" I complain.

"That's dudette to you," she says. "Stop avoiding the question. I was patient enough to wait until now." She doesn't mention that that's only because my parents were in the house when she came, and she thinks I have some juicy details that I wouldn't share in front of them.

"It was . . . fun," I say.

"Argh," she groans.

"Don't even think about it," I say, spinning and seeing that she has another small piece cocked and aimed.

"Then spill," she threatens. "Details, not generalities."

"Fine," I sigh, smiling as I turn away from her. Of course I'm going to give her the details, who else would I share with? I just like messing with her.

"Let's see," I say, turning on the water and running the meat beneath. "First, we went to this Italian restaurant."

"What did you order?" she interrupts.

"Really?" I ask, glancing back at her. "You want that much detail?"

"Hey, I've never been on a date outside this fabulous little berg, my friend. I'm living vicariously through you right now. And let me just tell you, that is a phrase I never thought I'd be saying concerning you."

"Vicariously, huh? Big word," I grin at her.

She shrugs. "Gotta start using them if I want to get into college."

"Alright, I ordered the linguini with clam sauce, and—"

"That's my girl," she cheers. I look back at her questioningly. "What? I hate it when girls go out on their first date, and order a dinner salad because they don't want to seem like a pig, or greedy by costing too much. *Clam sauce* . . ."

she muses.

I roll my eyes at her, then drop the first piece of chicken into the seasoned flour mixture. "I was planning to pay for it myself."

"What? Why?" she demands, sounding offended by the idea. "Wait, never mind, you can explain that little piece of stupidity later. Just finish the story."

I shake my head at her. "He ordered lasagna. Enough food detail for you?" I ask, glancing back at her again. She just narrows her eyes sardonically at me. "And we played the people game. It was fun. Then we—"

"Okay, whoa there. What in the world is the people game?"

"You know, where you make up stories about the people sitting at the other tables."

"You have a misguided sense of fun, my friend."

I choose to ignore her comment.

"We went to the movie—which *I* paid for. And he held my hand." I stop speaking, waiting. It takes several heartbeats, and then she's next to me, spinning me away from the counter, chicken juice and flour flying from my hands, spattering the floor—giving me another thing I'll have to clean before tonight.

"He *held* your *hand*?" I can't help the grin that splits my face as I nod. "Wait till the double-H and all those silly juniors hear this!" she exclaims.

"No, Stace," I say. "I don't want anyone to know. I mean, it may not have even meant anything." I think about the strangely intense heat of our hands pressed together, the butterflies it sent shimmering through me. "He might have just been being nice."

"Oh, come on," Stacy gives me a shake. "Boys don't hold hands to be nice. At least, not boys like Sam."

"Maybe they do," I argue weakly. "He's not from here. Maybe that's how they do it in New York."

Stacy opens her mouth to argue, but really, she doesn't know any better than me. She shakes her head. "No, I don't think he would. I've seen the way he watches you."

I can feel the heat climbing my cheeks. "Yeah, well, that's probably because he's watching for flying cookies," I mutter. Stacy laughs.

"So, your first date and first hand-holding, all in one night, with the hottest guy in town, immediately making an enemy of every chick between the ages of fifteen and thirty," she finishes ominously, tone in contrast with her grin.

"Stace, come on. It was probably nothing. So it's not going to matter anyway."

She looks at me for a long minute, reading me as only she can. "You liked it?" she asks with a knowing smile. I give a tiny nod. "You like *him*?" she asks more seriously. I think about her question for a minute, and realize that I do, probably more than I should. I have no experience with boys, so this is way outside of my comfort zone. I give the same tiny nod, and her grin widens.

"Then hurry up and finish playing with that chicken so we can pretty you up," she laughs.

✻ ✻ ✻ ✻ ✻

Stacy on a mission is an unstoppable force. That's how it is that I end up with curled hair, perfect make-up, and high heels when Sam and Shane arrive. I feel silly; it seems clearly contrived for him. However, by the time Stacy finished with me and I finished dinner, I didn't have time to at least wash some of the make-up off, maybe pull my hair up into a ponytail.

"Welcome to our town, and our home," my mother is gushing at Shane. It seems she's under the same spell as Stacy—who's standing uncomfortably close to Shane's other side—regarding Sam's uncle. Sam grins at me and winks, as if in on the joke, and I feel the blush stealing up my cheeks again. Sheesh, I *never* blush, now it seems that's all I do.

"Let me get you a drink," my father offers, steering Shane away from his fan club—who follow closely behind. I shrug at Sam, and he takes my elbow, giving it a light caress with his thumb, leading me after them. And there goes the stupid blush again.

The heat in my face deepens when he leans close as we're walking and murmurs, "You look amazing."

"Well, there's no stopping Stacy when she gets an idea in her head," I mutter. He lifts one copper brow at my words, a smile on his face, but he doesn't comment.

An hour-and-a-half later, after Shane finally manages to eat his dinner between answering the questions pelted at him by his adoring fans, we move outside. The evenings are getting very cool now as autumn takes a firm hold, but my father has already remedied this by getting a fire going earlier for us to gather around. That's one of the perks of living on a farm—a campfire anytime you want.

Shane finds himself firmly wedged between Stacy and my mom on the stone bench. He's such a kind man, or at least a good sport, as he tolerates their fawning. I sit with Sam on the log, lower to the ground. My father, always restless, remains standing, regaling them with stories of their travels, which is all fine and well until he brings me into it.

"So there we are," he laughs, "sitting in this fabulously wealthy sheiks home, with all of his wives, and Niahm says—"

"'Daddy, why does that man have so many *daughters*?'" he and my mother finish together, laughing. I groan, which causes an already chuckling Sam to laugh even harder.

"All right, that's my cue to go get our dessert," I say, standing up. "Help me, Stacy?"

She shoots me a pained look, and Sam comes to her rescue. "I'll help you," he offers. He follows me into the kitchen, scrubbing Bob's head as he pushes up against Sam's leg, making it difficult for him to walk.

"Guess you have your own little fan club there, huh?" I nod my head toward Bob as I open the fridge, bending to retrieve the pies. I lift one hand in the general direction of the backyard. "You'll have to tell Shane sorry about my mom and Stacy." I turn toward the counter, a pie balanced in each hand.

"I don't think he's too stressed about the attention," Sam

grins. He moves over next to me, picking up the knife I laid on the counter and cutting one of the pies now sitting on the countertop, slicing it into evenly sized pieces. I'm impressed.

"I guess he gets that everywhere he goes, huh?" I look up at Sam, realize he's standing closer than I thought, and immediately start stuttering. "You know, women . . . um, falling over him . . . I mean, falling *all* over him." He gives me a funny look, and I realize the senselessness of my question. Sam gets that as much as his uncle. I feel like smacking my head in consternation. Instead, I walk around him to get the small plates out of the cabinet. As he cuts the second pie, I start placing pieces on the plates.

"What kind do you want?" I ask distractedly, "Apple or peach?" When he doesn't say anything, I glance up at him and see his sardonic look.

"Guess," he says, and I grin at him, still embarrassed at my complete overreaction before in regards to my pie.

"I'm surprised you want to have anything to do with me," I mumble as I turn back to the cabinet, getting out a tray.

"Why wouldn't I?" he questions.

"I haven't exactly been nice to you. I don't know if I'd be as patient as you've been." I turn to him, curiously. "Why did you stick around, keep trying to be my friend? Especially when you had every other girl in town hot to be the center of your attention."

A peculiar look crosses his face, and he glances away from me. After a moment, he looks back and grins. "I'm a sucker for punishment?" he offers.

"I don't think so," I laugh.

"I've been angling for another pie?" He ducks as I lob an apple at him, swiped from the basket on the counter, neatly catching it above his head.

"Try again," I say.

He shrugs, and looks at me more seriously. "I thought you were cute. Which—" he holds up a finger to silence me when I open my mouth to protest, "—would not have kept me coming back, just so you know. I'm not that shallow. But I saw how much your friends cared for you, the way they listen to you, and I decided there was more to you than you were letting on."

"Oh," is my brilliant response.

He steps closer to me, and I instinctively step backward, my progress stopped by the sharp hardness of the counter. I reach back, resting my hands against the edge. He places both hands on the counter, trapping me between them. My heart immediately starts to race.

"Have you ever been kissed?" he asks quietly.

I swallow the lump in my throat noisily, which Sam hears if his grin is any indication, unable to answer. One of his hands slips underneath mine. I wonder if he's going to kiss me, my mind frantically racing as I try to decide how to handle it. I don't want him to kiss me . . . do I?

No, definitely not. I don't think. I'm pretty sure . . . I don't know. No, absolutely not. No, not now that we're getting along. I don't want to ruin—

My rambling thoughts are abruptly cut off as he chuckles, as if he read my mind. I narrow my eyes at him, but he's already moving away, placing the plates of pie onto the tray.

"C'mon, friend," he says over his shoulder as he pushes out the door. Bob, who apparently thinks that Sam was talking to him, bounds happily behind him. I don't move, except to take deep breaths, trying to calm myself.

"Silly girl," I chide myself. I push away from the counter, only slightly shaky, and return to the fire. Sam has already passed the pie out, and is sitting on our log. I think about sitting somewhere else, but he holds a plate of pie out to me, and I can't refuse to take it from him. Once I'm next to him, it seems ridiculous to not sit where I'd been before, so I sink down.

"Amazing," Sam says, savoring a bite of his pie. Stacy shoots a look my way, probably wondering if I'm going to shove mine in his face.

"Thanks," I tell him, giving Stacy a look to say: *See, I can behave.*

Sam scoots closer to bump his shoulder against mine, then stays in place, his arm pressed against mine. I hope the dark sky hides my red cheeks.

Chapter 17

Sam

O ver the many years I've lived on the earth, I've learned to appreciate certain things. One of those things is the amazing amount of talent that people have. Some of them recognize and share their talents with the world; too many keep them hidden, or even undiscovered.

Goshen is a very small town, but it's packed full of talent. I'm impressed by the magnitude of the production these few seniors are putting on. Some of the younger kids audition for minor parts in the play, sworn to secrecy about details of the production—which doesn't seem strange at all to any of them. It shouldn't seem strange to me, but I admit, I've never seen anything like it. And that's saying something.

When Niahm opens her mouth and sings the first note, I'm floored. Her voice is clear and true, as pure as any I've heard. And yet, she seems completely unaware of just how good she is. We spend a few weeks in intensive rehearsal, while performing double duty helping plan and construct the stage, with help from some of the parents. As soon as Shane signs on, the number of females volunteering increases. Makes me glad I get to play the part of the teen.

As if in deference to the upcoming show, the teachers lighten the homework load. That means weeknights and weekends are spent with me at Niahm's, helping her to complete the overwhelming number of chores she has assigned to herself.

"Let's take a break," I tell her one Saturday as we finish raking and bagging enough leaves to compost an entire city—a real city, not a small one like Goshen.

She looks at me as if I've lost my mind. It's beyond her comprehension to "take a break". I stretch my back, as if it's sore, and watch the slight guilt flit across her face. Of course, my back doesn't hurt in the slightest, and I'm completely aware that she feels some guilt for my help. She's tried to convince me to stay away, but I keep showing up anyway.

"Okay, if you want to," she concedes, reluctantly. "What do you want to do?"

"Let's take a walk," I say, nodding toward town. "Maybe grab an ice cream at Hornsby's."

She shrugs, and I wait while she takes off her work boots, and replaces them with sneakers, putting a jacket on against the chill air. I realize I've never seen her wear cowboy boots, as many of the residents do.

"So, tell me all about Goshen," I say to distract her from thinking about her waiting chores, which I can see she's doing by her puckered brows. As soon as I say the words her forehead smooth's out and she smiles at me.

"You might not believe this to look at it now, but Goshen was a pretty happening place at one time."

"Oh, yeah?"

"Yeah. Back when the mines were open. Once they closed, people started farming, which still kept the town booming nicely." I glance over at her, see the animation that lights her eyes as she speaks. "But then, the world changed. *Farming* changed. All the ranches got smaller."

She looks over as if gauging whether I'm listening or not. I am.

"The largest ranch left is the Rocher place, which is about a hundred acres. The Stanton place—I mean, the *Coleman* place," she corrects, glancing at me with an apologetic smile, "is the next largest at eighty. But it hasn't been farmed in years. Do you think you and Shane will?"

"Farm it?" I evade, doubting we will. We never knew when we might have to move again. At most, we could stay for a decade before suspicions arose. "I don't know. We haven't really talked about it much."

"Well, if you do," she continues, not noticing my hesitancy, "we mostly grow wheat, corn and potatoes around here. And sheep," she adds. "So you might consider something different if you want to make any money."

She glances at me again, curiously, and I decide I can't wait any longer to find out exactly what she's thinking. I slip my hand into hers, feeling the surge of energy immediately, only with effort managing to keep the surprise from my face. I thought maybe the first time was a fluke, the strength of the transfer. Images wash through my head, and I force them back.

"Is this okay?" I ask, seeing the pink climbing her cheeks.

"Um, yeah," she murmurs. I can feel the shyness that's pinging through her mind, tinged with pleasure. I can also feel her desire to ask me about money—which would account for the look she gave me after her last comment—but overlying that, her refusal to ask what she considers an intrusive question.

"And then," she continues, trying to cover her feelings of awkwardness with her recital of facts, "when they put the interstate in ten years ago, any money the town received from travelers disappeared." The interstate was twenty-five miles east of town, too far for travelers to go out of their way, I knew. "Main Street was actually a pretty cool place at one time—lots of little shops for the tourists. But I guess you've seen that those are mostly all boarded up now, covered with some graffiti. We still get some motorcycle riders during the summer, who are trying to avoid the interstate."

An interesting thing is happening. Niahm is reciting these facts, her voice full of the passion she has for her town, but her mind is occupied elsewhere . . . on our touching hands, particularly. I can see her warring thoughts about that. She's pleased, happy to be holding hands, but also reticent, wondering what it means. I pull out of her mind with effort. It's not fair for me to cheat by peeking, and I'm afraid I may answer her unspoken questions without thinking. The heat in my palm slowly recedes.

We step onto the end of Main Street, which is mostly deserted. As we pass the library, a woman steps out, nearly bumping into us.

"Oh, hey, Mrs. Thorne," Niahm says, stopping. "Have you met Sam Coleman?"

She turns to smile at me as the elderly woman peers over the top of her spectacles, as if I were a specimen to be studied. "You the new folks in town?" she asks in a whispery voice.

"Yes, ma'am. My uncle and I purchased the Stanton place." I've learned by now that's the way to refer to the place we purchased, not by saying "the place on Herbert Road."

"Well, welcome," she whispers, turning and reentering the library. I look at Niahm, and she just smiles and shrugs at the strange encounter.

"That's Mrs. Thorne, the librarian. I don't know exactly how old she is, but I suspect she might've known Moses." I laugh at her assessment. "She's strict about keeping it quiet in there, but she's a sweet old lady. And she knows *everything*. If there's something she might not know right away, she can find it for you lickety-split. Sometimes, I think the woman is immortal," she says, and if she notices the slight jerk in my frame at her words, the tensing of my muscles, the fight or flight instinct that kicks in before I push it back, she doesn't say anything.

We continue through town, as she tells me about some of the more prominent residents. Dan Smythe, who cuts hair in the same shop as his father did, for the slightly inflated rate of five bucks, as his father only charged two-fifty.

"But I wouldn't let him touch my hair," she says. She glances up at my flaming mop. "I wouldn't let him cut yours either, if I were you. Unless you prefer a short buzz or a bowl cut."

I don't tell her that I am not in the habit of having anyone cut my hair other than myself or Shane. Too much risk of having someone question why I color my hair . . . though right now it is its natural color, which I haven't worn since before Niahm was even born. I glance at her again, wondering what she would think if she knew that little piece of Sam-trivia.

We arrive at the store . . . which, incidentally, seems to be purely a remaining tourist attraction. The real store is a few blocks away, larger and better stocked than this one. This store carries overpriced specialty items, drugstore items, and has an ice cream counter in the back. There is not a head of lettuce to be seen.

Old Man Jones is parked in his rocking chair out front. He's been there every time I've been down this road, and I wonder if he's paid to sit out here, smoking his pipe, telling stories to anyone who will listen. Niahm stops to tell him hello, and introduces me.

"Is he always there?" I ask, pointing toward the front of the store, as we sit at the counter.

"Unless the weather's bad," she confirms. "He's usually got a bunch of his old cronies with him. Guess they're taking the day off."

Officer Hill enters as we place our orders, and I force myself to remain relaxed. He is the deputy of Goshen, under the jurisdiction of the state Sherriff. However, he's the only officer that resides in and patrols the town—something Shane and I checked out before moving here. He also mans the jail, which, according to what we found, is usually empty.

Several ATV's loudly pass on the street outside. Those and horses seem to be the main modes of transportation around here. Horses and ATV's going down the road are a more common sight than cars. Niahm told me that if you're raised here, you can ride a horse or an ATV with equal skill, and you will have been riding both since before you could even walk. Some people still even travel to participate in rodeos, though, she informed me, no one had won anything of importance in about a dozen years or so.

Niahm is relaxed, sitting here in Hornsby's, eating a banana split. Clearly she has left thoughts of her chores behind. I wonder if getting her to talk about her beloved town is the secret to relaxing her. And love this town, she does. Even if I couldn't peek into her head and see it, I would hear it in her voice.

I decide I had better learn to love it as much as she does. Because in some way, shape or form, I'm going to have to stick around, for as long as she is here. Unless she asks me to leave; then I'll have to hide out. I curse the stupid bond that holds me to her, and the creativity that will be required to stay by her side.

And stay by her side I will, whether I want to or not. I look at her, this stubborn, temperamental, hard-working, complicated, amazing-pie-baking girl, and realize that I'm very much starting to want to.

Chapter 18

Niahm

The play is a success. Of course, it can't really fail when the entire town either knows or is related to someone participating. The entire town closed up so that everyone could turn out to watch. That's normal. Whether it's a play, a wedding, funeral or graduation, Goshen closes so that everyone can support one another.

I will never admit, even on threat of torture, that I really had fun doing it. Heather had written a kiss into the show, between mine and Sam's characters, and I didn't want my first kiss ever to be in front of all of my friends, in rehearsal. I was trying to figure out how to explain that without sounding like a complete idiot, when Sam told her we should skip the kiss, keeping it absolutely PG. Before she could protest, he had charmed her into thinking his way, and she insisted we keep the kiss out. It was weird, as if he could tell how uncomfortable I was with it.

Part of me also wondered why *he* wanted to keep it out. I kinda thought he liked me, but maybe I was wrong. Maybe the thought of kissing me repulses him. I probably would have kept thinking that if he hadn't been spending so much time with me, holding my hand often, to the point where I now miss it when we're together and he doesn't take my hand.

Now that we've closed the final curtain on the play, we head to Blake Barton's house—along with most of the town. Blake's parents have opened up one of their already harvested, but not yet replanted fields to the after party. Everyone brings food, and John Matthews has set up his large speakers, which are blaring music from his attached iPod.

I set one of the two plates of cookies I made onto the table with all the rest of the food, and turn away.

"Not sharing today?"

I turn to see my copper-headed costar grinning at me. I hold the plate out toward him.

"I made these for you," I say.

"Oh yeah?" He walks closer. He takes the plate, pulling one cookie off and placing it in his mouth. "Mmmm, these are fantastic," he mutters around his mouthful of cookie. "Bet they make great grenades, too."

My eyes narrow at him, but he's laughing.

"Just kidding!" he protests, popping another cookie into his mouth.

I give in to his humor and smile. "To be honest, they are kind of an apology."

He looks at me, perplexed. "For?"

"Well, partly for, you know, throwing all of those other cookies at you before. I mean, those were really good cookies, and I wasted them."

"That was a while ago, Niahm. I'm hardly holding a grudge." While we've been talking, he has guided me away from the table, to a more quiet area. "You said 'partly'. What else could you have to be sorry for?"

"For taking up all of your time. You spend so much time helping me, you haven't had time to . . . well, to do your own things . . . whatever they are."

His brows come together in consternation, though his smile doesn't leave his face.

"Your brain works in the strangest way," he says.

"Why?" I can't help it, I'm a little offended.

"Because," he steps closer after setting the plate of cookies down on a nearby chair, "you seem to forget that you didn't ask it of me. I'm there because I want to be there."

"Oh." Another brilliant response from the strange-brained girl. Then, before I can stop myself, I blurt, "Why?"

He takes another step closer, pulling one of my hands into his, bringing his other up to brush his thumb lightly along my jaw. I feel that strange heat flare up between our touching hands. He leans down a little closer to me, and I immediately panic, wondering if he's going to kiss me. I want him to . . . I think. No, I don't, not here. Not now. Okay, maybe now will be fine. A small smile appears on his face, in contrast with the intensity of the moment.

"Because I like you," he says quietly. "I like being around you."

His words vaguely register over the anxiety. I try to remember what I've eaten today, whether my breath is bad or not. I know I brushed my teeth . . . I'm pretty sure, anyway. How should I hold my mouth, should I turn my head? Oh, man, I definitely should have asked my mom about this. Then the thought of actually asking her about kissing fills me with mortification. No, not her. Stacy, then.

Sam suddenly chuckles, and I freeze. Does he know my thoughts? I don't think I spoke aloud. Did I? No, I'm pretty sure I didn't. I open my mouth to ask him what's so funny, and instead hear myself say, "Are you going to kiss me?" in a tone both curious and demanding.

Humiliation floods me from the top of my head to the

minutest end of my toes. I try to pull back, but Sam holds me firmly, not letting me hide in shame.

"I am," he says, and my heart stops. "Soon," he qualifies.

My mouth drops open slightly at his words, and he laughs again.

"Wanna dance?" he asks, not waiting for an answer. Good thing, since I don't think I could form a coherent sentence if I tried. He leads me out to where others are dancing, pulling me into his arms. He's a very good dancer, though I shouldn't be surprised. What does surprise me is that he holds me at a distance even my dad would find respectable, keeping one of my hands in his, tucked up to his chest. He doesn't take his eyes from mine, his shining with humor from a joke only he understands. I wonder if *I'm* the joke. The smile drops from his face and he leans down, putting his mouth near my ear so that I can hear him over the music.

"I really do like you, Niahm. Don't doubt that for one second."

I look at him, stunned. Can he read my mind? He grimaces, and closes his eyes briefly, as one does when they are trying to control their temper, or something. Is he angry at me? He smiles down at me, and I can't read any anger on his face.

I feel the strange, intense heat between our hands begin to fade, and I'm relieved. I'm not sure why it keeps happening, that weird heat, but I definitely don't want him to think I have sweaty hands. He might not want to hold hands with me anymore if he did.

I glance over his shoulder to see Stacy watching us, a knowing smirk on her face. I can live with that, but I also see the Double-H right next to her, both glaring daggers my way.

Chapter 19

Sam

I walk in the door, and see Shane sitting at the table. It's an unusual thing to come in and see him like this so often. Shane, for the most part, is a doer. He's always got to be on the move, active, doing *something*. Maybe he's more tired of running than I'd thought.

"Hey," I acknowledge, jerking a chin at him as I head to the fridge, pulling it open and grabbing the juice bottle.

"Use a glass," he says mildly, without looking up from his Sudoku. I let out a sigh. There's definitely something on his mind—he gets very parental when there is. I fill a glass, sit down across from him and wait.

He's silent for so long, I finally say, "Out with it."

He glances up at me, tapping his lip with the pen, as if debating whether or not to share. My eyes drop—briefly—to his hand lying on the table, and he finally speaks.

"Don't even think about it."

I grin. Yeah, I knew there was no way he'd let me in *that* way. He knows all too well what I can do.

"All right," he lays the pencil down and turns his full attention on me. "I wasn't sure if I should say anything. You're old enough to make your own decisions."

"You think?" I shoot back sarcastically. "Many people would consider 465 nothing but a baby."

Shane rolls his eyes, though there is some truth to that. Shane is fifty years older, and we don't even come close to being as old as many of the immortals that we know of.

"*But*," he interjects, "you may be too close to see this." He sighs, and picks up the pencil again, rolling it between his fingers. "I've been watching you with her, with Niahm. You're letting yourself get too close."

I want to argue with him, tell him he's wrong . . . but Shane has his own gifts, and trying to fool him is an exercise in futility.

"You know the consequences of allowing yourself to fall in—"

"I know," I interrupt him, slamming the glass down on the counter a little harder than necessary. The glass shatters, and thin trails of blood seep from my hand. We both ignore the blood, though Shane raises a brow at my reaction. "I know," I say, calmer. "I've thought of that. Trust me; it has never left my mind. But there's something different about her . . ."

Shane's gaze remains steady. I think of the only other time I truly loved a woman. I *know* the consequences only too well.

"I wasn't expecting to like her, really," I tell him. "I mean, she was pretty unpleasant. But, come on, Shane, you know how hard it is to remain distant from someone you find yourself bound to."

"I do know," he confirms. "There are ways to fulfill the binding without growing too attached. You know this as well as I do, Samuel."

I push back from the table, pacing with agitation. I haven't felt so much like the teenager I pretend to be as I do right now.

Shane reaches behind him and casually tosses the kitchen towel my way. I wrap it around my bleeding fingers.

"Samuel," Shane's voice is quietly forceful, commanding my attention. He opens his mouth to speak, closes it, opens and finally sighs. I wait. I have all the time in the world to wait, I think acerbically. "You know there isn't any way to know . . . for certain, I mean, if she's . . ." he stands, folding his book closed and placing it and the pen in the drawer behind him. "Just don't pin your hopes on something that could be nothing," he says, leaving the room.

He's right. I know he's right. I'd be giving the same advice to him if our positions were reversed. But somehow, Niahm has become central to me, more than is required by being bound to her. I would never tell Shane, but it terrifies me.

I walk to the sink, wash the blood from my hand. The think pink line, that had been a gash only a few minutes earlier, only serves to remind me of how *wrong* I am, how wrong my life is. Even as I watch, the water running wastefully down the drain, the pink line slowly fades, leaving the skin perfectly unblemished. I turn back to the table, pick up a piece of the jagged glass, and hold it against my skin, wanting the laceration to return—*needing* it to return.

Finally, without drawing it across my healed skin, I drop the glass back to the table. I could cut myself all night long, and it wouldn't matter. I'd still wake up, exactly the same.

"And, Samuel?" Shane calls from the other room, "clean up that mess."

His words force a small, grim smile from me. Heaven save us from overbearing parents.

Chapter 20

Niahm

Brrr," I shiver, looking out the barn doors at the gray skies.

"Cold?" Sam asks redundantly, rubbing down the sides of the Irish. He's just finished working him in the paddock. He was able to place a saddle on the stallion's back today, after the past few weeks of leading him around with a blanket on his back. Of course, the Irish threw a fit, and tried bucking the thing off. Sam just waited patiently, keeping him close with the lead until he grew accustomed to it.

"Why would you assume that?" I shoot back, rubbing my arms. It's not his fault I was more worried about looking cute in my thin blue jacket rather than putting on something that would buffer me against the cold day.

Sam just chuckles at my response, not even looking up

from his task. He finishes, giving the Irish a final pat on the neck as I scoop up an apple and hand it over the low door to him, which he then presents to the Irish. Sam backs out, closes the door behind him and turns my way. I realize how close I'm standing when I have to crane my neck to look up at him. He begins rubbing my arms rapidly, the friction warming me—or maybe it's his nearness. He leans down, and I wonder yet again if he's going to finally kiss me. Not that I, you know, want him to, or anything. It's just that there have been so many times I thought he was going to, when he leans in close like this. Yet, he always pulls away.

"You should wear a warmer jacket, Niahm, when it's cold outside."

I narrow my eyes at him, but he just laughs again as he turns to clean up the rest of his gear.

"Want to go to the diner and get something to eat?" he questions.

"No, absolutely not!" I exclaim. Then, realizing how it sounds as his eyes jump to mine, I soften my tone. "We can eat here. I already have some chili cooking."

"Good," is Sam's only response, but I know what it means. It means he's happy. Sam is very vocal about his enjoyment of my cooking. I push down the self-satisfied feeling I always get when he reacts in such a manner.

Sam has taken to holding my hand quite frequently now—in public. At school, I manage to keep my hands bound up in carrying my books. He seems to have divined my hesitancy, and doesn't push the issue. But when we're in town, he always either holds my hand or has his arm draped across my shoulders. It almost feels like he's . . . I don't know, staking his claim, or something, though that could just be wishful thinking. I've been getting some hateful looks, especially from Hilary and Heather, when he does. I try to avoid being seen in town with him—not because I don't want to hold his hand. I *do*, more than I should. I'm just not fond of making enemies of my lifelong friends. Hence, my reluctance to eat at the diner.

Cindy C Bennett

"Your parents going to be there?" Sam asks, pushing himself up from his squatting position where he'd been organizing the bucket of cleaning items. I grunt. Sam and my parents get along far too well for my contentment. Sometimes, I think he prefers spending time with them, especially my father, talking about all of the places he's been. Sam is either well-travelled, as I'd once accused him of being, or well-read about other countries. I suspect it's the former. Their conversations can be extremely long, and extremely boring.

"Yes," I confirm, and his face lights up.

Chapter 21

Sam

We head inside just as darkness spreads itself across the land. The aroma in the kitchen is mouth-watering—spices and yeast. I watch as Niahm places the tray of rolls into the oven then pulls items from the fridge to make a salad.

It isn't long until Jonas and Beth have joined us—looking dapper in their "tea-time with the Queen" clothes, as Niahm calls them—and we're all sitting at the table. As usual, Beth invited Shane, but he cried off, claiming work. A blatant lie, but knowing what he's really doing, I could hardly call him on it.

Niahm and her parents talk almost constantly as they eat, and I get the feeling they are trying to make up for lost time. Still, it's been so long since I've felt like a normal part of a family, that I can't help but be grateful for the talking and laughter. I also genuinely enjoy time spent with Beth and

Jonas—they remind me of my own parents.

"How many times have you been to Jamaica?" I ask Jonas, always fascinated by his stories of travel, always trying to find somewhere he hasn't been. Niahm kicks me lightly under the table—she hates it when Jonas, Beth and I begin talking about their travels. Niahm has heard the stories many times, and so is annoyed by being forced to hear them yet again. I grin at her and, slipping my shoe off, rub my foot lightly over her ankle, bringing an immediate blush to her cheeks.

"Only once, actually, about two years ago," Jonas says, handing me the basket of rolls, which I gratefully accept, not noticing his daughters pink cheeks. "Fascinating place, fascinating people. We went for pleasure more than work, but of course we couldn't escape the work."

"The work *is* pleasure," Beth says, eyes lighting as she talks. I have clearly noted that neither of Niahm's parents share her unusual eyes. A crushing disappointment, realizing that her own eyes are likely just a fluke of nature, without any real possibility.

"Is there anywhere you two haven't been?" I tease.

"Russia," Beth says.

"Though that will very soon be remedied," Jonas says, taking his wife's hand and smiling at her.

"Oh, Jonas, we must be sure to get to Saint Basil's Cathedral," Beth gushes. "I know it's not really necessary for this particular book, but how can we go there and not visit?"

"Have you been to Russia, Sam?" Jonas asks. But I'm not paying attention to him; I'm watching Niahm. She has gone very still, lips thinning the tiniest amount, jaw clenched. Jonas follows my gaze, and upon seeing Niahm's stiff posture, he seems to droop, his shoulders sagging.

"Are you okay?" I ask, instinctively taking her hand, immediately wishing I could take the words back when she glances at me. In that glance I can see a maelstrom of emotion barely held in check. In her hand I can feel the pain, rejection, abandonment that drags at her.

"Niahm," Beth entreats, one hand snaking out toward her daughter, then pulling back when Niahm jerks away. "Honey, we were going to tell you tonight . . . " she trails off in Niahm's silence.

"When?" Niahm finally grinds out, quietly.

"Sweetie, we—"

"When!" she demands, pushing back from the table, standing, pulling her hand from mine.

"Next week," Beth admits, quietly.

Niahm takes a breath, as if to control her emotion.

"Baby, why don't you come with us?" Jonas cajoles. "You haven't been to Russ—"

"No." Niahm's refusal is immediate, firm. She turns tortured eyes to me. "If you'll excuse me," she says, sounding proper and stiff, controlled in a way I've never heard her speak before. With her words, she turns and walks out the back door.

I stand, intending to follow her, suddenly wondering if it's my place to do so. After all, this is between her and her parents.

"Oh, dear," Beth says, covering her mouth with a hand.

"She'll be fine," Jonas assures her. "She always is."

I look at them both, wondering why one of them hasn't already rushed from the room to comfort her.

"Should I?" I mutter, indicating the door she left from.

Jonas glances at me, as if just remembering I'm present. "Well, you can try, I suppose. It's usually better to just let her be."

I don't answer, just leave, hoping I can find her. She's in the stable, using a pitchfork to brutalize the hay. If I didn't feel so bad for her, I might be amused by the activity.

"Niahm?" I ask, and she glances up at me. I don't need to take her hand to see what she's feeling; it's written all over her face. She flings herself at me, wrapping her arms tightly around my middle as her tears come. I hold her, wishing that in all my years on the earth, I had somehow learned the proper words to say at this moment, to ease her hurt.

❄ ❄ ❄ ❄ ❄

"Are you sure you want me to come along?"

Niahm rolls her eyes at me. I've asked her the same question several times, and I guess she's tired of answering. I shrug and return to the house to haul another bag out to the truck.

It's a two-hour drive to the airport, one that Niahm doesn't usually make with her parents when they leave. She told me they typically drive and leave their car parked while they're gone.

"I feel this weird sense of . . . I don't know, foreboding, I guess," she explained. "I just have this overwhelming thought that I need to take them this time."

Because Niahm seems so firm in her conviction that something bad will happen if she doesn't do this, I don't argue with her. Instead, I'd volunteered to ride with her—later wondering if she needed the time alone with them. She's still angry, still hurt, but managing to hide it beneath a falsely cheery exterior. She wants me along, particularly, I suspect, since Stacy isn't available to make the trip.

The two hour trip to the airport is made with even more falsely cheerful conversation in the car, from both Niahm and her parents.

"How's school, sweetie?"

"Really good. I'm getting an A in biology."

"That's fantastic."

"A miracle, really."

I'm on edge just listening to the inane, senseless chatter. But it seems to be what they all need, so I don't say much—and definitely don't question Jonas about his travels, not matter how much I'd like to tell them some places to visit while in Russia. I can feel Niahm's worry, as palpable as her hand in mine, though I don't intrude on her mind. I'm tempted to, but I resist. She's told me her worry is unclear, nothing more than a feeling. I've decided it's just the stress of having them gone once again.

At the airport curb, Niahm clings to them.

"Sweetie," Beth laughs. "We'll be back before you know it."

Niahm shakes her head against her father's chest, eyes scrunched closed.

"Darling, we'll bring you back one of those amazing Russian dolls, the ones that stack inside one another." Jonas seems taken aback by Niahm's display.

"I don't want a doll." Niahm's voice is flat. "I just want you to be home."

"We will, Niahm—as soon as we possibly can." Niahm just shakes her head again and turns away from them, climbing back into the car.

The two hour trip back to Goshen is made with me driving, Niahm crying, pitifully silent as she gazes out the window, refusing to talk about their leaving.

✳ ✳ ✳ ✳ ✳

"Hey, Shane, you think we could slow down work on the stables?" I call, glancing out the window at the nearly finished structure.

Shane, having silently come into the room behind me, throws an arm about my neck, pulling tightly. I drop, throwing an elbow into his solar plexus as I do so, immediately grabbing his arm and flipping him over my head. I continue my descent over his prone form, driving my elbow toward his windpipe, stopping just short of actually hurting him.

"Very nice," he compliments, his breath wheezing. I hold out a hand, pulling him to his feet as I stand, grinning. It's only been the past couple of years that I've been able to defeat Shane, a source of great pride for me, and chagrin for him.

"You're an old man," I grin at him, "You sure you should keep trying to take me?"

Shane's fist shoots out, and I feel my shoulder dislocate.

"Uh," I grunt painfully, no longer grinning.

"Not so old, now, huh?" He smiles, grabbing my arm and pulling my shoulder back into place.

"Why don't we go out and visit that barn?" I challenge, rolling my sore shoulder, not wanting to destroy the kitchen.

"You mean the one you want me to stop working on so that you have a reason to go visit the object of your affection?"

"The very one," I say, grinning with what I hope is malice.

At the same time, we hear it—hooves galloping toward the house, and very quickly, at that. We turn and move at the same time. Without speaking we are plotting our defense if needed. As we step out the front door, I see Niahm's unmistakable blonde hair flying out behind her as she pushes Sheila toward our house. Shane relaxes, but my tension ratchets up in response to her body language.

Something is wrong.

I run out to meet her, Niahm throwing a leg over and sliding off the mare's bare back before she has even stopped. I catch her in my arms as she falls forward, horror and grief in every line of her body.

"What, Niahm? What is it?"

She opens her mouth to speak, but can't force the words past her intense dread. I snake my hand down to hers, and I see it.

Officer Hill walking up to her door, followed by two strangers, a man and a woman. I see the logo on their lapels; recognize that they are from the airline. I hear Officer Hill tell her, feel Niahm's panic as her brain tries to process his words, hear the representatives offering their condolences.

"No," I cry, releasing her hand and pulling her into my crushing embrace as she collapses, unable to withstand the burden any longer, knowing that now her parents will never again return home to her. In the back of my mind, underneath the overpowering concern for Niahm, I recall her intense worry over their trip, her need to drive them to the airport one last time.

Chapter 22

Niahm

Numb.

I lay on the couch, aware of Stacy and Sam's voices from the kitchen. They talk in lowered voices, but they needn't bother. I can't make sense of words anymore. Bob pushes his nuzzle under my dangling hand, a plaintive whine escaping him. It's a sound my own throat longs to release.

There's a knock at the door, I can hear that, divine the meaning of the sound. I try to muster the will to care who is standing on the other side, but the effort is too great, so I give up. Stacy passes me, her hand reaching out to squeeze my arm. She opens the door; voices that drone from her direction mean nothing to me.

Time passes. People stream in and out. They all come to me, touch me, say words to me in voices that grate on my nerves. I know them—have known them my whole life, but I don't care to pull their names from memory to acknowledge them. Finally, I pull a blanket over my head, hiding from them, hiding from the pain that keeps trying to surface. It works; they stop bothering me.

Sometime later, when the silence becomes oppressing, I pull the blanket back and see Stacy sleeping at the end of the couch, my feet resting in her lap. I didn't even feel her sit down, let alone pull my feet into her lap. A light snore from near my head pulls my attention there, where Sam sits in the chair with his head leaned back, also sleeping.

I study him. His cheek bones are angular, as if carved. Once, in India, I spent an entire afternoon sitting on a mat in the street, watching an old man carving a piece of wood with a small knife. When he was finished, he showed me the face he'd created, and I had been impressed by the symmetry and perfection of the cheek bones. I see the same perfection in Sam's face. With his eyes closed, I can see how long and thick his copper lashes really are, fanning across the high point of those perfect cheeks. His jaw is strong, masculine, freckled with stubble. His amazing hair glints in the dim light pouring in from the street.

I don't really know him all that well and yet it somehow feels right that he is here, in my life. In the short time he has been, it almost feels *essential* that he's in my life. As if he can feel the weight of my appraisal, he opens his eyes. He watches me in return for a few moments then slowly leans forward. He reaches out and touches my forehead lightly, fingers barely skimming the surface, and I feel a shudder start deep within my abdomen. I try to force it back, push it down to where I've managed to keep it tucked away. Then Sam moves closer and brings his other hand up, cupping my face, eyes full of sympathy and understanding.

A sudden recollection of his own family pushes to the front of my mind, how similar his circumstances—

I gasp, urgently trying to shove the thought away, but it

comes anyway. Sam's parents are . . . his parents are also . . .

Sam is kneeling next to me now, tears shining in his eyes as I stare at him desperately.

"I can't, Sam, I can't . . ." The shudder pushes its way up my spine, into my arms, down my legs. Shaking uncontrollably, I'm helpless as Sam pushes me into sitting position, sliding next to me. I'm aware of Stacy's now-awake warmth pressing from my other side, cocooned in the safety of two pairs of arms, safe to let the sound out, the one that's been trying to escape.

With the sound comes the grief that I've held at bay since that first day, when I could only think to go to Sam. Bob, at my knee, matches my grief with his own howling.

Chapter 23

Sam

I'm relieved that Niahm finally let herself cry over the loss of her parents last night. She hasn't cried since she first came to my place three days prior, wrapped in a silent, impenetrable wall. This morning she actually let Stacy pull her up off the couch, and get her into the shower. After she had fallen back asleep last night, sleeping peacefully for the first time since this had begun, Stacy informed me today was the day we needed to force her to make some decisions.

Niahm is escorted from her bedroom, hair damp, face clean, dressed in a black t-shirt and gray sweatpants, pulling a matching gray jacket on. She looks tired, grief etching deep grooves on her forehead and at the corners of her mouth. My heart thuds with dread. I'd give anything to not have to add to her distress.

She sits on the couch and eats half the sandwich Stacy's

made for her. When she's finished, Stacy shoots me a look over her head, letting me know it's time.

Stacy takes Niahm's hand, and I take the other. She grasps both ours tightly, as if holding onto a lifeline—a complete turnaround from the limp hands we've been holding for four days now. In those contacts, the only thing I had been able to read was darkness, hiding from the truth that lurked beneath the haze.

"Vee," Stacy begins, a slight hitch in her voice. Niahm turns her way, more response than we've had, but disinterested and vague anyway. "Sweetie, we need to make some . . . arrangements. Today," she adds firmly.

The only indication that she's even heard is in the slight tightening of her hand in mine, and I can feel her terror begin to rise. I squeeze her hand back and she turns to me, panic in the back of her unusual eyes.

"Niahm, it's going to be okay. I promise." I try to send her the sincerity in my words and she seems to believe me, giving a tiny nod before turning to Stacy again.

"Vee, your parents' bod—" she cuts herself off, dropping her eyes. I can feel that Niahm knows inside what she'd been about to say, but refuses to consciously acknowledge it. Stacy takes a deep breath, and begins again, "I mean, your parents are going to be here in two days."

Niahm's hand tightens on mine once again, and she turns my way, confusion darkening her eyes. I slide down to the floor, moving to sit in front of her near Stacy.

"But . . ." she trails off and I can feel the hope begin to rise in her mind. "But I thought that they were. . . . " When the hope becomes more visible, hope that she's somehow misunderstood what she's been told about them, I know I have to stop her now.

"Niahm." Her eyes come to mine, and I feel her surge of feeling for me, practically knocking me back in surprise. It nearly stays my words, only I know that not speaking them won't change the truth. "Your parents are going to need a proper burial." She jerks at the words, the darkness beginning to pervade her mind again.

"No!" I command, giving her hand a tug. She's shaking her head, tears gathering, but I can't let her go back to that place. "Niahm, you need to stay with me. You're their daughter. You need to do this for them."

As she processes my words, the darkness recedes and I feel the strength of will pushing through.

"Vee, I know how hard this is," Stacy reclaims her attention. "We have to do this—for them. And we will—all three of us. Okay?"

A shudder ripples through Niahm's body, tears spilling silently down her cheeks, but she nods.

"We need to go see Mr. Thompson," Niahm says, shocking both of us with her words.

"Yes, that's right," Stacy confirms, trying not to look as surprised as I know she is. "We can go today."

"Now."

Stacy's mouth drops open at Niahm's abrupt announcement. Lucky that Niahm is looking my way. I'd seen her determination rising, and had been a little more prepared than Stacy.

"Okay," I confirm, my relief palpable at the tiny smile that turns up one side of her mouth.

"Okay," Stacy reiterates, "I guess we'll go now." She seems to understand Niahm's strength better than even I do while cheating, because she stands, pulling Niahm up with her, Niahm's hand slipping from my own as she does. Stacy pulls Niahm into a quick hug, which Niahm returns fully, releasing her before Niahm can fall apart again at the gesture.

Stacy leads her to the door, putting Niahm's coat on her as if she were a child, Niahm not complaining at the gesture. Stacy puts her own coat on and, as she's leading Niahm through the door, turns back and says, "You coming?" Without waiting for a reply, she drags Niahm from the house, leaving me to hurry after them with a smile. I can see now why the two get along so well.

✳ ✳ ✳ ✳ ✳

Over the next couple of days, Niahm becomes a cleaning, cooking, baking flurry of activity, in spite of my protests. Finally Stacy pulls me aside.

"Let her go, Sam. This is how she copes. It's keeping her sane while we wait."

And she's right. Niahm is calm as long as she keeps busy. The animals had been cared for by neighbors while she lived in her fog, but now she's up and has the chores finished before they can get over. There's food enough to feed the three of us, as well as several of the neighbors. Stacy finally calls and informs Mrs. Harris to immediately tell everyone who had been asked to stop their own preparations for the post-funeral luncheon and instead to bring their groceries to Niahm's. This begins a steady flow of groceries being brought until there's nowhere else to put them, and a new stream begins to take the food to their own homes for storage.

On the day of the funeral, Niahm is up even earlier than usual. She's sleeping in her own bed again, Stacy next to her, while I huddle on the too-short couch. I hear the back door closing behind her, and follow her out into the cold morning air. Without words, I take a pitchfork next to her to begin tossing hay.

She glances at me, pale in the morning's dimness, face gaunt and troubled. She turns back to her work, shoulders tense. Silently, together, we complete the chores. When we finish, we head back inside and I sit at the table as she prepares a breakfast that would feed a dozen hungry men. I don't speak still, sensing that words will be her undoing.

Stacy wanders in, glancing at me questioningly. I shake my head and she comes to sit next to me.

"Good morning," she murmurs, though her words sound booming in the quiet.

"'Morning," I answer.

"Sleep well?"

"Fine. You?"

"Fine, thanks."

Silence reigns again, and in that same silence Niahm serves us, sitting to push her own food around on her plate, not taking a single bite. For the first time, Stacy doesn't comment on her lack of appetite, allowing her to keep up the pretense.

When we finish, Niahm rises to gather the plates, but Stacy catches her by the hand.

"Vee, it's time to shower and get ready," she tells Niahm firmly.

Niahm glances at me, and I give her a small smile. She nods at Stacy, and allows herself to be led from the room. I clean up breakfast, then put on the suit that Shane brought over for me the night before.

Stacy and Niahm descend the stairs as I let Shane into the house, who has arrived in a hired limousine. It's the only limo in town, driven by Thom James, who also drives the single school bus in town. I look up at Niahm, beautiful even in her tragic state, and wish I could tell her so.

We walk outside, Niahm not commenting on the car as she slides into the surprisingly luxurious interior. Stacy and I bookend her once again, each of us taking one of her hands, me pushing away the images that try to invade my mind. This day I feel she deserves absolute privacy with her thoughts.

The church is packed; it seems everyone in town has come to say goodbye. The two ornate caskets beneath the pew wrench my heart. Though their loss doesn't mean nearly as much to me as to Niahm, I will nonetheless miss the new friendship I had begun with the eccentric Jonas and Beth, his devoted wife.

Stacy and I had gone with Niahm to the mortuary when her parents' bodies had arrived. She had been counseled strongly to not view them as there had been fire and much bodily damage. I was grateful when she followed the counsel. I have seen horrors in my lifetime that I wish I could erase from memory, but which always remain. I don't want Niahm to have those images of her parents.

Rather than an organized service, Niahm has elected to open it up to allow anyone who wants to stand and recount their memories of Jonas and Beth. I don't think she knew that that would include nearly everyone. Many of the stories are humorous, all of them touching, and my heart swells with pride at the strength Niahm shows, standing to hug each person silently after their speech.

Four hours later we climb back into the car for the short drive to the cemetery outside of town. A prayer is given, dedicating the grave, and then Niahm—who's kept her eyes locked on the two coffins—is given a hug and words of love and support from those who are in attendance. Throughout all of this, she keeps Stacy and me by her side, holding onto one or the other of us the entire time.

The luncheon is attended by all, and Niahm manages to smile and laugh with her lifelong friends, though I can see the stress lines around her eyes. It's dark before the final person exits, leaving Niahm alone with Stacy and me once again. Niahm looks momentarily confused as she glances around. The house is spotless, having been cleaned up and re-organized by many of the women who had been in attendance.

Niahm stands, hands wringing, and Stacy and I both take a step toward her at the same time. Niahm jumps involuntarily, and moves toward the back door.

"I'm going out to see Sheila." She quickly exits the house, and Stacy shrugs in my direction.

"Guess I'll go shower, then," is her only response as she walks up the stairs, leaving me staring after Niahm. There is no hesitation in my decision to follow her.

She stands in the barn, forehead pressed to her mares. She doesn't look my way as I enter, but continues to stroke the side of Sheila's neck. I stop next to her, desperately wanting to take her hand. As if hearing my thoughts, she suddenly reaches a hand toward me, not changing position other than this. I hesitate for a nano-second, my conscience warring. I take her hand, but close my mind to hers.

"I want you to kiss me now."

Her words are spoken low, quietly, tremulously.

"Niahm," I say, giving her hand a tug. She turns my way, releasing the mare, stepping into my space, her face a mask of anguish. I take a breath, knowing I'm treading on thin, emotional ground here. "I won't let your first kiss be tied up with the memory of this day."

Rejection shades her face, but she covers it quickly.

"It won't, Sam. It will *replace* the memory of this day." She pauses, turns pleading eyes on me, "*Please.*"

"Ni—" before I finish her name, she pushes up against me, reaching up with both arms to pull my face to hers, awkward, urgent.

I move my head to the side, fighting the overwhelming urge to give her what she asks for. I wrap my arms around her, pulling her close to me, leaning down so her head is level with mine, cheek to cheek.

"There isn't *anything*," I say into her ear, "that will erase the memories of this day."

She remains still against me, and finally I lean back to peer into her face. She refuses to look at me, and even in the dim light I can see the high color in her cheeks.

"I'm a fool," she whispers, self-recrimination in her voice.

"No, you're not," my voice is urgent. I sit on a nearby hay bale and urge her down next to me. Not letting her escape my gaze, I cup her face and force her to look at me. "You're grieving. You've just lost the two most important people in the world to you. You're desperate for some kind of relief from that. You certainly would not be the first person to want to use physical contact in that manner."

Tears shimmer in her eyes, and she gives her head a small shake.

"How did you survive it, Sam?" she whispers.

I'm well aware that she believes the loss of my parents is

recent, has no idea that it's been over 400 years since they died. She also doesn't know that I remember full well the sharp pain that came as I stood watch over them during the wake: first my mother, only a short three months later, my father, and then buried them in the ground in crude wooden boxes. At the time of their deaths, they believed me to be their grandson, son of myself.

"You just do." Not a good answer, but I can hardly tell her what I really did after their deaths. "Life goes on, even when you think it shouldn't." Memories of the first Niahm slam into my mind, and I quickly push them away, wincing with the effort. "In the morning, the sun will come up, no matter how hard you wish for it to stay down. Bessie will need to be milked, your chickens will need feed, and everyone else in the world will get up and go about their days as if nothing has changed. You will probably be angry at everyone for going on, and that's normal." One tear slides down her cheek, and I wipe it away with my thumb. I lean down, holding her eyes with mine. "I promise, Niahm, that every day it will get easier. You won't think it is, won't notice it, but one day you'll realize that though you still ache for them, they are a happy memory instead of a painful one."

Niahm nods, taking a deep breath and blowing it out. "Okay."

Her acceptance of my words surprises me. I expected more tears, arguing.

"Niahm." She looks up at me, and I give her a wry smile. "You have no idea how much I want to kiss you."

She smiles tremulously, her slight hiccupping laugh leading to a gasp as the tears begin again. I pull her against me, holding her tight, wishing I could convey to her how very true the words are.

Chapter 24

Niahm

Bob slurps a long tongued lick into my dangling hand, pulling me out of the fantasy of Sam finally kissing me. Or rather, *almost* kissing me. Since I've never been kissed, I really can't get beyond the vision of him moving in before the image dissolves. Very frustrating, but losing myself in my unreal world keeps me from facing the pain of my all-too-real world.

I'm still humiliated by my gawky attempt to kiss him in the barn three nights ago. He hasn't mentioned it. I'm not sure if that makes it better . . . or worse. Of course I told Stacy about it, who had the good grace to not laugh at me, though I could see her biting the inside of her cheek, something she does whenever she's trying to keep herself from laughing or keep her mouth shut when she really wants to say something inappropriate.

Bob jumps to his feet, a low growl in his throat. This is something new he's begun since the day . . . I close my eyes against the image of my parents' coffins hovering precariously above the dark holes in the ground, balanced on thin straps of canvas. I couldn't concentrate as their graves were dedicated, unable to look away. I was afraid if I did the straps would snap, sending my parents plummeting into the dark depths. Bob growls again, reminding me that someone is here. I figure he's responding to some vibe I'm giving off.

The doorbell rings, and Stacy practically jogs in from the kitchen where she'd been sitting with Shane and her mom. I'm surprised she's willing to pull herself from his exalted presence long enough to answer the door, but she's been acting like an over-protective guardian dog herself.

She opens the door to two women, neither of whom looks familiar to me. One is an older woman, hair silver above an almost unlined face that seems much too young for the aged hair. Her slacks and flower-print shirt seems almost contrived to make her look older. She seems nervous.

The other woman is younger, in a crisp business suit, hair pulled up into a professional bun, the file grasped in her hand and spectacles completing the picture of a woman with a mission.

"Nee-uhm Parker?" she says, thrusting a stern hand toward Stacy.

"No," Stacy says at the same time the older woman says, "Niahm," in correction.

My eyes widen in surprise as I stand, though Stacy doesn't remark on the woman's correction. She doesn't realize how very rare it is for someone to know the correct pronunciation of my name. The older woman's gaze come to rest on me, and I'm suddenly uncomfortable, as if I need to escape before she can do or say whatever it is that is going to change my world yet again.

"Oh, um, well," the professional woman stutters, "is *Niahm* here, then?" Her corrected use of my name is punctuated.

"Depends. Who's asking?" Stacy demands, folding her arms in defiance.

Stacy's mom comes into the room at the same time that I'm getting ready to bolt. The professional woman glances in, sees me, and asks, "I assume you're Niahm Parker, then?"

"She is," Stacy's mom answers for me. "May I ask who you are?"

"May we please come in?" the woman asks, her tone letting us know that denying her is not an option. "We have something very important to discuss with her."

Stacy holds her position for long moments, until her mom says, "Stacy!" in a tone that brooks no defiance. Reluctantly, and with a glare of warning, Stacy steps aside to allow them to come in. My panic ratchets up at her capitulation, and the urge to run becomes stronger. Sam is outside, and I want to run to him, hide behind him. Vaguely, I wonder where Shane is.

Then the professional woman is striding toward me, hand outstretched. Behind her, the older woman has taken a tentative step into the house, looking around her, body saturated with some emotion I refuse to recognize.

"Hello, Niahm. My name is Susan McKay. I'm the case worker assigned to your case."

Okay, my attention is now firmly on the woman before me. I instinctively reach a hand out to stop her, which she mistakes and grasps firmly in her hard, unyielding hand, giving it a quick jerk, which I assume is her version of a handshake.

"My *what*?"

"Her *what*?" Stacy blurts at the same time.

"I'm from the department of Family Services. We've held off until after the burial to come forward, which turned out to be fortuitous, as it turns out. We've had a relative come forward, which means we won't have to find you placement in foster care."

She is smiling at me as if she's just told me the best possible news, but I feel as if I've been punched in the gut. The burial? My parents have become a synonym for *burial*?

"Wait," Stacy steps forward. "What do you mean, foster care?"

Stacy's mom steps forward and places an arm around me. "Why don't we all sit down?" Her voice is calm, her touch reassuring. I sink back to the couch along with her, Stacy coming to sit firmly on my other side, Bob positioning himself in front. The stiff woman looks around, slightly uncomfortable, and finally sits primly in the chair. The other woman stays standing, her eyes still skimming the room.

"Now," Stacy's mom begins, "why don't you tell us what you're talking about?"

"As I said, we were waiting until—"

"Yes, we heard that part," Stacy's mom interrupts firmly, and gratitude fills me at her defense. "Why in the world would you think Niahm needs to be placed in foster care?"

"She's a minor." The stiff woman sounds surprised, as if it should be obvious, and becomes "the bun" in my mind immediately when Stacy reaches up and draws the shape of said bun on the back of my head out of her line of vision.

"I'll be eighteen next summer." My voice is strong in spite of my still overwhelming desire to flee—and to laugh at Stacy's finger circling on the back of my head.

"Yes, well, in the meantime, you are still of an age which requires guardianship."

"But I'm always home alo—"

"She can stay with me," Stacy's mom interrupts, squeezing me tightly, in warning it seems.

"Well, Ms. . . . ." The bun trails off, waiting for a name.

"Bowen. I've known Niahm her whole life. I don't see any reason why she can't stay at our place until then."

"I can't," I tell her, "there isn't anyone to take care—" She squeezes me again, her words once more overriding mine.

"You don't need to worry about that, honey. We'll hire someone to take care of the farm."

"But, I—" Another squeeze, this one almost painful, stops

my words.

"There is a process for becoming a foster parent, Mrs. Bowen. It takes some time for your application to be processed. Niahm would have needed to be placed in the meantime—"

"Are you serious?" Stacy's mom practically explodes. "I've known the girl her whole life, have loved her as a daughter, and you'd take her from her home, from the town she lives in, to satisfy some—"

"No way!" Stacy yells, causing Bob to jump to his feet and begin growling in earnest. The bun shrinks back in the chair.

"Stop," I command, to nothing in particular other than the situation that is spiraling out of control. Stacy and her mom back down, Bob sinks back onto his haunches, though he keeps his teeth exposed for good measure, and my eyes rove unwillingly to the older woman who is now watching us all with interest bright in her eyes.

"I'm not leaving Goshen," I say to her, before turning back to the bun.

The bun gives Bob a cautious look before turning her attention back to me. "As I was *trying* to say," she emphasizes, shooting a look at Stacy and her mom, "that would have been the case, had a relative not come forth. We were under the impression that you no longer had any living relatives."

I cringe inwardly at her thoughtless words, swallow loudly, and say, "I was under that impression myself."

The bun regains her overly bright smile, and delivers what she seems to believe is happy news. "As it turns out, Niahm, we were wrong. Your grandmother came forth."

She sweeps a hand toward the older woman, and the desire to run once again flows through me. The woman is standing as if frozen, watching me with wariness. I slowly rise to my feet, Stacy and her mom matching my movement.

"No," I say, surprised at how steady my voice sounds. "I don't have a grandmother. They are both dead."

"No, Niahm, this is your mother's mother. She told me of

the falling out she had with your mother, of how many years it's been since she's been here." The bun sounds almost pleading, and I suddenly realize that any reluctance on my part will only make her job harder. She could care less about me—she just wants this wrapped up nice and tidy.

"No," I repeat, more firmly. "I don't know this woman. My mom—" I swallow over the painful word, try again. "My mom told me her mother died when she was a teen. This is *not* my grandmother. She's probably just some wacko who thinks she can get their money."

The bun stands defensively. "I hardly think that the department of Family Services is in the habit of handing children over to strangers. We required proof from her, and she has provided it beyond doubt."

"How?" I demand, turning angrily on the bun.

"Why . . . DNA, of course."

I stare at her for long moments then turn back to the other woman who is watching me with sadness reflected in her eyes . . . her clear eyes, I now notice. I feel a trembling begin in my knees, shuddering up through my torso. Her eyes . . . they could just be coincidence, right? And then she steps forward and holds her fisted hand out, turned downward. Without thought, I open my hand beneath hers, and she drops a ring into it. I glance down and my heart stops.

I know this ring. My mother had worn a ring like this in all of the pictures of her teen years. She told me that her mother had taken the ring to the jewelers to be fixed, as it was missing a stone, and that was the last she'd seen of her. Later they'd found her car, burned almost beyond recognition, the body within burned definitely beyond recognition. They'd only known it was her because when the car had struck the tree that sent it careening off the cliff, the front license plate had fallen off from the impact and remained on the road.

They'd never recovered the ring—identical to the ring that is now in my hand. My ears begin to buzz as the tremor slithers down my arms, my hand clutching the ring. There is only one way to know if it is the same ring.

I glance up in surprise as Sam rushes into the room, followed closely by Shane. Sam's eyes are on me, but Shane's are on the woman—my grandmother—and he slides to a stop, dropping into what looks like a combat position. Sam starts my way, glancing cursorily toward the bun, and then the other woman. When his eyes fall on her, he also freezes, dropping into a crouch and coming up with something in his hand. He leaps toward her, and there is no forethought, no conscious decision as I yell, "No!" and jump in front of him as his hand arcs upward.

A sudden pain just below my ribs takes my breath away, and it's too much. I give in to the darkness that claims me.

Chapter 25

Niahm

I slowly come awake as a wet sponge presses insistently and continuously against my chin. I vaguely wonder who could possibly think a sponge on my chin would do anything but annoy me as I hear the low, feminine, whispered voice, furious in tone from across the room.

"You might have *broken* her rib. She needs to be taken to the hospital."

"I agree," I hear Sam reply, his low voice wretched.

"Absolutely not!" This time it's Shane, his voice matching the anger in the woman's voice. "You know as well as I do what can become of that if—" he cuts himself off, and the woman utters a hiss. I nearly laugh, feeling as though I'm being treated to a melodrama, but the effort is too much. Breathing is painful in itself.

"Don't even speak it!" the woman commands. "What are the two of you even doing here? In Goshen, of all places? In my granddaughter's house?"

Her words send a shock wave of remembrance into my mind. The bun, telling me my grandmother is alive, the ring . . . Sam coming at me with something in his hand. I wonder idly if he stabbed me or hit me with something and I'm dying. Why is he still washing my chin with a sponge, then? It doesn't make sense.

"He's bound to her," Shane answers, his voice low, calm, resigned.

"No!" The woman's response is more of a gasp than an actual word.

A low whine near my ear makes me realize the sponge isn't a sponge at all, but Bob's long, wet tongue swiping at me. I decide it's time to wake and demand to know what's going on. I open my eyes and see Sam next to me, bent in abject misery as he holds my hand, rubbing his thumb across my knuckles, over and over.

Bob blocks my view as he once again comes in for his spit bath. "No, Bob," I gasp, reaching up to push him away. He's immediately shoved aside by a masculine hand.

"Niahm?" Sam's face fills my vision, and I smile in relief, until I notice the worry lines creasing his forehead. I reach up to sooth them out, and he catches my hand instead, pulling it to his lips, sudden heat between our hands.

"I'm so sorry." His green eyes beg for forgiveness. "You have to know I would *never* hurt you. I would protect you with my life."

I grin at him, taking a breath that, though still uncomfortable, is nowhere near as painful as it had been only minutes ago. "Well, that's a little dramatic, don't you think?"

Instead of my teasing bringing a smile to his face, he drops his head to my shoulder. "I'm so, so sorry," he reiterates.

I pull my hand from his, feel the warmth fade as I do, and bury my fingers in his glorious hair. I tighten my fingers and give a light tug.

"Sam, look at me." He hesitates, but then lifts his head, his face crestfallen. "Obviously you didn't hurt me, right?" Sam's ginger brows crash together in a strange mixture of defiant anger and deep sorrow, and I smile again.

"I hit you," he says, self-recrimination in every line of his body.

"On purpose?" I ask.

"Of course not! I just told you I'd—" His vehemence strikes me as funny and I laugh.

"Then help me up and explain to me why you were trying to hit anyone at all."

He looks at me for long moments, confusion written across his features. I laugh again and push him aside as I struggle to sit. He immediately hurries to help me.

"Get away from my granddaughter." The cold fury in the woman's voice draws my attention. I look at her, this woman who claims to be my grandmother, but who is as complete a stranger to me as anyone in a crowd. How dare she come in and act like she has the right to make decisions for me? I reach out and wrap my arm around Sam's waist, pull him near me. It's a pretty bold move for me, and I choose to ignore Sam's lifted brows.

"Sam's my friend. I want him to stay," I say firmly. "I don't know *you*, and you don't know me, so maybe you should let me make my own choices. I don't even know your name. How do I even know you're my grandmother, as you claim? Where have you been all my life?"

Her anger drains, and she shuffles nervously—which would have been strange enough, except that Shane and Sam both have similar body language. Finally, she takes a tentative step toward me, hand outstretched. I make an unthinking move backward, but stop when I feel Sam's arm slide around my shoulders. I don't know how, but I have a firm knowledge that he will protect me from harm.

She stops in front of me, and turns her hand palm side up,

opening it.

"My name is Jean," she says quietly.

I look down at her hand, and my heart stops as I gasp. I roughly swipe the ring from her palm, the same ring she'd handed me before, remembrance and disbelief throttling through me as I stare at the unusual ring. A green stone cut in the shape of a sideways teardrop centers the silver ring, surrounded by smaller blue stones which look teal in the cast of the emerald. Two copper colored vines twine down the band. I lift it, closing my eyes as I turn it over. I don't want to look, but I have to know. I slowly open my eyes—and there it is. Engraved inside are the words *mo chuisle*[1].

"Where did you get this?" I demand angrily, tightening my hand around it.

"It belonged to my daughter." Her response is calm, though she does seem to be a little wary of standing so near Sam.

"No . . . how could you be . . ." I trail off, unable to speak over the tears that clog my throat.

Jean looks at Sam, "Could you give us a few minutes alone?" After several heartbeats, she grits out reluctantly, "*Please*."

"No!" The word is out before I even have time to consciously decide to protest. "They stay."

She takes a calming breath, but gives a terse nod. *As if she had the decision*, I think irritably.

"My mom told me this disappeared the night . . ." I look at her, and see her eyes have filled with tears.

"I know," she says. "I was taking it to get repaired. There was a stone missing, right above one of the leaves."

I open my hand and look at the ring again—now whole.

"I had it fixed."

"Why?" My question is not why she fixed it, but a much bigger why, which she comprehends well enough.

"I had to go away." When I open my mouth to protest, she holds up a hand. "I can't tell you why. I can tell you it's the

---

[1] my heart

hardest thing I've ever done."

I remember the story my mother told me, about how they'd found the ring when she was only ten. They had never been able to find its owner, and so she'd kept it. She told me the words inside meant *my love*, and became Jean's nickname for her. Then one of the stones had fallen out when she was seventeen, and she'd still worn it for nearly another year. Finally, her mother told her she'd take it to be fixed. She'd never returned.

Two years after her mother's death, my mom had met my dad in college, and eventually moved with him to Goshen to escape the memories, the constant need to search for her mother, even though she'd believed her dead.

My gaze flies to hers. "The car . . . there was a body. Whose was it?"

Is this woman, who claims to be my dead grandmother, some kind of psychotic killer?

"I don't know," she says. "I parked at the bluff, intending to walk away. I left that night with the intention of never returning home." Her voice catches, and I shove down the flicker of sympathy that ignites. "I couldn't do it. I couldn't leave them even if it meant . . . " She looks at Sam, then Shane, a plea in her eyes, and I wonder why she's so worried about what they think when clearly she has animosity toward them. She takes a deep breath, and turns her attention back to me.

"When I came back, the car was gone." She's calmer now. "I suppose I shouldn't have been surprised. I left the keys in it. Within moments I heard the crash. By the time I arrived, the car was down the hill and burning. There was nothing I could do. I could feel the intense heat from where I stood. It seemed like an answer, confirming that it was time for me to go. I knew they would think it was me, would assume . . ."

When she doesn't finish, I shake my head.

"No, this isn't right. I mean, anyone could know about the crash, could come back and claim to have been mistaken for being in the car. I mean, what, you've had amnesia all these years? Just now remembered who you are?"

"No, Niahm. I've known full well all along who I am." Again, she speaks to Sam and Shane, in spite of having said my name, heavy meaning in her words. "More than anything I wanted to come home, but it was impossible."

"Why? Why was it impossible? Do you know how much my mom mourned you?" I spit out.

She flinches at my words. "Yes, I can imagine. We were very close." She gazes at me. "You still don't believe I am who I say."

Instinctively, I pull Sam closer. Deep inside I can feel the truthfulness of what she says, of who she is.

"I found that ring when your mother was ten. We were at the park. I told her it was calling to me." I jerk. She couldn't have discovered that particular detail. No one had ever known besides my dad and I. "The words inside, *mo chuisle*," I feel Sam tense next to me as she says the foreign words, "became my pet name for her. Because she always was that: my heart, my love."

"Yeah," I snarl at her, "because that's what you do to people you love—you walk away and never return."

She glances at Sam again, and I can't help but follow her look. Sam is surprisingly pale, jaw clenched, mouth tight.

"It's . . . complicated," is her only response.

"No, it isn't," I argue. "You love someone, you stay with them—no matter what."

She grimaces in pain, and nods. "You're right, Niahm. I should have stayed. I should have dealt with the consequences. I should have been stronger."

"No." I glance up in surprise at Sam. The word seems forced from him, and he now looks regretful at having spoken.

"What do you mean?" I ask.

He shakes his head. "Nothing. I just . . . I mean, there might be circumstances beyond ones control . . ."

A trickle of fear beads in the back of my mind, and I wonder if he's saying he'll leave, should *circumstances* force him to.

Somehow, in this short time, he has become vital to me. Part of me recognizes that I'm clinging to him in grief, but another part of me realizes it's also something more.

"Niahm," Jean speaks, reclaiming my attention. "I know you're angry that I've never been part of your life, but I'm here now. I know that Beth would have wanted you cared for, not taken from your home and placed in a new town with strangers." I can't deny that I agree with her, but I also decide I don't need to open my mouth and confirm it either. "I'll just stay through the end of your school year. You'll be eighteen by then, and I'll go." I'm stunned by her pronouncement. It's almost as if she's only here to provide me the means to stay on the farm, and in the end, that's what's important to me. If I have to tolerate her for a while, I decide I can—as long as she stays out of my way, that is.

"However," she says, interrupting my musing. "I intend to take care of you, *protect* you," this said with a firm look at Sam and, weirdly, Shane. "I'm your only choice besides leaving Goshen. That means you'll have to accept me as your *guardian*." I feel like I'm missing some important part of the play, here, that there is some kind of subtext that everyone but me understands.

"I guess I don't have much choice, do I?" I grumble. "Still, I've been on my own for a long time, and I don't need to be babysat." I glare at her. "And Sam stays."

Her eyes widen. "He *lives* here?"

I roll my eyes. "Of course not, id—" I stop myself from completing the automatic insult. "He lives with his uncle. But he's here quite a bit." A pause as inspirations strikes. "He helps out on the farm." Sam swallows a grunt next to me. Sounds kind of painful.

Her eyes drop to where our arms are entwined.

"*And* he's my friend," I respond to her unspoken question.

"Hum," she responds noncommittally.

"You guys wanna stay for dinner?" I ask with faux brightness, taking Sam by the hand, catching Shane's as I pass, and pulling them both from the room behind me, leaving her standing there watching after us.

"Got any pie?" Sam asks, grunting as I elbow him in the ribs.

Chapter 26

Sam

The guilt I feel over having harmed Niahm is almost more than I can bear. Centuries of training and perfecting my reflexes are the only reason she doesn't have a fatal knife wound—or even realize it was a knife I held in my hand. At the last second, I recognized her intention, and was able to turn my hand, burying my fist in her ribs, rather than the knife. Still, it was a violent blow. I'm surprised she doesn't have a broken rib, seems to have recovered quickly, with no lingering effects. I looked into her mind, saw that she has no malice or anger toward me for what I did. She doesn't need to. I have more than enough for both of us.

It would be enough, dealing with hurting her on top of her grief, but then to see her grandmother, know what she is . . . . She recognized us—Shane and I—immediately, as well. Not who we are, but *what* we are. We can all recognize one another.

Knowing that Niahm's grandma is immortal fills me with conflict. Hope, larger than before, that Niahm herself might be immortal as well. Fear that all of my hope will come to naught, and I'll be forced to watch her die. Dread that I'm now confronted with dealing with a new, paranoid immortal.

We immortals are a suspicious lot. There aren't many of us who can coexist together peacefully. Many immortals have become arrogant and malicious, fearing no consequence for any of their actions, no matter what they do. Death, the worst thing most humans can imagine, is not an option for us. Those particular immortals are the reason the Sentinels exist, to eradicate those who would use mortals for their personal pleasure or gain. The Sentinels are the only mortals who know how to kill us.

The problem is the Sentinels don't know who is who, and therefore try to kill any immortal they come across. No, that's not right. They don't "come across" us—they hunt us. And they, though mortal, are not beyond corruption themselves. Some of them simply hunt us for the sport, for the achievement—and for the padding of their bank accounts. The Sentinels don't care about the right or wrong of what they do. They simply use it as justification for their own evil deeds.

Jean, in her short time as an immortal, has learned to be fully suspicious of other immortals. This makes me question why, wonder if she's already losing her conscience. She wouldn't be the first to lose it so quickly. Now I have even more reason to worry about Niahm. If Jean even suspects that Niahm could be like us, she might decide to stop her before she can become a threat. I can't take the risk of that happening; I also can't do anything that would further hurt Niahm. I could see—when I took her hand to read her non-existent, as it turned out, hatred for me—that though she's angry with her grandmother, there is an instinctive love that resides within her for this one last living relative she has.

"Earth to Sam," Niahm says lightly, waving her fingers in

front of my eyes. I give the Irish one final pat, and turn toward her.

"Finished?" I ask, nodding toward Sheila, who she'd been grooming.

She nods, seeming almost shy, shuffling in the hay that litters the floor of the stable.

"Everything okay?" I say, lightly running my thumb across her cheek.

She glances up at me, and I'm struck once again by her eyes.

"Do you think . . ." She clears her throat, and begins again. "Do you think it's too soon to go back to school?"

I'm surprised by her question, and then realize she probably thinks I'm a good one to ask, having lost my own parents. I can't tell her that not only was I not in school at that time. It's been so long I can't really give a timeline as to how long I grieved. It's been ten days since her parents were buried—three since Jean showed up. Three of the longest days of my very long life.

I place my hands on her shoulders, rubbing lightly up and down.

"Niahm, only you can decide that."

"You think people will talk . . . think I'm unfeeling?"

I smile at her. "Everyone in town knows you well enough to know that is as far from the truth as possible."

"I haven't always been the nicest person." She grins wryly. "You should know that better than anyone."

"Yes, but I also know as well as anyone that it's all bluster. You are a kind, loving person who loved her parents. Not one person will doubt that—now or ever."

Tears shimmer in her eyes. She doesn't let them fall.

"I just feel like I'm going crazy sitting around here all day. I spend all my time trying to avoid Jean, which gives me too much alone time. I need to keep busy, keep my mind occupied. I need my friends."

I pull her close and give her a hug, which she returns

without hesitation.

"I'll pick you up in the morning."

She leans back and grins happily up at me. I move my hands up to caress the sides of her neck. I can't help myself; I lean down and kiss her lightly. She freezes in surprise for a moment. Then innocently she returns the kiss, her arms tightening around my waist. It's the most amazing sensation I've felt in nearly five centuries, taking all my strength to keep my knees from buckling with overwhelming feeling. With my thumbs I urge her to slant her head, which she readily does, allowing me to deepen the kiss.

The true depth of my loneliness has been kept from my awareness until this moment. Centuries of doing nothing more than existing, waiting for this feeling, seem suddenly crushing, unbearable. In the far reaches of my mind, I comprehend the vulgarity of giving Niahm her first kiss in the middle of a smelly barn, standing in dirt and hay, both of us smelling like horses. I no more have the strength of will to stop than I do to walk away from Niahm without her command. I do have the strength, however, to keep from pouring my feeling, my passion, into the kiss. That would surely terrify her, send her running from me faster than I could chase.

I finally manage to pull back, blinking to keep the intense emotion from showing in my eyes. Niahm's eyes have tears in them as well, and I immediately worry that I've hurt her again. Or scared her. Maybe I wasn't as restrained as I'd thought.

Then she smiles at me. "Well, it's about time," she laughs.

Chapter 27

Niahm

I grin foolishly as Sam drives away, as I enter the house—even the sight of Jean sitting at the kitchen table doesn't wipe it away—as I breeze past her and up the stairs, as I fall asleep. I even wake with the grin still on my face. I can't help but wonder why in the world I waited so long to experience such an amazing thing. Then again, maybe it's only because it was Sam who kissed me that makes it so amazing.

I relive the kiss, the feeling of having his mouth pressed against mine. At first light, almost a butterfly's touch—until he tilted my head. Then it became more like a stampede, the steady pounding of hooves beating along my nerves in a way that left my head spinning.

I'm still grinning as he picks me up, and he smiles back with something like relief in his face. I know he still feels guilty about hitting me, no matter how many times I've told him I hardly blame him. It was an accident. He claims he only went after her because he thought I was in danger. It seems a lame excuse, I mean, how could one little old lady be a threat? Of course, if I'm being honest, Jean isn't exactly some withering little prune. She's strong and vital, and looks much younger than her true age.

Luckily, the social worker apparently wasn't concerned enough to stay to make sure I was okay. Glad I'm not relying on her to take care of me. I let it go because even Jean doesn't want to talk about it, brushes it off as unimportant, a misunderstanding. It's all a little strange to me, but my euphoria over the kiss overrides my suspicions.

As I walk through the school doors, and am immediately surrounded with hugs and sympathy by the double-H, followed by almost the entire rest of the school body, at least those who are in the upper grades, my grin fades. I feel a moment of deep remorse for my happiness. How dare I feel so happy when my parents are gone?

Sam takes my hand, gives it a squeeze as if he knows what I'm feeling. Maybe because of the sympathy for me I don't receive a single glare from any of the other girls all day in spite of the fact that Sam is constantly at my side, and always either holding my hand or encircling me with his arm. Beneath my guilt, I feel a worm of pleasure at the gestures.

The overpowering grief—which feels like it is here to stay for the duration of my life—is in a maelstrom of turmoil with guilt at my strong, consuming desire for Sam to kiss me again, and wondering how soon he will. By the end of the day, I'm exhausted from the emotional turbulence, and from the false assurances I'm required to give everyone, telling them that I'm fine, when I'm anything but.

Sam comes home with me, of course, but he heads to the barn to prepare to work with the Irish again. I enter the house, determined to complete my homework quickly, then my chores, so that I can be with him.

"Niahm."

I cringe at the sound of my name coming from the woman who has interrupted my life and reminds me by her very presence that my mom and dad will never be coming home again. My father will never again sing with me in his horrible, off-tune—

"Niahm," she repeats, and I turn angrily toward her, swallowing the tears.

"What!" I demand.

Jean flinches at my tone, but steps toward me, anyway.

"We need to talk." Her voice is calm, which, of course, only serves to irritate me.

"Not now, I've got homework," I say rudely, turning toward the stairs. Her hand on my arm startles me. How in the world had she crossed the room so quickly, so quietly?

"Now," she says firmly. I might have refused again, except that for one moment, she sounds—and smells—eerily like my mother. Desperate for anything that reminds me of her, I follow her to the kitchen table. Once seated, however, her face reminds me that nothing will bring back the one I long for, so I sullenly cross my arms and lean back against the chair, hoping my body language will convey my irritation and boredom to her.

"I know things are bad—"

Her words compel me out of my chair. This is a conversation I *definitely* don't want to have with her.

"Please," she says, quietly. I sink back down into the chair, emotions barely contained beneath the surface.

She takes a breath, seems to consider her words as she watches me, and finally begins anew.

"I know you don't like me," she begins, and I interrupt her.

"I don't know you well enough to like or dislike you," I say.

"Hmm," is her sardonic response. "Well, then perhaps we should rectify that."

I nearly roll my eyes at how I've painted myself into a corner with this one. The last thing I want to do is spend time with the woman who abandoned us all.

"Look, Niahm, this isn't easy for me, either. You seem to forget that Beth was my daughter. You've lost your mother, and I've lost my daughter." Her eyes cloud with tears. Oh, this is too much!

"You mean your daughter that you abandoned all those years ago? The one who thought you were dead, who grieved for you like I grieve for—" I stop, refusing to give her my emotion.

She takes another deep breath.

"I think she knew I was alive."

I scoff. "Delude yourself if you must," I laugh harshly. "She would hardly tell me you were dead, stop looking for you if she thought . . ." A thought enters my mind even as I say the words, and I suddenly know it's the truth.

"She wrote to me," she says, apparently not noticing the panic that envelopes me. I struggle to push it back. I have to finish this conversation, so that I can talk to Sam. Then her words penetrate and I shake my head.

"What do you mean, she wrote to you? How would she know where to send a letter?"

She smiles, not at me but at some distant memory, and her smile is that of my mother.

"When she was little, we used to play a game. We would write notes to one another, hide them in the crook of the tree behind our house."

"What are you saying? That she left you notes in your tree, that she would travel to the city just to . . ." Of course she would, each time she and my father flew into or out of the country. And it fits in with the theory that continues to grow in possibility in my mind. Jean simply watches me, waiting. Another trait shared by her daughter.

"Where are they?" My words are quiet.

"I have them. And I found the ones I'd written to her in her armoire."

A surge of anger flows through me, that she would dare

search my mother's belongings. But of course she would, she was her daughter. The anger is as much at myself for not having looked through her things before Jean was able to. And at my mother—why didn't she ever tell me?

I stand up again, walking to the back door. I need to speak to Sam *now*.

"I don't want you to see him anymore."

Her words freeze me. I turn back, putting as much ice into my eyes and my words as I'm capable of.

"My mom might have known you were alive, but there had to be a reason she kept it hidden from me. She obviously didn't ever intend for you to be a part of my life. If you weren't my only choice, I wouldn't abide having you here now. But be very clear on this, *grandmother*, I have no ties to you, no obligation to you, and on the day I turn eighteen, you will walk away from me as you once did her, and I will never think of you again. There will be no notes, in trees or otherwise. In the meantime, I've lived my life so far just fine without you, and will continue to do so. You have zero right to tell me who I can hang out with," my voice is rising, but I don't care if the whole world hears. "I will decide who is in my life and who is not. Sam is *definitely* in, and you . . . you will soon be definitely out."

I turn away, slamming the door unsatisfyingly behind me, and hurry to the barn, hoping to catch Sam before he starts his training.

Chapter 28

Sam

"Can you *believe* the *nerve* of that woman?" Niahm demands.

Niahm has recounted her conversation with Jean to me. Part of me, the part that feels the natural enmity toward this intrusive immortal, wants to agree with Niahm, to insist she throw her out, send her far away where she can be no threat to Niahm, or to Shane.

The bigger part of me, the overwhelming part that will do anything for this fascinating girl standing before me, knows that whatever else she is, Jean is Niahm's only living blood relative. I understand better than most how precious that gift is.

"She's only trying to protect you," I murmur, nearly choking on the words.

"What?" Niahm swings toward me, stopping mid-stride in

her pacing to stare at me incredulously.

I clear my throat.

"I mean, she's your grandma, right?" Niahm's eyes narrow. "Look, Niahm," I walk to her, sliding my hands down her arms, avoiding the temptation to take her hands in mine. "I don't particularly like her, either, but I can understand the desire to protect those you love."

"She can't love me," Niahm argues. "She doesn't even know me."

"No, she doesn't know you," I agree, "but you are the flesh-and-blood of her own daughter. That brings a sort of innate love with it. She sees me as a threat; she wants to make sure you are kept safe."

Niahm scoffs at that. "How could she see you as a threat? She doesn't know you, either."

If only you knew, I think. Instead I say, "I did go at her the first time I met her."

A small giggle escapes Niahm. I pull her into my arms, and she relaxes against me, wrapping her arms around my waist.

"Sam, do you think that's why they travelled so much? She was searching for her mom?" I can hear by her tone that she already believes this to be the truth.

"I don't know," I answer honestly.

"Because I would do that, if I thought my mom were alive. I'd search every corner of the earth, trying to find her."

I don't answer, just squeeze her tighter. She's silent for long minutes, and I wait.

"Sam?"

"Mm?"

"Do you think . . ." she trails off, and I can hear the reluctance in her voice.

"What?" I ask, giving her a little, teasing squeeze. She shakes her head against me.

"Never mind," she mumbles. I push her back, see that her face is coloring, and she refuses to meet my eyes. I'm mystified by her reaction.

"Niahm, you can ask me anything. I won't laugh or make fun of you. Promise."

Still refusing to look at me, her next words are the last thing I expect to hear.

"Think you might ever kiss me again?"

I can't help it; I laugh. Her eyes fly to mine then, anger sparking.

"You said you wouldn't laugh!" she accuses, trying to pull away.

"I'm not laughing," I say, laughing more. She glares at me, and I pull her close again. "Niahm, I'm not laughing," I say, running one thumb along her jaw. That stops her fighting me, and she relaxes into me.

"I think I might kiss you now," I say, leaning to within a hairsbreadth of her mouth. "Or, maybe later," I tease, stepping away from her. Her mouth drops open in shock, and she looks ready to punch me.

"Okay, I'll do it now," I say, laughing again, kissing her before she can get a good swing going. She doesn't resist the kiss for even a moment, stunning me with her trust and acceptance. I might feel bad about teasing her, except that I'm as caught up in the experience of kissing her as she seems to be.

✳ ✳ ✳ ✳ ✳

"What do *you* want?" Jean watches me warily, dropping casually into an offensive stance, body taut with alarm. Looking at her, I suddenly realize that in her very short life, she has had two definite things happen.

She's had a run-in either with another immortal, or with a Sentinel.

And she's had training.

Most immortals live decades, if not hundreds of years, to get to the level of suspicion that Jean has acquired—not to mention having the tactical moves she seems to have. I move to the recliner, sitting down as casually as possible, lifting one leg to cross over the other, moving slowly, indicating I mean her no harm. It's a potentially foolish move on my part. I'm vulnerable, unable to get up fast enough to defend myself if she has had the training I suspect she has. I simply wait, watching her as she stands between me and the front door—a smart place to be, I can't help but think admiringly.

Finally, she relaxes fractionally, not going so far as to sit, but standing up straight, though she does not lose the tenseness in her body.

"Fine. I get it," she says. "Out with it."

I almost smile at her impatient words, reminding me so much of her granddaughter.

"I can't leave." She opens her mouth to protest, but I hold up a hand. "No. That's not right. Let me rephrase: I *won't* leave."

"Because you're bound to her." It's more statement than question.

"That would be reason enough," I confirm. "But it isn't all."

Confusion flits through her eyes, followed by understanding, and then fury.

"Do you dare tell me you are *in love* with her? It's forbidden!"

"Not forbidden," I shake my head. "Just frowned upon. We could go into the long list of reasons as to why that is, but it doesn't really matter, does it? The fact is I will stay by Niahm's side as long as she will have me. Not you, or an army of Sentinels, will change my mind. There's only one person who can compel me to go—which you would understand had you ever experienced bonding yourself."

Jean gives a slight shudder at the thought, her eyes like daggers as she glares at me.

"She's my granddaughter," she says, words laden with meaning.

"I'm aware."

"She has my eyes."

I swallow, having known this topic would come up, still

unsure of how to deal with it.

"Again, I'm aware."

Jean drops slightly again, into her attack position and I wonder if she's even aware she's done it.

"If you even consider—"

I'm out of the chair before I can stop myself, which does nothing to ease her tension.

"I would never—" Seeing her fists clench as she crouches even lower stops my motion. I quickly drop back into the chair, forcing my voice to calm. "I would never hurt Niahm, not even for my own selfish purposes."

She watches me cautiously, weighing my words. She relaxes fractionally, standing erect once more, but not relaxing her fists.

"Why? If you know there's a chance . . ."

"Because there's always the chance for error," I answer, an image of Niahm hurt and bleeding, her mortal life draining from her, shoving its way into my head. I push it away, sick at the thought, frantic at nothing more than imagination. As if she can see what I'm seeing, Jean blanches.

"You're telling the truth," she states.

"Yes."

"You can't ever tell her," she says, her tone brooking no argument.

"I can't promise that," I answer.

"You have to! You *cannot* tell her, cannot bring her into this nightmare."

"Lying to her is already almost impossible." Another side-effect of bonding. I can lie by omission. I can even lie to protect her, even from emotional hurt, but if she suspected, if she asked outright, I could not lie.

"She's already suffered so much." Her words are whispered, anguished.

"I know," I say, allowing the accusation in my voice. "I know better than anyone."

"I went to the site of the crash," Jean says, moving to sit in the window seat. It's as close to letting down her guard as she can get without sitting down next to me like old pals, I muse wryly. "I found them. I watched as they took Beth away, followed, and stayed with her in the morgue for three days." I grimace; that's a full day longer than necessary. If the change is going to occur, the longest known time is forty-eight hours. "I refused to let them touch her. I kept hoping . . ." As if just remembering who she's speaking to, Jean glances at me, clears her throat.

"Well, obviously she didn't change," she says, trying for emotionless but not quit getting there. "She's dead. That means there's a very good chance that Niahm is not immortal, either."

"Do you think I haven't thought this through a million times since I first saw her eyes? And a million more since the accident?" I shake my head. "It's the worst kind of torture, being bound to her, and loving her on top of that, knowing that there's a chance, that I may never know if . . ." I look at Jean, allowing her to see my vulnerability for just one second, to assure her that I will not act, will not attempt to take Niahm's life just to see if she's immortal or not. If she's not . . . the image comes again, Niahm bleeding and lifeless, and I know that I would not survive that.

Jean gives one sharp nod, indicating her acceptance of my words. "But you'll tell her?"

I shrug. "I don't know. I don't think so. I just can't make the promise."

"If you tell her, I'll set the Sentinel's on you myself," she promises.

"No, you won't," I say, "Not as long as Niahm stands in the line of fire."

"No," she agrees, "Not as long as she's in the way." Her unspoken words are loud and clear: once Niahm is no longer here, I'll have her tracking me, ready to inform the Sentinels the moment she finds me. I know I'll be able to avoid her; I have centuries of hiding skills. But I also think that once I no longer have Niahm, I won't care if they find me.

"I don't trust you," she says.

"Nor I you," I answer. "But because you are Niahm's grandmother, I give you my word that neither Shane nor I will harm you. In fact, as long as Niahm wishes it, we'll protect you."

"As long as she wishes it. As long as she's around," she clarifies.

"Yes."

"I can't make the same promise in return," she says, and I smile grimly.

"Well, I suppose that speaks to which of us loves her more, doesn't it?" I say, standing and turning my back on her as I leave the room, enter the kitchen and exit by the back door. I expect the point of a knife or a bullet to enter my exposed back, but all I get is the heat from her angry glare.

Chapter 29

Niahm

Today, Sam mounts the Irish. Which would be excitement enough for me, but even better he has asked me to help. I've never broken a horse myself. I know the procedure, but haven't even seen it firsthand. So to say I'm excited is about as much of an understatement as saying Bob has a slight liking for chasing the chickens.

Autumn is heavy in the air now, the days cool, leaves changing from green to brilliant yellows, reds and purples, in preparation for their falling from the trees for the sole purpose of causing me more work in raking them up. Other than that un-fun activity, I really do love the fall. The colors, the smells, not to mention the best apples of the season, are all benefits of the season.

Sam backs out of the stall, handing me the longe line that

he's already secured to the Irish. I glance at him, questioning. "Lead him to the paddock, would ya?" he asks, as if I've ever done such a thing with a wild horse.

Not wanting to let him down, I take the rope, pushing the nerves back to keep the stallion from sensing them.

"Alright, Hercules, let's get you out to begin the newest torture," I tell him, directing him toward the gate. He doesn't like having me at the controls, used to Sam as he is, but I don't give him a break, even as he tosses his head wildly. He decides I'm not messing around and follows me.

Once in the paddock, Sam gets the halter on him then puts the blanket over his back with the saddle. He's been getting the horse used to the saddle, so he barely flinches at this.

"Okay, are you ready?" he asks me. I grab hold of the halter, bolstered by the trust Sam has on his face as he watches me. He stands up on a block, and leans across the Irish on his belly, giving him his weight. The Irish isn't thrilled with this, and takes a few steps to the side.

"Hold it there, Hercules," I command, grasping the halter tighter and showing him the whip—which I would never use on him, but *he* doesn't know that. It works and he stops moving, settling for tossing his head and blowing loud breaths out between his lips.

Sam removes and reapplies his weight a few times until the Irish stops tossing. Then he places his foot into the stirrup and calmly lifts his right leg over until he's seated on the saddle. The Irish complains again by stomping a few times, but doesn't try anything else. Sam climbs off and on a few times, then says, "Okay, Niahm, let's walk him."

"What?" He's kidding, right?

"Let's walk. You've got him by the harness, just lead him along."

"You wearing some padding?" I'm only half-joking. Sam just laughs. I shrug and take a step. Amazingly, the Irish follows.

"Good boy, Hercules," I murmur.

"Why do you call him that?" Sam asks a few minutes later,

relaxing in the saddle, one hand resting lightly on the pommel, the other on his hip. He has more confidence in me keeping control that I have in myself.

"I don't know," I answer, leading them around the perimeter of the corral. "You haven't named him yet, and I was tired of thinking of him as . . . well, *him*. He seems big, strong, and demi-god-like, so I just kind of nicknamed him Hercules."

Sam smiles. "It's a good name."

I glance back up at him, the sun glinting off his copper hair, his smile directed my way, and shake my head. "Only for Greek myths and cartoon characters," I say.

"It's a good name," he repeats. I might have argued further except that Bob chooses that moment to chase an escaped chicken into the corral. The Irish *definitely* doesn't like this new development and rears up, ripping the halter from my grip. I manage to grab the longe line, but Sam, who'd been unprepared and relaxed flies off the backside of the stallion. I hear him hit the fence, and instinctively release the line. The Irish, not one to pass up an opportunity, races to the opposite side of the paddock, away from me, Sam, Bob, and the squawking chicken.

"Sam!" I exclaim, rushing to his side, followed closely by Bob who has forgotten the chicken in his concern for Sam. Sam sits up, laughing as Bob manages to lick his face from jaw to hairline.

"Gross, Bob, stop," I say pushing him away.

"It's fine," Sam refutes, scrubbing Bob behind his ear.

"Are you okay?" I ask, worried that he's hurt.

"It's not the first time I've been thrown. Probably not the last, either," he grins.

I smile, relieved that he's fine. I'd heard him hit the fence . . . or, I *thought* I had. Then Bob gives a little whine, and nudges Sam's arm with his nose. That's when I see the blood saturating his upper sleeve.

"Sam, you're hurt," I say, grabbing his arm. He glances down, then looks at me with alarm. Huh, I've never seen Sam panic over an injury before.

"It's fine," he says urgently, "just a scratch."

"How can you know?" I tease, trying to calm him. "Let's get inside and I'll clean it up for you."

"No!" His answer is quick, sharp, and I flinch. "I mean," he says more calmly, "it's no big deal. I'll just go home and let Shane take care of it."

"Sam, don't be silly. I'm hardly a squeamish girl. If it doesn't need stitches, I can bandage it for you."

Sam looks anxious, and I'm admittedly surprised. He's always calm in emergency situations. But then, I've never seen him hurt, so I guess maybe he's just calm with others, but doesn't deal so well when it's himself.

"What about the horse?"

I glance over at the Irish, contentedly pulling weeds from the ground now that he's been set free.

"He's fine for a few minutes. Let's get you inside."

Sam hesitates, looks around as if searching for an answer, and then finally sighs.

"Okay," he says, standing and pulling me up with him.

We walk into the house, and he immediately excuses himself to use the restroom. I begin gathering supplies—a wet rag, bandages if it's small, gauze if it's a larger cut, and some ibuprofen for any pain. Jean walks into the kitchen at the same time Sam emerges from the bathroom.

"What's going on?" Her tone is suspicious, accusatory.

"Sam hurt himself when the horse threw him," I answer. "He's fine. I'm just going to clean it up a little."

Jean's face tightens and she steps toward me. "Let me do that," she commands.

"I've got it," I say firmly, standing my ground. She looks at Sam, a pleading look in her eyes, and I feel once again like I'm missing some vital piece of the story here. Sam steps around her and peels his outer shirt off. I try not to check him out in his thin white T-shirt, but who am I kidding? I definitely look.

"Sit," I say, pointing to the chair. Jean steps closer, and I stiffen, wishing I could command her to go away. Instead, I turn my attention to Sam. I roll his sleeve up and wipe around the edges of the wound, glancing up to gauge if I'm hurting him. He has a tightness around his eyes, watching me warily and I get the impression that he's concerned for *me* more than himself. I glance back down at the wound just below his shoulder, which is spurting bright red blood still, and see how deep it is. I dab it with a piece of gauze, and he winces.

"Um, I think you're going to need stitches," I say. He only grunts, but Jean steps closer, peering over my shoulder.

"I don't know," she demurs.

Sam glances down. "I think you're right," he says, and Jean lifts her brows at that.

"Luckily, Shane can take care of that," he says, directing his words to her.

"Ah," she says, as if he'd answered a question for her.

"I think you should go to the clinic," I say, but he's already shaking his head, trying to pull his shirt back on.

"No. Shane is a medic. I'd rather he did it."

"Fine," I say, stopping him from pulling his shirt over the wound. "At least let me wrap it in gauze first. I don't want it infected, and I don't want you to bleed to death on the way home."

He grins at me, as if I'd made a joke, and I just shake my head at him, feeling again like I've missed something. He sits patiently, watching me closely as I bind his arm with a sterile pad and a strip of gauze, a slight smile on his face. When I finish, he looks down at it.

"Good job, Doc. Where did you learn such good bandaging skills?" He's teasing, but I feel a flush steal up my face and refuse to look at him as I pick up the remnants of the supplies.

"Nowhere," I murmur, turning away from him.

"Hey," he says, grabbing my hand. I glance back at him, then over at Jean who is watching us closely. There is no way I'll admit to him—especially in front of her—that when I was younger, I decided it was unfair that girls couldn't become Boy

Scouts. So I studied every merit badge requirement and passed them off—albeit to myself. A wide smile splits Sam's face.

"What?" I demand.

"Nothing," he says, still smiling. "Just, thanks." He lifts his wounded arm, as if I might have forgotten what he might be thanking me for. He leans forward, and I wonder if (hope) he's going to kiss me, but Jean shuffles, reminding us of her unwelcome presence, and he releases me.

"Just give me a sec and I'll be ready to go."

"Go where?" Sam and Jean both say at the same time, both sounding edgy. I turn back toward them, just catching the tail end of their look at one another.

"With you," I say. "I'm not letting you drive alone when you're bleeding."

"I'll be fine," Sam says.

"Yes, Niahm, you should probably—"

"I'm *not* letting him go alone," I interrupt Jean.

"What about Hercules?" Sam asks, and I roll my eyes at him.

"He'll be fine. He roams out there all the time. When I get home, I'll put him back in the stable." I pause. "And quit calling him Hercules."

Sam ignores my last comment, glancing at Jean once again.

"I'll call Shane and let him know you're coming," she tells him. I wait for Sam to tell her to leap off a cliff, he can do it himself.

Instead, he nods tersely and says, "Thanks."

Now I know he's lost too much blood.

Chapter 30

Sam

Shane waits outside as we pull up, like a concerned uncle. I glance at Niahm as she carefully maneuvers the truck into the driveway. She wouldn't even let me drive. I'd be amused if I weren't so worried about how we're going to explain my suddenly healed arm to her. It had taken my knife and some pain to reopen the wound in Niahm's bathroom before she took a look at it. I wanted to make sure it would stay for her inspection, but had cut too deep as she declared it necessary for stitches.

We walk into the house, Niahm watching me with worry etched across her forehead. I put my "good" arm around her and give her a reassuring squeeze. In the kitchen, I sit in the chair, and she sits directly next to me.

"Niahm," Shane says, professionally unwrapping his suturing kits to Niahm's widened eyes. "Would you do me a favor?"

"Sure," she answers immediately.

"In the hallway closet there is a small bin. Can you get that for me?"

"Okay," she answers readily, and I wince at the deception required to pull this off. She gives my shoulder a squeeze as she passes me then does as asked.

Without speech necessary, as soon as she is gone, I quickly pull my shirt off, and Shane uses a sterile scalpel on the now light pink line to recreate the wound. I grit my teeth against the pain, and he grunts in apology. His slice is much neater than mine, and not quite as deep. By the time she returns, the scalpel has disappeared into one of the pockets of his suture kit, and he's examining my arm.

"Thanks, sweetie." I raise my brows at his overly uncle-ish endearment, which he ignores. "Can you fill it with warm water from the sink? And put some of this soap in it." He hands her the bottle of sterile soap. She fills it, hands it to him, and returns to sit next to me.

"You're bleeding again," she notes, looking slightly pale.

"His shirt was a little stuck," Shane says. "Reopened it a little." He dips a sterile piece of gauze into the water, and cleans the wound quickly. He has to work quickly—otherwise he will soon be suturing nothing but my healed arm. She watches him, and I decide I need to pull her attention away from scrutinizing what I know will soon be happening.

"So, what's wrong with calling him Hercules?" I ask. Her eyes turn to me.

"It's a silly name for such an unusual, magnificent horse."

"You named the Irish Hercules?" Shane questions.

"Niahm did," I say.

"No, I didn't," she refutes. "I was just calling him that as sort of a nickname since he doesn't have one yet."

"Hercules was a magnificent man," I say, wincing as Shane stabs the needle into my arm. Niahm's eyes fly to my arm, and I regret reacting. "What else should I call him?" I ask, pulling her attention back to me. "Trigger? Mr. Ed?"

She grimaces. "Why on earth would you call a horse Mr. Ed?" Shane stabs extra hard for my blunder and I'm hard pressed to keep from wincing again. I sometimes forget that though a few decades mean little to me, Niahm has only been alive for a few years. Of course she would have no idea who Mr. Ed is.

"He was a talking horse on TV in the '60's," I say.

"You kind of like old movies and stuff, huh?" she says, and Shane coughs over his choked back laugh.

"I didn't say I *liked* it, I was just telling you who Mr. Ed is."

"Well, I doubt your horse is going to talk, so, no, I don't think you should call him that either." She starts to lean around me, to watch what Shane is doing. In desperation, I lean forward and plant a quick kiss on her lips. Her face reddens as she glances quickly at Shane, who is suddenly intent on his work. She looks back at me, then away, and I'm sorry for the action.

"Sorry," I whisper, "I couldn't help myself." She looks at me and I grin, reaching up to lightly caress her jaw. Her eyes widen a little, reminding me that she is not used to such overt displays of affection. But it's done the trick, diverting her attention from Shane suturing my wound.

"Done," Shane pronounces, pressing a gauze pad over his handiwork, and as Niahm had done, wrapping a longer piece of gauze around my arm. Niahm looks over, disappointed that he's already covered it.

"How many stitches?" she questions.

"Oh, uh . . . six." I roll my eyes at Shane's poor attempt at lying.

"Huh," Niahm answers. "Where did you learn to do that?"

"I used to work as a paramedic," Shane says, a story he's told many times. It's the truth; that is one of the jobs he has done. He can't tell her that he's also been through medical school—once in the 1700's in Europe, and again in the early 1900's in America.

"Why don't you anymore?"

He glances at her, and gives her his prepared answer. "A really bad accident, where I was unable to save a family. It shook me up so much I couldn't work effectively after that. So I decided to do something different."

"Oh." Niahm's small voice is laced with sorrow.

"Now that there's no danger of me bleeding to death," I say before she can question him further, "can I drive you home?"

She looks to Shane. "Do you think he should be driving?"

"He didn't lose much blood." She glances at the small pile of bloody bandages, and Shane smiles. "I know it seems like a lot, but it really isn't much. His reactions are all normal, his eyes are fine, his coloring is good . . ."

Niahm looks at me skeptically at that last. Granted, it would be a little hard to tell if I had lost any color with my naturally pale skin, the result of being a redhead.

"See, I'm fine," I say. "You, however, look a little pale."

She shakes her head. "No, I'm good. Let's go, then."

We walk out to the truck, and when we climb in, I'm pleased to notice that Niahm sits a little more to the center of the bench seat. I reach out and take her hand in mine, giving her a little tug. She smiles and scoots closer, and I close my mind to hers.

We pull around the backside of the barn, and see that the Irish is no longer in the paddock. We go into the barn and find him back in his stall, rubbed down, all the equipment stowed in the tack room. We both lift our brows and look at one another, well aware of who did this.

Niahm steps up to the half-door and shakes a finger at him.

"Bad, bad horse, to hurt Sam like that," she admonishes in a tone that sounds more like she's praising him. I walk over to the stall, and the stallion comes over to me—a first. Niahm slips an apple into my hand, which I then give the horse. He blows out a light whinny, as if in apology.

"See, I knew he was sorry," she says, as if I'd been angry

with him. How could I? He was only doing what was natural and instinctive to him.

"Is that right?" I say to the horse. "Are you sorry you threw me, Hercules?"

Niahm grunts, but the Irish tosses his head up once.

"Maybe I *should* name him Mr. Ed," I say to her with a laugh. He backs away a couple of steps, and I laugh. "Maybe not."

Niahm elbows me lightly in the arm, then horror crosses her face.

"Oh, I'm so sorry!"

I look at my arm, and remember this is my "wounded" arm—which is now completely healed beneath Shane's faux sutures and bandage.

"It doesn't hurt, Niahm." That much is true. She still looks worried. "I promise . . . it doesn't hurt."

"You don't have to be brave," she says.

"I'm not. It *genuinely* doesn't hurt."

"I'm sorry, Sam, for not holding on to him tight enough. I let him go and he threw you."

I shake my head at her skewed thoughts.

"You had no choice, Niahm. If you'd tried to hold on, you could have been seriously injured." I don't tell her that I threw myself as much as the horse threw me—I knew if I removed my weight, he would calm somewhat and stop his pawing which would be devastating to a mortal caught beneath. "I couldn't stand that, if you'd been hurt."

"Do you think I like you being hurt?" she questions.

I put my "injured" arm around her and pull her close.

"I'm not hurt. See?"

She's a little off balance at being so close, so I take advantage and kiss her. She melts against me, arms tight around my middle, returning the kiss with enthusiasm. Her innocence moves me. In the back of my mind, I wonder how I'm going to explain the lack of a healing wound and subsequent scar—bad enough to require stitches—to her.

Chapter 31

Niahm

Snow falls for the first time today. I love the first snow of the season. This year, it feels wrong. I can't run outside and play in the falling flakes with Bob. I can't call Stacy to go for a ride on the ATV's along the snowy paths. I can't take Sheila out for a run in the chill.

Because I can't call my parents and tell them about it.

A sob catches in my chest, and I swallow it. I can *feel* Jean behind me, typing furiously on her laptop, look up at me. Her stare is like a weight on my back.

I *can* go out and get the tarp secured over the chicken run. I *can* make sure the heaters are working in the coop and stalls. I can use the relative privacy of the barn to fall apart.

When I've finished crying, and completed the chores I set for myself, I return to the house. Jean is no longer in the kitchen, her laptop gone with her. I consider starting dinner, but I don't really feel up to it. I climb the stairs . . . and see the light on in my parents' bedroom. Fury flows through me as I hurry down the hall.

I shove the door open, and see Jean sitting on the floor, surrounded by papers, crying silently. I'm checked in my anger at the genuine grief creasing her face. Before I can retreat, she looks up and sees me. She lifts a few of the papers toward me.

"What . . ." I have to stop and clear my throat. "What are you doing in here?"

She takes a breath, controlling her emotions. Finally, she's able to speak.

"I think you should see these, Niahm."

With trepidation, I force my feet to move. When I reach her, I take the paper she hands me. The sight of my mom's handwriting drives me to my knees.

"What is this?" I gasp.

"She suspected I was still alive."

Her words turn my attention back to the papers.

> *Dear Mom (wherever you are),*
>
> *I wish you would come home. Dad tries, but he just doesn't know how to answer my questions—the ones I ask, anyway. Some of them, I refuse to ask him. He's my father. I need you, Mom. I don't know why you left— was it me? Did I do something wrong? I promise to be good, to do anything you ask if you'll just come home.*
>
> *I love you,*
> *Beth*

I look up at Jean, angry once again on behalf of my own mom as a young girl, desperately wishing for her mother. Her words could almost be mine.

"How could you leave your own daughter like that? How could you . . . stay away?"

"I haven't seen these before today."

"What? I thought you told me she'd written to you."

"She did," she confirms. "But not these letters—different ones. She was writing for all intents and purposes to a complete stranger. However, I suspected, from some of the things she'd written, that she thought it might be me she was writing to."

"Where did you find these, then?"

She smiles apologetically. "I broke into her files on her computer. She made reference to them, said she'd hidden them in the floor in her closet."

I glance past her and see where she's lifted the carpeting and a square of wood from the floor of their closet. And suddenly, a memory assaults me.

I'm a little girl. I walked into my mom's room, and saw her sitting in her closet.

"What are you doing, mommy?"

She turned guiltily, and I could see the hole in the floor.

"Mommy, there's a hole in your closet. Is the floor broked?"

"Broken," she corrected automatically, backing out and closing the closet door. "No, sweetness, it's not broken. Let's go make some cookies, hmm?"

Later, I snuck into her closet to see the hole, but it was gone. The carpet was in place and there was no evidence of it having ever been there.

I rise to my knees, push past Jean and look down into the hole. It's empty. The smells in the closet overpower my senses—my parent's scents. Why haven't I thought to come in here before, to smell them? I breathe deeply, hungrily, controlling my emotions before I back out.

"Everything is here," she says, indicating the mess around her. I sink back down, suddenly exhausted.

"Fine. Tell me," I say belligerently.

"The letters she left in the tree—they were more like journal entries in the beginning. I didn't plan to write back, but I looked forward to those letters, to know what was happening in her life. It wasn't safe for me to be there, I was always in disguise. Sometimes months would pass between visits, and I would find several letters."

She leans back against the closet door, pulling some of the papers against her chest.

"Then one day, I wrote back. A simple note, telling her I had found her notes and was intrigued by them. I gave her no indication it was me."

"Then what makes you think she believed you were alive?" I demand. "I mean, that one letter could have been written right after you left, while she was still in shock from your . . . death."

Jean shakes her head, as if the answer should be obvious.

"That was only the first." She points to a semi-neat stack of papers to her left. "Those are all similar letters. Only, as time passed, she became more and more angry at me."

I picked up the stack, flipped through them, overwhelmed at the pages of her handwriting. About halfway through, they became typed pages, and then printed pages. They weren't her handwriting, but in my hands I held my mom's words.

"You can read them all, if you'd like," she says. "But I think this is the one you should read now. This is the last one she wrote."

I take the paper she hands me, shaking at the thought that I hold the last thing my mom had created. I glance down at the date, and see that it's the day they left. I recall now her going back into the house after we had everything loaded in the car, claiming she had one last thing she needed to take care of. Was this it?

Dear Mom (wherever you are),

I glance up, shuffle through a few of the other papers, and see that she started them all the same.

You wouldn't believe how mad Niahm is at us right now. She's so angry that we are leaving her once again.

I wish I could tell her, could explain to her this insatiable need to travel the world, hoping that just once I might run into you. Whether in the Sahara Desert, or the jungles of Africa, I don't care. I'm not even sure how I'd react if I did—would I hug you, joyous to see you again? Or would I punch you square in the nose, tell you how rotten you are for leaving me? Leaving me . . . just as I leave Niahm. The difference is I will always come home to her.

I take a deep breath at the words, pain lancing through my whole being at the realization that she *wouldn't* always come home to me. Not anymore.

I have one last letter to leave in the tree. I think it's you I've been writing to all these years. Even if it's not, I've always pretended that it's so. It keeps me sane. Keeps that hatred I harbor for your actions at bay, the thought that you are still there for me. Why did you go? After this, I will no longer leave the letters. Even if it is you, it's far past time for me to move on.

I suppose this shall be our last excursion. Jonas and I have lived more adventure than most people do in their lifetimes. But it's time to be home, to do this for Niahm, rather than the constant searching that I do for me. I haven't spoken to Jonas about this yet. He doesn't know the reason behind my insistence on our travels. He loves me—he would do anything for me. I have used that to my own selfish ends. This will be the last time I indulge myself.

So, if you find the letter I will leave, I will hope that you honor my request to the best of your ability, to take care of Niahm. My Niahm has always had a sort of sixth sense about things, and she is worried about our leaving. I can feel her intense concern. That's the reason for the content of the letter, and the reason for, God

willing, my safe return to Goshen to live the rest of my days in peace.
  Beth

I clutch the letter, breathing heavily. She knew? I had no idea she could feel my concern. If she knew, if she believed it, *why* did she go? She couldn't give up this one last trip? It was only one, how much of a difference could that have made?

"Niahm?"

I look up at my name, see the worried look on Jean's face. I know I'm on the verge of losing it, but manage to pull my emotions back down to a manageable level, regaining control.

"Do you have it?" I ask.

She hands me another letter, this time in an envelope. Of course she would know what I was asking for, having read this herself. I just hold it, unable to take my eyes from the last thing my mom touched, at least that I have access to.

"I'll leave you alone," Jean says. "If you need me—" she breaks off, and changes course. "If you need anything, I'll be in the kitchen."

She leaves me there, among a side of my mom's life that feels like an opened secret—or maybe more like her own Pandora's Box left behind to destroy any sense of peace *I* might have.

❋ ❋ ❋ ❋ ❋

A few hours later I make my way down the stairs. Jean is back at her laptop, but looks up as I come in. She watches me warily, then stands and moves to the oven.

"I'm nowhere near as good a cook as you," she says. "But I manage."

She pulls a plate from the oven, and I recognize my mom's version of Shepherd Pie. At that moment I realize that it was never her version, but the version she'd been taught by Jean—a fact she'd never shared with me. Irritation fills me, but for once it's directed at my own mom, and not at Jean.

I sit at the table, and she places it in front of me. I wouldn't have thought I could eat, but as I take the first bite I'm suddenly ravenous. I finish it quickly as Jean sits silently across from me. When I finish, and make no move to leave, she leans forward.

"Did you read them all?" she asks. I nod. "Are you okay?"

I give a short laugh. Okay is not something I'll be for some time. But I will be eventually, I suppose. Even I can recognize it's my feelings of betrayal causing all of the hurt.

"Is that why you came?" I ask. "The last letter, I mean."

Jean doesn't answer for a moment, tracing the fleur-de-lis pattern on the tablecloth. Finally, she sighs and looks at me.

"Maybe. I don't know. I'd like to think I would have come anyway, after she . . ." She clears her throat. "But I just don't know. I'll be honest, I felt it was the least I could do for my daughter, after causing her so much pain."

She watches me, as if waiting for the anger, but it doesn't come. I respect her honesty, if nothing else.

"I'm going to bed," I say, standing up. Jean stands also. "Thank you," I murmur, turning away. I trudge up the stairs, wash my face and get ready for bed. I look outside once again at the softly falling snow, briefly frustrated at the shoveling that will be required in the morning. I slide between the cool sheets, turning on the bedside lamp as I read her last letter one final time.

> My name is Elizabeth Marta Parker, wife of Jonas Parker, mother to Niahm Jona Parker. Should something happen to Jonas and myself, where we are taken from this earth, every effort should be made to find my mother, Niahm's maternal grandmother, Jean Elizabeth Franza. She disappeared some years ago, but I believe she is still alive.
>
> Please tell her I would like her to go to Niahm, and care for her in my place. Tell her I know she will love Niahm as I do, and she is now Niahm's closest living

relative. Tell her to raise Niahm to be the strong, independent woman Niahm has already begun to be.
Niahm will need you. Please go.

Her signature rested beneath. The last two sentences haunt me as none of the others have. She knew that Jean would find this, that Jean would read those lines. I think she also knew that eventually I would see them, that I would need them to forgive Jean as she was never able to.

Chapter 32

Sam

"Sam, what are you doing?"

I turn from my task of shoveling the snow from Niahm's front walk. She's standing there, bundled up in her coat, gloves, and snow boots—and looking drained.

"Isn't that obvious?" I ask.

She stomps down the stairs, stopping right in front of me, leaning back to glare at me.

"I didn't ask you to do this." Her statement sounds like an accusation. I smile and lean down to kiss the tip of her cold, red nose.

"I'm aware of that," I say, turning back to my task. She steps in front of me, nearly shoveled off her feet at the forward motion of the wide shovel. Her arms windmill, and I grasp the front of her jacket, steadying her. "Are you trying to crack your head open?" I demand, immediately sorry as she pales at my harsh tone. I yank her to me, throwing the shovel to the side and wrap my arms around her, stunned as she bursts into tears.

"Niahm, I'm so sorry. I didn't mean it. You just scared me."

She continues to sob, shaking her head against me at my words. I've never claimed to know much about the female persuasion, but I'm aware that this type of crying from *this* particular girl probably isn't about my words or my tone. Something else is going on. My mind immediately goes to her grandmother, and I'm hard pressed to not storm into the house and cause the woman some serious pain.

Instead, I sweep one arm under her knees, and carry her to the barn, the best place I can think of for some immediate privacy.

"I'm sorry," Niahm says when I set her down on a hay bale and squat down in front of her. She wipes at her eyes and nose with her gloves, and my eyes go to those offending garments, wondering how I can get them off of her without raising suspicion why I want to hold her bare hand in the cold air, rather than with her gloves on. Her face is very pale and drawn, dark circles beneath her eyes. I rub a thumb across the smudges, as if I can wipe them away.

"I'm a mess, I know," she says with a sad attempt at a smile.

"You're not a mess," I say.

"I am," she refutes, "inside and out."

I take her gloved hand in mine—and get a flicker. Fuzzy images of white squares, anger, hurt, betrayal . . . I'm stunned by the discovery, disturbed by the feelings I catch from her.

"What?" She sounds slightly alarmed at my expression. I quickly school my features.

"I'm worried about you. You're upset."

She's silent, thinking, and finally pulls an item from her pocket. She hands it to me—a white square. An envelope. I look from the envelope to her and she gives it a little push toward me. I apprehend that she wishes me to read it.

My name is Elizabeth Marta Parker, wife of Jonas Parker, mother to Niahm Jona Parker. Should something happen to Jonas and myself . . .

I stop reading to look at Niahm again. Her face is creased with pain, as if she can hear the words. Considering the crumpled, worn look of the paper I assume she's read it many times and probably has it memorized. I read the rest of it, understanding her drawn look. I can also understand the feeling of hurt I got from her and maybe even the anger, but the betrayal stumps me.

"Where did you find this?" I ask.

"Jean gave it to me. She found it in the tree."

"The tree?"

Niahm tells me the story of the letters, both in the tree and the ones found in the closet. She keeps her gaze on her hands, which are twisting together nervously, during her entire recitation. I watch her face, emotions flitting across even though she tries to tell the story in monotone. She doesn't succeed—her voice expresses her wounded heart, the depth that she feels betrayed by her parents leaving her home to search for someone who'd willingly left, searching for someone who may or may not be dead, rather than stay home with the very much alive daughter who longed for them.

I'm not just getting these impressions from her tone, I *know* them, can *feel* them coming from her. How is that possible? I move to sit next to her, an arm about her as she leans into me.

"I wish I knew what to say to make this better for you, Niahm."

"I wish I knew why she preferred to search for a possible ghost than to be with me." She sighs. "And yet, I do understand a little. I mean, if I thought my mom were alive, I don't know that I'd ever stop searching for her."

I recall Jean's words about sitting with her daughter, waiting to make certain she wouldn't come back. I can feel that Niahm is thinking about Beth's search for Jean, which never bore fruit—and yet, Jean was alive. Beth had been right. Niahm is wondering about the possibility even now.

"Niahm," I hesitate, reluctant to extinguish that time flame of hope. "Your parents . . . I saw them. At the funeral home."

She shudders.

"I know." Her words are firm, but beneath them the shard of optimism stays strong.

* * * * *

"I have to tell her."

Shane finishes pounding the nail into the side of the barn before turning to me. He pulls the other two nails from his mouth.

"You just gonna stand there jawing, or do you think you might do something constructive?" He's been pushing to finish the barn, though he knows I don't have any intention of moving the horse—at least not yet. "Tell who what?" he asks, turning back to the task, replacing both nails between his lips and taking a third from the belt around his waist that he places against the wood.

I pick up a large sheet of plywood, and place it against the side of the barn, placing the nail gun against it. Shane is firmly against anything as innovative as a nail gun, preferring the old fashioned hammer-to-nail. So I don't feel exactly guilty about taking the occasional break. Even with long breaks, I still accomplish far more work than he does.

"Niahm," I answer after shooting a couple of nails in. "I'm going to tell her . . . what I am."

Shane lets out a string of curses, partly as a result of my statement, partly as a result of slamming his thumb with the hammer at my words.

"Are you insane?" he yells. "There are rules about that for a reason, Samuel. If you tell her, you put us both in danger."

"I know," I say, but he overrides my words.

"You put *her* in danger. If the Sentinels found out . . ."

He doesn't have to finish. I know exactly what would

happen if they found out.

"I would never put you in danger if I could avoid it, Shane, you know that. So if you need to go or if you want me to go—"

Shane's fist connects firmly with my jaw, sending me sprawling.

"You thick, fool eegit[1]! Ye think you're some kind of . . . hardchaw[2]? That ye can handle them alone, and protect her? Ciach ort[3]! Tá tú glan as do mheabhair[4]! Go hIfreann leat. O mbeire an diabhal leis thú[5]!"

I jump to my feet, my anger matching his, my carefully maintained American accent slipping in the face of his *Gaeilge*.

"He *'as* already ta'en me, Shane. Diabhal[6] took me centuries ago. My soul ta th' devil? 'Tis long gone! Tá mé faoi chrann smola[7]."

Shane's stance drops immediately from his aggressive position as my words register. It's an old argument, and he knows he's unintentionally just confirmed my side of the argument.

"Ye are no' cursed, Samuel." His words are still fierce, but in a protective way. He steps forward and gathers the front of my shirt in his fists, yanking me forward so that our faces are a hairsbreadth apart. "Do ye 'ear me, Sorley? Ye are *no'* cursed."

I push away from him and take some calming breaths, turning away from him. The years apart from Shane are the hardest to take, the loneliest. I don't want to alienate him, but I also won't give in on this point.

"I'll stay wi' her, as long as she'll 'ave me," I finally say. "I canna be wi' her in the way I want ta 'less she knows."

He's silent behind me for long minutes. The only sounds are the wind and Shane's breathing. Finally, he takes a few

---

[1] idiot
[2] hard guy or tough guy
[3] you are damned
[4] you're crazy/insane
[5] go reside in hell/the devil take you
[6] devil
[7] I am cursed

steps toward me. I brace myself for whatever his decision is.

"I canna change yer mind, then?"

I turn to face him.

"No."

His jaw clenches as he considers.

"I willna abandon ye, Sorley."

It takes several heartbeats for his words to register. I blink, give my head a small shake, not sure I heard right.

"You . . ."

His smile is grim.

"I do'na like livin' alone," he explains. "Yer an eejit, true enough, but I'll stick wi' ye."

Relief floods through me. He's right, this might be the most idiotic idea I've had. But I can no longer lie to her, hide who I am. If I want to be with her—*truly* be with her—it's time to tell her.

"You called me Sorley," I say, pulling my American accent back together. "You haven't called me by my real name in over a century." I grin at him. "You must be *really* mad at me."

Shane throws the hammer toward my head, which I catch neatly before it meets its target.

"I do'na remember when I've e'er thought ye a bigger fool," he says. "I also don' remember when I've admired ye more."

"*Admired* me?"

"Aye," he confirms. "It takes a great deal o' courage ta do wha' ye propose. Be sure ye know wha' yer doin'."

He pulls me into a bear hug, then leaves the barn, done for today. I watch him go, fear suddenly taking up residence in my gut. I *don't* know what I'm doing. All of my hope lays in Niahm's love. What if I'm wrong?

Chapter 33

Niahm

I sit at the kitchen table, doing my homework. Normally, Sam would be with me, but he said he had some things Shane needed him for, so he'd see me in the morning when he picked me up for school. Besides the powerful wish to be with him every possible moment comes the realization that when he's here, Jean makes herself scarce.

Tonight she sits at the desk with the laptop, too close for comfort. Since the discovery of the letters—of which I've read all by now, both Jeans and my mom's—there's been a sort of calm in the house. That doesn't mean I'm ready to have a grandma. She's still an unwelcome intruder.

The letters were a revelation. The correspondence between Jean and her daughter made it seem clear, to me at least, that she suspected it was her mother she was exchanging letters with. She'd asked for advice, which Jean gave. The letters my mom had written and kept were something else. In them, she poured out her anger, frustration, and betrayal. In them, I read her reasons for the constant searching. Yet, as frustrated and hurt as I was by being left behind by her searching quest, I couldn't blame her.

Jean, whose back is to me, stretches and tips her head back. I literally do a double take at what I see—her roots are *dark*. I blink a couple of times as she returns to her upright position. That can't be right. Roots are gray to one's dark dyed hair, not the other way around.

I stand up and she turns my way, a small smile directed to me. I normally would just say goodnight and go upstairs, but I've got to know what's going on with her hair. I don't know what expression is on my face as I look at her, but her smile drops and she rises with some alarm.

"Everything okay, Niahm?" she asks warily.

"I don't . . ." As I see her now, standing, her hair looking perfectly gray, I suddenly feel silly at my imagination. What am I going to say, *Do you dye your hair gray? Are you a young imposter pretending to by my grandmother?* It's ridiculous, of course. To what end would she do that? The entire inheritance is irrevocably mine. Besides, I saw her grief—it was real.

"Um, nothing," I finally say. "I just remembered . . . uh, I have this big test tomorrow. And, um, I should have been studying for it. So I guess I'll go up to my room and do that now."

Her eyes narrow suspiciously, but I hurry and gather my books, jogging up the stairs. It's stupid to have imagined the dark roots. Why would I even think I had seen such a strange thing? I flop down on my bed, covering my eyes with my arm. I must be exhausted. I mean, of all things to hallucinate—*dark roots*? Definite lack of imagination, there. I laugh at myself, rolling toward the window, listening to the wind howl.

A tightness resides in my gut, no matter how silly I tell myself I'm being. Something isn't right.

Cindy C Bennett

✳ ✳ ✳ ✳ ✳

"How's your arm?" I ask Sam as we throw hay. This is one of my least favorite activities during the summer, but during the cold winter, I don't mind it at all.

"Good," he says, not turning my way.

"Stitches out yet?"

"Uh . . ."

"Can I see?" I tease.

"No. It's . . . I still have stitches."

I stop moving, and tip my head at him. He barely glances at me, definitely acting strange.

"But it's been a month. Shouldn't they be out?"

"No. I mean, they were, but now . . ."

"Sam," I say firmly, and he finally turns my way, refusing to meet my eyes. I suddenly have an idea of just what happened. I've watched him and Shane often enough to know how they are together. "Did you reopen the wound?" He looks at me, but doesn't answer.

"Let me guess," I say. "You and Shane wrestling, right?" He shrugs, and I walk over to him. "You didn't want to tell me? Thought I'd be mad?"

He swallows, looking slightly miserable. "I don't want you to have to worry about me," he says.

I rise up and kiss him, which he doesn't seem to mind, throwing his rake to the side to put both arms around me.

"I always worry about you, silly," I tell him. "You don't have to be afraid to tell me things. I'm not that fragile, you know."

Even as I say the words, I realize how true they are. The grief and pain are still lodged in my chest, as I suspect they will be for the rest of my life, but I'm learning to live around that. I'm dealing with what was left behind by my parents, including an unwanted grandma. I'm getting up each day, and if my first thoughts are of them and how much I miss them, at least I'm smiling and laughing—and not falsely.

He looks conflicted as he gazes down at me. I know he's still worried about me, that I'm going to fall apart again at any moment. It's kind of nice having someone besides Stacy worry so deeply about me.

"Christmas is next week," he says, immediately derailing all my thoughts as the pain breaks loose and shafts through me.

"I know," I murmur, tears rising in my eyes. "Think there's any chance to avoid it?"

Sam squeezes me. "I'm sorry. I didn't mean that to come out so abruptly. I wanted to talk to you about it, find out what your plans are."

I grimace. Thanksgiving had been a lonely affair, even though Jean and I had spent the day at Stacy's house. Like that wasn't completely uncomfortable spending the day with a stranger who calls herself my grandma, and a family who was unnaturally subdued in order to try to spare my feelings. I haven't even bothered to put a Christmas tree up this year. That's an activity usually taken care of by my dad, and I have no desire to do it without him. Jean offered to get one, but I suppose my glare relayed to her my answer as she hadn't brought one home.

"I was planning to hide in my room and ignore the day completely."

"Or you could spend it with me," he says. I begin to shake my head, but he says, "Hear me out. Shane and I are alone. You and . . . Jean . . . are alone." I can't help but notice he stumbles over her name. "Why not spend it together and be a little less alone?"

I glance up at him. "That's your argument for spending Christmas together? Less alone?"

He scowls. "I did this completely arseways."

"You did it what-ways?" I ask, confused. He flushes.

"Uh . . . I mean, I completely botched it." He takes a breath, and I realize he's nervous. No wonder he's acting so strangely. "It's just . . . I really want to spend the day with *you*, Niahm."

"Okay," I capitulate, wanting to let him off the hook. "Why don't you come here and I'll cook?"

He shakes his head. "No, Niahm, I don't want it to be a day

of work for you."

I smile at him. "Sam, how long have you known me? Since when have you known me to consider cooking work? Besides, it's tradition." My voice hitches a little on the last word. This will be the first Christmas I haven't cooked for my parents. Suddenly, I decide that's exactly what I want to do. Sam's eyes are full of sympathy, so I push away from him and turn back to the rake, picking it up and stabbing at the hay.

"I'll invite Stacy and her family." Stab, toss. "I'll make all of the things I've made every other year." Stab, toss. "Then everything will be okay." Stab, toss.

Sam steps up behind me and wraps his arms around my waist, leaning his cheek on the top of my head. He pushes the rake from my hand and slips my gloves off, entwining his fingers with mine. I give a shaky laugh.

"All I do is cry, anymore," I say. "I must be wearing all my friends out with my pathetic-ness."

Sam chuckles against my hair. "I don't think that's a word."

"Well, neither is the one you used before. What was it? Arseness?"

He stiffens against me. "Arseways," he says thickly.

"What does that mean?"

Pause. "It means making a mess of something."

I squeeze his hands, which warm mine much better than the gloves.

"Where did you learn that?"

He doesn't say anything for a long moment. Just as I'm about to turn to discover the reason for his hesitancy, he speaks.

"I knew a guy who used it all the time. He was Irish."

"Mm," I answer. I suppose he must have known a lot of immigrants and foreigners in New York. Sam makes a slightly strangled sound.

"Are you okay?" I ask, worried that maybe he shouldn't be out here working so hard if he's reinjured his arm. He grunts, and not for the first time I wonder if he somehow knows what

I'm thinking.

"What should Shane and I bring?" he says, ignoring my question.

"Bring for what?"

"For Christmas, silly."

I turn in his arms, releasing his hands to wrap mine around his shoulders, my tears gone. Sam always manages to pull me from the brink of falling apart.

"A tree?" I say.

Chapter 34

Sam

Shane and I are on Niahm's doorstep first thing Christmas morning, loaded with gifts—and a tree. Niahm smiles at me, her eyes soft as I drag the pine into the festive-free house. It takes some time to set it up, drag the bulbs and lights from the attic, and decorate it. Shane then brings more boxes down, and we decorate the mantle, railing, tables, and every other surface we possibly can. Stacy and her family come during this, and between us all, the house soon feels like it should on Christmas morning.

Niahm stuffs the turkey we brought, and puts it in the oven, shooting me a look at the size of the massive bird. She, Stacy, Mrs. Bowen, and even Jean head to the kitchen to prepare the rest of the food.

I figure Niahm's going to be plenty angry with me when the doorbell rings in the early afternoon admitting the first of a large group of invited guests. I hadn't told Jean what I was up to, but Stacy and her mom were aware. They'd given me the list of who I should invite. I definitely don't want Niahm alone today. When the house is full to the tune of thirty people, I feel I've accomplished my goal.

Many of the men are gathered around the TV, watching a football game. I walk to the kitchen doorway, and see Niahm surrounded by friends from school, and other townspeople who love her. Bob dances happily around everyone's feet, quickly snapping up any morsel that drops to the ground.

The best part of the scene is Niahm herself. She's in top form, bossing everyone around, organizing the chaos of so many people in a relatively small space. Even better, she's laughing and smiling as she does so. As if sensing me watching, she turns toward me. She smiles, then mouths *thank you*. Maybe she won't be as furious as I'd figured.

Tables and folding chairs are pulled out of the garage and set up anywhere we can fit them. After a noisy, chaotic dinner and time spent cleaning up, Stacy leads Niahm to the living room, and plops her down onto a chair in front of the tree. As others gather around, Niahm looks wary.

"Niahm," Stacy says after quieting everyone down. "We knew that this was going to be a hard day for you." Niahm's wariness turns to anxiety as she looks around. Stacy takes her hand. "We decided that rather than give you a bunch of useless presents, we wanted to do something to hopefully make it easier."

"Like overrun my house with more people than it was meant to hold?" Niahm asks shakily, and everyone laughs.

Stacy pulls out large, square, heavy book wrapped with a ribbon and places it on Niahm's lap. Niahm's anxiety ratchets up to panic. I can feel it from where I stand across the room. I walk over and sit on the floor next to her chair, casually taking her hand in mine. Her mind is a riot of alarm, wondering what pain they want to inflict on her now. I pull her hand to my mouth and behind the guise of kissing it, look up at her and say, "It'll be alright, Niahm. Trust me."

She stares at me, holding my gaze, searching. I pull my mind from hers. I can feel when she begins to relax nonetheless. I frown from her utter trust in me—I don't deserve it.

"We all wanted to share with you memories of your parents," Stacy says, then hurries on, not giving Niahm a chance to react. "In that book are stories from most of the people in town." Niahm's eyes drop to the book. She runs one hand over the surface lightly. "All of ours are there, also, but we wanted to tell you while we're here."

Niahm takes a deep, steadying breath, giving a minute nod.

"I'll start." The deep voice belongs to Mr. Franklin, who grew up with Jonas. He lives on a small farm on the opposite side of town. "When Jonas and I were boys, we had a penchant for . . . well, let's just say for getting adventurous." All of the people who knew Jonas as a boy laugh. "One time, we decided it would be fun to go down to Mrs. Brown's and see if we couldn't steal a pie from her window sill where she left them to cool." Niahm's eyes jump to mine and twinkle at the mention of a pie.

"She had this big bull terrier, so we took some bacon from my mother's fridge to bribe him. We didn't take into account how quickly a big dog can down bacon." Another round of laughter and the corners of Niahm's mouth begin to curve upward. "We got into the backyard and all the way up to the house before that dog finished the bacon. Jonas had hoisted me up on his shoulders and I was just reaching for the pie when we heard growling behind us." Several people are leaning toward Franklin, apparently having heard the story before, in anticipation of his next words.

"Jonas swung around at the same time my hand touched the edge of the pie, bringing it down on his head. He began running, cherry pie filling dripping down his face, me still on his shoulders, holding on for dear life."

I open my mind to Niahm once again, and see that she

knows this story. She is anticipating Franklin's telling of it as much as anyone. She has a small smile resting on her face, and I can feel her contentment, see the memory she has of Jonas telling her the same story when she was younger.

"Mrs. Brown comes out to see what the commotion is, and see's Jonas running around with what appeared to be blood covering his face, me clinging to him. She screams and runs back in, coming out with a shotgun. 'Let him go," she screams at me, but I can't because he won't stop running." I feel a slight jolt in Niahm at the image of her father covered in blood, but just as quickly it's gone, and she's back into the story.

"Thank heavens Mrs. Brown is the worst shot in the world," Franklin says, everyone laughing. "At least the sound of the shot brought Jonas to his senses, and he stopped running so that I could jump down. Then he was bowled over by that dog, who began licking the filling from Jonas. Mrs. Brown screamed again, and about that time Mr. Brown moseyed on out from where he'd been watching TV."

Another round of laughter. In Niahm's mind, I see that it's common knowledge that there isn't much that will pull Mr. Brown from in front of his TV. Apparently it takes a gun shot.

Franklin smiles warmly at Niahm. "Jonas and I spent a great deal of time that summer cleaning the Brown's yard, and weeding her garden to pay for that fiasco. But I'll tell you, Niahm, it wasn't the punishment our parents had hoped. Jonas managed to make everything we did into a game. I'll never regret the day that I said yes when a funny kid named Jonas came up to me in first grade and asked me to be his friend. He was my best friend. I'm so grateful for having him in my life."

Niahm stood and went to hug Franklin. She hugged every other person when they finished telling their memories of Jonas and Beth. Each time she returned to her chair and took my hand, I felt the further peace and contentment she experienced. Stacy, whose idea this whole thing was, sits beside Niahm. I'm overwhelmed with gratitude that she's accomplished what I could not.

Chapter 35

Niahm

It's tradition in Goshen to hold the New Year's Eve bash in the school gym. There's a big pot-luck dinner, followed by a talent show mostly starring the younger kids. There's a pseudo New Year's call at nine for the younger kids, who are then taken home by their parents and either left with a babysitter, or with a neighbor who swaps years with one another.

That's when the music starts, with dancing and a few of the adults breaking out champagne. No one under fourteen is allowed to this party. Sam dances with me, but also with some of the other girls from school. I'm not jealous, because when he's dancing with them, he's watching me.

Everyone goes out of their way to make sure Shane and Sam are having a good time, since this is their first party. Of course, Shane's mostly being mobbed by the women, which amuses Sam—and irritates Stacy. I just shake my head at her. She's obsessed.

Just before midnight, someone puts a slow song on and Sam pulls me into his arms and out onto the dance floor before he can be claimed by anyone else.

"Having fun?" I tease.

"I am." He sounds surprised. "How about you? You seem like you are."

I lean my cheek against his chest. "I almost feel guilty that I'm having fun," I tell him honestly. "Maybe it's because there were a lot of years when they were already gone on their next adventure, so it's not that unusual to be here alone." He doesn't ask who *they* are; he doesn't need to. "Plus," I say, smiling up at him, "this is the first year I've had *you* here, so that's a bonus."

He laughs. "When you first met me, did you imagine you'd ever be glad to have me here?"

I think back to the first time I met him, when he insulted my pie. It's only been about four months, but it seems much longer. "You scared me," I tell him.

His eyes widen. "I *scared* you?"

"Well, yeah. I mean, I've always been pretty independent, determined to only marry someone who would stay in Goshen with me. And even then I had no plans of getting serious with anyone until I'm at least twenty-five." I shrug, and feel the strange heat begin between our palms.

"When I saw you, it was like there was this weird pull toward you, as if you were a danger to my plan. Probably just because I couldn't get over your amazing hair," I tease, lifting my hand from his shoulder to ruffle his copper head. When I glance at him, he has a strange look on his face. Part horror and part . . . hope. Suddenly I realize how this must sound to him, as if I'm saying we're destined to be together. For the first time, I question his feelings for me. Maybe it really has been based on pity. Maybe he'd been planning on dating someone else when my parents . . . and then he felt like he had to stay. Maybe he really wants—

"Niahm," he says sharply, interrupting my thoughts. When I look up at him, I make the decision to let him off the hook now, break up with him—if one can break up with someone who they aren't even sure feels any kind of commitment to them.

"I felt the same thing," he says with some amusement as I open my mouth to speak.

"What?" is my brilliant response. "You liked my hair?"

"No. I mean, yes, I do. That's not what I mean. I felt the same thing," he repeats, "when I first saw you. Why do you think I kept coming back when you made it clear you didn't want me around?"

I cringe as I think of how horrible I had been

"Why did you keep coming around?" I ask. "Most guys would have run the other way as fast as they could."

"There was just something about you," he says, amused.

"My apple pie?" I ask.

"Well, there *was* that." I elbow him lightly and he laughs. "And now . . ."

"Now *what*?" I demand impatiently when he doesn't say anything.

"Here you go," someone interrupts, nudging us with their tray full of sparkling grape juice. "It's almost midnight."

Sam releases me as he takes two of the plastic cups and hands me one. I feel a sinking disappointment that he didn't finish his sentence. Then I look up at him, see the flush in his cheeks, the hesitant look on his face and realize that maybe *he* was going to break up with *me*.

"Time for the countdown," Officer Hill booms from the stage that was set up for the DJ. "10-9-8 . . ."

Stacy hurries over to us, followed by the double-H and a few other kids from school. I'm a little surprised that she isn't near Shane.

"Hey, guys. Another year in paradise," she enthuses sarcastically. "Cheers."

I narrow my eyes at her, but laugh anyway.

"3-2-1. Happy New Year!"

Everyone cheers and lifts their plastic cups as someone begins singing Auld Lang Syne. Sam watches me intently, and I wonder what he thinks of all this. He takes my hand and pulls me from the room, which Stacy and all my friends notice, of course. But none of them follow us.

Outside the building, we can still hear the loud singing, and Sam and I laugh at it.

"I want to finish what I began to tell you," he says, and my stomach clenches.

"Kiss me first," I say. I figure it might be the last time I get to request a kiss from him. He accommodates me, cupping my face with both hands as he leans down, smiling just before his lips close on mine. Sam's kiss is deep and warm. I stretch upward toward him, as if drawn by his very being. Heat tendrils curl up from the pit of my belly to my throat as he wraps his arms around me and holds me tightly against him. When he pulls away, my head is spinning.

"Don't freak out," he says, and I immediately feel the panic begin to rise. "Shane told me not to do this, that it's too soon, but I don't care." My heart cracks, and I bite the insides of my cheek to hold back the tears.

"I'm in love with you, Niahm."

My mouth drops open. I just stare at him, unable to find any sense in his words.

"I know it's not what you want to hear," he says urgently. "And if it frightens you, I'm sorry. But I had to say it. I've had to stop myself from saying it so many—"

I launch myself at him and, unprepared, he stumbles back but manages to keep us from falling as he wraps his arms around me. I can't stop the stupid tears from falling.

"Whoa," Sam says, rebalancing. Then he looks at me, and brings his hands up to thumb the tears from my face. "I'm sorry, Niahm, I didn't mean to make you cry."

I laugh through the tears. "Don't be sorry. I'm so relieved."

"Relieved?"

"I thought you were going to . . . break up with me," I say. The words sound inane as I say them.

"Niahm, I *can't* ever—" He stops himself, as if he were going to say something he's changed his mind about. "I *love* you. The only way I'm going anywhere is if you ask me to." Something in the way he says the words makes me think he's trying to say something else.

"Then I hope you're planning to stay for a while," I say. "Somehow, in the short time I've known you, you've become . . ." I search for the right word, ". . . *essential* to me. I don't know how I would have survived without you."

Sam pulls me close again, and I relax into his arms.

"I love you, Sam," I say, wondering how one annoying, frustrating, auburn headed boy has managed to so completely derail all of my carefully laid plans in such a short time. Then he leans down to kiss me again, and I don't *care* how, just grateful that he did.

Chapter 36

Niahm

Sitting next to Sam in his truck as we drive down the old, unused, mostly deteriorated road is something I couldn't have imagined six months ago when he first moved to Goshen. A cloud of dust billows up behind us, surprising me. Though only patches of snow line the road and fields, most of the ground is still heavy with dampness. The past few days have been unseasonably warm, which I suppose accounts for the dry layer of dirt on the thin, cracked pavement.

An old building comes into sight. It looks a little like the Bates hotel from *Psycho*, and just as I'm about to remark on this, Sam turns into the nearly-non-existent parking lot. New weeds sprout between the cracks of both the parking lot and the sidewalk that runs in front of the rooms. A sign out front proclaims the place for sale, and I glance at Sam. Maybe this is his surprise that he promised me, that he's going to buy the place and refurbish it. He knows how important it is to me to stay in Goshen, so maybe this is his way of letting me know he's in for the long haul. I'm going to have to tell him that there is no point in buying the place. We have one small motel in town that has six rooms. If they have one of the rooms occupied, they consider the place to be overflowing.

Sam opens my door, helps me out of the truck, taking my hand. I wait for the weird warmth that comes most of the time when we hold hands, but it doesn't come. I mentally shrug as he leads me toward the somewhat creepy building, still silent. I'm bursting with questions, but don't voice a single one, not wanting to spoil whatever surprise he has for me.

"So, is this the latest venture in the Coleman dynasty?" I tease. He's told me about the business ventures that Shane has been involved in, which is how they've accumulated their fortune. Shane is quite the business man, and neither he nor Sam would have to work the rest of their lives if they chose not to.

"I want to show you something," Sam says, pulling a key from his pocket.

"Okay," I say, deciding he's already bought the building, so the least I can do is support him in his venture. We stop in front of the door that has a number three hanging askew on it. He unlocks the door, then turns to me.

"Before we go in, I want to tell you something," he says, looking decidedly worried. "I want you to remember that I love you, and that no matter what happens, everything is going to be okay."

I feel the first tinge of uneasiness at his words—and his expression. It's the first time he's said "I love you" that hasn't completely sent my heart skittering off into bliss. He says it quite often, and I never tire of hearing it.

"Okaaay," I say. I decide to question him, in spite of the absolute trust I have in him. "Is everything okay, Sam?"

He smiles and pushes the door open. Curious, I step around him. The inside of the room is completely refurbished, and quite nicely. It does not fit with the outside at all. With a sick feeling, I begin to wonder if he thought . . . the bed seems to loom in front of me. Sam and I have talked about this. He knows I refuse to take any chance that might put me in the dreaded category of "unwed, pregnant teen." I turn to Sam, knowing I have to stop this before it goes too far.

"No, it's not . . ." he says, even as I say, "You know how I feel . . ."

I laugh nervously. Sam smiles and places his hands on my shoulders.

"I do know how you feel," he says, squeezing my shoulders lightly, "and I would never do anything that would cause you to compromise your values for me. I didn't really think about how this would appear."

I smile at him. I should have known better, should have known Sam would never do anything to hurt me. I put my arms around him, leaning against him.

"I know that, Sam. I shouldn't have doubted you." I look up at him, and I'm rewarded with a kiss.

Sam pulls one of the chairs away from the little table near the door, and nudges me, giving me the hint to sit. He backs away, stopping near the bed.

"I want you to trust me," he says, desperation tingeing his voice. "Just stay there, just . . . wait. And remember what I said before: everything is going to be okay."

Excited again to discover the surprise he's promised, I wait. Then he pulls a gun from his pocket. Fear slides up my spine at the sight.

"Sam, what—" Terror binds the words in my throat as my mind races, trying to imagine what he plans to do with the gun, here alone in this room—where no one knows we are.

"I'm not going to hurt you, I promise." His words are at odds with his actions as he opens the gun, turning the back of it toward me. I can see a single spot of silver within the cylinder. "Only one bullet," he says, as if that should reassure me.

Cindy C Bennett

I start to rise, unable to remain seated like some resigned victim, dread coupling with the fear now. I have that feeling I sometimes get when something bad is about to happen.

"I think you should stay sitting," he says calmly, which is how insane people always sound, right? He doesn't sound crazy, but he's also not putting the gun away. I begin moving toward the door, slowly, trying to control my panicked breaths, suddenly desperate to not be in the confines of this room, threat heavy in the air. I can't decipher where the threat is coming from, my mind refusing to process that Sam could be the threat. It doesn't feel right, that he could be the danger here, but *something* is, maybe something *inside* him.

"Sam, I don't know what you're planning, but I think this has gone far enough." I try to speak as my mom used to when she was trying to calm me down, firm but understanding. He snaps the gun closed, and I flinch at the sound, cold clamminess inching up my neck. I reach for the knob; if I can just open the outside world to us, this surreal scene will disappear.

The knob turns, but the door doesn't open, and my panic ratchets up.

"Sam," I say, trying to sound even more stern, desperately trying to hide my abject terror. "Unlock the door. I want to leave now." Sam's face changes a little at my words, and for one second I think he's going to capitulate. Hope and relief comingle. I see the exact moment when his eyes harden, determination shining from his face.

"Just trust me—" My stomach clenches at his words, and he stops himself. "Just *give* me ten more minutes," he says. "Then I'll let you out, and we'll go home."

"I don't like this. I want to go now." I can hear the begging in my tone, but I don't care. I suddenly, desperately need to be out of here. I need *Sam* to be out of here. Even as I think the words, he turns the gun toward his own chest.

"No!" Instinctively I'd known this was his intention, and terror suffuses every cell of my body. I take a step forward, feeling as if I'm in a nightmare, feet stuck in quicksand, despairing at the thought that I will never reach him in time.

"Everything will be okay," he says again. "Remember, Niahm, everything is not as it appears. Don't forget that. *Please.*" A loud, quick, explosion unlike anything I've heard before fills the room, reverberating off the walls. I recoil intuitively, the immediate ringing in my ears painful as my hands come up to cover them. The deafening silence following is worse than anything I've heard before. I'm crouched in the corner facing the door, frozen, unable to move, overwhelmed by the smell of the gun powder.

For long moments, I wait. There's no sound behind me, and I somehow know that if I turn around, my world will be irrevocably changed. I'm gasping like a fish out of water, unable to draw oxygen into my lungs.

"Sam." The word is whispered—croaked, really—from deep within my throat. I begin hyperventilating, horror shrouding me, holding me in place. No sound, no movement in the room. That scares me more than what I might see if I turn around.

"Sam." Louder this time as I lift my head. Still no response. "*Please,*" I whisper, not sure what I'm asking for—and all too aware of what I'm asking for. I take a breath, and slowly turn toward him.

A scream rips from my throat at the sight of Sam, covered in blood, lying at an unnatural angle next to the bed. I'm propelled from my place on the floor before I'm conscious of my intention.

"Sam!" I scream, collapsing next to him. I shove my arms beneath his shoulders, pulling his limp form into my arms. His eyes stare lifelessly at the ceiling, my heart contracting with a grief that runs deeper than the grief I'd felt at losing my parents. "Sam, please," the words tangle over the tears clogging my throat, "please, wake up. Wake up!" I command, yelling, as if I can compel him by the force of my will alone. I shake him, and he rolls bonelessly to the side. In desperation, I look around.

My cell phone!

I awkwardly wrestle my phone from my pocket, my bloody fingers slipping against the plastic. I shove the realization of why my fingers are slipping from my mind; I can't deal with that particular horror right now, even as the despair crawls up my throat, releasing as a half-choked wail. I have to get help for Sam. I try punching the numbers, my slick finger unable to make any kind of significant contact. Hopelessness engulfs me as I force myself to my feet, and stumble into the bathroom. I grab the white towel hanging by the sink, dropping it in my haste. A moan escapes as I scoop it back up, wiping the phone quickly. I punch 9-1-1 and put it up to my ear, trying unsuccessfully to calm my breathing enough to speak.

Nothing.

I pull the phone away from my ear. No service.

"No," I moan, running back out into the room. I hurry from corner to corner, holding it above my head, watching for a bar—any bar—to indicate coverage.

Nothing.

With a rage born of pure fear, I throw the phone against the wall, where it shatters. Now what? I look around desperately and see the chairs in front of the window. I pick one up and slam it with all my might against the window, a surge of hope filling me as the glass shatters. I grasp the curtains, pulling them from their rod—

—only to see that the window is covered with bars. A furious cry is followed by placing my head as near the bars as I can get it.

"Help!" I scream repeatedly, knowing as I do that no one is coming, no one is going to hear me. I scream until my throat is raw, and the sound coming out is pitiful at best. I scramble to the door, twisting the knob and pulling with everything I have. It doesn't budge, thick and sturdy, nothing like the doors in the hotel in town. The key hole catches my eye, and I realize that Sam probably has the key, that I should have looked there first.

I rush back over to him, refusing to look at him. I can't look again, even though the sight of his motionless face will be forever burned into my brain. I begin searching through his pockets, revulsion thrumming through me at the act, as if I were nothing more than a pickpocket, and Sam nothing more than a random victim. It's only my desperation to get him help that propels my actions, even if I know deep inside that it's already too late.

"Where's the key?" I demand of the universe hoarsely when my search turns up nothing other than his truck key, which is alone on his key ring. I rush around the room, tearing open drawers, dumping their contents that seem as if someone lives here instead of empty as they should be, ripping the bedding from the mattress, then shoving the heavy thing to the side to look beneath, pulling up every loose item in the room that I can find.

Finally, dejectedly, with a sob wrenched from the depths of my soul, I stop searching. In anger, I sweep the lamp from the bedside table and send it crashing against the wall. Tears sheet down my face unchecked as I collapse in the same corner, next to the door, where this nightmare began.

Chapter 37

Niahm

The shadows deepen as time passes—how much time I don't know. It feels like an eternity. Exhaustion drags at me. Collapsed against the wall in the corner, I long for sleep to take me from this new, horrifying reality I couldn't have imagined in the furthest recesses of my mind. But my mind won't let me rest. Where did I go wrong? Were there warning signs that I missed? I go back over the time I've known Sam, trying to maintain a clinical distance, to look at everything objectively.

At times he acted oddly, or looked at me with something deeper than whatever he said, but at no time did I think him depressed. Sam was innately happy and cheerful whenever we were together. Maybe that was a cover.

My mind goes to Shane. Did Shane know something? He

didn't seem too happy when Sam told him we were going—

My heart stutters. Did Sam tell him where he was bringing me? I try to remember the exact conversation.

"We're going now," Sam had said.

"I don't think this is the right way to—" Shane sounded *troubled.*

"I know what I'm doing." Sam was firm. *"There isn't any other way."*

I search my mind, trying to discover if I missed some essential part of the conversation. I remember thinking it was a little strange, but I've gotten used to feeling like I'm out of the loop with half the conversations going on between Sam and Shane . . . and even Jean.

With trepidation, I crawl back over to where Sam lays. I notice with a small measure of relief that his eyes are now closed. I didn't know that happened naturally, but I'm grateful that I don't have to see his eyes open and staring.

Emotionally drained, I sit next to him, and slip my hand into his, wishing desperately for that strange heat to begin. His hand is warm and limp, and idly I wonder why. I thought that when someone was . . . well, I expected him to be cold, stiff. Numbly, I feel the tears slipping down my cheeks again. Exhaustion weighs on every inch of my body, my mind refusing to accept that he's gone.

After some time, when the reflection of the sunset lights the sky outside the window with an ethereal pink, I begin to hallucinate. I imagine Sam's hand warming in mine into the familiar heat, the sounds of his light breaths, tiny, gasping. I scrunch my eyes closed, and imagine his hand moving slightly in mine. *Please, stop.* My mind refuses to let me go as the heat intensifies. I know that letting go will end the illusion, but I can't. I keep his hand clasped firmly in mine, feeling the phantom tightening, ever so slight, of his hand on mine. A rustling sound, as if Sam had moved his leg, comes into my mind and the grief rears up again.

"Sam," I whisper. A deep gasp of breath startles me into

opening my eyes, my gaze flying to Sam. His eyes are open again. But not just open—moving. His hand clenches weakly against mine and in terror I tear my hand from his, reeling away from him. He turns his head and looks at me, my heart thudding in fear.

"Nee—" The sound, the beginning of my name, issues from his mouth and a half-scream on my huffed breath escapes as I push further away from him, my feet propelling my sitting body across the carpet, my legs lacking the strength to stand.

He rolls to his side, grimacing in pain, and suddenly I realize—I was wrong! He wasn't dead as I'd thought, just unconscious. Relief rushes through me, intense and powerful, unlike anything I've ever experienced, mingled with guilt over my inaction to help him before now.

"Sam," I enthuse, voice raw, crawling quickly back over to his side, helping him into a sitting position as tears begin anew, this time tears of joy. "Sam, you're alive! I thought . . . It doesn't matter. You're alive."

I throw my arms around him, aware that this could be nothing more than an extension of my delusion, that there's a possibility I've completely lost touch with reality. I don't care though, as his arms come up around me, pulling me close.

"I love you, Sam, I love you. You're not dead. Thank you, God. Thank you." I know I'm gushing, unable to stop myself in spite of the soreness of my throat. I kiss his cheeks, his neck, his forehead until finally he captures my face and pulls my mouth to his. I may be hallucinating, but if I am this kiss is as real as any he's given me before—maybe more so.

"You're not angry?" he asks, hands cupping both my cheeks as he pulls back to look at me.

"Angry?" I ask incredulously. "How can I be *angry* that you're not—" I stop, as if someone has thrown a switch cutting off my speaking ability as his words sink in, and memory rushes back. Sam, with the gun . . .

"You killed yourself," I accuse as I push away from him.

"I'm sorry," he says. Not, *Of course I didn't, I'm sitting here just fine*—which brings immediately to mind the fact that he shouldn't be sitting here, just fine. His blood soaked shirt is clear evidence of that. I scoot further away as a new kind of fear shoots into my heart.

"How can you be . . . I *saw* you. You shot yourself, and you were . . ."

"Niahm," he says, holding his hands toward me—trying to calm the insane person, I think cynically. "Please, let me explain."

"Explain what?" I explode, voice cracking from the stress of my previous screaming, rising to my feet in one smooth motion. "Explain what, Sam? Explain why you shot yourself? Explain how you could be lying there, looking dead, and now you're . . ." My eyes drop to his chest, to the place I saw him put the gun barrel. "How did you stop bleeding?" I whisper.

Sam pulls the front of his shirt up, and I reach out a hand as if to stop the motion, unable to tear my eyes from the sight of his blood covered but clearly unwounded chest—other than the angry red circle surrounded by a purpling splotch.

"Was this some kind of trick?" I demand, fury coming up to replace the fear. "Is this your idea of a *joke*?"

"No, Niahm, of course not," he answers quickly. "I would never do something so—"

"Don't!" I exclaim as he begins to stand. He freezes, and sinks back down to his sitting position.

"Niahm, please, let me explain."

"I want to go home," I demand, ignoring the undertone of begging.

"I wanted to *show* you," he pleads. "I knew you wouldn't believe me if I just told you."

"Told me what? No, wait, I don't want to know. I just want to go home."

"Niahm, I—"

"Stop!" I yell as he begins to rise once again. He holds his hands up in supplication as he continues to stand.

"I'm getting the key for you," he says softly, his eyes

Cindy C Bennett

beseeching me. I look away from them, refusing to give into the love and desperation I see there. He takes a step and I smash myself back against the door.

"Niahm, you needed to know what I am," he says as he stumbles toward the head of the bed. "I want to be with you . . . *stay* with you as long as you'll let me." He puts one hand on the wooden cap of the headboard. "Which for me means forever."

He watches me closely, and his words penetrate through the terror and rage that grip me.

"What?" I finally say. "What are you saying?"

"I'm an immortal," he says, and I burst out laughing. The sound is maniacal, lacking any humor, leading me to believe that this whole thing might be nothing more than the most vivid of delusions, or dreams, or . . . something. His face falls at my laughter.

"And I'm the tooth fairy," I gasp. He takes a step toward me and my laughter dies immediately. "No," I command, "don't come any closer. Don't you ever come near me again."

Pain shoots through his eyes, but I refuse to give in to his agony. He turns away, and with a violent wrench he pulls the cap from the bed post. I look around frantically for a weapon, but he simply turns back and pushes his fingers inside the hollow wood. When they come out, a key is clasped between his first two fingers.

"Niahm, please, I—"

"The key," I interrupt wildly. "Give it here."

His face drops, and he tosses me the key. Unprepared for him to actually give it to me, it hits the wall and falls to the floor. Keeping my eyes on him, I stoop, feeling around until my fingers touch it. As I stand and fumble to get it into the keyhole with my shaking hands, he puts his own hand into his pocket and I freeze, panic causing me to drop it once again. I know his pockets are empty, I checked them all myself, but that doesn't stop the alarm that he's somehow hidden something there that I didn't find, something that will hurt me.

~ 206 ~

He pulls his hand out, and I see the truck key in his hand. I don't even recall placing it back in his pocket. He tosses that to me, and better prepared, I catch it.

"You can go," he says. "I'm not going to hurt you. I would *never* hurt you. You know that."

I *thought* I knew that, but now I know differently. I don't tell him that, though, stooping and quickly snatching up the room key once again. I turn my eyes away from him long enough to fit the key into the lock. With a turn, the bolt snaps open and I'm able to open the door.

Dusk's fading light seems bright as I back out of the room, keeping my eyes on him as he watches me with sorrow lining his body. I pull the door shut, wondering if I'm locking him in. Distractedly, I decide I'll let Shane know. I run to the truck, stumbling in my haste. The door opens easily and I climb in, slamming my hand down on the automatic lock button. I jam the key into the ignition, missing the first time because of the violent shaking of my hand, and the engine turns over. I heave out a sigh. I suppose I thought he might have done something to the truck to keep it from starting. In my haste, I pull the shifter beyond reverse into neutral, and have to push it back. I stomp on the gas pedal, not waiting for the truck to come to a complete stop before pulling the shifter into drive and peeling out in the loose gravel that litters the parking lot. I glance in the rear view mirror. Nothing moves at the motel as I pull away, dread filling my heart as I watch it fade in the distance.

Chapter 38

Sam

I'd forgotten how much it hurts to get shot. If I'd remembered, I would have chosen a different method to get my point across. I would have chosen something quicker to recover from, having seen the abject terror and profound grief that Niahm suffered while I recovered when she held my hand. I could have spared her some of that.

I couldn't have spared her the rage she now felt.

I wad the bloody shirt up, pulling a clean one from the top of the closet where we keep an emergency stash of clothing. Odd that in her tearing the room apart, Niahm had missed this. I walk into the bathroom and catch sight of myself in the mirror. Blood stains my chest and belly, splattered across my jaw, dark and flaking.

"*Bloody eejit,*" I curse myself, rinsing the white towel that's also stained with blood until it's mostly clean then use it to clean myself up as best I can. I pull the clean shirt on and stare at my pale face. Self-recrimination stares back at me, and well deserved at that. I'm still weak, will be for a day or two while my body replenishes the blood it lost. I walk back into the room, and pull the secondary key from the cap of the footboard, letting myself out of the room.

It's not likely I'll make it back to town in my weakened state. I drop to the bench that rests near the doorway, dropping my head into my hands. We'll have to go now, leave Goshen before Niahm starts spreading the rumor, before the Sentinels get wind of it themselves. We'll have to erase every sign of having been there, to protect Niahm and the rest of the town. Jean will have to go also. She can't be discovered here, living with Niahm.

I groan at the mess I've created by my stupidity. I should have told her, given her some kind of forewarning at least about what I was going to do. I laugh cynically at the thought. That would have simply sent her running sooner.

Niahm.

Her name comes unbidden into my mind, a shaft of pain like lightening striking my heart with it. How will I go on without her? Even now, the pull to get up and go to her is so strong I can barely resist.

Time, which has very little meaning to me anymore, passes slowly. The shadows haven't grown all that much when I hear a vehicle coming toward the motel. Warily, I sit up. It's rare for any cars to come this way, since the road isn't used anymore, and has fallen into extreme disrepair. Nonetheless, I need to get back to town quickly, try to stop some of the damage if possible, which means I need to flag this car down.

I'm stunned when I see my own truck coming back up the road. I look up at the sky. I don't *think* Niahm has had time to get all the way back to town, drop the truck to Shane, and for Shane to come all the way back again. The truck stops at the edge of the parking lot, and with astonishment I watch as Niahm opens the door and slides from the truck. I move to stand, then think better of it and relax back.

"What is *wrong* with you?" she yells, guilt filling me at the raspy, strained tone of her voice.

She bends down and picks up a rock, and hurls it at me. I duck to the side as it hits the wall of the motel behind me. I stare at her, shocked as her expression looks. Then, resolutely, she shrugs her shoulders a small amount, chin jutting up, glaring at me, daring me to say anything.

I try to create as unthreatening a pose as possible as she walks slowly toward me, caution in every line of her body. When she's a dozen feet from me, she stops. She simply stares at me, confusion warring with disbelief in her expression.

"How is it possible?" she finally asks.

"I don't know," is my honest answer.

She shakes her head, as if answering an internal question.

"Tell me you're not lying," she says. "Tell me you're telling me the honest to God truth."

"I swear it," I say. "I wouldn't lie about something so . . ."

"Unbelievable," she provides angrily when I don't finish.

"Right," I say, grimacing. "Niahm, trust me, I know how hard this is. Imagine how I felt when I first realized I was . . . not dead. I mean the first time, when I realized I couldn't die."

She takes two steps closer after scooping up a rather sizable rock, still watching me cautiously.

"Does Shane know?"

I sigh as I contemplate how much to tell her.

"Yes," I finally answer simply.

"Then he's not your uncle?" she asks.

"He *is* my uncle," I say. Before she can question it, I say, "He's my great-uncle."

"But how can . . ." I watch as understanding dawns. "You mean he's . . . like you?"

"Yes."

She looks around, as if to find an answer in the cracked and lifting asphalt. She takes a few steps closer once again. I wonder if she's even aware of her movement.

"How did you . . . I mean, when . . ." She takes a deep breath, blows it out, and begins again. "How . . . how old are you?"

I lean forward, resting my arms on my thighs, and notice that while she flinches a little at the movement, she doesn't take a step back.

"I was born in 1544."

Her mouth drops open and she quickly slams it closed, her teeth clacking together. She takes a few more deep breaths before speaking.

"1544?" she squeaks.

"Yes. In Ireland."

Her eyes snap to mine at that. She takes a few more steps, until she's within a few feet of me. I can see that she's trying to be calm about this, but forceful panic resides just below the surface.

"Maybe you should sit down," I say. "I'll move." I stand, only wobbling a little. Her eyes fill with concern that she quickly covers and she waves me back down, sitting on the opposite end of the bench, as if unable to stand any longer.

"This is so . . ." She glances up at me, as if searching for some kind of indication of my true age. "So, you're like an old man?"

I nearly laugh, but bite it back. Somehow I don't think she'll appreciate any humor in this.

"I suppose so," I say, "Trapped in this body."

"How old *are* you?" she asks curiously.

"I'm four hundred and—"

"No," she interrupts, closing her eyes against the number as if to erase it, one hand up to halt my words. She opens them again, leveling her gaze at me, her eyes striking me once again. "I mean, how old were you when you . . . became how you are."

"I was nineteen, almost twenty when I died the first time."

"The first time?" Her voice squeaks on the question again.

"I guess that's not the right way to say it," I explain. "To become immortal, we have to 'die' the first time. Then, after we wake, we can suffer a sort of mortal death, I guess you'd call it, but we can't ever really die."

"Ever?"

I think about the Sentinels, about the method they have for killing us. I decide this isn't the time to tell Niahm about that.

"Trust me, I've tried." It's cryptic, but since it's not an *exact* lie, I can speak it to her.

She thinks about this, then looks at me oddly.

"You said 'we'. There are more of you, more than you and Shane?" When I nod, she asks, "How many more?"

"I don't know exactly. We don't have a census taker." I don't tell her that there are records, kept by the Sentinels, and that last any of the immortals knew, the count was up to around four thousand. And who knew how many have managed to stay hidden, are unaccounted for? Or who were new.

"Oh, yeah, that makes sense, I guess," Niahm says, sounding like it doesn't make sense at all to her. She glances down at my chest. "Does it hurt?"

"Not anymore," I say. When she continues to stare, I slowly pull the front of my shirt up, not wanting to startle her. She watches, as if unable to look away. Where the wound was is now a circular bruise, yellow in color. Her eyes come to mine, stunned. I let the shirt fall back down. "I lost a lot of blood, so I'll be weak for a couple of days. But that'll regenerate, also."

Her eyes flash a moment's sympathy, quickly gone, then she shakes her head.

"It's a lot to take in, I know," I tell her.

She huffs out a sarcastic laugh. After a few minutes silence, while she studies her shoes, she turns to me again.

"Couldn't you have just told me rather than force me to go through that?" Her gravelly voice rings with accusation and hurt, and I cringe at the memory of what I'd seen as she'd held my hand while I came to.

"Would you have believed me?" I ask. She stares at me, not

backing down from the question.

"No, I suppose not," she grunts.

"I'm so sorry, Niahm. It probably wasn't the best way to tell you. I would not *ever* want to purposely cause you to suffer. I just didn't know how else to do it."

She nods stiffly then looks off toward the mostly dark horizon. I stand and walk in front of her to lean into the room and turn the outside light on. To her credit, she doesn't shrink away from me in disgust as I thought she would. I walk inside and pull a bottle of water from the small fridge.

When I return to the bench, I hand her the water, which she eyes before finally taking. I sit down a little closer to her, testing. She doesn't acknowledge the move. She twists the top off and gulps the water, and once again I'm filled with recrimination for what she's suffering. When she speaks again, her voice sounds a little better.

"How many others have you told . . . you know, before. Before me, I mean."

I don't have to hold her hand to know exactly what she's asking. The flush in her cheeks is the first hint; that I know her so well gives me the rest. I turn toward her, so that she can see me fully, so that she will know I tell her the truth.

"None, Niahm, I've never told anyone else. You're the first."

She watches me, weighing my words, deciding on the truth of them.

"Why me?" Her voice is small.

"I should think that would be very obvious, Niahm," I say. When she continues to watch me, not apprehending my meaning, I clarify. "You're the only one who's meant enough for me to tell. It isn't something I do lightly."

I watch as she processes my words, watch the change in her eyes as she understands. She scoots a little closer to me, cautious and hesitant, and finally leans into me. Gratefully, I put my arm around her shoulders, holding her tightly.

"I don't know what to do about this, how to feel," she says.

"My mind is numb."

"I know."

"I'm really angry with you. That was a jerk thing to do. And then to find out you're . . ." She takes a breath. "I'm going to need some time." She sits up to see what I think of her words.

"I can give you as much time as you need," I say. "But I don't know that I can stay away."

Niahm sighs and leans against me again, exhaustion in every line of her body.

"I don't know that I want you to," she says.

Chapter 39

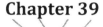

Niahm

Sam stops the truck in front of my house. I gaze at it, wondering how it can look the same when everything is suddenly so different. Sam waits silently. I look at him, admittedly frightened at the knowledge of what he is. My world is suddenly tilted, everything I thought I knew to be true I'm now questioning. I don't know what's real anymore.

"I guess I'll see you tomorrow?" I ask, unsure. Sam usually comes by on Sundays . . . actually Sam comes by every day.

He lifts his brows a little. "Well, yeah, if that's okay."

I realize he's surprised that I want to see him. I don't know how I feel about what I now know, and I don't know that I'll ever be able to reconcile it in my head, but I'm not quite ready to give him up, either.

"Okay, then, um . . ." I glance at him. Usually I would kiss him goodnight. He leans the tiniest bit toward me and I panic, grasping the door handle and pushing the door open quickly. "Bye, Sam. See you tomorrow." I slam the door closed and hurry into the house.

Jean looks up from the couch where she'd been sitting, reading. I try to calm my nerves at the sight of her. I can't face her right now. I'm grateful for the large jacket Sam had given me, which falls to my knees and covers the evidence of my night.

"Niahm? Is everything okay?" she asks, her brows puckered with worry.

I shoot her a smile, then realizing a smile will just seem odd to her, I quickly drop it.

"Yeah, of course. Why wouldn't it be?"

I jog up the stairs, and as I turn toward my room I glance back to see her watching me, a puzzled look on her face.

I quickly change out of my blood spattered clothes, stuffing them in the bottom of my hamper, still completely freaked by the whole thing. After a hot shower, scrubbing my entire body until I'm red and raw, I flop on my bed, my mind whirling. I have about ten-thousand questions for Sam—but I'm as afraid of asking them as I am of *not* asking them. I try to imagine what it would be like, to know that you can never die, that no matter what you do you'll survive . . . what kinds of things you might do.

To live over four hundred years. Alone.

I sit up. What if he hasn't been alone? It would make sense, right, that a guy who's been on the earth for so many years would have been with someone at one point or another. Jealousy suffuses me, both for those he's been with in the past—and those he'll be with again in the future.

A knock on my door startles me, and for a brief second I imagine Sam will be on the other side of the door as I open it. Of course, it's just Jean, still with that same concerned look on her face.

"Can I come in?" she asks. As if I can stop her.

I turn away and sit on my bed. She pulls the chair from in front of my desk and turns it toward me, sitting down. I force myself not to groan aloud. *Now* she wants to talk? When I want nothing more than to be alone with my thoughts? My anger? I glance at her as I realize how angry I *am* at him. My look seems to encourage her.

"You seem . . . upset," she begins.

"Nah, I'm good," I say, trying to look like that's the truth, pretending my voice isn't gruff.

"Listen, Niahm, I know that you aren't particularly thrilled having me here—" I can't stop the little noise that comes from my throat at that, but she ignores it. "But it seems that we are all that one another has." I open my mouth to protest, and she holds up a hand to halt my words. "We seem to be one another's last living relatives."

As she says the words, I think of Sam. Does *he* have any living relatives? Besides Shane, that is. Does he have descendants? I look at Jean, my mother's mother, and suddenly I want to tell her everything. I want to tell her what I now know, and cry in her arms, and have her tell me everything is going to be okay.

But of course, I can't do that.

She scoots the chair closer, hesitant, and I feel some shame that she has to feel this way around me. If my mom were still alive, she'd be angry at me for being such a brat toward the person that she explicitly asked to take care of me.

"Do you want to sit?" I ask, patting the bed next to me. She looks surprised, but then quickly moves and sits down.

"Are you okay?" she asks again.

I take a breath, twisting my hands together in my lap.

"I'm fine, Sam and I just—" I feel her tense at Sam's name. When I don't continue, she turns to me.

"I'm sorry," she says, her tone implying she's speaking of her reaction to him.

"Why? What is it with you two? Do you know each other? From before, I mean."

She opens her mouth to speak, but says nothing. Finally, she blows out a breath.

"I know *of* him," she says. Then, with urgency, "You need to stay away from him, Niahm. There are things . . . you don't know, can't imagine."

I think about what I *do* know, and what *she* can't imagine.

"Like what?" I ask, recalling my earlier thoughts about what it would be like to know you could never die, what sorts of thing one might . . . "If there's something you know, you *have* to tell me."

She looks at the walls, the floor, everywhere but me, and I feel a tightness begin in my belly. Finally, she glances at me.

"It's not so much *Sam*," she says with a half-smile. "It's his family."

So, he *does* have family. "What about his family?" I ask.

She shrugs. "It's not my place to tell you, Niahm. It's his."

"But if you think they might be a danger—"

"No," she says, "not to you."

"But they are a danger?"

"Some people think so. But then, those people don't really have any idea."

"This is a very cryptic conversation," I say.

"I'm sorry, Niahm," she says, raising one hand and resting it on my back. "I don't mean to be. But, as I said, it's—"

"—his story to tell, I know." She smiles at my disgruntled tone.

Suddenly, a thought strikes me. Does she know about Sam? Does she know that he's immortal? Is that where she sees the danger? But how could she . . .

The image of her *dark* roots flashes into my mind, that she felt she had to leave home all those years ago. Why? To protect whom? Her husband and daughter . . . or herself, because she knows she'll never age? I'm propelled to my feet. I can feel the look of horror on my face, and I can see it reflected in hers. She stands also.

"Niahm? What is it?"

I back away from her, as if seeing her for the first time. Her unlined skin, not even laugh lines around her eyes, how she never gets tired or worn out, how she walks as tall and strong as . . . no, *more* strong than my own mother.

She raises a hand toward me in alarm. "Niahm?"

"No!" I say, holding my own hand toward her. "Don't."

She stops, and a wary look comes into her eyes—the eyes so much like my own.

"What would happen," I begin slowly, "if you were shot?"

She blanches at my words. "Why, Niahm, whatever do you . . . you know what would happen."

But I can see it now, in her eyes, her face, even her body language.

"Would you die?" I demand. "What if you were stabbed, or hit by a car, or . . . went off a cliff in a burning car?"

"Niahm! Why would you ask that?" Her words are right, but her tone is completely wrong. I can see her processing, see that she knows I know.

"Or would you live," I say, my conviction growing strong. "Would you live to dye your hair gray, to cover the fact that it's dark as it was when you were young?"

She's staring at me now, stunned.

"Answer me," I say, my voice low, not letting her break eye contact.

"What did he tell you?" Her voice is a whisper, barely heard.

"Not about you," I say.

"I told him not to tell you," she says, fury suffusing her voice. Then, as if realizing what she's admitting, she turns pleading eyes on me. "Niahm, please, I—"

"Get out," I say through gritted teeth, rage and betrayal cutting through me.

"Please let me explain—"

"Get out!" I yell.

She takes a breath, then turns and leaves, tears shining in her eyes. I resist the urge to throw something at the door as it closes behind her. With a shuddering sob, I slide down to the floor. She knew about Sam all along, and he . . . he knew about her. He knew, but he didn't tell me, even after he told me about himself.

I pull my cell phone out of my pocket and hit the speed dial.

"Well, look who's decided to pull herself away from her boyfriend long enough to remember she has a best friend." Stacy's voice is teasing, but the undercurrent is pure anger, and guilt cuts through me at how little time I've given her.

"Stacy," is all I can manage.

"Vee? What's wrong?" The anger is gone, replaced by concern. When I don't answer, she says, "I'm on my way."

Chapter 40

Sam

Shane stares at me, his silence thunderous in the room. It's far worse than his yelling, worse than even when he curses at me in *Gaeilge*. Waves of disapproval roll off of him.

"*That's* how you told her?" he finally says. I've just finished telling him everything that happened at the motel. I nod in answer. "You do realize that this girl just buried her parents four months ago, right?"

I twitch at his words. Of course I knew that, but I didn't really think . . . I mean, it's been several hundred years since I myself have buried anyone who meant as much to me. I sigh, misery and self-recrimination flowing through me. I hunch forward, dropping my forehead into my hands. I can't believe I didn't stop to think what it might do to her, how it would make her feel so close on the heels of her parents deaths.

"I didn't think about that," I try to explain. Then, realizing how lame my words are, I say, "I didn't think at all. I could only think of showing her in a way that would make it clear that I was telling the truth, that she would have to accept it as truth."

"So to recap," he says, "you took an emotionally fragile, seventeen year old girl to a motel, locked her in and, to her way of thinking, killed yourself, without any kind of warning or explanation that you wouldn't really be dead. Then you let her sit there with your corpse for over an hour. And *then*, like a zombie, came alive again."

I don't have to try to imagine what it felt like to her sitting trapped in that room with what she thought to be my lifeless body, I'd *seen* it.

"Could you just beat the crap out of me, please?" I beg, deadly serious as I glance up at him.

"Not that I wouldn't love to for your complete and utter idiocy, and for causing the girl unnecessary psychological harm, but no. I don't think so. It wouldn't really help in the long run, would it?"

"It would help me now," I groan, wretchedly miserable in a way that I didn't think I was capable of anymore.

"Then you definitely don't deserve it." He stands and walks past me, squeezing my shoulder sympathetically as he passes, which only makes me feel worse. "You'll be lucky if she ever forgives you," he says.

And I didn't think I could possibly feel worse.

Chapter 41

Sam

When I walk into the barn early the next morning, planning to do Niahm's chores to hopefully soften her attitude toward me a little, I find her already there, saddling Sheila.

"Niahm." Her name escapes me in surprise. She jerks at the sound and turns my way. At the sight of her face, I take an instinctive step forward, but halt as she visibly tenses. Her eyes are red and puffy, her cheeks pale and drawn, her mouth pulled tight.

"I'm going for a ride," she informs me, as if I couldn't divine that myself by her actions.

"Should I?" I lift a hand toward Hercules, who has retained the name despite Niahm's protests and disgust. He's an amazing stallion to ride, mostly broken though he still has his moments of wanting to return to his wild nature.

"No, I want to go alone."

"Okay," I say, though it's anything but. "Are you alright?"

"I don't want to talk about it now," she says listlessly. "I just want to ride."

"Okay," I say again. "Is there anything I can do for you while you're gone?"

She looks as if she'll refuse, but instead says, "Yeah, I haven't milked Bessie or fed the chickens."

The flatness of her tone worries me as much as how she looks. Her words worry me even more. Niahm never does anything until all of her animals are taken care of. The thought reminds me that I haven't seen Bob. As if sensing my wondering, he gives a little whine from where he crouches in the corner. Apparently his mood is a reflection of his mistresses.

Niahm leads Sheila from the barn, her body language reflecting none of the joy that it usually does when she's about to ride. Bob lifts his head in her direction, giving another whine before settling back down. She swings up into the saddle outside the barn, and they take off at a run. Now I *know* how upset she is; she would never start Sheila at a run without walking her first.

I crouch down, holding my hand toward the dog, still watching where she was just moments before. Bob belly-crawls over to me. I scrub him behind the ears.

"That bad, huh?" I ask, and he whines again, confirming my question. "Wanna help me feed the chickens?" He perks up, his tail thumping the ground twice. He turns his head toward the opening where Niahm led Sheila out, and gives a small bark.

"She'll be gone for a while. You'll be okay. You can chase all the chickens you want."

He stares at me, as if processing my words, then stands up and wags his tail with enthusiasm.

"That's more like it," I say with a grin. Bob leads the way to the chicken coop, ready to play.

❋ ❋ ❋ ❋ ❋

Two hours later, chickens fed, cow milked, horses fed, and still no sign of Niahm. It's been thirty minutes since Bob took up his position at the edge of the barn, staring in the direction that she went. My own gaze hasn't wandered far from the same.

With a sigh, I give up. There's a lot of run-off, and the creek is running high and fast. Add to that the slick muddy ground that can take a horse down without warning, and I can't just keep waiting, no matter how furious she'll be.

I quickly saddle Hercules, and lead him from the barn. Bob is standing, wagging his tail expectantly at me.

"Don't worry, I'll bring her back," I say, lifting myself into the saddle.

*****

I find her near the creek in the same spot she and I had sat so long ago, when I first tried to convince her to like me instead of hate me. Feels like déjà vu. She's curled up on the damp ground, knees pulled up to her chest, while Sheila wanders nearby. I slide off Hercules and approach her.

"Niahm?"

She doesn't move, and as I walk around to where I can see her face, I see she's fallen asleep, hiccupping lightly, her face still damp. It's clear she's been crying and my heart contracts. I've been beating myself up since dropping her off last night. I didn't really think through how she'd feel, watching me die without any warning, so close on the heels of her parents' death. Niahm shivers violently, and I pull my jacket off, wrapping it around her as I pull her upper body off the ground and into my arms, pulling her onto my lap.

"Sam?" she asks, stiffens momentarily as she realizes it is me, then relaxes against me as her tears begin again. Her capitulation doesn't feel like acceptance or forgiveness, though. More like she just doesn't have the energy to pull away.

"I'm so sorry," I whisper, pulling her cold hands into my

warm ones. I'm assaulted immediately by her feelings of deep, cutting betrayal. I see her conversation with Jean, her realization that Jean is like me, and her anger at being lied to—particularly by me. I mutter a curse under my breath. I should have known she'd figure it out. Niahm is nothing if not intelligent.

"Why didn't you tell me?" she accuses. I consider pretending I have no idea what she's talking about, but decide right then that I won't lie to her anymore. Anything she asks, I'll answer.

"I should have," I say. "Honestly, I felt it was her—"

"Don't you dare say it was her story to tell," she says angrily, pushing harshly away from me as she slides off my lap.

I have no defense, so I don't even try. She glares at me, wiping her tears away.

"I'll answer any questions you have, Niahm. No more lies, no more secrets." She narrows her eyes in disbelief. "Starting with this," I say, swiping my green contacts from my eyes. Her own widen in disbelief as she stares at my eyes, so like her own, only with a much smaller rim of green instead of gold.

"How . . ." she breathes. She shakes her head, scooting further from me. "Does that mean I . . .?"

I shake my head. "Not necessarily. It can be an indication, but it's not a guarantee. Eyes like ours are passed down through our genes. Without them, we know there's no possibility. With them, we know that it *is* a possibility, but no more than that."

Her face reflects her dismay at this information. I can't really blame her. I can practically watch her thoughts flit through her expression, shock and horror at this information. Her fists clench and she squeezes her eyes shut, taking deep, deliberate breaths. After a few moments, she clears her throat, that admirable courage coming through once again as she keeps herself together. I think if it were me I'd be freaking out.

"So," she begins, her still-hoarse voice shaking a bit, "when would someone know, then?"

"Only when something happens to cause their mortal death. If they wake, then they know."

"But sometimes someone with eyes like . . . *this* . . . might just die?"

"Yes."

"What if it happens when you're old? Would you be old forever?"

"No. If something doesn't happen before your fifty-third birthday to cause your mortal death, then you won't become immortal. "

"Why fifty three?"

"No one knows for certain, though there are several theories. In numerology, the first number, or five, represents man. A star has five points which represents a man standing arms and legs out. It was the fifth day of creation in which God created man. Adam, the first man, was immortal until he fell. It's also a number which ends in itself when raised by its own power, making it a circular number. A circle is endless, or eternal."

"Huh," Niahm says. "I didn't know any of that. What about the three?"

"Well, the number three is considered to be the first true number and has heavy meaning in magic. It represents the past, present, and future. In geometry it's the first number of sides on a shape which creates an enclosure—as in a triangle— making three sides also endless or eternal. It also represents the beginning, the middle, and the end."

"Kind of freaky," Niahm says, sounding absolutely fascinated.

"If you add them together," I say, "you get eight. Of course the number eight turned on its side is the symbol for eternity. It also represents regeneration or rebirth. The eighth day of the week is the new beginning, or the revival of the week."

"You've spent some time studying this?" she asks with a small upturn at one corner of her mouth.

I shrug. "I was curious. No one has ever known of an

immortal that changed after that age." I glance at her. "Immortals tend to look younger than their mortal age, anyway."

"*Immortal*," Niahm mutters, looking at the stream as it flows by. "I can't believe I'm having this conversation." A thought strikes her and her eyes fly back to mine. "Is that why you've been with me? Because you saw my eyes and knew I might be like you?"

"No," I quickly negate. "I didn't really see your eyes until that day in the barn? Remember?" I watch as the memory comes to her.

"But do you think on some subconscious level you recognized that I might be?"

"No. Not that. But there is something else."

Her eyes turn wary as she weighs whether she wants to know or not. Finally, beaten, she mutters, "What?"

"As an immortal, on rare occasion you meet a mortal that you become bound to."

"Bound to? What does that mean?"

I try to find the words to explain while making sure she doesn't doubt that my love is true. "Uh, basically, you meet the person and you feel this pull toward them. As time goes on, if you spend more time with them, the feeling intensifies, until it becomes impossible to leave them—unless they ask you to. If you go away when you first feel it, sometimes you can walk away and avoid the binding, but not always."

She swallows loudly, and I don't need to hold her hand to know what she's thinking.

"So you are bound to me?" she asks in a small voice.

"Yes," I say honestly. "But it's different with you."

"Different how?" she asks skeptically.

"I won't deny the initial pull I felt with you," I begin. "But I've never had it become so intense so quickly. It wasn't long at all before I knew I couldn't go."

She turns her face away, but not before I see the hurt in her eyes.

"Niahm," I say gently, but she refuses to look my way. "Being bound and being in love are two separate things." Now she looks at me, bewildered. "An immortal can be bound to men or women, and it's almost always just a deep, protective instinct. It's kind of hard to explain. It's an inescapable need to watch over them, and keep them safe. We usually try to befriend the person, because it makes it easier to stay near them." I scoot closer to her, and reach out to touch her arm. "I've never been in love with someone I'm bound to. Until now."

Tears form in her eyes again, but she blinks them back.

"Are you lying to me?" Her voice is barely above a whisper.

I smile. "That's another thing about being bound. Once it's taken firm hold, it becomes impossible to lie to the mortal. That can be rather inconvenient at times."

"But you did lie to me," she says. "You didn't tell me what you are, or what Jean is."

"Had you asked, I couldn't have lied. I can withhold information, but I can't straight up lie."

Niahm shakes her head again. "So you can lie, just not when you're directly answering a question."

"Nor when I'm volunteering information," I say. She looks doubtful. "I didn't expect to love you, Niahm. I knew I was bound tightly, especially since it was so fast. Love, though, should never have come into the equation. I personally don't know any other immortals who have loved their bind, though there are some who are rumored to. Even if I weren't bound to you, Niahm, I would still love you."

She sighs.

"This is all so weird and confusing."

"I know," I say. "Imagine being me, thinking I was dead, then thinking it was a miracle that I was alive, never suspecting what I had become. Eventually it became impossible not to notice that I was not aging, even as my wife grew old."

"What?" Niahm shoots to her feet, at the same time I realize what I've said. "You're *married*?"

I quickly gain my feet, mentally beating myself for my usual stupidity.

"Of course not," I say then qualify, "Not anymore."

"What does *that* mean?" she demands, hands on hips.

I remind myself of my newfound resolution to not withhold information from her, no matter how much I'd rather not share this with her.

"Can we sit down again?" I say, indicating the grass. She seems about to refuse, so I say, "It's a long story."

She debates internally—it's as if I can watch the entire argument she has with herself while I wait. Finally, she drops back down. I slowly join her, take a breath, and begin.

Chapter 42

Ireland, 1563

Sorley Ó Clúmháin swung his axe down in a final, powerful arc. The blade remained buried in the stump as the two smaller pieces of wood fell evenly to the side. He rubbed his bicep before bending to retrieve the pieces. He added them to the rest, tying the twine tightly before hefting the entire bunch over his right shoulder. He leaned forward against the weight, hoping it would be enough to keep her while he was gone.

When he arrived at their small hut, he neatly arranged the wood against it. He went inside to see her as she squatted in front of the fire, stirring the pot of soup. She turned as he entered, a wide smile lighting her face.

"*A ghra mo chroí[1]*, Padraig," she said as he pulled her into his arms for a thorough kiss. She was the only one who called

---

[1] love of my heart

him by his middle name.

"I'll miss ye, wife."

"As I'll miss ye," she said. "At least ye won' hafta worra' for me as I wi' worra for ye."

Sorley shook his head sadly. He wanted nothing more than to stay in their little hut, raising babies—though he was beginning to wonder if that was a possibility. They'd been wed two years, and still no bairn[1] had blessed them.

"Go now," she commanded, "before I refuse to let ye."

He scooped up his small pack and slung it over his shoulder, the weight much less than his previous load. With his sword strapped to his side, and his battle axe in hand, he began the long walk, glancing back once at the edge of the forest. He had the sudden feeling he might never see this place—or his beloved wife—again.

"Go dté tú slán[2]," she called. Sorley swallowed over the lump that had formed in his throat as he lifted his axe in farewell.

✳ ✳ ✳ ✳ ✳

The battle had been raging for nearly half a year. Sorley was cold, wet, hungry, and exhausted beyond what any man should have to withstand. The fact that every man within eyesight shared the same misery stayed his tongue from complaint. At least he wasn't wounded—much. He dipped the filthy rag into the water that wasn't much cleaner and retied it around his thigh, not looking too closely at the slash the English scum had put into him three days prior.

He downed a mug of brew, cringing at the bitter taste. He hadn't had anything of substance to fill his belly for too long. Weakness dragged at him.

"Deifir! Deifir! Siad ag teacht[3]!"

---

[1] baby
[2] may you go safely
[3] hurry! hurry! they're coming

Sorley jumped to his feet at the warning cry and bolted from the thatched hut housing the wounded before the words had really registered. His sword had been lost a fortnight past, so he ran toward the fray, axe raised high as the first Englishman came into view. With a cry upon his lips, he swung his weapon down.

✻ ✻ ✻ ✻ ✻

Pain, deep within his side, roused Sorley from his sleep. He didn't remember laying down. He got his fists beneath him and pushed himself slowly away from the icy wet ground. He must've been exhausted as he didn't even have his thin blanket over him. When he gained his knees, he lifted his head and froze at the sight before him.

Men lay slaughtered as far as the eye could see, the ground stained red. Not just men—Irishmen. Men he'd been fighting side-by-side with for so long. He glanced to his right to see FitzGerald, his closest mate, lying with his eyes wide, the gash in his neck telling why. Sorley's stomach heaved at the sight, his empty stomach having nothing to expel, his gut wrenching sobs and loud wailing cries reaching for the heavens.

He pushed away from FitzGerald, stumbling over the dead man to his left. He refused to look and see who it was. He stumbled across the massive field, his anguish growing at each man he passed, their numbers seemingly endless.

Three days later he crested the hill above his thatched hut. He dropped to his knees at the sight of the thin tendril of smoke rising from the chimney. It felt like lifetimes since he'd last crested this ridge. Overcome with emotion, he couldn't move, couldn't stand and make the last three hundred meters it would take to put him back into her arms.

The door to the hut pushed open from within and Sorley's stomach lurched at the sight of her walking out into the yard with a bucket. She walked over to the edge of the river, dumping the contents, then refilling it with clean water. She turned back toward the hut, stopping to stretch her back before picking the bucket up again. The flatness of her belly was obvious even from this distance, and Sorley was suffused with a mixture of both regret and relief.

As she walked back to the hut she glanced up to where Sorley knelt. In panic she dropped the bucket and ran inside. He painfully pushed himself to his feet and began the long walk toward his home. Moments later she emerged again, axe raised high. Sorley groaned with a mixture of amusement and exasperation as she came his way. Did she really think her questionable skills with the heavy weapon would protect her?

"Who are ye?" she called. "State yer name, now." Sorley wanted to call to her, take the fear from her face, but words locked within his throat. "My 'usband will be right behind me, so I tell ye again: state yer name."

"*Grá[1]*," was all he managed. Her face changed at the sound of his voice.

"Padraig?" Her voice was hesitant, disbelieving.

"Aye."

She stepped cautiously closer. Sorley knew how he looked, six months without a shave or haircut, thin and emaciated from the constant hunger, his clothing hanging like rags, covered with blood.

As she reached him, she bent down, axe still raised in preparation, and peered into his face. As she caught sight of his unusual eyes, her own widened. She gasped and flung the axe to the side, launching herself at him.

"Padraig!" she screamed, her enthusiasm knocking him back. It was only with great effort that he was able to keep them from falling to the ground. "*A chuisle mo chroí[2]. Buíochas le Dia[3]. Fáilte ar ais, céad míle fáilte, mo shíorghrá[4].*"

Sorley simply held her, crushing her against his chest as tears of gratitude slid down his face.

---

[1] love
[2] pulse of my heart
[3] thanks be to God
[4] welcome home, a hundred thousand welcomes, my eternal love

Chapter 43

Niahm

I have no words as Sam tells his story. It's as if he's telling me a fairy tale, something not real, and yet the emotion on his face as he speaks of the fighting, of leaving his. . . *wife*. . . and then returning to her when he should have been dead, speaks of the truthfulness of his words.

His wife.

Immortal.

I hug my knees to my chest. I feel as if I've been lifted out of reality and plopped firmly into an alternate reality full of pain and fantasy. I wonder idly if I can find my way back to my reality, if my parents will be there waiting, and Sam and Jean will be nothing more than my imagination.

"For several years we lived hap—" He cuts himself off with a glance my way. "We lived gratefully, without knowing what I was. I stayed away from the fighting. I felt that I had done my duty and that God had spared me for a reason, among all those men who'd died around me. The wars raged on, especially when the *Deasmumhain*—uh, the Desmond's, began their rebellions. But I didn't care about politics anymore, I just wanted to stay home and raise children, and try to erase the horrors of war from my mind."

"Children?" I gasp. His tortured gaze comes to mine.

"We didn't have children. I could no longer have them once I was immortal, but of course I didn't know that at the time." I feel the suffocating panic beginning to rise again at his words. He can't have children? I manage to push the panic back to a manageable place.

"You can't have children? *Ever*?"

"No, I can't," he says, watching me closely at the disclosure of this information. I can't decide if I'm more upset for him for this loss . . . or if this should be *the* deciding factor for me of what to do about him. I always knew I'd get married and have kids. If I stay with Sam, I won't have babies, or even anything resembling a normal life. I can't think about that right now. It's too much on top of everything else.

"So, when did you . . . know?" I ask.

He looks away again, lost in his memories, and it occurs to me that he's lived a whole lifetime—several lifetimes—before now. He *isn't* seventeen.

"I can't really pinpoint an exact *when*. There just came a time when it became clear that she was aging, and I wasn't. We went to see my parents when they were quite old, because I hadn't seen them for many years." He pushes to his feet, and I jump involuntarily at the abrupt movement. He paces back and forth in front of me. "They thought I was a ghost, an evil spirit. They called me the devil." I wince at the deep hurt behind his words.

"What did you do?" I breathe.

"I convinced them I was my own son." He laughs, but there is no humor in the sound. "They believed me, or at least convinced themselves that that was the truth. We returned home after a time. We lived far from anyone, so it wasn't that hard to keep the secret, even if we didn't understand it."

"Then how did you know? I mean, didn't you just think you weren't aging?"

He looks at me again, and I can see a flush of humiliation climb his cheeks.

"After she . . . died," his voice catches on the word, and I'm filled with a mixture of deep sympathy for his pain, and burning jealousy that she can inspire such feeling from him, even now. "After she died, I—" He swallows, but seems determined to tell me. "I tried to kill myself."

I can't help the small intake of breath as the remembrance of him turning the gun on himself in the motel room invades my mind, and panic tries to push its way forward again.

"It didn't work, obviously, no matter how many times I tried, no matter how many ways." He sounds bitter. "After some time, I realized that I *couldn't* die, though I didn't have a word for what I was."

He comes and sits down near me again.

"What did you do after that?"

He takes a deep breath, and says, "I'll tell you if you want me to, Niahm. I'll tell you everything." He looks away from me, a flush stealing up his cheeks. "I did a lot of things during that time that I'm not proud of. I was angry—no, I was *furious*. I didn't know why I couldn't die, which was what I wanted more than anything. I'd rather not give you the details," he turns to me, "but I will if you ask it of me."

I think about his words. Part of me wants to know, is *desperate* to know, but a bigger part knows that everyone has secrets, things they are ashamed of, things they don't want anyone to know, ever—me included. So I decide not to ask.

"You refer to her as 'she.' Your . . . wife, I mean. What was her name?"

He hesitates as he gazes at the stream. I'm beginning to think he won't tell me when he looks directly at me. "Niahm."

"Yes?"

The slightest smile lifts his mouth. "No. I mean, that was her name as well. Her name was Niahm."

Shock filters through me. I examine it, trying to decide if I should be angry or not. Is that why he was drawn to me?

As if sensing what I'm thinking, he shakes his head. "It has nothing to do with you, Niahm. I knew I was bound to you before I knew your name. It was a shock finding out you shared her name. I didn't expect to find anyone *here* with such a name."

I remember back to when he first knew my name, how I'd thought he was saying I couldn't have such an exotic name. Really he was simply stunned to find it out.

"Do you think of her when you say my name?" I ask, bracing myself for the pain that will come if his answer is yes.

"No." At my skeptical look, he says, "I can't lie to you, Niahm. I don't think of her. I did the first time I saw your name, of course. That's only natural. But you are completely different than she was. And . . ." He leans slightly toward me, one hand reaching out but then dropping before touching me. "She never meant as much to me as you do. It might sound heartless, but it's true. I loved her. I won't deny that. But with her it wasn't the same as it is with you."

Not sure what to say, I blurt the first thing that pops into my head. "It probably just feels different because you've been alone for so long."

"No, Niahm," he says, shaking his head firmly. "I've never felt about anyone the way I feel for you. Not my wife. Not my parents. Not even Shane. Only you."

His words cause a funny tightening in my heart, but I'm still not ready for any of this . . . no matter how much I want to lean into his arms right now.

"How did you find Shane?" I ask, clearing my sore throat and changing the subject.

He watches me for a few moments, probably trying to figure out how I can let his words pass without reply. I feel a little bad about that, but I just can't respond to him yet.

"He found me," he says. "And a good thing it was, too. He saved me from myself. He'd been around for quite a bit longer than me, and knew what we were. He'd been trying to keep track of members of our family in case he found another who was immortal. It took him so long to find me because I had been so rural, and then had been on the move after realizing what I was." He pulls his knees up, looping his arms loosely around his legs, looking at me with puzzlement on his face.

"What?" I ask defensively.

"You need to know . . ." He trails off, contemplating. Then, making up his mind, he begins again. "You need to know that there are immortals out there who aren't . . . who *like* the fact that they can't die, who feel like they are above the law, I guess, above morality or consequence for their actions."

I shudder at his words as I recall my thoughts the night before.

"And there are others—mortals—who hunt people like me."

His statement, given so nonchalantly, stuns me.

"What? What do you mean, *hunt* you?"

He blows out a breath.

"The call themselves the Sentinels. They feel, rightly so, that we are an abomination, and that it's their duty to remove us all from the earth."

I just stare at him, trying to process his words. There are people trying to *kill* immortals? Deliberately trying to kill Sam?

"But . . . I thought you said you can't die."

He looks away from me, watching the stream that flows quickly by.

"I can't kill myself. There are ways," he says, "that they know of. I can be killed, we all can." He looks directly at me. "Please don't ask me to describe how they can kill us." I shake my head quickly, having no desire to hear of whatever horrible thing might have to be done to kill someone who can survive a gunshot. "They don't care if you're evil, or if you're just trying to live a decent life."

His words recall his earlier statement.

"What did you mean when you said they *rightly* believe that you're an abomination?"

He shakes his head, tucking his chin against his chest. Just when I think he won't answer, his voice comes, low and quiet.

"How can I be anything but, Niahm? How can I be one of God's creatures, when I'm unnatural? I can only belong to the devil."

As angry as I am at Sam, as shocked as I am by his having been married, I can't let his statement go.

"Sam." I reach out and lay my hand on his arm, and his gaze moves to my hand before meeting my eyes. "I don't know why you are the way you are, but if there's one thing I *do* know, it's that you are *not* of the devil. You are good, and kind, and pure. I don't believe for one second that you aren't one of Gods children. Not you, not Shane . . . not even Jean."

He watches me closely, and while I can see that my words don't change his mind, I can see that he knows I'm not just trying to make him feel better.

"You honestly believe that." It's not a question, but a statement. His arm under my hand is warm even through his sleeve. I wonder if that's some kind of immortal thing, how warm his hands and now arm always seem to be. Just as I move to pull back, he covers my hand with his own. "I'm sorry, Niahm, *so* sorry for the brainless way in which I went about telling you this. I didn't fully consider how my actions would hurt you. At my age, I should have known better, I should have taken the time to think it through more thoroughly. Instead, I acted like the rash, reckless seventeen year old I pretend to be. And because of that, you're suffering."

Tears prick my eyes, and I don't know whether I want to punch him, or throw myself into his arms. I don't do either.

"If I could reverse time, I would take it back. Not the telling you," he clarifies, "I would still do that. I've wanted to tell you for some time now. But I would definitely do things differently."

I swallow, not reaching up to brush away the tears that manage to escape.

"That really was brainless, Sam." He nods in agreement. "Worse was that you lied to me for so long about Jean. You knew her, but didn't tell me."

"I didn't know her," he says. "I didn't know she was your grandma, either. But I knew what she was. And I thought she had come to harm you. I mean, what are the chances of another immortal showing up in Goshen? Unless she'd come here for a specific reason—and it seemed that reason was you."

"Are you saying most immortals don't get along?"

He smiles, his thumb lightly caressing the side of my hand. "I'm saying most immortals are suspicious of one another. Remember the bad ones I was telling you about before?"

I sigh, and turn my hand over, wrapping my fingers around his hand. His eyes come to mine in question.

"I'm still not sure how to feel about all of this, Sam. And even though I can kind of understand why you did what you did, it doesn't change the fact of what I had to go through during the time I thought you were . . . I mean, couldn't you have given me some kind of warning? I don't know if I've ever been so terrified in my life—and that's saying a lot since I've slept in jungles with lions and other predators."

He squeezes my hand lightly, the heat between our hands intense.

"I will never forgive myself for what I made you go through, Niahm, so if you can't ever forgive me, I can't blame you. I should have tried to explain at least, though it would only have made you believe I was crazy, and you still would have thought I'd killed myself."

I go back to when we first arrived at the motel, and try to imagine how I would have reacted had he told me he was immortal and then shot himself to prove it. He's right; I would not have believed him.

"It's going to be hard to trust you again," I say.

"I know. And I understand. I hope you can believe me when I tell you that I won't ever lie to you again. I *can't* lie to you, but even if I could, I wouldn't. Not now."

I can feel that he's being utterly honest, and feel the tiniest portion of my anger slip away.

"I should get back," I say. To my surprise, he doesn't argue. He stands and pulls me up by my hand that had been resting on his arm, which he hasn't released.

"Niahm, can I please . . ." he stutters, unsure of himself. "I know it doesn't mean anything to you, that it's not saying . . . but, please, can I please just hold you for a minute?"

I consider refusing, just to see if I can, but then I step forward and wrap my arms around his waist. His arms close tightly around me, sheltering and safe, and for a few minutes as we stand that way, swaying slightly, I pretend that all is right with my world.

Chapter 44

Niahm

Sam rides back to the house with me, and after brushing down the horses he leaves. I've been avoiding Jean all morning. I'm not quite sure what I'm going to do or say when I see her.

Stacy came last night, and held me while I cried. I knew she was frustrated by my refusal to tell her what was wrong, but really, what could I say? *Hey, guess what, my boyfriend shot himself today to prove he's immortal. And, oh yeah, my grandma is immortal also.* She left this morning when I told her I needed to be alone. I'm feeling amazingly guilty over how good a friend she is, and how much I've neglected her.

I walk into the house with a dejected Bob trailing me. I don't feel too sorry for him though. If the two or three feathers hanging from his belly are any indication, he had plenty of fun while I was away.

"Hi."

I jump as Jean's voice comes from the backside of the kitchen table where she sits. I guess she's trying to be unobtrusive.

"Hi," I say, unsure of how I feel about her. Then, deciding I may as well get it over with, I pull out a chair and sit down opposite her. I can't miss the overflowing plate of homemade cinnamon rolls sitting in the middle of the table, especially as my growling stomach reminds me I haven't eaten yet today. I consider refusing them just on principal, but decide it won't help my pride if my stomach continues to protest loudly. I drag a napkin from the holder, plopping a large roll on top after taking a big bite.

"Are you okay?"

I glance up at her. There isn't an easy answer to her question, so I just shrug.

"Did Sam find you?"

I nod.

"Do you want to talk? Ask me some questions?"

After swallowing another large bite, I say, "I don't know what questions to ask, because I'm not sure what all I want to know." A thought strikes me. "Can you lie to me?"

She smiles grimly. "He told you about that, huh?" At my nod, she continues, "I'm still pretty new at this, so I don't really know exactly how it all works, but I believe the only thing that prevents one from lying is being bound to another. I'm assuming he told you about that, as well?"

There's a slight edge to her voice, as if she's trying hard not to be angry at Sam herself.

"Yeah, he did. So, you've never been . . . bound, I guess?" I grunt at the strangeness of this conversation. That surreal feeling comes over me again.

"No." She takes a cinnamon roll and bites it before placing it on the napkin in front of her. "From what I understand, it's rare."

That was what Sam had said. Or something like that.

"How rare?" I ask.

She shakes her head. "I really don't know, Niahm. Sam or Shane might be able to answer you better than me." She pauses as she takes another bite. "You know, I'm furious with him for telling you."

"Really? Why?" I'm genuinely curious. Is she just angry that I know about *her*?

"Because he has put you in danger." Her words surprise me.

"The Sentinels?" I guess. Her face changes at my question, as she shoves away from the table, standing in the same motion.

"He *told* you about them?" she demands.

"Well, yeah," I say. She stares at me for a minute, jaw clenched before she sinks back down into her chair.

"He would," she mutters.

"Shouldn't you have?" I ask. "I mean, you're my grandma, you're supposed to be watching out for me, right?"

Tears swim in her eyes, but never fall as she answers me. "I wouldn't have come back if I hadn't found Beth's letter." I raise my brows at her comment. "I would never have put you in danger that way."

"But you're here now. You put me in danger by coming here, right?" I'm mostly guessing but her guilty look tells me I hit it right on the head.

"I couldn't ignore her final plea. It was hard enough ignoring her pleas while she was alive."

"Yeah, but you managed to ignore them," I spit out. "What's different now?"

She takes another bite of her roll before answering.

"She included a picture of you once, when you were maybe five or so." She glances up at me, holds my look. "I saw your eyes."

"So you came back to see if I am . . . like you?"

"Yes," she says, and at my dropped jaw, adds, "and no."

"Do I want to know what that means?" I mutter.

"Of course I was curious, but I could have easily waited until I heard of your death before coming back to see."

"But?" I ask when she pauses, her words hanging on an unfinished thought.

"But mostly I wanted to meet my granddaughter. I knew that you wouldn't know me, that I could come and look the way I do, and not have you question it."

"Look young, you mean," I say.

"Yes."

"I noticed your dark roots before. But I couldn't find any rational explanation, so I convinced myself I was crazy."

Jean smiled. "I don't know if I just got lazy at keeping up the scheme, or if I subconsciously wanted you to figure it out," she says.

"I doubt I would have figured it out," I argue. "Who could possibly imagine such an explanation?"

She shrugs, taking another bite of her roll, which I mirror.

"How did you, uh, die, I guess?" I ask.

A pained look crosses her face, and she sets the roll that she had just lifted to her mouth back down without taking a bite.

"That's a long story," she says quietly.

"I've got time," I say, leaning back in my chair as if to prove it.

"Stubborn like your mother," she says. "Alright, I'll tell you."

I lean forward again, surprised. I really didn't think she'd capitulate.

"You have to understand that there were a lot of things that your mother wasn't aware of," she began. "My husband wasn't who she thought he was. He was a great father, I'll give him that. But he wasn't a great husband."

She clears her throat, stands and crosses to the fridge, where she pulls out two bottles of water which she brings back to the table, setting one in front of me. "He tried, he really did.

But he just couldn't love me in the way I wanted to be loved. When he was a boy, he'd been . . ." She glances up at me, looking as if she's debating how much to tell me. When I don't say anything, she sighs and continues. "He'd been molested by an adult relative."

I gasp at her words. She couldn't have surprised me more had she confessed her secondary ability to fly.

"It went on for quite some time, and it really messed with his head."

"Well, duh," is my brilliant response.

"He could be a great father, and love his daughter to no end, because it was an entirely platonic relationship. With me, it was different of course." She grimaces at the painful memories. "For the first year of our marriage, he really made an attempt to have a normal relationship. But I could always feel the hesitancy, the wall that he put up whenever I came near. Eventually, he quit trying. I found out shortly after that I was pregnant. We only had one child because after I became a mother, he told me that he couldn't be my husband any longer. When he told me why, I thought that maybe if I loved him enough, I could change him."

She shifts uncomfortably in her chair. "I convinced him to stay. And he did, because he loved his daughter, and I think he even loved me a little—just not as a husband should love his wife. Weeks of waiting for him turned into months, and then years. I was lonely. I felt like a failure, as if I were undesirable and unwanted. I became depressed."

She glances up at me again, then stands and walks to the sink, where she picks up a lone plate and begins to wash it. She rubs the soapy cloth against the porcelain for far longer than necessary, her back to me.

"I knew that if I left him, he wouldn't blame me. But because I had let so much time go by without seeking help, the depression was deeply rooted. So I got into the tub one day, slit my wrists, and waited to die."

A shudder of shock runs through me at her nonchalant

narrative. She was *suicidal*? When I say nothing, unable to speak as my mind tries to make sense of her actions, she turns my way.

"When I woke up, I was lying in a deep pool of blood, weak from the loss, but alive."

"What if my mom had come in and found you?" I demand.

"She wouldn't have," Jean says. "She was gone away to camp for the week. I wanted *him* to find me, to know what he'd driven me to." She shakes her head. "I was not in a good frame of mind, Niahm. It's hard to understand unless you've been there."

I swallow over the lump in my throat, trying to push back the feelings of betrayal on behalf of my young mother who would have been left motherless.

"So what made you think you were immortal?" I ask, not exactly kindly.

"I didn't. Not then. I thought God had spared me for some reason. I didn't want to be spared, though, so I took several bottles of pills a few days later. All that resulted in was a lot of vomiting and horrible stomach cramps. So I walked down to the cliff—the same one that the car went over—and jumped. When I woke from that, I was sore everywhere, covered with bruises, but still not dead."

I shake my head, wanting to stop her words. I've heard enough. I lift my hand as she says, "A few days after that, I took his gun—"

"Stop!" I yell, coming to my feet. Her words immediately bring remembrance of Sam and his own gun, and I *definitely* don't want to hear this part. "No more," I whisper, sympathy for her plight cutting me. "I get it. You kept trying to commit suicide, but couldn't. I don't need any more details. *Please*."

"I'm sorry," she apologizes. "I didn't mean to upset you."

"Really?" I scoff. "You didn't think it would upset me to know that my grandmother was suicidal? In the *extreme*?"

"I . . . I didn't think that part through, I suppose," she stutters.

"Must be some kind of immortal shortcoming, not thinking things through," I mutter. "I just don't know why I have to be the one who pays for it."

"Did Sam—"

"No," I interrupt her abruptly again. "No, you don't get to bring Sam into this side of it," I say, feeling nauseated.

"I'm sorry," she repeats, and she actually sounds sincere. "I just wanted you to see that it wasn't a fluke that I figured it out so quickly. I mean, relatively quickly compared to most immortals from the stories I've heard. I should have figured it out much sooner."

"So you left?" I say, changing the subject, not wanting to dwell on her story any longer.

"I felt I had no choice," she answers. "It had been several years since my failed . . . attempts. I was frightened by the knowledge of what I was. I actually only thought to go away for some time, try to figure things out. At least, that's what I told myself. I think deep down I always knew it was going to be permanent. When my car was stolen and then driven off the cliff—"

"So that much is true, at least?" I interrupt.

"Yes, that part is true. It seemed divine intervention, so I took it. I've told you how close I was to deciding to go home."

"After you'd been gone a while," I say, "didn't you ever think about going back?"

"Every day," she says firmly, the conviction in her voice convincing me of the truth. "But by then I knew about the Sentinels, knew about other immortals who were dangerous, knew that I couldn't bring that home to my daughter. Then she married and moved here." The look she gives me is equal parts pleading and defiance. "She was happy. So was my husband, because he didn't have to pretend anymore, could live as a loner without having any personal relationships other than his daughter, and that was long distance."

"He died young," I say, as if it were somehow her fault.

"Yes," she says. "He had a heart attack, and no one found

him until it was too late. I went to his funeral." I can feel that my face shows the surprise I feel. "I cried for him, for his lost soul, and for my daughter who now thought she was an orphan." The corners of her mouth turn up slightly as she remembers. "But she didn't need to be cried for. I watched her with her young husband, saw how much they loved one another, saw the way he looked at her with such love and devotion, with everything I had always wished for from my own marriage. And I knew then that she was going to be just fine."

"Yeah, right, fine other than spending her entire life searching for her lost mother."

Jean shakes her head again. "I didn't know that was what she was doing. I knew how often she travelled, knew that she was in the city quite often to leave letters in the tree. I didn't know *why* she was doing those things. I just knew her life afforded her the opportunity to travel, and I was so grateful for our strange correspondence that I didn't stop to question it."

As much as I want this to be her fault, her words make sense to me. What I wouldn't give to suddenly start receiving letters from my mother now. Besides, I can understand her unwillingness to bring danger to my mother's doorstep. I would have done the same thing.

"Niahm." Her use of my name brings me out of my thoughts. "I'm genuinely sorry for the hurt I caused Beth, and you. I would do anything to not have this curse, to have had a normal marriage, to have been able to watch my daughter as she became a woman, a wife, a mother. I would do anything to keep you safe now."

Her fervent speech moves me against my will.

"I'm sorry, too," I concede. "For having been so horrible to you since you came. I know my mom would have wanted me to treat you . . . differently. I've dishonored her by being such a brat. But—" I lift a finger to stop her when she opens her mouth, a hopeful expression on her face. "This is all very weird, and I don't really know how to deal with it just yet. I need some time to process, and decide what I'm going to do with what I now know about . . . all of you."

She nods solemnly, but the hopeful look remains.

"Do you want me to go?" she asks. "Just for a while, give you some space?"

I consider her offer. It would be nice to be alone, without anything trying to influence me in any way. Honestly, though, I won't be alone. My thoughts won't leave me be. Sam and Shane are here and in a small town like this, it would be impossible to avoid them. And as much as I want to tell Stacy everything, and let her be my support, I know that's impossible. If by some chance she *did* believe me, then I would be endangering her. That's one thing I definitely won't do.

"No," I say, making up my mind. "I'd rather you stayed."

She nods, unable to stop the grin from splitting her face.

"I'm exhausted," I say, and I am. Not just physically, but emotionally. Actually, mostly emotionally. "I think I'm going to go take a three day nap," I inform her.

"Okay," she says. "I'll keep things quiet so you can rest for *four* days." I give her a half-hearted smile. As I head up the stairs, she calls out, "Just don't forget you have school in the morning."

I shudder at her words, the same words my mother would call to me as I went off to bed, as if I didn't know, or didn't get myself to school on all the days she was gone. If I'd had any doubt she was my mother's mother, I no longer did.

Chapter 45

Niahm

School feels surreal after my weekend—almost pointless to be honest. Why do I need to know what absolute convergence is or what a demonstrative adjective is when there are immortals running around the world, and some crazy dudes called Sentinels hunting them? Not to mention suicidal grandmas. What's next? Werewolves and vampires? I think about asking Sam or Jean about them, but shudder at the thought of what answer they might give.

"Hey, Niahm," the double-H call simultaneously as they round the corner. I take a breath and paste a smile on my face.

"Hey," I say back, although not much enthusiasm accompanies the word. They don't notice.

"You've been M.I.A. a lot lately," Heather grins, winking suggestively. "Been wrapped up in a certain red-head?"

I cringe at her words, not really wanting to think about a certain red-head until I've decided what to do about him.

"C'mon, Heather, give her a break," Hillary says, saving me from responding. "If it were any of us dating him, we'd have disappeared also."

Guilt rears up again, amplified when Stacy comes over to us. She still looks a little angry with me, her face grim as she greets everyone, mostly ignoring me. Stacy is an amazing friend who came at my urgent call without a second's hesitation, and I then blew her off first thing in the morning to go and lick my wounds—all without revealing a thing about what was going on.

"We're all going to the movie Wednesday night for a girls-night-out since we have a long weekend," Heather says, singing the last two words. "You should come."

They all look at me doubtfully, as if it's a foregone conclusion that I'll say no. Suddenly, more than anything I want a girls-night-out at some movie that the rest of the world saw weeks ago, because that's *normal*. That's the way life is supposed to be, at least here in Goshen.

"Sounds fun," I say. "Tell me where to be and when, and I'll be there."

They all three narrow their eyes at me.

"You do know it's a *girls* night out, right?" Stacy asks, not exactly kindly.

"That means you can't bring Sam," Hillary clarifies, in case I missed Stacy's point.

"No problem," is all I say.

"Speaking of Sam," Heather pipes in, "Where is he today? Usually wherever you are, he is."

"Um," I say, not sure how to answer. I had actually been thinking the same thing, both relieved and worried that he wasn't here. I might have wondered a few days ago, but now, knowing what I know, my mind begins to go to dark places. Have the Sentinel's found him?

"Girls, girls, girls," Kevin sings, doing a decent imitation of

Mötley Crüe as he and Jon come up to us, throwing their arms around Hillary and Heather. "No dawdling in the halls. We don't want to be late for class, do we?"

He's doing his not-even-close impression of Mr. Hale, the science teacher, which usually amuses me with its ridiculousness. Not today. I'm afraid maybe not ever again. I glance over at Stacy as the double-H allow their giggling selves to be led away. The hurt in her eyes tears at my heart.

"Stace—" I begin, hand held out in supplication. She turns away to follow the others without even acknowledging me, and I'm left empty handed.

After school—to which Sam never does show—I catch up to Stacy.

"Stacy, please, wait," I say, grabbing hold of her arm and forcing her to stop.

"What?" she demands, impatience in her voice.

"Stacy, I'm so sorry. I've been such a horrible friend."

"Ya think?" Her sarcasm burns me as she turns away and begins walking, though not so fast I can't keep up.

"No, I don't think. I *know*."

"So, what, you and Sam have broken up so now you want me back?"

"No." My denial is immediate, surprising me. "We haven't broken up."

That stops her. She turns back my way.

"You haven't?" When I shake my head, she says, "Then what was all of that this weekend? You wouldn't tell me what was wrong, so I just assumed . . ."

"Nothing like that," I say, thinking she can't begin to imagine how far off the mark any of her guesses would be. "Stacy, what if you . . ." I glance around at all the other students still milling about. "Can I walk home with you?" I ask. "I don't want to talk here."

She seems about to refuse, but then gives a terse nod. We begin walking away from the school, quickly, hopefully to discourage any others from joining us.

"What if I what?" she asks when the silence stretches.

I'm confused for a second, before remembering what I had begun to ask her earlier.

"What if someone told you something that was a secret?" At her glance, I clarify. "Not just any secret, like Hillary saying she wears a padded bra, but a serious secret?"

Stacy grins briefly at my analogy before turning somber again.

"What kind of secret?" she asks.

I take a breath. "The kind of secret that could threaten their lives if it were to get out to the wrong person."

Now I have her full attention. She stops and turns so that she's facing me.

"Then you'd have to keep it to yourself," she says firmly.

"Even if it meant not telling your best friend, and she was so mad at you that she wouldn't even speak to you."

Her mouth tightens, she glances away, arms crossed, and finally brings her unwavering gaze back to mine. "Yes. Even then. A secret that big that is entrusted to you should stay with you."

"Really?"

"Really." She gives a decisive nod. "But you said 'their lives.' Does that mean this affects more than just Sam?"

"I never said it concerned Sam at all," I say.

"Oh, yeah, I guess you didn't. I just assumed again."

"But yes," I say. "I guess I can tell you it's his secret, and that it does affect more than just him."

"It must be bad," she says.

"Why do you say that?"

"Because you were a mess the other night. I haven't seen you like that since—" She cuts herself off, but I know what she'd been about to reference.

"It's bad," I confirm, the vision of Sam raising the gun to his chest flooding my mind. I shudder with horror and shove the image away. "I wish I could tell you, Stace, because it would

Cindy C Bennett

help so much to ask someone what I should do. But I can't."

She nods again. Suddenly she reaches out and pulls me into her arms. I cling to her, relief flooding through me at her forgiveness, her willingness to accept my words and to support me even if she has no idea what's going on. Guilt sluices through me again at how much I've ignored her over the past few months.

"You want me to come over and we can bake cookies?" she asks as she releases me.

"I really do." I smile at her, brushing my tears away.

"Then let's go." She hooks her arm through mine, and with a lighter step, leads me home.

Chapter 46

Sam

I'm in the paddock with the horses when Niahm and Stacy come home from school, laughing together. It feels like years since I've seen Niahm smile like that, even though it's only been a few days.

They don't see me as they disappear into the house. I can hear them in the kitchen through the windows Jean opened to let a fresh breeze in. They are banging around in the kitchen, clearly preparing to cook something or other. I hope it's cookies or pie or anything sweet—then realize I may not get to taste whatever they're making if Niahm is still peeved with me.

I move closer, Bob at my heel, to spy on them. Just then, Niahm opens the doors and calls Bob's name. She stops abruptly, one hand still on the door handle when she sees me.

"Hi," I say, unsure of how to proceed.

Bob bounds forward and jumps up on Niahm, happily

nosing her neck and chin. She turns her attention to the dog, scrubbing him behind the ears and talking her nonsense to him that he loves. She glances back up at me.

"Hi," she finally says as Bob drops down and pushes past her into the house.

"Bob! No!" I hear Stacy scolding him. I grin at the sound, and Niahm does as well.

"You'd think he'd know better than to aggravate her," I say.

"Well, she hasn't been around much lately, so I guess he's forgotten." I see the pinch at the corner of her eyes as she says it, can feel the guilt she's suffering with. I share in that guilt. I've been happy to monopolize all of her time without a thought for how it might be affecting her friendships.

"That's my fault," I say, and she shakes her head.

"It was my choice."

I can't help but notice she said *was*. Stacy comes to the door.

"What are you doing out her, Vee? Your terror of a dog is out of control without—Oh, hi, Sam," she says upon spying me. She sounds friendly enough. I realize how much *I've* missed Stacy, my comrade in arms when it comes to taking care of Niahm. She glances between Niahm and myself, and finally says, "Wanna come in and make cookies with us?"

I'm as surprised by her offer as Niahm apparently is, if the look on her face is any indication.

"Um, well, I . . . yeah, I'd like to . . ." I pause, trying to read Niahm, but I'm too far away. "But maybe I should—"

"Come on," Niahm says, standing back and opening the door wider. "It'll be fun."

"The Three Musketeer's ride again," Stacy says with a laugh, stepping back and turning to chide Bob once again, who looks at her in abject innocence, his nose covered in white flour. I follow them in, and Stacy shoots me a cryptic look, sideways from beneath lowered brows and I suddenly wonder if Niahm has told her. Does she understand the danger this puts Stacy in? More than ever I wish I had the freedom to walk over to Niahm and take her hand.

The two of them make the dough, and I find I'm only in the way. It's clear they've done this many times together, each doing their part without even talking of who will do what. I retreat to the table and watch them, smiling at their silly laughter. At one point Stacy turns on the radio which is playing an old, upbeat song from the fifties.

"Ugh, horrible music," Niahm moans.

"What? You're crazy, this is amazing music," Stacy argues. I have to agree with her.

"Come on, Sam," Stacy laughs, taking my hand and pulling me up. "Let's show Niahm how great this music is to dance to."

I admit I'm showing off a bit as I twirl her into a swing dance—which she manages to keep up with, apparently having been taught by her dad. That memory is front and center. The entire time, I'm listening to her, watching to see if Niahm has given her any information she shouldn't have. I skim over memories that aren't related to Niahm, go a little slower whenever Niahm makes an appearance. Finally I reach their interaction of the past few days, and see that Niahm has kept our secret. I'm a little surprised by Stacy's acceptance, and her advice to Niahm to keep the secret. It comes completely from a place of love for Niahm. That's something I can relate to.

"Whew!" Stacy exclaims as she drops onto one of the chairs. "You should give some of the boys around here lessons. Where did you learn to dance like that?"

Niahm looks at me oddly, and I can't meet her eyes as I tell the lie. "In New York. They gave us lessons one year in school."

Stacy nods, accepting my words. "Dude, you have the warmest hands of any guy I've ever danced with. You don't have a fever, do you?"

I realize I may have overdone it on the brain-picking, not quite sure how to answer.

"That's normal for him," Niahm says. "He has hot hands." Then, blushing at her words and Stacy's laughter, she says, "I mean, his hands are always hot like that."

"Weird," Stacy proclaims. "I've never felt anything like that before, at least on hands that aren't sweaty in the process."

I look at Niahm, see that she's watching me, a thoughtful, questioning look on her face. Thank the heavens the oven timer chooses that moment to go off, taking her attention from me. Somehow, though, I don't think she's going to forget about Stacy's words calling her to the fact that the heat she feels from my hands all too frequently isn't exactly normal.

❋ ❋ ❋ ❋ ❋

"Stay."

I look at Niahm, for one second wondering if she's speaking to Bob. But she's looking right at me. Stacy just announced her intention to leave, after we've gorged ourselves sick on the cookies they baked. I stood to leave also when Niahm speaks the word. I can only nod, hoping she wants me to stay for a good reason.

Stacy and Niahm hug, then Niahm closes the door behind her. She turns to me, an unsure look on her face. When she hesitates, I say, "If it were possible, I'd probably gain about forty pounds from the amount of cookies I ate. But it'd be worth it."

"You . . . you can't get fat?" she asks, surprised.

"No." I hope a simple answer is the best way to keep Niahm from freaking out.

"That seems unfair," is her only response. She walks over to the couch and sits down. I follow and sit in the chair next to the couch. She leans forward, elbows on her thighs, twisting her hands together in front of her.

"I wanted to tell you," she begins, not looking at me. She glances up at me from beneath her lashes, and I'm struck once again by her eyes. I envy her not having to wear contacts to cover their strangeness. She still has enough of a rim for them to appear unusual but not alarming, as mine do. People tend to cringe away from my eyes, as if they can sense something isn't right with me. She takes a deep breath and blows it out. A trickle of apprehension creeps up my spine. I can't read her very well right now. I believe she may be trying to find the words to break up with me. I decide to give her a break. It's the least I can do after everything I've put her through.

"Niahm, it isn't easy knowing what you now know," I say. "I've had years of learning to live with it, and it still is hard for me. There isn't any blame for not wanting to be part of it. I promise. And you know I can't lie to you," I smile at her. She's simply staring at me, a ridge of confusion puckering her brow. "It will be hard to walk away, but I'll do it. For you. It won't change my feelings for you at all. But eventually you'll be able to forget about me, and you'll have—"

I stop when she brings her hand up, palm toward me.

"Sam," she says, shaking her head a little. "Let me finish, okay?"

I nod.

"I don't *want* to forget about you."

A spark of hope ignites. "You . . . you don't?"

"No," she laughs. "When I told you I love you, I wasn't kidding. This is all very weird and sci-fi channelish, and I don't know what will happen down the road." She shrugs. "Maybe it will be too much at some point, when I'm getting wrinkles and you're not, or maybe even before then. I don't know. There's a lot to consider. But for now, for today, I'm not ready to give you up."

I slide from the chair so that I'm kneeling in front of her.

"Are you saying . . .?" I take hold of her hands, nearly floored by the wave of feeling she has for me. I can see the confusion beneath it all, see conflicting thoughts of giving up her idealistic future including a family, see her fear of being old and hunched with me next to her looking the same as I do now. I know I should let her go, so that she doesn't have to deal with those fears, but I'm just selfish enough not to.

"Thank you," I whisper, leaning forward to kiss her. She pulls her hands from mine and wraps her arms tightly around my neck. My own arms about her waist pull her close to me, until she's kneeling on the floor in front of me, kissing me back with all the passion she has.

"I love you," I say, pulling back to caress her cheek with my thumb.

"I love you, too," she says, kissing me once again.

Chapter 47

Niahm

On Wednesday, as promised, I go with my girlfriends to the movie. I've been wrapped up in Sam for so long that I've forgotten how much I like just hanging out, being a silly girl. Sam came back to school on Tuesday after our cookie making night—and making out night, if I remember right.

I decided that I shouldn't be so stubborn. Yeah, what he did was about the worst way he could have decided to tell me what he was, but I can't forget how relieved and grateful I was when he woke up, and I first realized he wasn't dead. Or how I felt when I thought he was.

"Someone's birthday's coming up," Hillary sing-songs. I give her a half-grin in response. I hadn't ever imagined I would celebrate my eighteenth birthday without my parents being by my side.

"Got any plans next Friday?" Heather asks. Stacy rolls her eyes at me. A few years ago we all decided that we'd do surprise birthday parties for everyone when they turned eighteen. At the beginning of the year, the Double-H decided that if we didn't speak of it, no one would remember when their birthday came.

"I'm all yours," I say, no matter how much I want to spend the night at home, curled up in a sobbing ball.

"Well, maybe we can go see a movie or something. It's your birthday, what do you want to do?" Hillary asks, I suppose thinking I have no idea she's setting me up for the surprise party.

"I'll let you pick, Hill," I say, ignoring Stacy's smirk. "Surprise me."

When I get home, Jean is sitting at the computer in the kitchen again. I'm dying of curiosity to know what she spends so much time doing on there, but when I asked her once, she made up some lame excuse that was clearly a lie, so I haven't asked again.

"Hey," I say, stepping into the room as she minimizes the window she had open.

"Hey, yourself. Did you have fun?"

"I really did," I say. "I'd kind of forgotten how much fun it is just to hang out with the girls."

"Yeah, well, cute boys will always turn your head, won't they?"

I glance at her, hearing the slight edge in her voice. But she's smiling at me, no malice reflected on her face.

"You're calling Sam cute? Since when do you give him compliments?"

She laughs, shuts down the computer, and walks over to me. "I don't like that an immortal is anywhere near my granddaughter, but . . . he's not a bad guy, overall."

"Huh."

"'Huh' what?" she asks.

"Two compliments. Without any irony, I might add."

"Should we change the subject while it's still good?" she says with a wry grin.

"Good idea," I say. "My friends are having a surprise birthday party for me on Friday."

"If it's a surprise, how do you know?" she asks, looking at me sideways as she opens a cabinet to pull a glass out.

"They've had one for every person who's turned eighteen this year. There's only one more after me."

"Ah, gotcha," she says, filling her glass with water.

"Is that . . . necessary?" I ask, eyeing the glass as she tips it up against her mouth.

"What? Water?"

"Yeah. I mean, you can't die, right?"

"No, I can't die," she says sardonically. "But I can be pretty miserable if I don't eat and drink."

"Sam says you can't get fat."

"Really?" She sounds surprised.

"You didn't know that?"

"No, I didn't. That's good news. In that case," she pauses with her hand above the plate of cookies we made the other day, "may I?"

I laugh and wave permission toward her.

"What do you want for your birthday, Niahm?" Her question is casual as she sits at the table, but my stomach clenches as I prepare my response, one I've been thinking about for a while now. I sit across from her, one foot propped beneath me as I rock back and forth minutely with nerves.

"I was thinking that maybe, since I have a long weekend with it being the end of the quarter and all, that you and I could drive to the city. We could stay there and, I don't know, shop, go to a movie, eat out, things like that."

Jean stops with the cookie poised halfway to her mouth and stares at me. She lowers the cookie back to the plate and swallows loudly.

"Just you and me?"

"Well, yeah." I look at the table, trace an imaginary pattern on it. "I thought it might be kind of fun, you know? Just to kind of get away, get to . . . get to know each other a little better."

When she doesn't say anything I glance up and see her watching me, her hand at her throat, tears shining in her eyes and a small up-tilting at the corners of her mouth. My breath is pulled from me as I realize how very much she looks like my mother.

"I think that sounds absolutely wonderful," she says, her voice not far above a whisper.

I nod, and without another word walk to the bottom of the stairs.

"Goodnight," I say, looking back to see her standing in the same position. I hurry up the stairs, and into my room, closing the door behind me as my breath whooshes out. The enormity of my request is no more lost on me than on her. Basically, I've just asked her to stay in my life.

Jean.

My grandma.

Chapter 48

Niahm

"No need for so much subterfuge, Sam, I know what you're up to."

"Maybe I'm having fun," he says, kissing me before putting the bandana across my eyes. "I've never been part of a surprise party before."

I pull the bandana up so I can look at him. "Really? Never?"

"Don't feel bad for me," he says, tugging the blindfold back into place. "I've done and seen a lot of things most people never get to in their lifetime." When I open my mouth to say something, he lays a finger across my lips. "Not all of it has been bad," he chuckles.

"All right, let's get this over with," I grumble.

"At least pretend you're having a good time," he says, leading me to the truck. "Don't be a fun vortex."

"A fun *vortex*?" I ask, squeaking in surprise when he sweeps me up into his arms and plants me in the truck.

"A quagmire?" he asks before slamming the door closed. When he opens his door on the other side, I turn my head toward him—a waste of time since I can't see anything. "Black hole?" he says as I hear him climb up into the truck and close his own door behind him. I'm grinning, but refuse to give him an answer. "Quick sand? Vampire?"

I laugh at the last one. "How am I a vampire?"

"They suck the life out of everything, right?"

I punch in his general direction and completely miss. He laughs and pulls my hand into his, giving a little tug to encourage me to scoot closer, which I gladly do. The gesture brings to mind something I've been meaning to ask him.

"Hey, Sam, what's the deal with your hands?"

"What?" I can hear the confusion in his voice.

"The heat thing," I say, and feel him stiffen next to me. "It doesn't happen all the time, only sometimes. I just wondered what causes that, or do you even know?"

I can feel the rigidity in him, feel his hesitancy to answer.

"I'm not going to like the answer, am I?" I ask.

"Probably not," he says, voice strained.

"Then don't tell me yet." I can't see it, but I can sense his head turning my way. "I mean, I still want to know, I guess." That's a bit of an understatement. His absolute tension has me more curious than ever. "But let's wait until after the party. I don't want to suck any more fun from your night," I tease. He doesn't respond, other than a slight tightening of his hand on mine. My curiosity ratchets up to worry.

My party is the same as every other party thrown for everyone who's turned eighteen before me this school year, down to the recycled party decorations. It's fun anyway. All the seniors are there along with the juniors and sophomores as well. Stacy's mom baked the cake, and most everyone else brought something their moms made as well. It's sort of like the junior version of the after-church potlucks. We play music, dance, and laugh at the boys who suck the helium from the balloons and sing in chipmunk voices, and underneath it all is Sam's edginess, making it hard for me to concentrate on my friends.

Whatever the heat thing is, it's clear he doesn't want to tell me, but he will. He can't lie about it. And I'm suddenly not sure if I really want to know. I try to imagine what it can be, but have no idea where to take that imagining. What comes after immortality?

Finally, years later, or what feels like years, everyone leaves. No one has a curfew when we have an event like this, so it's 2 a.m. before we finally head back out to Sam's truck. Sam is reluctant to be alone with me if his body language is any indication.

We drive toward my home, but before we get there, he pulls off the side of the road down a small dirt path. He turns toward me and in the ambient light I can see the stress written in every line of his face. He *really* doesn't want to tell me.

"All right, spill," I try to tease, though my voice comes out wavering and nearly as tense as he is.

He takes my hand in his, and slides his thumb up and down across the back of my hand, watching the action. "You sure?" he asks.

"No," I answer honestly. When I don't say anything else he looks up at me and blows out a resigned breath.

"Most immortals develop a kind of . . . skill, I guess, after they become immortal."

"What kind of skill?" I ask, confused as to what this has to do with his hot hands.

"Depends. It's different with everyone. Usually an immortal begins to develop the skill before they become immortal; they just don't recognize it for what it is."

I think about his words. "You mean, like, flying or . . . or someone who can grant wishes?"

He smiles—it's a small smile, but a smile nonetheless. "I haven't met anyone who can fly *or* grant wishes. Which, by the way, is a strange place for your imagination to have gone. No genies among immortals."

I narrow my eyes at him.

"So what kinds of things are you talking about, then, since you're not exactly being forthcoming with information here."

"I've known immortals who are incredibly strong, or who can move things just by thinking about them. Some can start fire with their hands, or create ice. I knew one who could transport from place to place, but not through time. And some," he pauses, pushing his hand against mine until we are palm to palm, threading his fingers through mine, "some can read minds."

That strange heat begins, intense, and I decide he must be the fire creating guy.

"Nope, not fire," he says.

Guess it was easy to figure out what I was thinking.

"It's never easy to figure out what you're thinking, Niahm."

My eyes widen as realization hits. "You can read minds?" I ask.

"Yes . . . and no," he says. "What I can do is more being able to see what's in someone's mind. I can see everything a person has ever done, or thought, every conversation they've ever had. I can see what they're thinking." He glances at our hands again. "But only if I'm touching them. Particularly if I'm touching their hand."

I follow his gaze to our hands, my mind processing his words. If he can see what someone is thinking just by touching—I rip my hand from his, suddenly feeling very exposed.

"The heat?" I ask.

"I can always feel the heat, but usually the other person can't. I was surprised the first time you told me you felt it."

His words freeze me. The *first* time? I try to think back to the first time I felt the heat . . . at the movie, in the dark, the first time he held my hand.

"You can see everything? Know everything?"

"Yes, even things the person has forgotten."

"So every time you were holding my hand, every time I could feel that heat between our hands . . . you were . . ." I look up at him, betrayal saturating every pore in my body, "*spying* on me?"

"No, Niahm, I wasn't . . . well, perhaps I was. I didn't mean to hurt—"

I push away from him to the opposite side of the truck, horrified.

"You had no right." I push the words out, an angry whisper.

"Niahm, please, I—"

"No! No, Sam, you don't have an excuse for this one. This wasn't a lack of planning, or not thinking what a moments action might do to me like when you—" The vision of him turning the gun on himself rips through my mind and I shake my head, trying to clear it. "This was something you *planned* for, something you did continually, over and over, stealing my *privacy*. You didn't give me the chance to decide whether I wanted you to know something or not. You just *took* it."

He holds a hand toward me in supplication, misery on his face. I stare at his hand in horror. As if realizing what the gesture must mean to me, he drops his hand back to his side.

"Niahm," he says, despair heavy in his voice. Nothing more. Just my name.

"I wasn't sure, Sam, if I could deal with everything." I laugh sardonically. "But then, you already knew that, didn't you?"

He shakes his head mournfully.

"There isn't much I can tell you that you don't already know, is there? Except this: I will *never* forgive you for this, Sam. All this time, you've known exactly what to say, exactly what to do that would make me happy, make me love you, when you didn't deserve it. Trust is a pretty big issue with me—as I'm sure you know." I can't keep the mocking sarcasm from my words. Then again, I don't really care to. "You went into my head, without permission, and you took everything from me." I pull the handle, opening the door. "I have nothing else to give." I slide out of the truck, slamming the door behind me.

Sam shoves his own door open, right behind me as I stalk toward my house, my arms folded tightly against my chest, against the heartbreak that I can feel coming. He reaches out, putting his hand on my shoulder.

"Niahm, please, let me—"

I swing around on him, shoving his hand from me with all the fury flowing through me.

"Don't touch me," I growl, putting all the anger I can into my words. "Don't ever come near me again. You said you'd go away if I asked it. Go away, Sam. Go away and *never* come back."

I harden my heart against the pain on his face and turn away from him. He doesn't follow me this time as I hurry away.

Chapter 49

Niahm

Stacy rides to the city with us. She'd been planning to go anyway for some college interviews, was just waiting for her mom to have time to take her. I offered for her to ride with us. She promised to keep out of our hair for the weekend and let us have our "bonding time" as she called it. She was going to get a motel room even, but that was silly. Jean has a house there, with plenty of room for her to stay with us. Much safer, too.

Some of my joy in the trip has been taken by Sam's revelation. I haven't told Jean what happened. I'm sure she knows something is up, but she hasn't asked. I'm a little leery of her, wondering what *her* power is. Stacy just thinks that Sam and I broke up. I told her that he and Shane were going to be moving away from Goshen.

I'm furious with Sam, and that's the only thing holding me together. If I let go of that, I'm afraid I'll fall apart. So I'm holding it tightly. My mom always told me that anger shouldn't be a bedfellow, but I can't help it.

When we get to the house, Jean gives Stacy a key to her second car sitting in the small garage behind the house. Stacy has an appointment with counselors at a couple different colleges. Her phone has GPS, so Jean isn't too worried about her. We make plans to meet her later for dinner, over Stacy's protests that that hardly keeps her away from our weekend.

"Well," Jean says, "what do you want to do today?"

"Shop," I say immediately. In my agitated mood, I have a strong desire to spend money on myself. This trait I *know* I get from my mom.

"I know just the place," she grins.

We bundle up and she takes me to an open air mall that sprawls across three city blocks. We buy new clothes, shoes, and spring jackets. Then we stop in front of a day spa.

"Let's go in," I say. Jean shrugs and follows me through the tall glass doors. We decide to spoil ourselves and get both a manicure and a pedicure. As we're sitting in the massaging recliners with our feet soaking in the scented water, I look over to where there are a few women having their hair done. I look at Jean.

"You should get your hair done," I say.

She grimaces. "I don't think there's much they can do with this," she says without lifting her eyes from the magazine in her lap, lifting a frazzled gray portion of her hair and dropping it back to her shoulder.

"They can color it back to what it's supposed to be," I say.

Her gaze snaps to mine. Her eyes narrow slightly, as if trying to decipher the meaning behind my words.

"Why would I want to do that?" she asks slowly.

"Why wouldn't you?" I counter. "I mean, most women color their hair nowadays. How many grandmas actually have gray hair?"

She continues to watch me then finally shakes her head.

"No, I don't think that's a good idea. Everyone knows me with the gray hair. If I suddenly show up looking . . . well, younger, that might raise some suspicions."

"C'mon, no one will think anything. We came to the city to have fun, went to the spa, got our hair done. I'll get mine done also so it doesn't get too much notice." She still looks unsure, so I say, "Please. For me?"

She sighs, giving in. "Alright."

I grin.

Jean dyes her hair brown with lighter highlights at my urging, and I add highlights to mine. As the hairdresser's getting ready to trim my hair, Sam's face flashes before my eyes, my hand heating phantomlike. I decide to cut my hair off. Or maybe not quite off, but so that it resides just below my shoulders. Jean just raises her brows at my request, but says nothing.

When we're done, I look pretty much the same with shorter hair, but Jean looks amazing. I can definitely tell that she's my mom's mom, but it's not painful for me to look at her, her features just different enough. She's actually very beautiful.

Stacy meets us for dinner and oohs and ahs over our hair and nails. We all head back to the house, and Stacy heads immediately for her room to call her mom with news about her interviews. I go and sit by Jean on the couch where she's reading a book.

"Fun day," I say.

"It really was," she answers, putting her book down next to her. "Thank you, Niahm. I know I don't deserve to have such a fun day with you, but thank you, anyway."

My heart sinks at her words. She thought she had to walk away from her family to protect them from what she is, and has spent all this time living alone. When she finally does reconnect with a family member—me—she gets nothing but rejection and hatred. Tired of trying to maintain all my anger at her, I scoot closer and lean against her shoulder. She tenses for a moment, before relaxing, leaning her cheek against the top of my head.

"I'm sorry I've been so awful," I say.

"Niahm, you haven't—" She cuts herself off at my grunt. "You had a right to be," she says.

"No, I didn't. I can understand now why you felt you had to leave. I think in that same situation, *anyone* would do the same thing. But you came back. For me. And I've only made it hard for you. You're my family, all I've got left. I don't want you to go away again."

Jean's hand covers mine, and I can feel her shaking with emotion.

"Thank you," she whispers.

After a few minutes of silence in this position, I say, "Can I call you grandma?"

Jean laughs. "Honey, you can call me anything you want."

Her hand moves to caress my arm. Then, with reluctance in her voice, she says, "Stacy told me you and Sam . . . broke up?"

I turn my face toward her arm, not wanting her to ask me, but knowing that more than anyone, she'll understand what that means. I nod against her shoulder.

"What happened?" she asks.

I take a breath, hold it, then blow it out. "He told me he can read minds by holding someone's hand."

"What?" Jean sounds stunned. I sit up to see that she clearly didn't know. She's as surprised as I was when he told me.

"He said that he doesn't just read minds, he can see every memory a person has, know everything they've ever thought, or done."

"He's read your mind?" she asks, anger and sympathy warring in her tone.

"Yes."

She looks as if she wants to explode, seems to be searching for the words she wants to say as she looks around the room.

Then her eyes come to my face, and all the anger drains out of her.

"That's pretty rotten for him to do without your permission," she says without malice.

"Yeah, I know."

"You're angry at him?" she asks.

"Furious," I say, the word coming out sounding pathetically forlorn. I can feel the pain at the base of my throat fighting its way up.

"He loves you," she says, surprising me. I shake my head in denial. "He's caught in a strange place with you. He's bound to you, which forces him to need to protect you. But he also loves you, which makes you even more precious to him."

"You're defending him?" I should be affronted, but I only feel amazed by her defense.

"No." Her denial is immediate. "Yes, I suppose I am just a little." Her half-smile is apologetic. "I haven't ever been bound, but he and Shane explained it to me. It's not really an emotional thing, but more of a duty thing. An immortal might be upset when their bind dies, but it isn't the end of the world for them. What Sam feels for you goes beyond that. It *is* emotion for him." She reaches up and wipes my tears away. "His need to protect you and keep you safe goes deeper than anything he's ever known." She shrugs. "If I had that power, who knows, I might be tempted to use it on those I cared about as well if it meant the difference between keeping them safe or not."

"How does spying on my mind keep me safe?" I ask.

"I don't know," she answers honestly. "Maybe it's more for him, to make sure you're happy. But he might have a good reason. You should ask him."

"You're being pretty magnanimous toward him when you've only ever shown him dislike."

She puts her arm around my shoulder and pulls me against her side.

"I've changed my mind about them both. I think they're

good people who would go to any lengths to protect you. How can I dislike someone who would do that for my granddaughter?" She squeezes my shoulder. "You don't seem all that upset about this," she observes.

"I'm trying to stay angry so that I don't start screaming," I say. "Since I've known Sam, my life has been an emotional rollercoaster. I guess I'm just kind of tired from it all."

"Do you still love him? Even knowing what he did?" she asks. I have to think about her words. Immediately my mind says yes, of course I still love him. But there's so much more to the answer than that.

"I wouldn't ever be able to have secrets from him," I say.

"Secrets aren't all they're cracked up to be," she murmurs.

"I wouldn't have *privacy*," I say.

"Okay, that would suck," she says and I choke on a half-sob, half-laugh.

"Yeah," I agree. "And I don't know if I can trust him again. He lied to me for so long. He didn't ask if it was okay to take my memories. It was like he just swooped in like a buzzard and picked what he wanted without checking to see if it was his or not." She nods against the top of my head. "Staying with him would mean leaving Goshen eventually." I pause. "I can't have children with him," I whisper.

Jean kisses the top of my head as my tears begin anew. "I wish I could tell you what to do, Niahm, but this one has to be your own decision."

Yeah, I think, and that's what *really* sucks.

Chapter 50

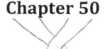

Niahm

We manage to talk Stacy into spending the next day with us. We go to a movie, but in a different theater than the one I went to with Sam all those months ago. I have no desire to walk into that place and those memories. We gorge ourselves on ice cream, and find a Farmer's Market in one of the city parks. As evening closes in, Stacy goes back to Jean's house, leaving us to go to dinner on our own.

Jean takes me to a Chinese restaurant that she says she went to quite often when she lived with her husband and daughter, like a "real" person she says. It's a bit of a dive, everything inside red and gold and covered with a light layer of dust.

"I don't think they've cleaned this place since I was here twenty-five years ago," Jean says. "But it's still the same owners, so the food should be good."

We order too much food, and Jean shows me how to use chopsticks, which I can't really master too well. I decide that must be the reason Asian people are always thin, and that if Americans could just start eating with chopsticks, we might all be thin as well.

The front door opens, the little bell over it announcing the arrival of new customers. Jean stiffens in alarm as she looks toward the door. I instinctively follow her gaze, and see two men standing there. They are dressed in casual suits. One is tall, with dark, slicked back hair, quite good looking, the scar that runs along his jawline adding to his looks rather than detracting. The other is shorter, a shock of silver hair on his head sticking out in deliberate spikes. There isn't anything particularly menacing about them.

I look back at Jean and see genuine alarm is evident in her expression. She's lowered herself in her chair a bit, her hand up next to her face as she brings some noodles to her mouth with her chopsticks. She's purportedly watching what she's doing, but it's clear she's watching them. A thrill of fear runs up my spine.

"What is it?" I ask. "Do you know them?"

"Who?" she asks, trying to feign innocence, but the fright in her voice is obvious.

"Je—I mean, Grandma, you know exactly who I'm talking about—those two guys who just came in."

She looks at me, and my fear ratchets up to terror to match her own.

"We have to get out of here, Niahm. Now."

"Okay, uh . . ." I turn back toward the door and see the hostess leading them to a booth not far from the door. *Crap*. I look around. "There has to be another exit somewhere." I lean toward her. "Who are they?"

She swallows, and as if afraid to say the word aloud, she mouths, *Sentinels*. I jerk in shock. *Those* are Sentinel's? I somehow imagined them to be hulking thugs with horns, scars, and missing teeth. Not a couple of average looking business men.

I gasp a couple of panicked breaths. *Okay, okay, the important thing is to get Jean out of the restaurant safely.* I look around again. A server comes through the swinging kitchen door and I get a glimpse of an emergency exit sign at the back of the kitchen.

"There," I say, pointing just above the table top. She glances behind herself, a look of confusion on her face. "An exit, at the back of the kitchen."

"I can hardly go traipsing through the kitchen," she whispers, her voice tight with tension. "And I'm not going to leave you."

I wave the server over.

"Hi," I say with a note of beseeching, lifting my eyebrows, silently asking for understanding. "Listen, one of my gr— friend's old boyfriends just came in. It was a really bad break-up, you know?" I watch her face change from polite interest to sympathy. "Do you think it would be possible for you to sneak us out through the kitchen?"

She's already shaking her head, "I ca—"

"Please?" I ask, handing her a hundred-dollar bill. "If she tries to go out the front and he sees her, it could get . . . ugly." I drop my voice menacingly on that last note and her eyes widen. She glances at Jean, then back to me and down at the money.

"Okay," she says. "I'll take her out that way, but I can't take both of you."

"No," Jean's denial is immediate.

"Gra—Jean," I say firmly, changing the word I almost called her, aware that it might seem a little strange for this young woman to be my grandma. "They don't know me. They have no idea who I am. I go up front, pay, and leave. They won't even look at me twice. I'll meet you at the car." She's shaking her head, but I don't acknowledge it.

"Go with her," I urge, pleading now. "Do you have our bill?"

I ask the server. She fishes it out of her pocket and hands it to me. "Thank you," I tell her sincerely. She nods and turns toward the kitchen. "*Go*," I say, squeezing Jean's hand, trying to look confident in the plan, which I am anything but.

"Be careful," she whispers.

"You, too," I say. "I'll stand up at the same time to block you. Don't look that way, just go."

She nods and we both stand. She follows the server, who is glancing nervously over her shoulder. I take a breath and turn toward the register at the front. I make my way over, trying to be casual, trying not to break and run as I'd like to. I have to wait a couple of minutes for the hostess to come up to take my money, minutes that feel like eternities as I force myself not to look their way, not matter how much I want to.

Finally, the woman comes over and takes the bill from me.

"Excuse me," a masculine voice says. I glance over my shoulder and see the scarred Sentinel right next to me. My heart stops dead even as blood rushes to my head, filling my ears with a whooshing sound. "Can I get a menu?"

"Sure," the woman says, pulling one from the slot on the side of her desk. "You change your mind?"

"My friend is rethinking his choice," he says, smiling at her. He glances quickly at me, a polite stranger's glance to include me in their exchange. My blood turns to ice. I quickly look away.

He takes the menu and returns to his table as she takes my money. I've given her way too much, but say, "Please give the change to our server for her tip." The hostess raises her eyebrows a little at the gesture, but I need to go now before I make some stupid mistake.

I move to the door, and as I'm stepping out, I glance behind me. The man is watching me. His look could easily be interpreted as benign, but I don't know that for certain. I step through the door, forcing myself not to rush to the parking lot which is on the side of the building. The car is already running and I breathe a sigh of relief. I open the passenger door and slide in.

"Let's go," I say, glancing over—at Sam. "What are you doing here?" I demand angrily.

"I called him," Jean says from the backseat. I look at her, see that though she's still worried, she's slightly more relaxed. I know I should be grateful she made it out okay, but I'm furious. I turn my gaze back to Sam.

"What, you have some kind of transporting power also that you forgot to tell me about?"

"He was already here," Jean says. "Please, let's go."

Sam continues to watch me for a few seconds before putting on a baseball cap and shifting the car into gear.

"Get down, Jean," he says, and she lays herself flat on the back seat. As we pull around the building, I see the two men exiting the restaurant. They look at us, Scars eyes meeting mine. He acts casual, but it seems as forced as when I was doing it. Sam also looks over at them, though he looks quickly away, as if dismissing them as casual strangers.

"This isn't right," I say.

"What do you mean?" Sam asks.

"They shouldn't be leaving the restaurant yet. They haven't been there long enough to eat."

"Take out?" Sam questions.

"I don't know. Maybe. But I kind of doubt it since they were seated at a booth."

"Okay, well, let's just remain calm, not panic yet," he says, glancing in the rearview mirror.

We drive in tense silence for a few minutes.

"Why are you here?" I ask.

Sam's jaw clenches, as if he's fighting answering.

"I followed you," he finally says.

I huff out an affronted breath, but before I can say anything, Jean says, "I asked them to come."

"*Them*?" I say.

"Shane is here also," Sam says.

"Niahm, I knew there could be some danger in coming

here," Jean says.

"Why didn't you tell me?" I ask, turning toward the backseat where she's still lying, though now propped up on one elbow.

"Are you kidding?" she laughs. "I wasn't about to pass this trip up. I just thought it wouldn't hurt to have a little backup."

"But you knew that Sam and I were—" I stop, not quite sure how to finish.

"Yeah, but I didn't know why."

"Even if she hadn't called, I still would have followed," Sam says.

Before I can respond, Jean says, "I was hoping you wouldn't have to know they were here."

Her words bring back to mind our current situation, and I glance behind us.

"Yeah, they're back there," Sam confirms. He pulls his cell phone out and punches a single number. "Shane, I think they're following us."

He's silent for a moment, then hands the phone to me. I stare at it blankly.

"Just hold it for a sec," he says distractedly. "We're going to see if they keep following us. See that black SUV a few cars back?" I look back and see it. I nod. "Keep an eye on it and tell me if it follows us."

He makes a sudden right turn, without any warning. The SUV, being some space back, has more time to make the turn without it seeming so abrupt.

"Still behind us," I say.

Sam takes another left then right again. I watch the SUV follow, fear crawling up my spine.

Sam grits something out beneath his breath that sounds garbled and foreign. He gives up trying to appear casual and speeds up. "You're going to have to tell Shane where we are, tell him every time we turn and what street we're turning on."

It takes me a few seconds to realize where we are. "Hello?" I say hesitantly as I bring the phone up to my ear.

"What are your coordinates?" Shane demands.

"Uh . . ." I look out the window, trying to spy the street signs. "We're on 4800 west," I say. "We're just going through the intersection of Fredondo Avenue."

"Which direction?" Shane's abrupt question deflates my pride in telling him where we are.

"I don't know." I turn to Sam. "What direction are we going?" I ask him.

"North."

I repeat the information to Shane, and suddenly Jean sits up and takes the phone from me. "Hey!" I exclaim.

"I know the area well," she says. "I can give him a more accurate idea of where we are."

"Aren't you supposed to be hiding?" I ask.

"I think it's a little late for that now, don't you?" Her gaze is unwavering and full of fear. I open my mouth, but she says, "Don't argue with me, Niahm. Let's get safe first and then you can lecture me all you want." I swallow over the lump lodged in my throat and nod.

Sam says some more of the strange words more vehemently. The SUV closes on us. Jean shouts speaking directions into the phone. Unthinkingly, I reach out to Sam who is gripping the steering wheel with both hands. His eyes scan my face. His intense worry for me is deeper than any emotion directed toward me, including from my own parents.

"Hold on," he says, turning his attention back to the road. He stomps the gas pedal and we jump ahead. The SUV doesn't hesitate to follow suit. We rocket around other cars on the road, then through a red light, brakes squealing as another car avoids hitting us. The SUV weaves around the stopped car in the intersection. Reality has been suspended and I've been thrown into a stereotypical action movie.

"They have guns," Jean warns frantically as we swerve around another corner near an industrial area, away from traffic. The buildings are large and flat, empty this time of day. A loud pop sounds, and suddenly our own car is fishtailing out of control. Sam frantically pulls at the steering wheel, trying to retain control. The car is leaning unnaturally to the side. Time slows for me to watch my own destruction and that of the two people I love most. The car flips up onto its side, sliding along the pavement, sparks flying. Sam grips my hand in his. I grasp his desperately, realizing that the screaming I can hear is my own.

A loud, grinding metal sound drowns out my voice as I realize we are now upside down. I have time to gasp out one word before my world goes black.

"Sam."

Chapter 51

Sam

The car finally stops its movement when it slams into the side of one of the buildings. Before it stops I'm unbuckling my seat belt. With an *oof* I drop to the ceiling of the car. Niahm's eyes are closed and she's not screaming anymore. I fumble with the buckle holding her suspended, catching her as she falls. In the back, Jean is moaning. She hadn't been buckled in and so her fall had been a bit more painful than mine.

"Jean, move," I command. She nods and crawls toward the shattered windshield. The SUV has screeched to a stop. We have seconds at most. I slide out the opening, ignoring the pain from the tears in my skin caused by the twisted metal of the windshield frame, trying to protect Niahm's fragile skin. Once through, I reach behind and pull Jean out. She's still sluggish, but recovering.

With Niahm in arms, I run toward the nearest warehouse,

Jean on my heels. I pull the gun from my pocket and shoot at the nearest glass door which explodes inward. I continue past the door as Jean shoots me a questioning look, but I don't have time to explain. We round the corner of the building, not slowing.

Behind the warehouse are some large storage sheds. I run behind them and slip between the building and the sheds. In my arms, Niahm moans, rousing. I stop and turn back toward Jean who hurries forward to touch her granddaughter.

"Niahm, sweetie, are you okay?" she whispers as she brushes her hands down Niahm's cheeks.

"What . . . where . . ." Niahm's eyes finally focus on me, and then Jean. I watch as memory rushes through her mind and she looks around. "Where are we?" Her voice is too loud in the silence, and Jean immediately lays a hand across her lips.

"Shh," she hisses at Niahm. Niahm silences.

"We're behind some sheds, but the Sentinels are behind us," I whisper. "We need to find a place to hide until it's safe to escape."

"Okay, put me down," she whispers back, more calmly than I would have expected. I let her legs down but retain my hold on her until I'm sure she has her balance. Jean gives her a quick hug as she pulls away from me, and I'm insanely jealous that I can't follow suit.

"We need to hurry," I say more harshly than needed. "Follow me."

I continue down the small alley in front of Niahm, Jean behind. We don't need to speak to know that this is the best way to keep her alive. We come to a gap between two of the sheds and I peer around the corner. No movement, so I follow this new path. When we get to the front of the sheds, I look around the corner. I can't see the Sentinels but I can hear them. I reach behind me and take Niahm's hand which she immediately rips from my grasp. I cringe but don't look back at her.

Across the lot there is another warehouse with a metal

door on the side for entrance that is only held closed with a padlock. To my right is a pile of rebar. I send a silent prayer of thanks to the sky and turn toward Niahm and Jean.

"I'm going to grab one of those rebar and see if I can open that door," I say, pointing. Niahm immediately begins shaking her head frantically.

"No, Sam. You'll be out in the open, they'll see you."

I brush a thumb across her jaw, gone before she can react. "We're sitting ducks here. If we can get inside we have a chance." I look at Jean.

"Go, Sam. I've got her," she says, wrapping her arms around Niahm. I give Niahm on last look, trying to convey my concern for her before I slip stealthily around the corner. Staying tight against the front of the sheds, I manage to reach the rebar without incident. As I lean down to pick one up, I hear movement behind me and dart behind a forklift.

"They're here somewhere," I hear a man's voice say, low. They aren't near me, but I hear them clearly.

"I'm aware of that," another answers impatiently. "How long before police show to investigate the accident?"

"Doesn't matter," says the first. "We're concerned citizens who saw it happen, and stopped when we saw the driver and her passenger run away."

"Who's the girl?" the second asks and my gut clenches in anger and alarm for Niahm.

"I don't know, but Jory's on it. He'll get the tapes if they have any."

I throw another prayer heavenward that the restaurant doesn't have any kind of security cameras for *Jory* to look at. Even if they don't, they'll find something somewhere else. Niahm's life is now in danger.

A beep sounds, and the two men turn back toward the first warehouse whose door I shot out. They begin running, and I take the opportunity to move. I pick up one of the metal rods and hurry toward the warehouse. It doesn't take long to pop the lock off. I've had a bit of practice. I run back to where

Niahm and Jean wait and once again we sandwich Niahm as we run toward the warehouse.

Once inside we bypass the offices and enter the area in the back which is piled high with large wooden crates. We hurry down between them ducking between two high stacks.

"Do you have the phone?" I ask Jean. She pulls it from her pocket and I give her a kiss on the forehead. I quickly punch in some numbers and wait while they send. After thirty seconds, it vibrates and I get the confirmation I was looking for. "Shane's on his way with the van," I say and Jean grins at me.

"What van?" Niahm asks, confused.

"Bullet-proof," I say. Niahm blanches. I curse myself once again for my thoughtlessness. "It's what will get us all out of here alive," I say.

Yelling and the metal door slamming open let us know the Sentinels have arrived. Jean and I both grab one of Niahm's hands and we begin moving again, quickly but quietly. This time Niahm doesn't pull her hand from mine. We wind down between the crates, watching and listening for the Sentinels. But they are now being stealthy themselves, no doubt aware that they have us trapped. As we round another crate, I stop. We've reached the back corner of the building with nowhere to go. Instinctively, we turn back but a nearby footfall stops us. I push Niahm behind me into the corner, taking a stance in front of her with Jean helping to complete the wall. After a few tense moments the footsteps move further away.

Suddenly, Jean grasps my hand. I look at her and she is staring at me intently. Immediately understanding, I open my mind.

Can you hear me?

I nod.

We aren't going to be able to get out when Shane comes, not from where we are. You know that, right?

I think about arguing, but finally nod. Behind her clear thoughts she's sending my way, I'm seeing everything else that resides in Jeans mind, her childhood with a cruel father, her loveless marriage and feelings of worthlessness, the despair that drove her actions.

I'm going to distract them so you can get her out of here.
No!

Her eyes widen. *So you can project thoughts as well?*

I nod, jaw clenched.

She has a better chance with you. You know that. I'll do everything I can to get away.

I shake my head. *She'll never forgive either of us.*

Jean's mouth quivers a bit as she nods, acknowledging my words. Abruptly, she turns toward Niahm and pulls her into her arms. Niahm fearfully clings to her. Jeans hand shoots out and I grasp it tightly.

Tell her, she thinks frantically, *tell her this was my idea. You have to take her away, Sam, keep her safe. They'll figure out who she is.*

I nod.

In six months I'll be here. She sends a picture into my mind of Bryce Canyon, at Rainbow Point. I know it; I've been there. *I'll go every six months until you have the chance to come.*

I'll be there, I send to her.

Only when it's safe, she admonishes. *I know you love her.* I nod fervently. *I'm counting on that, Sam. I'm counting on you. Make her understand and keep her safe.* The last three words are thrown at me, as if she's thinking them as separate words with an exclamation point after each.

I will, Jean. And . . . thank you.

She nods again, letting go of my hand to wrap both arms tightly around Niahm. Then she releases her and begins to move away. Niahm grabs her arm, alarm on her face. Jean looks back at her with a small smile. She takes Niahm's face between her palms and then leans forward to kiss each cheek. She whispers something in Niahm's ear, and though Niahm still looks terrified, she nods.

Jean moves quietly away, peering around the corner before moving out of sight. Niahm and I listen quietly. Tension thrums through my blood. After a few stress-filled minutes pass with nothing, Niahm grasps my hand tightly. I keep my mind closed, but I don't have to open it to know how frightened she is. Not for the first time I wish I could go back in time and not enter her life so that she wouldn't now be in this predicament.

Then, the metal door slams loudly. Niahm jumps and the tiniest squeak escapes her. Two sets of footsteps run in the direction of the sound as one of them curses. They noisily slam through the door themselves. I don't waste time. Keeping hold of Niahm's hand I pull her toward the front of the stack. I look around the corner and don't see or hear anything. I put a finger to my lips to remind her of the need for silence and she nods, eyes wide. We hurry along the front of the crates toward the front office, bypassing the metal door which has swung back to rest within inches of being closed.

We move into the front office area and toward the front door as I punch a couple more numbers into the phone. The front door is glass, but the office is dark. I urge Niahm into a crouch as we near the door. Then I see it—the van screeching into the parking lot, not even making an attempt at stealth. Shane brakes and turns the wheel, forcing the van into a squealing circle in front of the office. The sliding back door of the van gapes open and I wrap an arm around Niahm's waist as I push the bar which allows me to shove the door open. An alarm immediately sounds.

Niahm pulls against my grip for just one second, clearly intending to not leave without her grandma. In that second, a shot rings out as I unceremoniously toss her into the van, following closely and shoving the door closed behind me even as Shane stomps down hard on the gas pedal, sending Niahm and I tumbling toward the back of the van.

As I right myself, I look to see Niahm still crumpled in the corner. I quickly crawl toward her, knocked back a bit as Shane sharply corners the van, the feeling of two wheels not quite making contact with the asphalt clear.

"Niahm, are you okay?" I ask as I finally get to her side.

"Jean," she moans.

"She'll be fine. They won't stick around with the alarm going off. When she's safe, she'll find us," I say. Niahm nods sluggishly at my words. "Did you hit your head?" I ask with concern. She isn't responding as she should be.

"Get Stacy," she says, her words garbled and slow.

"Shane," I call to the front of the van.

"Got her," he says back. Stacy peeks around the front passenger seat, pale, lips pulled tight. She glances at Shane.

"Just sit tight a few more minutes," he says in answer to her unspoken words. ""We'll be in the clear soon, and then you can have your reunion."

Stacy narrows her eyes slightly at him, though the gesture is rather unthreatening in her fear-filled face. She doesn't unbuckle or try to come back though.

I turn back to Niahm who is lying with her eyes closed. "Niahm?" I ask. No response. I'm worried about a possible head injury between the way I threw her in and the tumble she took as Shane sped off. I reach down and slowly, gently probe her skull. I can't feel anything obvious, so I do the thing I know will infuriate her. I take her hand and listen.

All I see are confused images overlapping one another. Images of Jean, Stacy, and myself rotate and merge. Then I see it . . . *feel* it really. "No," I mutter, pulling her up from the floor of the van, pushing my hands frantically against her back. Sticky wetness greets me. I don't need to pull my hands up to know it's blood, but I do anyway. My hand is covered.

"No, no, no," I moan, pulling her limp form into my arms.

"Samuel?" Shane questions as Stacy's gaze comes back around.

"Shane, you've got to get us to a hospital. *Now*." I'm pleading with him, pleading more desperately than I ever have before. "Niahm's been shot."

Chapter 52

Sam

We can't do that," Shane says calmly as Stacy, who managed to unbuckle herself and move into the back of the van in one fluid motion turns back to him with a horrified, "*What*?" Perhaps it's a good thing she's not within striking distance of him, because I think she might have belted him if she were closer.

"If we take her to a hospital, she's dead," Shane replies.

Stacy swings frantic eyes back to me. I know he's right, because I've seen it. Without help, she's dead anyway.

"Sam!" Stacy exclaims, the single word demanding and pleading all at once.

"*Mac an donais*[1]!" I mutter. "He's right," I admit miserably.

"What do you mean?" she practically screeches, leaning

---

[1] Gaelig curse

down near Niahm and soothing her hands across her hair.

"Those men . . ." I begin.

"What about them? What do they want, Sam? Why are they after Niahm?"

I pull Niahm up into my arms, tight against my chest.

"They don't want Niahm," Shane says from the front. "They were after Jean. And now us."

"Then go to the hospital," she demands, confusion lacing her voice. "I'll take her and you guys can get away."

"Too late," I moan, rocking Niahm as her breathing becomes labored.

"They know her now," Shane says. "Her life is in danger. And yours if they see you with us. We have to get you to a safe place where we can let you off. We'll give you money to get home."

"No way," Stacy says firmly, her eyes locked on Niahm. "I'm not leaving her."

"Shane, please," I say, not knowing how else to express what I need.

"I know, Samuel," he answers. "Okay, I'll find somewhere safe where I can look at her."

"Why in the world would that help?" Stacy asks. Before he can answer she leans toward Niahm. "Sam, she's not breathing right," she gasps. "She's going to die if we don't help her."

"I don't think they've followed us," Shane says, turning to glance at us quickly. His eyes drop to Niahm before returning to the road. "I don't have my equipment, Sam."

"Anything," I say. "Anywhere."

He nods. He knows what I'm asking. A few long, eternal minutes later, after several turns, he stops the van. He climbs into the back of the van and pushes me out of the way. I move, but retain hold of her hand. The images are fading, becoming more discombobulated and obscure. He turns on the overhead light. Stacy whimpers when she sees the blood covering the floor. I'm not altogether sure that I don't join her.

"Samuel. Sam!" Shane says when I don't look up at him the

first time. "This is a clinic," he says. "You know what to do."

Stacy turns questioning eyes on me. I move as quickly as I can to the sliding door. When I open the door, I'm facing a rundown clinic, windows barred, graffiti, dirt, and oil smudging the sides of the building.

"Sam, wait," Stacy calls worriedly. I step out, slamming the door behind me. I look around for a weapon, not to defend myself but to slow anyone who would try to stop me. A rusted hammer lies on the ground beneath the barred windows and I scoop it up. At the front of the clinic, the metal door is locked tight, a doorbell and camera facing me. I press the doorbell several times.

"What do you need?" A tough-sounding female voice crackles out of the ancient door speaker.

"I need help," I say, trying not to sound threatening.

"Hold your hands up and turn in a circle," the voice commands. "Lift the back of your shirt so I can see your pockets, pull your front pockets inside out, lift your pant legs so I can see your socks."

I drop the hammer and do as she says, trying not to look and sound rushed. The last thing I want to do is panic and blow my only chance of getting inside. Once I've followed her instructions, my mind ticking down the amount of time that is passing, she asks, "What's wrong?"

"Shot," I say.

"We don't have no narcotics here."

"I don't want any," I answer.

Long seconds pass before I hear the multiple bolts being opened from the inside. A burly man opens the door and holds a gun on me. He looks me up and down, the blood on my clothes obviously convincing him of my claim. He waves me in.

"Back here," the tough voice calls, waving me to the hallway next to her. She doesn't look as tough as she sounds, standing maybe five-four, rounded body, hair pulled up into a black bun, ebony skin gleaming in the florescent light. The look on her face would be convincing enough, though. The clinic is in dire need of paint, flooring, and new chairs. But it's clean. I hurry back and she waves me into a room.

"Where you shot, honey?" she asks, her words at odd with her tone.

"I'm not," I say, and she opens her mouth to call for the guard. "Please," I beg, holding my hands up toward her. "I don't want drugs, either. My . . . *friend*, she's outside in the van. She's been shot. Shane can help her, but he needs equipment. Please, she'll die. I have money."

She looks skeptical, and I reach into my back pocket, a look of threat and worry crossing her expression. I hold one hand up in supplication, and pull my wallet out. I pull out all the money within and drop it on the exam table. Her eyes widen. She looks at the impressive pile of money before turning suspicious eyes on me.

"*Please*," I beg. "Please don't let her die." I don't add that *I* won't let her die, even if it means hurting her and the burly guy to get what I need.

"Bring her in," she says.

"No, we can't, we need to—"

"Bring her in," she repeats firmly, overriding my words. I stare at her, but decide it's not worth the fight. I nod. She steps to the door and commands the burly guy to go out to the van to get them. I call Shane and tell him what's going on.

"Who's Shane?" she asks as soon as I hang up.

"My uncle," I say. "He has some medical training."

"Uh-huh," she answers, clearly not believing me. "My name is Mary."

"Sam," I say, then hear the commotion of Shane entering the clinic. I hurry from the room and see him carrying Niahm in, her face more pale than I've seen it. He's followed closely behind by Stacy who looks terrified and worried in equal measure.

"Good heavens. Get that child in here quickly," Mary says as she sees Niahm's still form in Shane's arms. Shane carries her into the exam room and lays her on the bed. He starts spouting off supplies he needs, and Mary seems to recognize his knowledge. She doesn't question, simply hurries to get what he needs.

Shane pulls Niahm's shirt up, exposing the hole where the bullet exited on the front lower quadrant of her abdomen, cursing under his breath. Stacy moans and moves to sit in the chair in the corner of the room.

The clinic is poorly equipped, an old EKG machine providing the information that her heart beats. A loud beeping begins as Shane probes within, looking for any bleeding that needs to be stopped. I step forward in alarm. Shane sticks a stethoscope against her chest as Mary pulls out a mask and Ambu bag and begins forcing air into Niahm's lungs. Shane begins pushing on her chest. My own chest tightens in response. I hurry to stand near her head.

"Breath, Niahm, breath," I plead. "Don't leave me now, please, don't leave." I continue saying this over and over as Shane and Mary fight for her life. Finally they both stop, and I look at Shane with terror spiking throughout.

"She's breathing," he says. I release the breath I didn't know I was holding.

"This girl needs a hospital," Mary says.

"No," Shane and Stacy say at the same time. Mary's brows raise suspiciously.

"There are some bad men after us," Stacy says urgently. "If they find her, they'll finish what they started."

I decide Shane must have given Stacy a little history while they waited for me. For Mary's part, I doubt it's a strange story in this world she lives in. She shakes her head and hands Shane some sterile gloves.

"Let's get her sewed up, then," she says. "Otherwise, this little girl is going to bleed to death."

✳ ✳ ✳ ✳ ✳

It's over an hour later by the time Shane snips the final suture. Mary has placed an oxygen mask on Niahm, checking the printout on the EKG machine occasionally. Blood and IV solution drip slowly into her arm. Mary turns to the sink and wets a washcloth, and begins cleaning the blood from Niahm. There's so much of it—too much.

Mary glances at her watch. "Well, the clinic is closed for the night. Normally I'd kick y'all out, but I suppose with this little deposit," she pats her pocket which holds the money I'd dumped on the table, "I suppose you're trustworthy enough."

"Thanks, Mary, you're a gem," Shane tells her, kissing her cheek, causing the tough Mary to blush. She waves a dismissive hand at him and pulls her jacket on.

"You're gonna want to lock the door behind us," she says. "I suppose you'll still be here in the morning."

"If we can move her, we'll go," Shane says. Mary nods as if she'd been expecting that answer.

"Call this number," she hands a card to Shane. "Joran is the night watchman who comes by to check the place. I'll let him know you're here, and that you'll call if you're leaving. He can come lock up."

"Thank you, Mary. You've been amazing." Shane squeezes her upper arm.

"You wanna come work here?" she asks, only half-teasing him. "We always need anyone with any kind of medical expertise."

"I'd consider it just for you," he says.

"Sure you would," she laughs, following the burly man out the door. I hear Shane lock the door before coming back to where Stacy and I stand over Niahm. I have no doubt Stacy is willing her to live as hard as I am.

"We should try to get some sleep," Shane says. Both Stacy and I give him a look which he interprets easily enough. "Fine, I'll get some sleep while you watch over her. All we can do now is wait." He pauses. "She's lost a lot of blood. I didn't see much internal bleeding, but without the proper equipment, I can't say for certain."

He crosses the narrow hallway into another room and I

hear the gurney creak as he lies down on it. I turn my gaze to Stacy, who is pale and drawn.

"Stacy, you should try to sleep," I say gently.

"What about you?" she shoots back.

"I don't need much sleep," I say honestly. "Shane doesn't either. He'll be back in here within the hour. We can watch her."

Stacy shakes her head. "I'm not going anywhere, Sam. I would like some answers, though. For example, where is Jean? Why isn't she with you guys?"

I look down at Niahm's inert form, washed out and bloodless, her chest barely rising and falling. I'm not sure how much she can hear, so I don't want to say anything that might interfere with her recovery.

"She created a distraction so Niahm could escape," I say.

"What kind of distraction?" she presses.

"She's fine, I'm sure," I say. I think if they had her they wouldn't have kept pursuing us." It's a blatant lie, but I can't say what I really believe, that she couldn't have possibly escaped.

"Why were they after her?" Stacy asks.

"Old enemies, I guess," I say.

"So, we're all enemies by association?"

"Yeah, I guess you could say that." I know the answers I'm giving her are incomplete, but I don't have good explanations for her without the full truth. "They haven't seen you though, so you should be safe."

"But, why would they—" Her words are cut off by the high pitched alarm of the ancient EKG machine going off. Both our eyes fly to Niahm.

"Niahm!" I shout, searching out her pulse even as Shane comes flying into the room. He puts the stethoscope in his ears and curses loudly. He rips the oxygen mask from her face, replacing it with the Ambu bag.

"Squeeze this every five seconds or so," he directs me. He begins chest compressions. Stacy pushes back against the wall, horror on her face. She looks how I feel.

"Niahm, don't do this," I command roughly. "You've gotta hold on. Please. Don't leave me." The last words are whispered.

"Stacy, roll that cart over here," Shane yells. Stacy immediately does as she's told, rolling the red cart that, ill equipped as it is, holds the keys to bringing Niahm back. "You're going to need to take over for Sam," he says. "Samuel, get over here and do chest compressions."

Stacy takes the bag, calm now. I hurry over and begin pressing down on Niahm's chest, cringing with each compression, feeling the hairline cracks in her ribs at my touch on her bare skin. Tears run freely down my face and I don't care. Shane fills a syringe and plunges it into the IV line. Nothing. He grabs the paddles and yells, "Clear!" as he shocks her. Nothing. He repeats everything he knows, jaw clenched as each new procedure yields no results in the flat line printing out of the machine.

"Stop!" Stacy screams. I look at her, see that her own face is covered with tears. "Don't do anything else to her. *Please.*"

"No," I yell, refusing to stop now—or ever.

"Samuel," Shane says. "There's nothing left." He reaches out to touch my shoulder. I shove him with both fists, sending him flying across the room, crashing into a mobile shelving unit before turning back to Niahm. Stacy is backing away, eyes glued to Niahm's face.

"Keep going," I shout at her, but she ignores me. With a curse, I lean down to blow air into Niahm's lungs. Then Shane is leaping at me, tackling me to the floor, Stacy screaming. I fight with all I have, but he manages to restrain me.

"She's gone, Samuel. There is *nothing* left."

"No." This time it comes out as little more than a wailing moan, and I have a glimpse of what it must have been like for Niahm, thinking I was dead on the floor of the motel room. Suddenly, Stacy is in my arms, and with Shane holding both of us, we allow our grief to explode in the room.

Chapter 53

Sam

"Samuel." Shane's voice penetrates the horror filled fog I'm hiding in. "Samuel, there's still a chance." I try to decipher his words. Still a chance to what?

"Samuel." I look up at him. He pulls me away from Stacy and into a standing position. Stacy watches us from her supine position, sobs hiccupping from her. "There's still a *chance*," he repeats with an eye flick toward Niahm. I look at her myself, forcing my eyes to go to her still form.

Stacy seems to comprehend his meaning before me as she pushes herself up. "What do you mean, Shane? You mean there's still a chance for her to live? What? *How*?"

Suddenly his meaning comes clear, and I gasp in a breath as I go to Niahm.

"What are you talking about?" Stacy demands loudly. "Tell me!"

Shane looks at Stacy, then moves to the opposite side of Niahm. I take her hand in mine, searching desperately for *anything*. All I see is blackness. Stacy shakes my arm.

"Sam! What is he talking about? Are you some kind of . . . vampire, or something?" That gets my attention and I look at her. There is fear and disbelief in her eyes, but also hope. "If you are, Sam, and you can . . . I don't know, bite her or whatever to save her, then do it."

"I'm not a vampire," I say.

"Then what?" Her voice brooks no refusal to answer.

"We can't die," Shane says. Stacy's gaze flies to Shane.

"Why?" I think it's an odd question. She should have been asking *what?* in disbelief.

Shane shakes his head. "We don't know, really. There isn't any magic trick, or—"

"Then why do you say there's a chance? Can you give her something?"

Shane shakes his head again. "No. If she's immortal, she'll wake on her own."

"If she's . . ." Now Stacy's voice reveals her skepticism. "Why would you even think she's . . . you know, what you said."

"Her eyes," I answer. Stacy's gaze returns to me, and I swipe the contacts from my eyes. She gasps as she sees my eyes that are so like Niahm's.

"Yours, too?" she asks Shane.

"Yes. And . . . and Jean's as well."

"Her *grandma*?" Stacy's shocked. "Jean is . . . um, she can't die either?"

I nod. She looks at Niahm.

"So, what do we need to do? How do we save her?" She's all business.

"We can't do anything but wait," I say.

"We need to get out of here," Shane says.

"How long?" Stacy asks.

"It can take as long as three days."

"*Three days*?" Stacy looks at me again. "Did she know? About you, I mean?"

I nod. "I showed her."

"You showed . . . wait, let me guess, this would be about a couple weeks ago when she spent the night crying and wouldn't tell me why?" I nod and she says, "So is that why she broke up with you?"

"No," I admit. "Something else."

"Something you're not going to tell me."

"No," I say. "Not now. Now we need to get her out of here. We need to go somewhere safe while we wait."

Shane drops another pile of money in the drawer with a note for Mary to replace the supplies we used, apologizing for leaving such a mess, and instructions that they need to update some of their equipment, which he will arrange to have sent as soon as he can. He goes out and pulls the van around to the front door after calling Joran to let him know we're leaving.

I carry Niahm's limp form out and place her in the back of the van on a blanket. I sit next to her, pulling her head into my lap, her hand clasped firmly in mine, looking for any flicker of awareness. I'm exhausted in a way I haven't been for centuries. I want to hope, try to keep my faith alive, but it's near impossible. Her rims were still too wide. Even if she were immortal, it's probable that she died too soon. Despair threatens to overwhelm me.

I can feel Stacy's eyes on me, watching me and Niahm in equal turn. Shane is driving, too far away to be included in her scrutiny. I can feel that she wants to ask questions, but her concentration on willing Niahm alive is nearly as intense as mine.

Three hours later Shane pulls into the lot of the motel outside of Goshen. He's taken a roundabout way getting here to be certain we weren't being followed. He opens the door to the very room I'd taken Niahm to, waits for us to enter, then moves the van to hide within the rundown shed behind the motel.

He returns and locks the door, setting the alarms which will inform us of anyone coming near the premises. He closes the metal shades that will hide the light from the outside world.

"Stacy," he says, turning to Niahm's friend who holds her hand tightly across from me. "If Niahm . . . well, if Niahm wakes, I think it would be better if . . ." I'm surprised at how Shane stumbles over his words. He's always calm in an emergency. He moves to the closet and pulls out a sweatshirt and sweatpants. "There are washcloths and towels in the bathroom."

Stacy understands his intention. "Yes, okay, but you two leave."

I consider arguing. I don't want to leave her, not for one second.

"Go, Sam," she says. "Give her this dignity."

I can't argue with those words, so I follow Shane to the connecting door between this room and the next. Shane forces me to shower, arguing that it won't do Niahm any good to see me covered in blood either. It seems pointless to me. She isn't going to wake. Not now. Not ever.

The shower gives me a place to fall apart, though, without the eyes of Shane and Stacy on me. This is my fault, all of it. If I had never come into Niahm's life, she wouldn't be in this predicament now. She wouldn't have been locked in a room with what she thought was my corpse, she wouldn't have known that her every secret had been exposed to someone. She wouldn't now be lying in the next room, dead.

When the water runs cold for long enough to penetrate my numbness, I step out and dry off. Shane has placed a clean pair of jean and a t-shirt for me on the counter. I quickly dress and walk out.

"Left me a cold shower?" Shane asks. I don't answer. He walks past me and lays a hand on my shoulder. "Samuel, don't give up. Just try to retain some hope, because there is hope yet."

I nod though I completely disagree with him. He disappears

into the bathroom. I look at the door connecting the rooms, wanting to go over, hold her hand, search more. I stand and grasp the handle between the rooms, but don't turn the knob. I simply stand with my hand on the knob. When it turns beneath my hand, I step back. Stacy opens the door and waves me in.

Niahm is as motionless as before, though now she is clean, dressed, and her hair has been brushed. It feels far too much like preparing a body for a wake—something I've done many times in my life. I lay down on the bed next to her, pulling her hand into mine. Nothing.

Stacy lays down on the other side and takes Niahm's other hand. She's staring at Niahm face as I am, but her eyes lift to me.

"Is she going to live, Sam?" she whispers.

"I don't think so," I tell her honestly. Tear well up in Stacy's eyes, but she blinks them back. "I'm so sorry for this."

"For what?" she asks.

"It's my fault she's here," I admit wretchedly.

She props herself on one elbow. "How do you figure?"

"If I had never come into her life . . ."

"If you had never come into her life, she'd still have gone to the city with her grandma."

"She only went because she was so angry with me."

"No, Sam. Niahm made that decision based on a desire to get closer to Jean. She would have gone anyway, but she wouldn't have had you and Shane there."

"They shot at *me*," I argue.

"You got her out of that warehouse, right? While Jean distracted them. She would never have gotten out otherwise. And if they had found her, they would have made sure she was dead."

I narrow my eyes at her. "How do you know all this?"

"Shane gave me a rundown while you were in the shower."

I close my eyes. Whatever she says, I know it's my fault.

"The sun's coming up," she says. I open my eyes and see

that she's right, the room is beginning to lighten. I enclose Niahm's hand with both of mine.

Please.

I send the single word into her mind. I see nothing in response. So I send it again, and again. Stacy closes her own eyes across from me and slips into a fitful slumber. I keep sending the word, the plea, over and over into Niahm's mind, hoping that somewhere in there she still resides, but knowing the desire is moot.

✳ ✳ ✳ ✳ ✳

Sam

I open my eyes and look at Niahm. Her eyes are still closed and she doesn't breathe. Guilt over having fallen asleep while watching over her consumes me.

Sam.

"What?" I whisper, lifting my head to look over at Stacy. She's still sleeping. I watch her for a moment, wondering if she's really awake or if she's said my name in her sleep.

Sam.

My gaze flies to Niahm. Did she . . .? I squeeze her hand tighter.

Niahm, please, tell me that was you, I send into her mind as forcefully as I can.

Sam. The word comes again, clearer. I roll toward her, letting go with one hand to touch her cheek.

"Niahm?"

Stacy sits up at the sound of my voice. "Sam? Is she . . .?"

"I don't know," I say, unable to keep the smile from my face. "But I think I heard her."

Shane moves to the end of the bed. "What did you see?" he asks.

"Nothing," I say. "Just my name. I thought it was Stacy."

"It wasn't me. At least, I don't think so. But I didn't hear anything."

"You wouldn't," Shane says. "Samuel can hear thoughts by

touching someone, particularly their hand."

"What?" Stacy looks at me as if I've sprouted two heads. She shakes her head, then looks at Niahm's hand in mine. "Wait, so you're saying you *heard* her? She's . . . alive?"

I sit up, place both hands around Niahm's once again. Once again, I get nothing, not matter how much I plead with her.

"I can't hear her now. Maybe it was just wishful . . ." I can't finish, the thought of her never coming back after imagining her there is too much. Suddenly, Stacy thrusts her hand at me.

"What am I thinking?"

I just stare at her, not sure where this is going. Why now? I take one hand from Niahm's and grasp Stacy's.

"You're thinking you don't believe I can read minds," I say. Stacy gasps. "You also don't believe we are immortal. And yet, you somehow believe Niahm will live again." She simply stares at me, mouth agape.

Finally, she says, "What else?"

I look again, then shake my head sadly at her. "You don't think any of this is my fault. And you think Niahm would agree."

She pulls her hand from mine. "Can someone lie in their mind?" she asks.

"Yes, but I can always see the truth beneath the lie."

"Did I lie?"

"No," I say. "That doesn't make it the truth."

She reaches out to touch my arm in comfort, but then draws back. I grimace at the action. "Now you know why Niahm broke up with me. In fact, she ordered me to go away and never come back."

"This?" she asks, looking at her hand. At my nod, she says, "I can totally see how that would tick her off." She grins. "How many times did you do it without her knowing?"

I shrug and Stacy shakes her head. "That many, huh?" This time she does touch my arm. "Sam, if you looked into her mind, you know that if there's one constant about Niahm, it's that she doesn't hold a grudge. She gets angry, but then she forgives and forgets. She loves you, Sam. This wouldn't be the thing to drive her from you." She pauses, then continues. "Fear would. If she knew about you, she knew she wouldn't be able to have her happily ever after in Goshen that she's always imagined." She squeezes my arm and releases it. "If she knew that *she* might be . . . the same . . . that would have scared her more than anything else. That would definitely screw up her plans. Unlike the rest of us who can't wait to escape, Niahm was doubly determined to stay."

"You know her pretty well, don't you?"

"Yeah, well, we've been besties our whole lives," Stacy smiles as she caresses a hand down Niahm's face. "There isn—" She stops speaking abruptly, her face changing from a musing look to one of shock.

"What?" I ask urgently.

"Her face," she says, turning to look at me. "It's warm."

I look at Niahm, touch her face myself. It's true. She should be cold to the touch without blood flowing through her veins.

"Shane?" I say, but he's already pushing past Stacy, stethoscope in hand. He places it against Niahm's chest, listening intently. I'm doing the same by clutching her hand. Silence. Then . . .

One single beat. Faint, almost non-existent, but there nonetheless.

Shane's gaze meets mine. A matching grin lights his face as Stacy shifts from foot to foot impatiently behind him.

"What?" she says. Then, more fervently, "What!"

"A heartbeat," Shane says, turning toward her. "Only one, fairly weak, but a heartbeat."

Stacy drops to her knees by Niahm's feet.

"C'mon, Niahm," she says. "Give us another one."

Shane and I both listen intently, Shane waving Stacy to silence to better hear. And then . . . another beat, still faint but slightly more clear.

Niahm, I project, *come back to me.*

Sam.

Chapter 54

Niahm

Sam calls to me, repeatedly. I can hear him, but I can't find him. I'm looking for him in every way I know how, but all around me is darkness. Actually, darkness isn't the right word. It's nothingness. Thick and intangible, seen and unseen. I'm lost, with only his voice as any kind of compass point. I try to call for him, but my voice is absorbed by the nothingness around me. I feel like if I can just call him, he'll be able to reach me and save me from this dreary place.

I crouch down, crossing my arms over my chest, fists clenched, centering myself. I can't tell up from down, but feel I must by sitting upright. Closing my eyes reinforces the feeling. I take deep breaths which pulls no oxygen into my lungs. The action gives me something to do, though, so I continue. When I feel balanced I put everything I have into one word.

Sam.

I hear myself. He doesn't answer, so I repeat the procedure and call again. This time I feel as if he's listening. I call once more and finally hear him responding, calling my name back to me. Keeping my eyes closed, I stand and follow the sound, depending on my hearing rather than my sight, which is useless in this environment. He continues to answer my calls with his own. He's pleading for me to find him.

Like a miracle, he's there. I see his hand reaching for me. I grasp his hand desperately, and with a wrenching, painful jerk I'm hauled into the light.

❄ ❄ ❄ ❄ ❄

My eyes open, my vision filled with the sight of Sam grinning at me, tears running from his eyes so like my own, rimmed in green instead of gold. His copper hair is a mess, made more so as I reach up and thread my fingers through it. I pull his mouth to mine, hungry for the sensation of life after the desolation.

His mouth on mine is desperate as he hauls me up into his arms, clasping me tightly against his chest. My return kiss is just as frantic, my fingers urging his mouth closer to mine. Finally he pulls back a little, resting his forehead against mine as he stares into my eyes.

"I love you," he says, his voice full of fervent emotion. "You came back to me."

"You found me," I answer. "I was lost, and you found me."

He pulls me close again, hugging me as if he's afraid he might lose me if he let go. I return his embrace, my eyes closed against the brilliance of my love for him. I've loved him for a long time, but I've never felt this strongly for him, as if he is the center of my existence, as if I must protect his life with my own if I'm to survive myself.

I become aware of another hand grabbing mine. I open my eyes and see Stacy there, tears streaming down her face.

"Stacy," I breathe, and Sam releases me so that Stacy can

take his place. Behind her back I grasp his hand, refusing to let him move further away. I don't know where I am, or why, but I remember what he can do with my hand, and I don't care.

"Niahm, I thought you were dead. But you're not. You're here, you're really alive," Stacy gushes as she holds me. "I didn't believe them when they told me what they were, what *you* were, but it's true."

Her words penetrate my cloud of happiness and I push back from her, but still not relinquishing my hold on Sam.

"What? What did you say?" I ask her. Her face changes, and she glances uncertainly at Sam. Sam gently takes her arm and urges her out of the way so that he can sit next to me once again.

"Niahm, what do you remember of the past few days?" he asks me.

"I . . ." I trail off, trying to remember. I remember my trip with Jean, Stacy tagging along for her college interviews. I remember our day shopping, our visit to the spa. I remember the Chinese restaurant—

"The Sentinels!" I exclaim. "Jean, where is she?"

"I don't know," Sam says. "Do you remember being chased through the warehouse?"

I didn't until he said it, then it all comes flooding back.

"Oh no," I breathe on a sob. "They took Jean?"

"I don't know," Sam says again. "Can I show you something?"

"Okay," I acquiesce reluctantly, and immediately the warmth begins to flow between our hands. Only this time he's showing me the messages Jean had sent him as she stood in the warehouse, hugging me. "She left for me?" I ask. Sam nods. "They might have her?"

"I don't believe they do," Shane says. My eyes go to him for the first time, and I can see how tired he is. Suddenly, I realize how tired all of them are. "I don't think they would have kept pursuing us if they had her."

"You think she managed to get away?" I ask doubtfully.

"They came back after the two of you. That's how you were shot. They wouldn't have done that if they'd had who they were after to begin with," Shane says.

I look at Sam, who's watching me with sympathy. "She said she'd meet us," he says. "All we can do is wait, be there when she says she will." I reach up and sooth a thumb beneath his eye.

"You look exhausted," I say. "I didn't think you could get tired."

"I can get tired," he says. "It just doesn't come from lack of sleep."

"What, then?" I ask.

"Worry," he says, which bring my thoughts immediately back to the details I've been trying to ignore.

"I was shot?" I say.

"Yes," Sam answers.

"Where?" I ask.

Sam reaches behind me and places his finger on a spot on the soft area of my back, where my kidneys reside. "Here," he says, moving his finger to the outside edge of my abdomen. "It exited here."

I lift my shirt, and see a small bruised circle on my abdomen. How long has it been? Long enough for the wound to heal, and . . . suddenly, I look around, aware of just where I am. Not in a hospital, not home in bed. In the motel, alone with Sam, Shane, and Stacy. No medical equipment surrounds me.

"I . . ." I swallow over the lump that's formed in my throat. I take a breath, not wanting to ask but *needing* to know. "I'm . . . like you?"

"Yes," Sam says, watching me cautiously.

I shake my head, denying it, tears starting.

"I'm so sorry, Niahm," Sam begins, but Shane moves to sit on my other side.

"I tried to save you, Niahm," he says, sorrow and candor in his words. "We all did. We couldn't take you to a hospital, not with the Sentinel's . . . Even then, they couldn't have saved you, Niahm. There was too much blood loss."

"Show me," I say through my tears, pushing my hand into Sam's, closing my eyes. He does, beginning with our running to the van. I'm horrified at what he observes, at his feelings of utter despair and guilt at the whole incident. He shows me everything, all the way to the moment my eyes opened. I open them once again, letting my vision fill with the pure vision of Sam.

I don't know how to feel about this. I don't want to live forever, I don't want to spend eternity looking over my shoulder for Sentinels. I don't want to leave my home. Then I realize that even more than all of that, I don't want to lose Sam. I don't ever want to be away from him again, even if it means moving around the world more than my parents did. For the first time I have some clarity as to why they did it.

My mom had searched for someone who meant so much to her, and my dad had followed because he couldn't imagine living without her, even for a couple of weeks at a time. I understand now why they did what they did, that it had nothing to do with me, that they were driven by forces beyond their control. I understand because I'm now willing to do the same for Sam.

"I'm sorry," he whispers again.

"I'm not," I say, meaning it. His beautiful copper brows lift in surprise, but I give his hand a squeeze. "Look," I say.

He shakes his head. "No, Niahm, I told you I wouldn't do that again." Then he laughs. "Of course, I did it the entire time you were wounded and then . . ."

"Now, Sam," I say. "I'm asking you to look now."

He does, and like the sun coming out after a cloudy day, his face clears, his eyes regaining the sparkle and humor I've never been able to see quite so clearly thorough his contacts.

I love you.

My answer is a kiss that confirms how very much he loves me as well.

Chapter 55

Niahm

It's complicated trying to leave my life in Goshen. I'd always lived in a permanent way, so it isn't easy trying to extricate myself from my home. My heart breaks as I realize I won't even be able to graduate with my friends, the people who have been an integrated part of my life from my first memory. But we have to go now, before the Sentinel's come. We can't risk them finding us here and possibly hurting any of my townspeople.

I give Bessie to Stacy's dad, and the chickens to the Hill's. Sam arranges to have the horses picked up and moved to a stable until it's safe to bring them to us once again. I refuse to give up Bob. Sam doesn't even try to argue the logistics of moving a dog around with us. I think he's as attached to Bob as I am. No one knows I'm going so soon.

I know what kinds of stories will be imagined to explain my sudden departure with Sam and Shane. At first I'm upset about that, then decide it's okay. It will give everyone something to talk about for a while, anyway.

Sam and Shane put their ranch up for sale, but I can't bring myself to sell mine quite yet. I know I'll have to eventually, but there's too much loss to deal with already.

"Stace, are you going to be okay?" I ask her again.

"Yes, for the cajillionth time," she says, rolling her eyes. "I'm going to see you again," she says firmly. "Even if it's when I'm old and gray, and you're still young and beautiful, and I'll be insanely jealous."

"I'm going to miss you more than anything," I say, hugging her.

"I know," she says. "But you'll never forget me, no matter how much time passes."

"I won't," I say, looking at her, smoothing her hair back. "You've gone above and beyond as my friend . . . as my sister, really. You've saved my life, more than once—in more ways than one."

"Yeah, well, you made life in dull Goshen exciting," she says. "Think of the great stories I'll be able to make up for my kids about my immortal friend." Stacy is much more comfortable referring to me as immortal than I am. "Go," she says, looking beyond me to where Sam waits in his truck. "You have your own immortal waiting for you. How romantic is that? You guys genuinely get the happy forever."

I look back to where Sam waits, and can't refute her words. I clasp her tightly to me, no more words necessary to covey my love and appreciation. Then I turn and run to the truck. I climb in, sliding over to the middle, pushing Bob to the passenger seat and we drive away. I watch Stacy until I can no longer see her, then Bob and I both watch Goshen fade. Bob seems to understand that we are leaving, never to return. He gives on high pitched whine as it disappears.

Sam drives silently for a few more minutes, then without a

word pulls over to the side of the road, turning to take me into his arms. He holds me while I cry, his hands moving up and down my back in a soothing motion.

"Sam," I ask after a few minutes. "What am I going to do if you ever leave me?"

He laughs. "Niahm, it doesn't work that way. I *love* you. I've felt what it is to lose you, I won't put myself through that again."

"Yeah, but I can get pretty annoying," I say. "Sometimes I'm even sick of myself."

He puts his hands on my cheeks, ducking to look directly into my eyes. "Niahm, there isn't *anything* that will take me from you. Or you from me."

I smile at him, then narrow my eyes. "You seem pretty sure of yourself. What if I find someone I like better?"

"I always thought I was bound to you," he begins.

"You're not?" I interrupt.

"Oh, I definitely am," he says. "But I believe it's more. I didn't really recognize what it was until I saw it in you."

"Saw what?" I ask.

"Remember when you first opened your eyes, how overwhelming your feelings for me were? How you felt you couldn't exist without me?"

I nod, remembering those feelings clearly, feelings that returned each time I looked at him.

"It's the same for me," he says. "It was faster than the normal binding with someone, stronger. Neither Shane nor I recognized it because we've never even *heard* of anything like it before. It must be rare, but exists, and someone, somewhere knows what it is, has a name for it. It doesn't matter what the name is, though, Niahm, I only know that I *can't* exist without you. I won't, as long as I have any say in it."

"Do you think it only happens between immortals?" I ask, curious now.

Sam shrugs. "Maybe. Seems like it would be incredibly unfair for an immortal to feel this way about a mortal who would not survive for many years with them."

"Hmm," I say, my curiosity about it disappearing. "I don't need a name for it either. I know *what* it is, and that's good enough for me. It makes me your immortal, and you mine."

"Mm," Sam answers, lowering his mouth to mine, one arm behind pulling me close, the other resting alongside my neck, holding me a willing captive. When he releases me, he grins.

"I'm going to have to marry you soon," he says, slightly breathless.

"How soon?" I ask, completely breathless.

"Tomorrow?" he says.

"How about today?" I tease.

"I'll marry you whenever and wherever you say, Niahm Parker."

"Ditto, Sam . . . is that your real name?" I ask, the thought suddenly occurring to me.

"It's a close translation," he answers. "My birth name is Sorley Padraig Ó Clúmháin, Samuel Patrick Coleman. I try to keep some part of my real name in all of my incarnations. This is the closest name to my real name, which seemed appropriate since my hair is its natural color for the first time in a long time."

I look up at his gorgeous hair, filled with sadness that it will soon be covered by hair dye, as will mine.

"Okay, well Sorley Padraig O . . ."

"Cloo-waun," he pronounces slowly.

"Cloo-waun," I repeat. "I will also marry you anytime, anywhere . . . with our real names, though I may have to practice that a little."

"Deal," he says, kissing me again. Bob nuzzles between us, and Sam laughs. "Not to worry, Bob, you'll be best man . . . er, best dog."

Bob barks once as if in agreement. We laugh, and Sam puts the truck into gear as we pull back onto the road, heading off into the unknown, but at least we'll be facing the unknown together. Forever.

Authors Note

This is the first time I've attempted to write anything even slightly paranormal. My first two novels, *Geek Girl* and *Heart on a Chain* are both contemporary.

I began thinking about this story some time ago. I was riding down the road a couple years ago on my bike (Harley) and we passed through a small, charming town in Utah called Goshen (pronounced Goh-shun). A girl was walking down the street in the requisite Wrangler jeans and cowboy boots of many of the small towns in Utah. I immediately began forming a story about her in my mind, that being that she was content with her life, and determined to live her entire life in Goshen, in spite of the fact that her tow was dying. That was all I had, but I knew there had to be something, or rather *someone,* who would come along and shake up her ideals. Somewhere in the back of my mind I had the idea that Sam would be immortal, but I wasn't aware of it when I first began writing. Once I had that thought, I had an idea of how their story was going to go. Of course, things changed along the way as they always do whenever I'm writing a story.

There was never intent for this to be a series, or anything more than a standalone book. As many of you know by now, I exchange chapters with three other authors: Jeffery Moore, Camelia Miron Skiba, and Sherry Gammon. Sherry was the first to bring up the idea of this becoming a series, whether it be a series about Sam and Niahm, or about other immortals. Once I hit the 90,000 word mark and still wasn't quite done with the story, I began to think she was right. I have plans for another story starring Sam and Niahm, and ideas for some stories starring other as-yet-unmet immortals.

Being as paranormal is not my genre, I can only hope I've done it a small amount of justice, and have not shamed myself or the genre itself. I feel that though there are paranormal or supernatural elements, at heart *Immortal Mine* is a contemporary young adult romance.

I'd like to thank everyone who has helped push this book to completion, in particular my three "Wigz" partners in crime, the indomitable Jeff, Cami, and Sherry who as always have caused me to write a tighter, more cohesive story. Without them I would be floating adrift in an ocean of chaotic words.

I'd like to thank all of my beautiful, amazing readers who have not only spent a little of their hard-earned money on buying and then reading words I've written, but who have taken the time to either write to me to tell me they like my work, or have gone onto any number of sites and left me reviews. You have no idea how much I appreciate you!

I'd also like to thank all of the book bloggers. Without them, it would be almost impossible for any author to actually sell a single book. I have the highest appreciation and respect for the work that you do—willingly and freely—on behalf of all of us authors.

This journey into authorship has been the best ride of all!

About the Author

Cindy C Bennett resides in Utah with her high school sweetheart-turned-hubby of 25 years and two daughters. She also has two sons and two daughters-in-law. She is the author of three young adult novels. When not at her keyboard--which is rare--she can be found either reading, resting, or riding her Harley. Those are her "three R's". She feels very blessed and grateful for the opportunities life, and her amazing readers, have afforded her so far.

Contact Cindy at any of the following links.

Website: http://cindybennett.blogspot.com/

Facebook: http://www.facebook.com/#!/authorcindycbennett

Twitter: https://twitter.com/#!/cinbennett

Goodreads:
http://www.goodreads.com/author/show/4116333.Cindy_C_B
ennett

Amazon: http://www.amazon.com/Geek-Girl-Cindy-C-
Bennett/dp/1599559250/ref=sr_1_1?ie=UTF8&qid=132152025
1&sr=8-1

Or you can email her at fanmail@cindycbennett.com, and she promises to answer you!

12701167R00188

Made in the USA
Lexington, KY
22 December 2011